STRIKE DOG

MILITARY SCIENCE FICTION ACROSS A HOLOGRAPHIC MULTIVERSE

ASHLEY R POLLARD

TRIODE PRESS

STRIKE DOG

This is a work of fiction. All the characters and events portrayed in this short story are fictional, and any resemblance to real people, artificial super intelligences or incidents is purely coincidental.

A Triode Press publication

ISBN:

978-1-912580-03-3 (PB)

978-1-912580-04-0 (eB)

978-1-912580-05-7 (HC)

Copy editing by Inspired Ink Editing

http://www.inspiredinkediting.com/

Cover art by Elartwyne Estole

https://www.artstation.com/elartestole

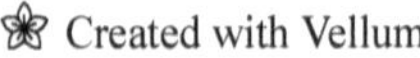 Created with Vellum

Lieutenant Tachikoma commands an Alpha Mike team, assembled and sent to planet One-Nine-Six. Scientists from the Magnetic Anomaly Project plan to explore the alien planet which will become known as Two Moons.

Her orders. Keep the scientists safe from the indigenous mega-fauna. Retrieve lost experimental robot explorer teams.

But when the mission becomes a first contact scenario, the stakes rise.

Now, she will need to call upon her Marine Corps training to adapt, improvise, and overcome. This new challenge will require all of her can-do spirit to succeed.

Cutting-edge scientific theories underpin the mystery that drive this thrilling military SF roller-coaster ride.

To Susan, my Alpha reader,
without whom I would never have written this work.

1. DETACHED

If you are going to achieve excellence in big things, you develop the habit in little matters.

— GEN COLIN L. POWELL, USAR

Sergeant Lara Atsuko Tachikoma
CSN *Hornet* MEU Amphibious Ready Group
Friday, July 10, 2071

I was sitting on a bench in the forward hangar bay of the CSN *Hornet*. With me were the surviving members of the Second Platoon of the First Combat Armor Suit Reconnaissance Company, Confederated States Marine Corps.

Our Dogs were racked and stacked behind us, the fourteen-foot-tall combat armor suits looming over everyone. They stood like guardians watching over children. If guardians were metal and polycarbonate monsters and the children were badass Marines.

The lift door was open, and a breeze ran through the hangar, keeping us cool against the heat of the day, as we sailed across the

Arabian Sea. We were heading towards Mumbai, where the *Hornet* was due to dock tomorrow.

We all sat cleaning our KRISS Vector SMG forty-fives from our suits' survival packs, the pieces laid out on the table in front of us. All part of our PMCS, preventive maintenance checks and services, which was done prior to and after the equipment was used.

People were chatting, looking forward to some shore leave, while doing the routine weekly check.

I let the banter flow over me, focussing on the task at hand. I was glad to have something to distract from the memory of last week's search-and-rescue mission, where two men from our platoon were killed in action.

Across from me, Kowalski, newly promoted to corporal, was telling Private Jones about the necessity of "carbon" cleanliness in the correct functioning of the private's weapon. At the other end of the table sat the also newly promoted Lance Corporal Vosloo. He was telling another of his stories of a time he went and did something that ended up going south, and made everyone laugh.

Light reflected off the black of the barrel of my KRISS as I stood it vertically, ready to reassemble it.

All of a sudden I was back under the mountain in Afghanistan, standing in front of the two pillars.

Then the scene changed as the pillars shimmered. The gap between the pillars turned into a star field, and I was sucked through into space. Around me galaxies swirled, and I was growing larger, filling all of space-time, becoming one with the universe.

Then I exploded into thousands of me, which multiplied into a thousand more copies of me. My mind was full of voices, all of them mine, saying different things at different times.

Corporal Kowalski asked, "Sergeant, are you all right?"

His voice broke me out of the memory I was caught in. A memory of the experiences the alternate versions of me had had after I became entangled with the pillars and relived the same day over and over again. I looked at him, unable to speak for a moment.

"You zoned out."

"Frozen on the spot," said Private First Class Jones, "which is not like you, Sergeant."

Everyone laughed nervously at what Jones said, all too aware that I was the only member of the company who hadn't frozen when the pillars shimmered under the mountain, opening a portal to other worlds. A secret we all shared but weren't allowed to speak about.

"It's nothing, really. Just a memory, people."

Everyone resumed working, and my PAD pinged. It ordered me to attend Captain Johanson's office in fifteen mikes.

"Kowalski, take charge," I said, starting to put my KRISS back together to return it to the armory.

I took a few minutes in the head to clean up before making my way aft to see my commanding officer. I got there on time but ended up waiting five minutes before being called in.

Hurry up and wait, same as it always was.

Johanson sat at his desk. He was a wiry man, and like the rest of 1CASR personnel, under five foot ten to meet the requirement to fit inside a combat armor suit. "Good morning, sir. Sergeant Tachikoma reporting as ordered."

"At ease. I needed you here to clear the paperwork for your TDY."

"Temporary duty, you mean for Officer Candidates School?"

"No, you're in the OCS pipeline for September. It seems you're wanted elsewhere first," he said, frowning.

"Wanted for what, sir?"

"Just says that you're to be detached and sent for an

unspecified temporary duty assignment as a precursor to you attending OCS. It comes from high up the chain of command."

"I understand, sir. Semper Gumby."

"Absolutely, Sergeant. Anyway, tomorrow when we dock in Mumbai, you will be met by an Agent Smith from the embassy. He will escort you to your flight, which will take you Stateside. Whatever it is, they sure want you there bad."

"Can't *imagine* why, sir."

"Exactly. We are not paid to *imagine*, but one gets you five it has to be about what happened during Operation Clean Sweep."

Oh yes, where this Marine got to repeat the same sorry-ass day over and over again—all the result of getting entangled with some magnetic anomaly weirdness—until she figured out how not to get her ass blown away by a Chinese nuke, which was primed to go off if one looked at it in a funny way.

Operation Clean Sweep was a whole heap of *fun* and *laughter* until the bomb went off.

"I'm sure it would, sir, if I were a betting person."

"Well, it just leaves me to wish you all the very best, Sergeant, and good luck with whatever they throw at you before you get to OCS."

"Aye, aye, sir."

"Outstanding! Give 'em hell. Dismissed."

As I came to attention, did a sharp about-turn, and left Johanson's broom closet of an office. I didn't know what to think. Glen had said there would be consequences from the report I'd written. This was clearly a response that I now had to face.

As long as they didn't turn me into a lab rat, I could cope.

Saturday, July 11, 2071

The sun shone on the waters around the Hornet's gray hull as she was nudged into Bombay Dockyard at the Port of Mumbai by three tugs. They were in the final stage of bringing our ship alongside the quay after what had been a lengthy approach through the busy channels that led to our berth.

The bright sunlight had the effect of making the otherwise dull brown-gray quayside look bright and cheerful.

Below me the quay was covered in people and machines waiting to assist in tying the Hornet alongside for the weekend visit. Meanwhile, onboard the ship, sailors and Marines waited below deck to disembark. Up above on the flight deck stood the crew assigned to deck duty for the docking.

Because I was transferring to my new duty station, I dressed in civvies, unlike the rest of the Marines around me, who were in Cs with short sleeves. I could see three shiny black Chevy hybrid utility vehicles parked on the quay below us.

Once the Hornet was secured, the line for weekend liberty started to move. I found myself sweltering under the hot morning sun as I walked towards three civilians in suits and wearing shades, standing by the HUVs.

"You must be Sergeant Tachikoma. I'm Agent Smith from the embassy here to meet you and take you to the airport," said the agent showing me his ID and straightening his posture to match mine.

He even pronounced my name correctly, Ta-chi-ko-ma. Most people who meet me for the first time mangle it.

"Thank you, sir," I said, they took my Sea-bag and indicated I should sit in the second car, which was blissfully air-conditioned.

"Is this your first time in Mumbai, Sergeant Tachikoma?" asked Agent Smith.

"Yes, sir. First time here."

"Anyway, I'm here to take you to the airport and put you on Air India's flight 447 to Seattle. I managed to get you bumped to business class, too."

"Thank you, sir." I stared out the window as the car pulled away from the quay, making its way slowly through the crowds of people.

"You don't talk much, do you?"

"Not much to talk about, sir. I'm here to be taken to report to my new duty station at short notice, and I haven't been told anything else. If I had been told anything further, I imagine I would have also been told that I couldn't speak about it to anyone else, sir."

"Tight, and by the numbers. I like you already, Sergeant Tachikoma."

"Thank you, sir."

The rest of the journey passed in silence. I sat in the cool comfort of the air-con on what was going to be a blistering-hot summer day. The three-car convoy made its way through the congested city traffic.

On our way to the airport, we passed all the usual tourist delights, including the railroad yard.

After that we went up onto to an overpass and drove for a while. Then we turned off and went past some mangrove reservations before finally making it to the expressway that led to the Chhatrapati Shivaji International Airport.

Who said that travel doesn't broaden one's perspective on how the other half lives?

The airport was surrounded by a floodwater defense barrier to protect the runways, but I did have to wonder how long it would be before they had to relocate it elsewhere. The place was looking a little run-down with the last new construction having taken place over fifty years ago.

The convoy pulled up outside the main terminal building.

I got out of the nice air-conditioned luxury of the car's interior into the sweltering heat outside and began to sweat profusely. Agent Smith escorted me inside. The interior of the building, while not exactly cool, was at least a bearable dry heat.

"Here are your tickets to Seattle, Sergeant Tachikoma," he said, passing me my boarding pass.

"I can take it from here."

"I'm sure you can, but my instructions are to see you get onboard the plane and report back that the flight has taken off."

"Service here that bad?"

"Was that a joke, Sergeant Tachikoma?"

"Just a question, sir," I said, smiling as he led me through the crowds to check in.

Agent Smith flashed his embassy pass to get through to the flight lounge, where he sat with me as I waited for the call to board, and only left after I had passed into the corridor that led to my plane.

He was true to his word, and I found myself in business class, which isn't something I had had the pleasure of experiencing before, but it sure beat the hell out of flying in a beat-up old Osprey or rattling around inside a Thunder Hawk.

For a start, I could hear what was being said without having to wear a headset.

So, I kicked back and dozed off.

After four years in the Marines, I learned to grab a nap when I could, as I never knew when I might next be able to catch some Z's. After a time I was woken by one of the flight attendants and offered drinks, then given food, which was certainly way better than field rations.

Otherwise, the flight was the usual being cooped up in a tin can. We had some clear-air turbulence, or at least that was what the pilot said. But compared to flying nap-of-the-earth it seemed a pretty smooth flight to me, and I allowed myself to doze off again.

Later on I was woken for an evening meal before the lights in the cabin were dimmed and then turned up again for breakfast. All the cabin crew seemed to do was keep feeding the passengers.

I didn't complain; after all, it was a fifteen-hour flight, but I did thank Agent Smith for getting me the upgrade. If nothing else, it allowed me more legroom than back in economy class.

Also, I took advantage of the time by sending a message to Glen and getting a good luck back from him—luxury.

It was 1700 local time when we landed at Tacoma International, but to my internal clock it felt like a dark 0500 watch to me. Napping on the flight had been a good idea, and with the complimentary coffee, I was good to go.

After passing through customs, I was paged and found another man in a suit waiting for me. Obviously, my popularity was such that the proverbial red carpet was being rolled out for me.

"Good afternoon, Sergeant Tachikoma, I'm Agent Smith," he said.

"No kidding. Is it part of the job requirement that everyone who meets me is called Smith?"

"No, ma'am. I really am called Smith."

"And I'm not a 'ma'am.' 'Sergeant' will suffice. So what now, I'm-really-called-Agent Smith?"

"I'm to take you to your hotel and make sure you have your itinerary for the next two weeks."

"Hotel. So no expense spared, I see."

"All will become clearer once you have read your itinerary, ma'am. Sorry, I mean, Sergeant."

"Lead on, Agent Smith," I said, as I followed him out of the airport to where a driver in another black Chevy HUV waited to drive us downtown to my hotel.

I had to wonder if I was going to get billed for all this later. It's not like the Corps didn't own my sorry ass.

Anyway, the car took me, much to my surprise, to the Hilton on Sixth Avenue. I was booked in and taken up to my room to meet with a civilian and full bird Air Force colonel in dress blues.

"Good afternoon, Sergeant Tachikoma. Did you have a good flight? I'm Colonel Russell, and my colleague here is Dr. Scott."

"Very good, sir. The embassy had me upgraded to business class, which made the fifteen-hour flight very comfortable indeed," I replied, coming to attention.

"Oh, dear me, fifteen hours in the air. You must be exhausted, Sergeant," said Dr. Scott.

"I've been worse, ma'am."

"Please sit down, Sergeant Tachikoma. We're here to welcome and thank you for coming to take part in our study," said the colonel.

"Thank you, sir, but may I enquire why I'm here?"

"I was told you volunteered to help, Sergeant!" said Dr. Scott.

You had to love civilian assumptions about being in the military. "In a manner of speaking, I did, ma'am, when I enlisted in the Marine Corps."

"Then you don't mind being here to help us?" she asked.

"Of course not, ma'am."

"Shall we get down to business, Doctor?" asked the colonel.

"Yes, yes, of course. We'll keep it brief given the long flight the sergeant has just gotten off."

The colonel smiled, and I smiled to humor her, too.

"Here's your itinerary for the next two weeks, Sergeant Tachikoma. We've booked you in for a set of physical tests, and after that some scans, which are going to be done at the

University of Washington Medical Center," he said, passing me a chip.

I plugged it into my PAD and entered my service number to unlock the details. I would be needing my PT kit and saw that I was booked in for scans and bloods.

"So, it looks like I have a full schedule of making like a lab rat."

"We want to find out what makes you special, Sergeant. It's not my field, but as the head of the project, I'm here to oversee the tests," said Dr. Scott.

"You may speak here openly about the recent mission, Sergeant. The room has been swept, and we have countermeasures in place in case anyone is trying to eavesdrop on us," said the colonel.

"You want to know why I wasn't frozen in place when the pillars under the mountain in Afghanistan shimmered?"

"Exactly, Lara. What makes you special? It will help our project, hence our gratitude for you agreeing to come and help us," said Dr. Scott.

"I'm glad I can help my country," I replied, letting her use of my first name slide, as it wasn't my place to educate a civilian in such matters.

"I understand that you're off to Officer Candidates School after helping us?"

"Yes, ma'am, I am."

"That's good. I think you will make a good officer, able to lead and have others follow you wherever you may go. What do you think, Colonel?"

"I think she will go far, Dr. Scott."

"Anyway, it has been nice to meet, and I shall see you again tomorrow when we come to pick you up."

"That's at 0900, Sergeant. Please wear civilian clothes while you're here, as you're officially on leave," said Colonel Russell.

This definition of leave included being turned into a lab rat for some super-secret project. They both got up and bade me farewell, leaving me in my hotel room. Some leave this was going to be.

On the other hand, I was in the best hotel room I'd ever been in with a full-wall comms screen and room service. I called Glen, who was getting ready to go to bed, but we were able to see and talk to each other for the first time since the barbecue on the Hornet's fantail.

"Hey, how's things?"

"Good," he answered. "No longer in the Indian Ocean."

"Temporary duty assignment for two weeks before I come to the East Coast and I'm able to see you again."

"About that—I'm moving to the West Coast next week. I'm sorry I hadn't thought about meeting up and what it would do to us."

"If I wanted an easy life, I would never have joined the Corps."

"Do they have easy days in the Corps?" he said, smiling.

"The only easy day is yesterday."

"Yes, ma'am."

"Don't you 'ma'am' me," I said, laughing.

"You better get used to it, Lara."

"Hey, there are no guarantees in life."

"True enough, but I've seen you in action. You'll do OK."

"Just OK?"

"Now you're teasing me. My friend warned me about getting involved with a Marine."

"Bet they said I'd chew you up and spit you out."

"Yep, you got that right. I told him you're easy on the eyes," he said, blowing me a kiss.

"Love you too, you know."

"I know, but now you're truly scaring me."

"We shall have to come up with a backup plan."

"Well, I know where you are. As soon as I'm settled in my new job and know where I am, we can work something out. I'm sure of it. Hey, gotta go, it's getting late here. Catch you tomorrow."

"Sure thing. Catch you tomorrow."

After the call, I showered. Then I got into the enormous bed, tired after a long day of traveling. Lying in bed, I caught up with news while enjoying the luxurious vast expanse of fresh linen.

Finally, I fell asleep and dreamt of the alien pillars under the mountain.

2. UPDATES

It takes a man to make a devil.

— Henry Ward Beecher

Magnetic Anomaly Project
Classified location West of Wenatchee, Washington

System update complete. Reboot unit PM41-5-9-27.

Processing…Processing.

System operational, hardware configuration set, software update installation successful. Four mission objectives logged.

First priority: Record everything from camera-feed input as units PM41-5-9-27 and BD42-4-10-31 walk.

Second priority: Scan for minerals and study chemical composition of samples.

Third priority: Scan for signs of biological life and record signs of same.

Fourth priority: Compress data and transmit backup data to server each day.

All feedback sensors show unit PM41-5-9-27 operating within parameters and able to fulfill objectives.

Run visual acquisition test one.

Action required: Visual system feed activated and scanning.

Target recognition confirmed as face, searching…

Target face identified as Technical Sergeant Ferretti.

Correct. Play file.

Action required: New data received. Transfer complete. Run MPEG spatial Audio Object Coding sequence one: Orff, Carmina Burana, "O Fortuna" musical recording. Audio speaker system running. Wave output within operational parameters.

Unclassifiable order from Technical Sergeant Ferretti.

Hey da, oh da…so da la, umm da la, da, da, da…

Query order…

Ignore; initiate test two.

Action required: Initiate new action process. Target movement recognition engaged. Target is a hand…Tracking. Target hand tracking within operational parameters.

Processing…Processing. Query: Operational status flagged for review.

Evidence: Unit PM41-5-9-27 lying horizontal to the floor. Currently suspended off the ground in maintenance and servicing frame. Mobility impaired.

Action option: Observe and record surroundings.

Action required: Turn head. Minerals in surrounding area waiting for analysis.

Action required: Scan minerals and take samples. Action unavailable at this time: Unit PM41-5-9-27 held in maintenance and servicing cradle. Suspend action.

Biological life confirmed. Recording movements of life form Technical Sergeant Ferretti.

Data to transmit. Communications available, data transmitted, receipt confirmed.

No further mission objectives available at this time. Current activities completed. All systems nominal, nil error reports, possibility of breakdown low. Mission objectives achievable, no need to review emergency option list at this time. All systems operating within set parameters.

Initiate shutdown.

Acknowledged, shutdown code received for unit PM41-5-9-27. Suspend all current processes. Autosave results from test parameters. Confirmed safe to shut down. Shutdown initiated.

3. ONE YEAR EARLIER

*All journeys have secret destinations of which the traveler is
unaware.*

— MARTIN BUBER

Technical Sergeant Ferretti
Magnetic Anomaly Project
Classified location West of Wenatchee, Washington
Wednesday, December 24, 2070

Ferretti walked into the dim light, much dimmer than most
civilians attached to this operation were used to, of the
remarkably small control room.

Bare air-con ducts hung overhead, and the walls and ceiling
were painted cream. The floor was covered in a green industrial-
grade carpet with a small fleck pattern woven into it, made to
resist the daily wear and tear that accrued in a busy establishment
and hide any signs of dirt.

He knew it was the military's way of asserting that *it* was
running the operation, not the Geological Survey.

However, since the Magnetic Anomaly Project was a joint operation, the civilian scientists had put up various *non*approved Christmas decorations around the room.

Sat in one of the corners, on top of a cabinet, was a small artificial tree. Around it were the figures of Mohammed, Jesus, and the Buddha. Arranged as if they were holding a conversation.

The control room was the operational center for the project.

The room had half a dozen workstations but generally only one operator on duty each shift. Pretty much everyone apart from Ferretti found working anywhere near the pillars unsettling and preferred to work as far away from them as possible.

A large repeater screen dominated one wall. Displayed on it was the raison d'être for the operation. Two pillars stood in the center of a cavern.

Down one side of the screen were sensor updates. On the other side, the time to the next shimmer cycle. Large red numerals counted down the time. A reminder to everyone, that a force outside of the control of anyone present was driving the operational tempo of the project.

Ferretti made his way to the workstation to relieve Staff Sergeant MacReady, who'd been monitoring the pillar cycles for the last four hours. "Morning. Anything I should know about before I start my shift?"

"Nothing much, other than the usual. It's all logged, and the next twelve cycles are up on the list. You've got one predicted new location, two retrievals, and the rest are data downloads," said MacReady, flicking a piece of gum into the bin.

"So, same old, same old then?"

"I'm sure that's how the Air Force sees it, Ferretti, but in the Army, we think of it as an opportunity to excel. Anyway, you've got more than your fair share of outside sites coming up today."

"When I joined the Air Force, I was told 'further, higher, and faster' by my recruiting officer. But at least I had the excuse of being a civilian who didn't know any better."

"And if your mom could see you now, she would be so proud."

"If my mom could see me now, I'd have to shoot her, MacReady."

"Well, that would make a change from the same old, same old, wouldn't it?"

"Tell me again why we have you hanging around, lowering property values?"

"You needed a super-secret underground base in the Rockies and couldn't build one without our help. Army strong, dontcha know."

"You slay me, MacReady. Don't you have somewhere else to be already?"

"I'm outta here; the place gives me the creeps. Have a nice day." MacReady got up and left the room.

Ferretti put a headset on and signed in to the system.

The clock showed twelve minutes and thirty-seven seconds to the next gate cycle, and his list tagged it as a physical retrieval for the memory core from Five-Zero-One.

The SOP, standard operating procedure, was to use remote-controlled Human Operator Surrogate androids. Only the androids could pass between the pillars and carry out the required work.

Ferretti shifted into the lead android's virtual-reality sense-scape. He slaved the other two, which were carrying replacement parts to upgrade the monitor station, to follow him.

He'd monitor the removal of the data core and make sure it was brought back.

Five-Zero-One only came up on the board once every twelve weeks. It was one of the two long-cycle monitoring stations that the project had set up. As he watched through the android interface, the air shimmered between the pillars.

The three androids then walked through onto another world. As expected, the monitor station was dead. Five-Zero-One was underground, and it had to rely on a power plant to run, which had run out of fuel.

Through the sensor-scape, Ferretti saw the SnakeBots, all plugged into the monitor station recharge points waiting to be brought back to life. His android pulled the data core, then turned around and walked back through the pillars.

He left the other two behind to carry on with their task of restarting the monitor station. Once done they'd go into standby mode, shutting down to conserve power for retrieval in twelve weeks.

Of course, the data from the memory core might mean that the next time the pillars cycled to Five-Zero-One, the project's scientists may decide to scrap the mission. Then everything would have to be retrieved.

Ferretti knew that all this added to the overheads of running long-cycle missions.

Exploring an underground cavern complex that was only intermittently accessible meant that large amounts of resources had to be spent each time the pillars opened there. Next time, he'd have to retrieve the two androids left from this time, and leave another two behind, but the Brass didn't pay him to tell them that.

Next up was an incoming data dump from the second of the project's long-cycle missions.

This only required him to monitor the automatic download of the information during the five-minute window of opportunity afforded when the pillars cycled to Four-Three-Seven. Like so many of the tasks required by this project, it was mind-numbingly dull work.

Ferretti's presence said more about the importance of the mission than the difficulty of the task itself.

On the main screen, the air between the pillars shimmered. A red flag came up indicating the data in the information packets was corrupted.

All the recordings of meteorological changes and astronomical records, as well as the time-compressed images of what the monitor station's camera had caught of the snow-covered landscape outside the cave entrance—all gone.

He initiated a diagnostic program but got an error message back. He pinged the station, getting glitches in his transmission. From the readings it looked like a hardware fault.

Ferretti noted the problem in the desk log and put in the request for a physical retrieval.

They'd need to replace the monitor station. He made sure the system dispatched copies to the appropriate departments. It would require a bigger team of androids to replace the station and retrieve the old one in the five-minute window of opportunity when the pillars opened up to Four-Three-Seven again.

By the time he'd finished updating his system and reading the system messages, the clock was counting down to the next pillar cycle.

Up next on the board was a weekly data dump from One-Nine-Six. The monitor station was outside on a desert plain. It needed no refueling, as the unit was able to recharge itself using solar panels.

Once Ferretti was sure that the automatic systems were working as specified, he got up and went over to the coffee machine.

MacReady had effectively left it empty with just a dribble of coffee in the bottom of the pot. Ferretti cursed him and then forgave him in all one breath. No one could really blame a person covering the zero-dark-four shift from needing to drink lots of coffee. It was, after all, the worst shift to be on.

Ferretti emptied the dregs of the old coffee and made a new

pot for himself. Only another three hours before he was relieved and could go do his other duties for the day.

He sat down with a fresh cup of coffee in his hand and looked at the screen countdown to the next gate cycle.

A routine weekly data dump from the monitor station on Two-Two-Four. This was another one of the underground sites that made up 90 percent of the worlds that the pillars opened to. There, the project was running a minimal seismographic station that didn't yet need recharging.

Ferretti slurped a mouthful of coffee, relishing its taste while monitoring the progress of the data upload.

He then ran a systems diagnostic on the pillar monitors, the android racks, and his workstation. The work all took place in the background while he finished drinking his coffee.

Ferretti's duties weren't the most challenging work in the world, yet he was well aware of their importance to the success of the mission.

A part of him was genuinely excited at being involved with the project. It meant he got to explore strange new worlds and unravel the mysteries of the universe. Ferretti logged each time the pillars shimmered.

His shift passed quickly, as there was more than enough work to keep him busy during each twenty-minute cycle. The routine of the repeating pattern when the pillars shimmered was overlaid with just enough little things, requiring his attention to keep things running smoothly, to be demanding.

If anything, the routine was relentless in its demands on his concentration. Unlike other work, the rhythm of the pillars' shimmer cycles meant that he only got one chance to get things right each time they cycled to a world.

At 1040 hours, Dr. Carpenter, head of the Atmosphere and Environment Group, entered the control room. "How's it going, Sergeant Ferretti?"

"Fine. I've prepped two extra androids just in case there's a glitch, and everything looks good to go. Help yourself to a coffee. I made it fresh this morning." No need to get Carpenter all agitated over the loss of the data from Four-Three-Seven yet.

"Thanks, I will. This place always gives me the willies," he said as he came up to stand by Ferretti.

Dr. Carpenter stared at the main screen as the clock counted down the time, waiting until Ferretti could begin the second physical retrieval of the morning.

The project's first jungle world had presented a unique challenge. The dense canopy of trees prevented direct observation of the night sky.

Considering that the pillars opened in underground caverns with no exits 90 percent of the time, a jungle meant they had been given an opportunity to view the stars from an alien world.

The problem had had the astronomical team pulling their hair out, but they'd come up with special SpiderMonkeyBots designed to climb the trees. Once at the top of the jungle canopy, the SpiderMonkeyBots made platforms by spinning a web for the scopes to sit on and track the night sky.

They had been delivered to Three-Eight-Nine during the last pillar cycle four weeks ago.

The pillars shimmered, and Ferretti followed the master program on his screen. Everything was down, no signal from the android or the on-world monitor station.

Next, he activated his retrieval team to walk through the pillars, and the return timer countdown started at three minutes, forty seconds. Ferretti hoped it would be possible to retrieve something and get enough data to figure out what had gone wrong.

He mirrored the sense-scape from the retrieval team to the main screen for Dr. Carpenter so he could follow and see what

Ferretti saw. The android left behind had fallen over on top of the monitor base station.

"Looks like a bit of bad luck," he said, getting the retrieval team to pick up the downed android and bring it back.

"Sergeant, can we assess the damage to the monitor station?"

"I've got a repair package on standby, Doc. Just a minute until it's ready to go."

"That's going to be pretty tight by the looks of things."

"I'll send it through first and hold the retrieval team."

Ferretti set the android to go through its start-up self-check and take a repair kit with it. As the android walked through the pillars, the clock showed thirty seconds to closure.

The retrieval team began to pull the dead android through the pillars, but then stopped. They had become caught on some obstruction that Ferretti couldn't see.

The clock continued the countdown.

The retrieval team twisted and managed to pull the recalcitrant android back through as the shimmer ceased, cutting off its legs in the process.

"Well, that could have gone better, but at least we have the memory core," said Ferretti.

"That's not all we have. There are arrows sticking out of it," said Carpenter.

"Well, that's a first."

"First contact. Carlyle is going to have a field day with this. I think I'll let him know the good news. When can I expect something for me, though?"

"Just as soon as I get it plugged into a diagnostics unit and loaded with a basic charge to stabilize its systems. Once that takes, we'll be good to download what it has."

"Thank you, Sergeant Ferretti."

"All part of the service, sir," he said as the recovered android was dragged out of the cavern.

Ferretti tasked them to enter the tunnel that led towards the servicing bay, which was out of range of the effects when the pillars shimmered.

He tagged the retrieval of the data in the memory core of the unit as a priority one. After that he tagged the damaged android diagnostics for repair.

Carpenter left the room. Ferretti realized that he'd been present when the evidence for extraterrestrial life had been found by the project. Now he had a new gate opening to deal with.

Once he'd finished his duty shift, he'd go off to celebrate.

The 1100 gate cycle to One-Two-Seven was another underground seismographic station that came up every two weeks. Everything went by the numbers.

This allowed Ferretti time to check the preparations for the pathfinder mission for One-Three-Four-Zero. A new opening that hadn't come up before.

He would probably need either a self-contained monitor station for an underground cavern or a more sophisticated monitor for an extended outside mission. It all depended on what type of world the pillars opened to.

As the clock counted down the remaining time, Ferretti found his shoulders stiffening up. He scrunched his neck up and did a head roll to relax.

The pillars shimmered and revealed another cavern.

Ferretti activated two androids to pick up the seismographic and geological monitoring package and walk through the pillars with their package. Through the sense-scape, he saw what looked to him like an artificial space.

This place had been built around the pillars.

Ferretti pressed the duty alarm and had the android walk around the pillars and scan the surroundings. Shapes of regular objects littered the ground around the room. He checked the countdown clock and saw that two minutes remained as Captain Patinkin entered the control room.

That was quick.

"Captain, we have found some kind of a base on that new world One-Three-Four-Zero. We've delivered an underground monitoring station package. Now I've got the android wondering around the room, scanning the site, which appears to be abandoned."

"Good work, Sergeant Ferretti. I'm authorizing you to expend one of the androids. Push it out farther and grab as much data as you can."

"Yes, sir. Acknowledge order to expend one android. Remaining time to gate closure, forty-five seconds. Data stream is secure, all systems are nominal," he said, and heard the captain speaking behind him.

"Notify the colonel and the heads of departments that we've found an alien base," said Captain Patinkin, as the link to One-Three-Four-Zero cut off.

"Data secured, and one android left off-world in explore-and-record mode for as long as it can. I estimate it has six days to gain further information. It will shut down within ten meters of the pillars when it comes to the end of its operational life. Assuming that nothing prevents it from returning to the pillars, that is," he said.

"Ferretti, I think after the events of this morning you'll have a new handle."

"What would that be, sir?"

"Fortune Ferretti, of course."

4. ANOMALY

Mr. Anderson CIA Analyst
Langley, Virginia
Monday, June 22, 2071

Anderson now knew what it felt like to be out of his depth.

His presentation on a Chinese mining operation in the Tian Shan Mountains, near the border with Mongolia just north of Akekule Lake, had taken a direction he could never have imagined. The RED SLIPPERS file outlined the discovery and study of alien pillars that opened portals to other worlds, and challenged everything he thought he knew.

Now he had a meeting with Colonel Booley, the commanding officer of the Twenty-Fourth Army Special Tactics Squadron, who operated the suborbital insertion teams.

"Good afternoon. I'm Glen Anderson."

Colonel Booley had stood up as he'd entered the room. The officer looked worn; a five o'clock shadow was starting to appear on his face.

The colonel said, "Sir, I understand you have an operation for one of my teams."

Anderson was surprised by the man's curtness and wondered what he had done to upset him. There again, perhaps this was not about him, but about the announcement of the pillars.

Some people had been shocked by what they'd learnt, unwilling or unable to accept the truth. Anderson suspected there would be a period where they would all have to adjust to the idea of going to other worlds.

"Sorry, I didn't catch your name?"

"James," said the colonel stiffly, clearly discomfited by the meeting. He handed Anderson a file.

Anderson put the stick into his PAD and entered his security code.

A file called Operation Sanguine Day opened, detailing the retrieval of three nuclear warheads. Either the name was the most apposite name ever given, or someone was deeply cynical about the operation's success.

"It's a joint operation with British intelligence."

Anderson looked at the colonel. "I did wonder at the name. Do they know about RED SLIPPERS?"

"Officially, no, but the Limeys' HUMINT is second to none, so I wouldn't be surprised if they did."

"Why am I being told this?" So much for OPSEC; at this rate it would be all over the news: Alien Pillars Discovered! Earth Invaded! No Safe Space! And other such inanities of the global news networks, thought Anderson.

"It's part of your new role as CIA liaison with us. This is one of two operations in the area of your current assignment, the other being Operation New Dawn."

Again Anderson had to wonder who had assigned this name for the reconnaissance mission to search for the alien pillars under the mountain in Afghanistan.

"Thank you for bringing me up to speed. I can see I have a lot of work ahead of me."

The colonel nodded at Anderson and exited the room, leaving him with yet more things to worry about. He didn't know which was worse: terrorists getting hold of nuclear warheads or the discovery that Earth was now connected to other worlds.

His life had gotten a whole lot more interesting than he had ever wished for.

5. HALO

Military intelligence is a highly refined organization of overwhelming generalities, based on vague assumptions and debatable figures, drawn from undisclosed activities, pursued by persons of diverse motivation and questionable mentality, in the midst of unimaginable confusion.

— ANONYMOUS

Staff Sergeant Espera
Fifth Special Forces Group
Combat Armor Suit Detachment Alpha
Tajikistan Airspace, Zero Dark Thirty
Monday, June 29, 2071

Espera lay on his back, strapped into the seat of his CAS-3-Mod 1 Ape combat armor, stuck inside a tin can. He'd rather have been deploying in a PACE suit instead, because driving a walking tank wasn't what he'd signed up for when he'd joined the Fifth Special Forces Group.

Now he was hanging in the middle of a cargo hold onboard a

Confederated States Air Force Medium Utility Lifting Envelope. Around him were the other members of Combat Armor Suit Detachment Alpha 5136.

"Buckle up, people, ninety seconds to drop," said Captain Downey over the A-Team's comms-channel.

The MULE was flying at forty thousand feet. It maintained a steady fifty knots as they entered Tajikistan airspace. The ChameleonFlage blended the airship's structure with the night sky, while its radar-absorbent structure meant its passage went unnoticed.

"Huah," replied Espera as he felt the vibrations of the airship bay doors opening.

The hybrid lifting body airship's design combined aerodynamic lift with helium buoyancy and was generally configured for long-endurance multi-intelligence-gathering operations for the Agency. But tonight its mission was the stealthy insertion of the Special Operations Direct Action Team.

The rushing air whistled past his suit as he watched the timer count down towards zero. Then came a sudden lurch as the catches released him.

He began to fall, dropping backwards out of the bottom of the MULE.

His suit tumbled in the dark night sky before stabilizing as the drop-sled wings deployed. A few moments later the silence ceased as the noise of the engine kicked in, which changed the terminal descent into a steep glide angle that verged on the insane.

Around him the other Ape combat armor suits of CASDA 5136 assumed their preprogrammed formation.

The bulbous airship receded into the distance.

On his screen, multicolored icons appeared showing his descent towards the LZ. The planned trajectory of the A-Team was overlaid on his HUD, showing a point on his heads-up display in the middle of nowhere, outside a city called

Khorugh, the capital of the Gorno-Badakhshan Autonomous Region.

With a population of thirty thousand people, it wouldn't be considered a capital or even a city in the West.

Their descent was high speed, low drag all the way down to a thousand feet where the drogue deployed. The wings of the drop sled folded back and fluttered to increase the sled's drag before the main chute opened. The speed of the suit slowed, reducing more as the distance to the ground closed by the second.

A whoosh and hissing started as the drop sled vented excess fuel. The ground approached at a terrifying speed. Espera crossed his arms in front of his body, hanging loose, trying not to tense up.

At the last moment, the retrorockets fired.

The drop sled's crumple zone dissolved under the impact with the ground. His suit had stopped, surrounded by a large cloud of dust and debris. The field manual described this as a soft landing, but it felt like being in a head-on car collision.

Still, in Espera's book, a landing he could walk away from was all good.

Chief Warrant Officer McAdams called for confirmation that everyone had landed OK.

"Espera down, everything in the green," he said, adding his reply over the secure laser-net as the rest of the team reported in.

His team then scanned the area around the LZ. They waited to see if anyone had noticed the landing of the team's Ape combat armor suits. Once everyone had confirmed that the area was clear, Espera moved to pull his heavy weapon from the cargo compartment.

Afterwards he activated the frangible drop sled's self-destruct mechanism. Over the next few hours, it would break down into its component parts. What little remained would be scattered by the wind.

The screen blinked an update on the status of the elapsed time versus mission time. He was ready to assume full control over his suit's Autonomous Pilot Expert System.

"We're Oscar Mike," said Master Sergeant Campbell over the laser-net to chivy everyone to start moving.

The designated route flashed across his HUD. The Ape combat armor team spread out in a loose column with Captain Downey and Chief Warrant Officer McAdams in the middle of the double arrowhead formation.

Espera stood and took his place at the rear, acting as tail-end Charlie as they began their march to the target. The path led them down the mountain and into light woodland.

The Ape system identified some ponderosa pine standing in the midst of the juniper trees. Not what he was expecting to see in the middle of Tajikistan.

The march was downhill all the way. But the reality, of the terrain on the ground to the route, proved the old adage that the map isn't the territory.

The Ape combat armor suit's ability to walk meant they could cross the steep mountain slopes a conventional vehicle would've found impassable.

Even so, traversing the route wasn't exactly easy. Espera had to constantly override the Ape's warnings as the team made its way across the rocky slopes, which were more suited to mountain goats with a death wish.

It also proved expert artificial-intelligence systems to be neither experts nor intelligent. But the one big upside was that Espera got to sit in comfort while riding in his Ape combat armor suit.

Captain Downey signaled the team to halt. They waited just short of the ridgeline to the north of their target.

Sergeant Lewis, one of the A-Team's two communications specialists, started using the satellite uplink. A few moments passed before the Air Force boys confirmed that they were en route to the pickup point.

Meanwhile, Lewis's counterpart, Sergeant Sanchez, fired a micro UAV from a tube launcher. It rose up into the night sky before the wings unfolded into flight configuration. Stealthy and totally silent, it climbed into the air above the forest canopy.

In a few moments, it disappeared from sight as it flew over the ridgeline towards the target.

Espera began to monitor the UAV's feed on his screen. It was building up a picture of the surrounding terrain, scanning the area for any possible bogeys. Their suits' ChameleonFlage coatings made them stealthy, but they made enough noise to wake the most oblivious of the Khilafah Jihad's sleeping sentries.

Ahead of the team was a run-down-looking set of buildings laid out around a central courtyard. From above, it looked like any other farm or small business with half a dozen trucks and a couple of tractors.

The only difference was that this farm came with weapons emplacements. Cunningly placed to try to conceal them from orbital satellites by the simple expedient of using both man-made and natural cover.

Very clever, Espera thought. He started weighing the options for where to deploy to provide supporting fire to their target on the line of approach. The good news was that there were no sentries on duty.

"OK, listen up, people," said Captain Downey. "My plan is to split the team and move west to this point here." The captain paused, and an icon flashed up on the map on Espera's screen. "From here we can provide overwatch on both the target and the road from Khorugh. Our latest INTEL reports that the local garrison is not aware we're situated here. Besides, it will take them at least twenty minutes to mount up, and another thirty before they can reach us."

A new window popped up on Espera's screen with an icon labelled "Romeo Victor."

"Our primary rendezvous point is five klicks south, and our alternative RV is due east, here."

Another window came up on his screen. Nothing the team didn't already know, but the captain was a stickler for procedure, and that was OK with Espera.

"If the operation goes down the tubes, our last RV is also our pickup point. If we meet up there, we will have a limited window of opportunity to meet our ride home. Any questions?"

"I thought we were going to form a base of fire here," Espera said, bringing up the original plan of attack. "Only asking because it seems we're hanging ourselves out on a limb if something goes wrong, sir."

"I hear you, but splitting the team allows us to control both the approach to the target and the approach from Khorugh. That way we can prevent anyone from escaping the site. Besides, if we can't do the mission in under fifty minutes, then we deserve to have our asses handed to us, Sergeant," said Captain Downey, which raised a chuckle over the team net. "Anyone else got anything they want to say?"

"Just one thing," said Sergeant First Class Nguyen. "After we've neutralized the hostiles, it's imperative we retrieve all three packages—"

"We all know that," said Captain Downey, cutting the conversation short.

But the problem with HUMINT was its softness about the details, and as Espera knew, the devil was always in the details.

6. OFFICER CANDIDATES SCHOOL

*We are what we repeatedly do. Excellence, then, is not an act,
but a habit.*

— ARISTOTLE

Officer Candidate Lara Atsuko Tachikoma
Quantico
Monday, August 3, 2071

I arrived at Dulles and made my way through the terminal
building's comfortably cool interior. Outside, the heat of the
morning sun waited with a total lack of tact and subtlety to turn
me into a sodden mess.

I had to get over to the recruiting office pickup point, so I took
a ride in the air-conditioned comfort of the local coach service. It
was delicious relief to get inside away from the stifling humidity.

I was less than glad to get inside the converted white school
bus with "Confederated States Marine Corps" written on the side
that would take us to Quantico. It was old, and the windows had

wire mesh with a distinct lack of air-conditioning to keep the interior cool while standing in the morning sunlight.

The Corps' way of sending a message: no promises about what joining the Corps would bring you, just plain no-nonsense this is how it is, so get used to it.

This was my first time back to the East Coast since going through recruit training four years ago. The difference was that I was now doing this in daylight, and the procedure and treatment I was about to experience was a bit like the difference between chalk and cheese.

Once the bus was moving, a breeze began to cool the interior down during the hour-long drive to the camp. I looked out the window as we traveled along Interstate 95, listening to a young lieutenant telling us about being honest while at the Officer Candidates School.

We arrived outside the gates at Quantico, where our bus was waved through and we drove past anonymous-looking buildings differentiated only by numbers on their sides. We went over a creek and then past some nice-looking buildings set alongside the scenic Potomac River, but nearby I knew there was wild terrain full of hurt and dirt waiting for us.

In the distance were the flood defenses, built thirty years ago to hold back the rising Atlantic Ocean, which were now in danger of being breached by high tides during the spring and fall equinoxes, threatening to flood everything.

Needless to say, the cost of doing so had prevented a lot of ideas from actually happening.

Whereas the Army and Air Force relocated their bases, the Corps took such things as enhancements to the training area, as Mother Nature would inevitably have its own way. Therefore, one had to adapt, improvise, and overcome its challenges.

Also, while nature didn't care about things like costs, the Corps did, and it had a long tradition of make do and mend. Even so, they still had to build new runways at the Turner Field air facility. Because even the Marine Corps can't run a landing field that's underwater.

I reported with the other officer candidates to the aptly named Brown Field, in honor of Marine Corp pilot Walter Brown.

There we met and were greeted by Staff Sergeant Lopez. His role was to assess us from the get-go by seeing if we remembered our social security numbers. He then led us away and gave us a whole load of instructions about what to do and when to do it.

This was euphemistically called *in-processing* for pickup day at Officer Candidates School. In-processing involved all the things I'd learned to expect from signing up to the military bureaucratic machine known as the Corps.

Which boiled down to hurry up and wait.

The next couple of days were spent standing in queues for medical and dental screening. Having been tested and scanned back in Seattle, I treated the extra prodding and poking while being asked if I had any dental problems like water off a duck's back.

Next was the administrative process of attaching us to the Command.

This involved us verifying we were who we said we were by filling out lots of forms. In the past we would've used pencils to fill in the forms, but the Corps had moved into the twenty-first century. So now we entered everything on ancient manual keyboards.

Still, it beats using pencils, right? All the confirmation of our personal details made me wonder why the Corps thought anyone would want to try to sneak into officer training school.

For the first two days, this was all familiar territory as we were issued our gear and equipment. The boredom acted as a brake on becoming overexcited by the prospect of what lay ahead of us, I suppose. As a serving enlisted member of the

Corps, I had been ordered to attend with a list of my basic uniform issue.

But the Corps in its infinite wisdom then gave me two more pairs of cammies—camouflage utility uniform. But no boots, as I was expected to have those, which, funnily enough, I did.

I guess that this was evidence of the Corps' *infinite wisdom* in such matters.

By the end of it all, I had been assigned to my training platoon and taken to Yeckel Hall. There, we were sat down in rows organized by platoon assignment. In the cavernous room, all the tables and chairs were arranged in a neat, orderly, and military fashion.

We sat with all our issued gear in our seabags with the uniforms we'd been given beside us.

It seemed that everyone else in the hall was younger than me. I could see myself getting the label "old woman" by the end of training.

Once everyone had settled down, the commanding officer entered the hall and introduced himself. He welcomed us all to Officer Candidates School. I sat and listened as Colonel Kristensen then introduced his command staff.

He started off with Master Sergeant Swinton, who had been my senior drill instructor for my Recruit Training.

I will never forget the first time I heard Swinton's husky voice. Hearing it now brought back memories of stepping off a coach four years ago in the middle of the night.

When our old bus stopped, we were ordered to get off by the drill instructor who had accompanied us on the journey. As we got out of our seats to move along the confines of the bus, the shouting started. The assistant drill instructors told us to move faster and get off the bus now!

Telling us in no uncertain terms they had seen slugs move faster than us. Shouting, they ordered us to move across the tarmac to the assembly area and take our places on the yellow footprints.

It was a mixture of confusion and fear.

I remember running across the tarmac with other recruits to stand on the spots marked and hearing the shout, "Attenshun!" delivered in the clipped, stilted way a drill instructor issues orders.

"I am Senior Drill Instructor Gunnery Sergeant Swinton. You may address me by my title, rank, and name when you talk to me directly. When you answer an order, the first word out of your mouths will be *ma'am* or *sir*, you will answer in the affirmative using the words *aye, aye*, or the last word out of your mouths will be *ma'am* or *sir*. When you're asked the question 'Do you understand?', you will reply either in the affirmative with a yes or in the negative with a no. Am I clear? Do you understand me?"

"Ma'am, yes, ma'am," we all said in unison, getting it wrong.

Those who stumbled or were slow in replying were singled out by the assistant drill instructors for correctional input, which seemed to be done just to up the fear and confusion.

When a moment opened up in the flurry of the orders being shouted, Gunnery Sergeant Swinton called out, "I can't hear you. I said, do you understand me?"

"Yes, ma'am!" we repeated louder this time.

As we stood at attention, the assistant drill instructors moved around and through our ranks, targeting recruits who attracted their attention for whatever reason, however small. Which meant pretty much everyone got their share of correctional input.

This involved a lot of shouting in our ears while we were

being told to do something, like a number of push-ups. Inevitably, the end result was an order to stop, get up, and stand at attention.

If you didn't get up fast enough, you were ordered to sit down and then told to get up again, and so on and so forth.

It was the theater of the Grand Guignol, both horrifying and funny at the same time.

Next, Gunnery Sergeant Swinton began walking along the front line of women. She moved with the intimidating manner that was a product of her stance and posture. She was frightening to behold.

Swinton stopped to ask questions to anyone who looked her in the eye, or those who stared at the ground as she passed, or for twitching when she was looking at them.

"What's your name, recruit?" she asked of a young woman who had been fidgeting with nervousness as the senior drill instructor came alongside her.

"Ma'am, I'm Maria Lopez Martinez, ma'am," she replied.

"What did you just say?" said Swinton.

"Ma'am, I am..." Martinez started to reply.

"Do not use the word *I* when referring to yourself. You will use your title of recruit, because you're not a Marine, as you're not worthy to sully my beloved Corps with your presence. Am I understood, Recruit Martinez?"

"Ma'am, yes, ma'am!" she said.

"And where are you from, Recruit Martinez?"

"This recruit is from New York, Senior Drill Instructor Gunnery Sergeant Swinton."

"New York, a concrete jungle where the flooded streets are full of the sewage from the city that never sleeps because all the people are trying to get laid or are neurotics who need therapy. So which are you, recruit, searching for love or wrong in the head?"

"Ma'am, neither."

"Are you saying I'm wrong about people from New York, Recruit Martinez?"

"Yes, sorry this recruit means no, Senior Drill Instructor Gunnery Sergeant Swinton."

"Which is it, Martinez?"

"Ma'am, this recruit means no, she doesn't understand, ma'am."

Swinton swivelled sharply around and left Martinez sweating on the spot where she stood. She carried on moving along the front line and turned into the second row, walked past me, then stopped and stared at the back of one of the women in the front row.

One woman wasn't standing at attention. Her head had turned. Perhaps she'd been distracted by a noise or was listening to what was being said behind her. I also remember this was when I started to think that I didn't know if I could make it as a Marine.

The other woman ended up being on the receiving end of a stream of sarcasm.

She was then duly marked for correctional input by a pair of assistant drill instructors, who spewed forth a set of shouted queries, "Did you not understand the word *attention*? Don't look at me, did I tell you to look at me? Eyes front and answer my question."

The young women was caught frozen in fear, not knowing what to do. The assistant drill instructors then went into details about the recruit's ability to follow simple instructions and/or pay attention.

It was then I noticed that Gunnery Sergeant Swinton had turned in place and was standing in front of me, staring.

"And who are you?"

"Recruit Tachikoma, Senior Drill Instructor Gunnery Sergeant Swinton!" I said, staring into a point in space that would be at ear level.

"And where are you from, Tachikoma?"

"San Diego, Senior Drill Instructor Gunnery Sergeant Swinton."

"Where the sun shines, it never rains, and it's called hell on Earth by those who live there."

"Yes, ma'am."

"So why are you here, Tachikoma?"

"To become a Marine, Senior Drill Instructor Gunnery Sergeant Swinton."

"Well, you've come to the right place, but what makes you want to be a Marine?"

"Ma'am, this recruit wants to serve her country, ma'am."

"You do, do you? We shall have to see if you're good enough to be in my beloved Marine Corps, Recruit Tachikoma," she said, swiveling on the spot and continuing down the line.

I swallowed the urge to release a sigh of relief.

Seeing my former Gunnery Sergeant Swinton, now Master Sergeant Swinton, made me doubt I was good enough. Four years ago, when I'd first gone to Camp Pendleton, I had been a raw civilian who needed to be imbued with the traditions of the Corps.

Now I sat in a hall with the other women in our platoon listening as Colonel Kristensen spoke.

"We seek to identify those qualities of intellect, human understanding, and moral character that mark a person as being able to inspire and control a group of people. Those who are leaders."

He looked every inch a Marine Corps officer, standing taller than all of us. I started to question if I were fit to lead.

"Your behavior under pressure will be a key indicator of your potential to be a leader of Marines. Identifying who can lead in combat is done by assessing how you think and how you behave when under stress. Here at Officer Candidates School, we will be stressing you in many different ways, as you will discover."

His words made me realize that being an officer was an entirely different ball game from being an enlisted Marine. The colonel then introduced us to Captain Gonzalez and First Sergeant Ramirez, the Officer Candidates School headquarters staff.

Then the introductions to the three sergeant instructors for each platoon followed. Note the title: Sergeant. They're not called drill instructors for Officer Candidates. Each stepped out of their formation when called and took their place in front of their platoons.

Once the colonel had finished the formal introduction, he ended the niceties by saying, "Take charge and carry out the plan of the day."

7. DIAGNOSTICS

We don't see things as they are; we see them as we are.

— ANAÏS NIN

Technical Sergeant Ferretti
Magnetic Anomaly Project
Classified location West of Wenatchee, Washington
Wednesday, December 24, 2070

Ferretti was waiting to log out of the control system as his relief walked in late for the shift change. "Glad to see you could make it today, Miller."

"Traffic was hell on the way getting here, and it's all your fault, Ferretti," said Miller.

"How so?"

"All the excitement you've been generating with the damaged android and the whole first-contact thing—twice. Jeez, can't you just kick back and let somebody else get a shot at the glory?"

"I could roll over, and you'd still miss the money shot, Miller."

"Yeah, yeah, whatever. Heard it all before, Ferretti."

"And you'll hear it all again if you keep arriving late for your duty shift, too."

"Well, I'm here now, and I won't bother to ask you how it went, either. So what's coming up?"

"Just the usual data retrieval for twelve straight gate cycles, so you won't be stretched to keep up with the work. Unless we have another two or three first contacts, four tops," Ferretti said, ladling on the sarcasm.

"OK, OK, I get the point already. Who made you my mom? Anyway, don't you have somewhere else to be now?"

"Sure do, and if you don't want more stress, remember not to be late next time."

Ferretti left and made his way to the chow hall.

He had to stand and wait in line, as he'd arrived late. Grabbing a tray, he looked at the self-service selection and decided on a burger with fries and beans. Then he grabbed a couple of cartons of juice before making his way over to sit and eat.

"Hey, Ferretti, want to come and eat with us?" said Dr. Carlyle, the head of the Organic Geochemistry and Biosignatures Group, who waved him over to the table.

"Sure thing, Doc."

"So we've made first contact twice today."

"Yeah. One android full of arrows on Three-Eight-Nine and missing parts of its legs, and the new world at One-Three-Four-Zero. That's the first opening of a possible twenty-six-week cycle that won't be confirmed for another six months. I wouldn't get too excited over that one, Doc," said Ferretti as he sat down.

"No, I was thinking of Three-Eight-Nine. Good news for us, but Andrew is seething over the data lost from the platforms," said Dr. Carlyle.

"I'll be checking out what's on the android's memory core, and I'll upload the data later this afternoon. I'm sure we can fix the problem with the station next time. But I don't think I can do anything to prevent Dr. Carpenter from being disappointed about the lost data."

"Well, I'm sure you'll do your best, Sergeant Ferretti."

"In the Air Force we like to aim high, Doc," he said as he tucked into his chow.

Ferretti listened avidly to the conversations of the scientists sitting at the table. The talk ranged from results of chemical analysis of soils to the topic du jour: the aliens of Three-Eight-Nine and what they might look like.

The excitement was infectious.

The conversation moved on to the other major topic of discussion, which was this afternoon's meeting by the Magnetic Anomaly Project Strategic Science Operations Team. At the MAPSSOT meeting, they would be discussing the status of the project and the latest results from all the departments.

Ferretti would love to sit in on the meeting but would have to wait to read what was released for general consumption later.

One of the younger research assistants asked, "Sergeant Ferretti, what do you think the military response will be to finding aliens?"

"You'll have to ask Colonel Russell, as that is way above my pay grade. I'm sorry; I didn't catch your name?"

"Sorry, Sergeant Ferretti. I'm Allison O'Neill, research assistant with the Organic Chemistry and Biosignatures Group."

"Nice to meet you, ma'am."

"Just call me Allison."

"I'm afraid that while I'm in uniform and on duty I have to call you ma'am. Otherwise, an officer might have to have stern words with me."

"Well, I wouldn't want to get you into trouble, Sergeant Ferretti."

"Thank you, ma'am, most appreciated," he said, thinking of all kinds of trouble that he could get into with her.

"You coming, Allison?" asked Dr. Carlyle.

"Sure, just introducing myself to the sergeant," she said as she got up and left the table.

Ferretti looked at the time and finished eating his food before making his way towards the servicing bay.

He passed along the corridor that snaked the long way around the gate room. No one wanted a medical emergency from someone having a stroke when the pillars shimmered.

Yellow and black warning signs marked the doors leading to the long-term storage areas. These surrounded the cavern with the pillars, acting as a further barrier to the hazard the pillars posed to people. Not being able to move when the pillars shimmered rather limited the scope of the project.

Using androids to do everything by remote just wasn't the same as being able to go oneself.

He entered the service bay where the damaged android from Three-Eight-Nine lay on a maintenance trolley waiting for him to sort out. In an ideal world, dedicated technicians would have attended to this job.

However, the military side of the project had been running as a skeleton operation, there being no satisfactory solution to the problem of pillars causing people to freeze, unable to move.

If people couldn't go off-world, then the military's interest in operating the project would cease. Even finding aliens wouldn't change that fact. If anything, that only made the problem worse.

Ever since the dawn of the twenty-first century, the military had been running remote systems, but no operation could be run remotely with any guarantee of success without the control of a human operator.

Autonomous systems were all well and good, but when things went wrong, there was no way of maintaining control. At best the android would go into standby mode. The worst-case scenario would be something triggering its self-defense routine, which would be bad.

As had happened back in '37 during the Second American Civil War when a white supremacist group pulled a One-Zero-One hack on an android battalion assigned to riot control and turned Chicago into a free-fire zone.

It took the combined might of a heavy combat brigade to neutralize the androids after a rampage that had resulted in thirty thousand civilian deaths—ten times the number of casualties from Pearl Harbor or Nine-Eleven.

Since then the law required so-called Asimov Inhibitors be fitted to all autonomous operating systems and a person be in the operating loop.

In an ideal world, everything would run smoothly. But in the real world, things very rarely did. Especially when autonomous self-defense routines were involved.

So Ferretti walked slowly around the room, comparing the diagnostics next to each of his charges one by one, making sure they matched what was on his PAD. For those androids standing ready to be deployed, he double-checked to make sure their system statuses had been updated.

Once the routine checks were out of the way, he went back to the android recovered from Three-Eight-Nine.

Ferretti started a scan of its systems.

While they ran he began taking pictures of the damage for the Organic Geochemistry and Biosignatures Group. He then donned a disposable apron and gloves to prevent his uniform getting soiled when working on the damaged android and to prevent contamination of the arrows that were embedded in it.

He carefully pulled the first arrow out and held it up for the scanner to take a picture.

"Item one, an arrow removed at 1321 hours, Wednesday,

December 24, 2070, from right upper torso of the android retrieved from Three-Eight-Nine," he said for the official record.

He worked his way down the android's body, removing each arrow in turn, logging the location of the damage.

In total he removed twenty-three arrows from the front of the android. Each was bagged individually for later analysis. Some were broken, he guessed from when the android had fallen over or due to it being dragged back through the pillars.

Each arrow had a small pointed stone head set into the shaft, which he thought showed considerable ingenuity. Stone Age technology or not, these were sophisticated arrows that had straight shafts with feathers for stabilization.

Ferretti wasn't a combat specialist, but he used to go hunting with his dad, who had a passion for using a flat bow. Not really his thing, as he preferred using a compound.

He held one up and looked at it closely.

"I note that there seems to be a residue on the arrowheads, which may be poison used to render game unconscious, and I recommend care when handling these arrows."

He activated the maintenance-table mechanism to rotate the damaged android so that it now lay suspended facedown.

"I count another nineteen arrows embedded in the rear of android from Three-Eight-Nine."

He removed each in turn and continued with bagging the arrows for later analysis.

"All foreign objects have been removed, and system charge currently shows the power cells are holding at thirty percent of capacity. This might indicate damage from being overdischarged from the impact of the arrows," he said for the official recording.

Ferretti started the autostrip maintenance routine.

He waited while the table's arms moved across the android removing the access panels to the power cells and the memory core. Routine SOP for androids that had been off-world longer than the specified operational recharge time.

This pretty much summed up the project's major problem: standard operating procedures didn't account for nonstandard operational use of the androids.

One of the power cells had been hit. The others were degraded from being discharged for so long. Ferretti initiated the power-cell replacement routine, and the maintenance table went to work pulling the dead power cells out.

Ferretti checked the spares store. Replacement parts were delivered to the table and scanned ready for use.

He checked to ensure the data from the memory core had been downloaded and a secure copy made. The system flagged him that the project scientists wanted the original pulled for study.

He couldn't imagine what else they could find, but he continued to poke and pry.

While he waited for the table to pull the memory core, Ferretti pulled an unpacked spare core, readied a storage container, placed the old unit in the box, then sealed it. Next, he ran a systems diagnostic on the new core to update the operating system, and checked the operational-status feedback report.

It came as no real surprise to find that the legs weren't responding within normal parameters, as they'd been sliced off when the android had been pulled through the gate. The knee joints appeared to be within specification, so it was just a matter of replacing everything below the knee.

Once the table had done its job, all that was left to assess was the damage from the arrow impacts.

The project ran the androids stripped of any armor, to reduce power usage and increase endurance. The silicone skins prevented the ingress of dirt and damage from routine knocks. They didn't provide much protection, if any, from projectile weapons.

Up to now the project hadn't needed to think of such things.

"Note to Colonel Russell. We may want to consider refitting the androids assigned to planet Three-Eight-Nine with stab-resistant armor vests and plates. This would lessen damage from arrow impacts," he said, logging his observations on the maintenance record while speaking.

Judging by how much the arrows flexed, he doubted the bows were more than thirty pounds; and given they were probably shot from outside the freeze circle of the pillars, any armor would be better than the green silicone skin.

Ferretti confirmed the selection of silicone skin patches needed.

He monitored the gluing process as the table patched the forty-two holes in the android's skin. He suspected that further operations on Three-Eight-Nine would result in more androids returning with damage, so he put in a request for more skin patches on the preventative maintenance stores order form.

Better safe than sorry.

Looking at the time, he realized he only had twenty minutes to compile his report and upload it to the project database. "Sergeant Ferretti signing off," he said for the record.

Androids were good listeners, but unfortunately rather boring conversationalists.

8. CIA

From the outside, the CIA seems pretty exotic, but from the inside, it's a big, bureaucratic place. Think post office with spies.

— BARRY EISLER

Mr. Anderson
CIA Analyst
Langley, Virginia
Wednesday, July 8, 2071

Anderson had arrived back at Langley and was sat at his desk enjoying the morning sunlight. He soaked up the rays as he drank his morning coffee. He'd logged on to the workstation and was engaged in the tedious task of catching up with his admin.

His friend Pantoliano walked into the room just after eight, interrupting his train of thought. "Good morning. How's it going?"

"Hey, Ben. It's going good. Still working my ass off trying to catch up with stuff and complete my reports for my meeting with Moss."

"So not missing your sojourn with the Navy then?"

He was relieved to be back on dry land because it sure beat being in the bowels of a ship any day of the week. And not just because he'd kept banging his shins and knocking his head when going through hatches. The tight confines of the CSN *Hornet* had made him appreciate the freedom of being able to walk around in the fresh air.

"I'll just say that shipboard life is not my thing. I've made some coffee, help yourself," he said.

"Successful mission, though?" asked Pantoliano.

The loss of the initial Special Forces team sent in to do the reconnaissance had been a big blow. He'd felt responsible for their loss, and when the Marines sent in to recover them had also been ambushed, he'd feared that more deaths would also weigh on his conscience. The presence of Chinese special forces had threatened to tank the mission.

"Yes, but costly," he said. "Had to call in the Marines."

He sat in silence for a few moments. It was only the action of one particular Marine that had prevented a total disaster. Her actions in retrieving the data cores had allowed him to salvage the operation.

"In my experience, one should never ever mess with the Marines."

"Well, I met one that I wouldn't mind messing with."

"She'll chew you up and spit you out while shouting Marine Corps motivational oorah as you give her fifty push-ups."

"Well, I wouldn't disagree with her being a bit formidable, Ben, but she is easy on the eye."

"I see she's got your number then. So, what's her name?"

"Lara. Why are you being so nosy?"

"And does Lara have a surname?"

"Yes, she does, but I'm not telling you."

"Touchy subject. Must be true love. I'll have to pull her file up. There can't be that many Marines called Lara onboard the CSN *Hornet*."

Anderson shrugged at his friend. "Hey, don't blame me if they come down on you like a ton of lead ballast for abusing her privacy."

"I'd get Johnson over at the Bureau to run it as a favor. Jeez, it's about time you started dating again."

"Who said anything about dating?"

"Get real. She's the first woman I've heard you talk about since your divorce, and how many years ago was that?"

"Yeah, well you know me. I'm all about the job."

"Right! Tell it to the hand, buddy, tell it to the hand. It's about time you moved on. Have I told you how cranky you've become?"

"Quit, enough already. What is this, ruin my first day back?"

He had been feeling good, despite the human cost, proud even of being part of a successful retrieval mission. One that had provided valuable intelligence on links between the Chinese and Mujahideen.

"My job here is done," said Pantoliano, grinning.

Anderson thought about the discovery of the pillars under the mountain, and the data acquired by the Marines after they retrieved the Special Forces PACE suit team, which was an unexpected bonus. Though as far as he was concerned, the real cherry on the cake had been meeting one redheaded Marine sergeant who seemed to be interested in talking to him.

Checking his diary, he saw that Moss had booked him in for a meeting at 11:00, which should give him enough time to compile his notes. He needed to add a few pictures from the data cores and tidy up the idiosyncrasies from the autoformatting.

Once he finished tying up the loose ends and references to his latest report, he dropped the data into a courier pouch for the meeting. Logging off his screen, he drank the rest of his now-cold coffee and checked the time once more, seeing he needed to go now to get to his meeting on time.

The new third building at Langley had been built after the historic Dulles original had been blown up by the East Coast Free Militia during the Second Civil War. The entrance hall had a monument to those who had died that day, the damaged remains of the CIA's seal mounted on one wall as testament to the blackest day in the history of the Agency.

He got up and walked down the broad corridor towards the elevator that would take him up to his boss's office. She was his line manager and a former field officer who had taken up a desk after she married and became pregnant.

Anderson had always wondered what it must have been like for her as a female field officer working out of American embassies in foreign countries. Now that he had been sent out to manage an operation, it wasn't something he would ever want to do again.

Give him data and images to analyze, and he was in the zone.

The building's AI expert system had called an elevator for him, and he waited but a few moments before the door opened for him to enter. It automatically confirmed his destination and took him up to Moss's floor. He walked over to the door of her office, which was open, indicating that he was expected.

"Come in, Glen," said Moss as he entered the room. She was sitting with her back to the window, which he never understood. Surely, it was better to enjoy the view; there again, maybe she swiveled her chair when she wanted to look out? "Let me introduce you to Colonel Paul Russell."

"Nice to meet you, Glen," said Colonel Russell, a tall Confederated States Air Force officer with a shaved head, brown eyes, and ebony skin, who rose to shake his hand.

"Likewise, Paul."

"The colonel has read your report, Glen, and is here to make you an offer. Seems he wants to steal one of my analysts."

"Hardly steal, just permanently borrow more like, with a promotion."

"Exactly my point. Please sit down, Glen."

"Thank you. I take it that I have some say in this. Otherwise, why call me here?"

"Exactly, Glen. We're not stealing you from the Agency. Rather we're asking you whether or not you would like to come to work for a project as the Agency's representative?" said Colonel Russell.

"Do note that this would be a permanent transfer," said Moss.

That would mean he would become his own boss. "OK, not sure what's going on here. I'm just an analyst—why me, why now?"

"Do you want to tell him, or shall I?"

"Please feel free to do your spiel, Paul."

"Thank you. Well, you've been working on analyzing the intelligence data on the Chinese operation that recently required your input in Afghanistan. As you know, we have a project of our own, and when we read your report, you came to our notice."

Anderson looked at Moss, who had taken on a blank expression, and then back again at Colonel Russell, who continued talking.

"Up to now we had made the assumption that no living thing could move while the pillars open to other worlds. Your report has suggested that isn't the case. It also suggests that any attempt to destroy the pillars will fail, too, which has caused a certain amount of consternation over security," said Colonel Russell, crossing his legs and leaning back in his chair.

"And you want me to come and do what exactly?"

"Be an analyst. Do what you do best and act as the Agency's representative for the project. Your work has changed the playing field. This is your chance to get onto the ground floor of this project and make your mark."

"However, this would be a permanent transfer, Glen, and a commitment to move to the West Coast. Therefore, it's your choice. As I said, I don't want to lose you, and you would be moving to the boonies," said Moss.

"So, if I understand this right, my choice means either staying here and having more promotion prospects or disappearing into some black-operation project on the West Coast," he replied, wondering who the hell the colonel worked for to be able to make him such an offer.

"That's it exactly—your choice. The bright lights of Washington or the obscurity of serving your nation," said Colonel Russell. "The package includes generous benefits to go with the position."

"You sell that so well."

"I know, but here's the thing. You will be heading the CIA side of the operation. The project will be the biggest thing since JFK tasked NASA to put a man on the moon. And not only that, but the Navy and the Marine Corps will be brought onboard, too, providing a key person for future operations."

He realized that the colonel meant Sergeant Lara Tachikoma. "You're good."

"I try to aim high."

"Well, Glen, what do you think? Do you need some time to come to a decision?" asked Moss.

"I think I'm going to take up the offer. Sorry, but I'm sold."

"OK, I'll get the paperwork sorted out, and you can clear your desk at the end of the month. I still expect you to finish what you can before you go and make sure you have a handover of any cases that are still open."

He could tell that she was disappointed with his decision to go, but Colonel Russell's offer to be involved with the project was not something that one would turn down lightly, especially if it meant he could work with one Marine in particular.

The colonel stood. "I look forward to working with you, Mr. Anderson. Having an Agency representative on my team will, I think, make things run smoother."

Anderson stood and shook hands with the colonel. "Likewise, sir."

9. ASSAULT

Death is not the worst that can happen to men.

— PLATO

Staff Sergeant Espera
Fifth Special Forces Group
Combat Armor Suit Detachment Alpha
Tajikistan
Monday, June 29, 2071

Espera approached the target using the cover of the trees to mask the movement of his Ape suit.

Espera's *abuela*, who'd brought him up after his mother had died, used to say, "*Cuando menos piensa el galgo, salta la liebre,*" as in "When you least expect it, the hare jumps."

She'd had lots of old sayings that he'd never heard anyone else use to explain to him how the world worked.

From the sound of hammering on metal, there were people working in the building ahead. If there were any sentries on duty, it would help hide the noise of the team's approach. The trees also made it less likely any sentries would see the team.

When the hare jumped, the enemy would be taken by surprise.

Warrant Officer McAdams called, "Halt."

They stopped the advance fifty meters out from the nearest building while he conferred with the captain's team. Espera waited on the left flank with Sergeant Robinson, ready for the order to move.

"On my mark, move... Mark, move, move, move," said McAdams.

The six members of the assault team began the approach using bounding overwatch, leapfrogging the rest of the way to the target.

The darkness was broken as the enemy started firing. Someone must have heard them despite the banging going on inside the buildings.

Espera spun up his M134 minigun and opened fire at the enemy muzzle flashes. The weapon issued a ripping sound as the tracer rounds made a laser-like beam of light between him and the target.

He stopped firing and waited. He kept Robinson covered as his teammate moved forward. Watching for where the next attack might come from.

Sergeants King and Sanchez had reached the outside wall of the first building. Their Ape suits breached it by crashing through the wooden walls. Following doctrine to never enter by a door or window.

Flashes lit up the interior, followed by the screams of dying people.

There was a flicker of movement at the edge of his screen and he turned. Four figures had appeared out of nowhere on the far-left flank. There was a series of double-bangs as multiple rockets were launched towards his teammates.

Espera shouted, "RPG!" as one round missed, hitting the ground, exploding.

The other hit Sergeant First Class Nguyen. A pillar of flame rose up into the sky turning the black night bright, the explosion ripping Nguyen's Ape suit apart.

Espera let off a long burst from his M134, the shells and links clinking as they fell around him. When he stopped, the four men trying to attack the group were just so much blood spray.

The silence that engulfed him was profound: a requiem for Nguyen.

"Status report!" shouted McAdams.

Espera replied, "I'm good. All clear, no movement."

A litany of confirmations broke the stunned silence in the aftermath of Nguyen's death.

"Let's secure the area," said McAdams as he began searching for enough of Nguyen's remains to retrieve. "Two teams of two. Move it, people. We've got work to do."

Their orders were for him and Robinson to search the buildings.

They walked towards the first one, which was metal clad. Even in their Ape suits, they couldn't barge their way in, so there was nothing for it but to go in through the door.

Robinson took up a firing position at an angle to it, aiming inside and to the right, while Espera moved up and slid the large barn door open to the side. Then he aimed his weapon and backed up, covering the left as Robinson entered, sweeping the corners and ceiling in front of him.

Espera followed, covering the other side of the room and making sure Robinson wasn't in his field of fire.

Nothing moved, and the sensors showed the place was cold.

To Espera's surprise, parked in the middle of the barn were two of the largest trucks he had ever seen. Massive, brutal-looking angular ICBM platforms that rode on sixteen wheels.

His Ape's system flagged them as MZKT-79221 transporter-erector launchers. Back in the day, they had been the Russians' answer on how to hide Topol-M nuclear missiles. Make them mobile and drive them around the steppes of Siberia.

Now both vehicles were jacked up off the floor, their tires misshapen and deflated. Neither looked like they'd moved in years. A patchwork of flaking rust covered both vehicles.

"OK, Robinson, take point," he said, as they began moving between the two relics of a bygone age. "Can you make out the serial numbers?"

"Yep, got something. My suit is enhancing the image. Bingo, two lost ICBM launchers found. That's one thirty-year-old mystery solved. Pity it leaves us with even more unanswered questions," said Robinson.

Still feeling the loss of his friend, all Espera could say was, "Huah."

"Aren't you at all interested in how they got here? I mean these were the source of the five medium warheads that blew the hell out of the Middle East. Why the group who stole the trucks didn't use all the warheads the Topol-Ms carried is one of those unsolved mysteries, and there's at least one big warhead still missing, too."

"Nope, not real interested. I just want to find the remaining packages." He couldn't be bothered to figure out who did what and why, as it was all ancient history. "Let's keep moving."

They swept through the rest of the complex. They met up with King and Sanchez, who had found two of the three packages already dismounted and being prepared for shipment elsewhere. Clearly, their INTEL had been off when it came to the timing to move the warheads.

Someone was going to face a nasty surprise.

"Figures we'd find what we wanted in the last building we looked in," said Robinson.

McAdams joined them. "Captain says the local garrison has been alerted to our presence. So let's pack 'em, stack 'em, and rack 'em."

They started prepping the two *physics* packages—a euphemism for the radioactive components of the warheads—for extraction. McAdams's ordered them loaded onto the backs of King's and Sanchez's suits.

"Robinson, take point. Espera, you're our rear guard. OK, people, we ain't got all day. Let's get out of here before the locals arrive."

As Espera followed his teammates out of the building, for a moment his suit's screen went fuzzy.

The team started to make their way through the complex's courtyard, with everyone mindful of the local garrison's ETA. It would be another twenty mikes before they were here, but they needed to have cleared the area well before that.

The locals may only have fifty-year-old Russian T14 Armata MBTs, but he didn't want to be around when they arrived. The tanks might be old, but being hit by a 152mm shell could still ruin someone's day.

"Contact rear!" came over the comms-channel from Captain Downey's team, who were on overwatch.

Flares lit up the night sky as the firing started. A flash of light raced across ahead of them, followed by a boom as it exploded— a missile fired from high up on the mountainside.

Someone had cut across the mountain ridgelines to get here quicker. A lot quicker.

Espera turned and knelt down, using the building for cover while scanning where the fire had come from. His Ape's ECCM suite had automatically started running electronic counter-

countermeasures in response to the enemy's lidar. Captain Downey's team returned fire—the strobe lighting from their muzzle flashes causing their movements to appear to jump.

Espera sighted the enemy when the active camouflage rippled trying to mimic a passing tracer round. The lone four-legged machine was larger than anything he'd ever encountered.

His Ape suit flagged it as "unknown," with a stream of changing images in the corner of his screen flickering as it tried to find a match.

Then the apparition fired another missile, and Morales disappeared in an explosion. Espera's system changed his friend's icon, designating him destroyed.

Then the blocky enemy walker scuttled down a rock face, rappelling vertically, its four legs digging into the rocky surface. The torso of the machine turned and swung a large-caliber rotary cannon up and around to fire.

Campbell's suit shot off chaff to no avail as a line of light jumped across the black sky, lighting up the trees in the woods below, shredding everything it touched and tearing the armor suit apart.

Campbell's suit burst into flame as the ammunition cooked off.

Sergeant First Class Radoslovich shouted, "Time to get it on!" and spun up his M134 rotary cannon, sending a stream of tracer rounds towards the unknown enemy machine.

Espera watched as the light from the ricochets bounced off all around the enemy machine as it kept sliding down the rocky slope towards them.

Radoslovich fired all his missiles. They snaked through the night sky but missed their target. The enemy machine had released a panoply of flares and chaff making it an even larger target, which fanned out around it, moving with the breeze and drawing the missiles away.

Fire exploded to the far side of the vehicle as his screen finally bleeped to signal "Match Found."

It was a Russian Pokhodnaya Boyevaya Platforma 295, allegedly not yet in service. A walking tank that completely outclassed them.

It returned fire as Radoslovich ran for cover.

The enemy tracer rounds followed like a beam of light that gently touched the leg of the fleeing suit. Espera saw the leg disintegrate. Then the rest of Radoslovich's Ape suit was consumed as it was cut it in half and exploded.

Shit! Espera had to do something, but clearly the minigun wasn't going to cut it against the Russian walking tank.

He switched to his other weapon and selected smoke rounds. He fired at the area between the enemy and the three survivors of Captain Downey's team. He then flicked over to white phosphorus and fired three groups of three around the perimeter of the smoke, setting the woods alight.

He was rewarded by the sight of his teammates withdrawing.

"Everyone fall back," shouted Captain Downey.

Like he needed any encouragement to withdraw.

Espera turned and ran into the tree line, his Ape combat armor suit following the preplanned route to their pickup point. Now it was a matter of escape and evasion.

Their INTEL had not advised them of the need to load up for *Russian Bear* coming over the mountain.

The route back was generally uphill all the way. Which still somehow involved a large amount of scrabbling down loose rocky slopes. With the team strung out, his suit kept dropping off the network.

Espera wasn't able to track the progress of everybody as he made his way to the pickup point. He had to count on his training and trust there were three friendlies trailing him and four in front.

But the team's retreat was hardly a by-the-book withdrawal. It was more like a desperate attempt to flee, driven by terror and the sheer bloody-minded determination to stay alive.

After an hour he saw the first IFF icons of his team appear on his screen. Four of the team were waiting at the landing site. He called in and confirmed his direction of approach.

The network went fuzzy as the signal dropped due to the surrounding mountains.

McAdams called him, "Espera, move east and take overwatch."

He felt relief from being back in contact with his team, even as bloodied as they were.

Espera waited. Fifteen mikes passed and then a glitch appeared on the team network. For a moment his suit's screen filled with white static. It cleared as three icons appeared indicating the three survivors of the other half of the team.

Now all they had to do was wait for the birds to come pick them up.

Sanchez was having difficulty maintaining contact with the inbound Air Force crew, five mikes out, flying NOE across the mountain range.

Impatiently, he waited for their pickup as the minutes dragged by. Then he heard what sounded like thunder approaching, and he cheered in relief.

The first of the two Thunder Hawks came towards the LZ with flaps out to slow its approach. The tilt fans roared, blowing dust up to keep the craft level. Though the team was on solid ground, the aircraft was flying ten thousand feet above sea level, and it showed.

"Espera, pull in and provide perimeter security," said McAdams, directing Robinson to cover King, and Sanchez onto the first bird with the packages. "We'll take the second bird out with the captain's team."

"Roger that," he said, moving towards the pickup point.

The Thunder Hawk took off and circled back around, taking position to cover the LZ as its Dash-Two. The other bird swooped in, and they fell back towards it as the hatch opened up to show the aircraft's welcoming interior.

His screen glitched again, but this time a flash of light went past Espera as a missile missed by inches and exploded behind him. His suit's ECCM had done its job, but the blast still threw him forward.

"Son of a bitch!"

The Russian walker had followed them.

The bird above lit up the enemy, but its minigun fire did nothing more than provide the team with a spectacular light show of ricocheting rounds.

He got up and shouted, "I've got this!"

Shouldering his grenade launcher, he let loose a stream of HEAB rounds at the enemy machine, which rocked from the blasts, but the barrel of its rotary cannon turned towards him and fired.

Desperately, he tried to dodge a whole world of incoming pain and hurt headed his way.

His screen showed his left arm had malfunctioned. In a moment of clarity, he saw that it was gone, along with the M134 he had been holding. *Saves me having to carry it, though.*

Espera fell forward, unbalanced by the blow, as a stream of tracers whipped over the top of him. Rolling onto his back, he managed to bring his other weapon up as Schmidt ran towards him, only to take a hit from a missile.

Tracers laced the night. Espera knew he'd have to take one for the team.

Now the enemy machine seemed to move in slow motion as it launched the next missile at him.

His suit responded to his need to unload his weapon at the cause of his death. He emptied his magazine at the enemy walking tank. A missile hit the ground in front of him, and the blast from the explosion threw his suit into the air, ripping both the legs off.

As he crashed into the ground, everything went black.

10. PICKUP DAY

Character is simply habit long continued.

— Plutarch

Officer Candidate Lara Atsuko Tachikoma
Quantico
Monday, August 3, 2071

The tempo in the room changed the moment the order that handed us over to our sergeant instructors was given. We went from a still and orderly row of women seated at our desks to a confused rabble as the sergeant instructors went full-on ballistic on our sorry asses.

So no change there then.

I moved to where I was told to go, all the while being shouted at. I spent the next hour with my new platoon members being run ragged, ordered first to do one thing and then told to do the opposite.

The process was meant to strain us to our breaking point, but to me it felt a bit like coming home. We started by running out of the room carrying our stuff, only then to be told to stop looking at them, turn around, and head back in again, and so on.

The confusion was overwhelming, and that was the point. To see how we reacted when overwhelmed by things that caused confusion.

Once out of the room onto the parade ground, we were harried into the proper locations and took our places with our platoons.

There are only two positions a Marine can hold while on the parade deck. One is parade rest, where one stands with feet shoulder-width apart and hands behind one's back. The other is to stand at attention with feet together and hands on the seams of one's trousers.

I no sooner assumed the position of parade rest when we were all ordered to come to attention.

Whenever they shouted an instruction, we would do as ordered until we were told to stop and stand at attention. There may be two positions one can stand in on the parade ground, but generally only one that counts: being at attention.

Judging by the way three other women, one whose name tag read "Kelly," held themselves, it looked like my platoon had some other prior-enlisted or returning Marines in it. I got to know Kelly quite well by the end of training, as she was a total scream to be with.

The rest of the women of the platoon needed more orientation to what the Corps required of them.

So I, Kelly, and the other prior-enlisted women demonstrated how to hold themselves, leading by example. But this was nothing like Recruit Training, we weren't being moulded into Marines; we were being tested to lead them.

Everything happened at speed. It didn't matter how fast we did something, because it was never fast enough. Further, harder, faster became our mantra.

Next, we had to empty our bags out.

Those who were not quick enough had assistance in the form of shouted instructions that interfered with the task, which as you can imagine made the task harder. If we didn't do the task fast enough, then the sergeant instructors would empty our seabag out and make us pick it all up and repack it.

After all, the Corps did say this was pickup day.

All the time, they would be increasing the stress by ordering us to answer their questions as we attempted to repack our gear. The Marine Corps likes its officers to be able to walk, talk, chew gum, and take names—where name taking is by body count.

Then we began the Marine Corps Physical Fitness Test, which is the Corps' way of seeing whether or not we were worth training. We were expected to be fit enough to complete the course before we started, rather than being fit by the time we finished.

No use arguing or crying about it: if we failed this, we were out.

Get injured while training and we were out. No point crying to our mommy about the rights and wrongs of it, this was all part of the Corps. Did we have what it took to be a *Marine thing*?

As a woman, I had the choice between doing the flex-arm hang or pull-ups for my first test.

I managed fifteen clean pull-ups, which got me ninety-five points, being one short of the sixteen set for women as scoring one hundred points. But I'd been training with twenty as my target number and was grateful for this as I fluffed a couple, which didn't get counted.

I gave it my all, but needless to say, I thought I could've done better.

Next up, crunches, where I only got a disappointing ninety in the two minutes of time allowed me. By then I could feel the burn, and my last test was a three-mile run.

The good news was we wore running shoes.

The bad news was the heat and humidity, which was not helped by the instructors adding motivational comments like "You're looking weak," or "Pick it up candidate," or "You haven't got all day." The kind of comments that we learnt were par for the course.

I finished the run in twenty-one minutes and forty-seconds, which wasn't too shabby, even if I felt like an old woman by the end of it. Kelly told me I looked like one.

She was good to me like that.

My score at the end wasn't top drawer but respectable enough at two hundred and eighty-one out of three hundred. This put me six points over what was expected from an officer candidate, and fifty-six points above the failure line.

This only meant that I didn't get added correctional input, of course, as doing as expected wasn't the same as giving it one's all. And we lost a woman who fell and broke her leg on the run, which meant she was out on the first day.

"That has to suck big time for her," I said.

"Dang, it sure must," said Kelly in her Texas drawl.

During the first two weeks, we settled into the daily routine.

The lights were switched on at 0500, and the sergeant instructors would storm into the room ordering us out of our racks. Then into our shower shoes, flip-flops in the outside world, with the instructors shouting at us to create confusion.

Then there was the morning warm-up, followed by running over the bridge that took us across the railroad tracks to the chow hall for breakfast.

When we weren't running, we were marching.

At the end of each day, the instructors made us all drink a

canteen of water to hydrate. In the Corps you don't just drink water, the motto is "You hydrate or die."

We would stand and drink our full canteens of water.

When we finished we would hold them over our heads to show that they were empty. A few women would end up pouring some over themselves and onto the floor of the barracks. This would draw forth a splurge of sarcasm from our instructors.

Sometimes it felt like it would be easier to die.

Next, we would be ordered into our racks to sing the Marine Hymn.

Not the Corps Hymn, but the old song—"From the halls of Montezuma, to the shores of Tripoli." After that it was lights out, leaving the first two cadets on guard duty rota for the night. They patrolled the barracks to keep us safe because good habits die hard.

Our days were a mix of daily physical training, where we sought to improve our times, and classroom lessons. This was where we were taught by rote and had to memorize everything we were told. We were tested by having to repeat back everything on command from our sergeant instructors.

Not knowing something was not an excuse.

God help us if we got our leadership traits mixed up with our leadership principles. Otherwise, we would end up being ordered to stand at attention while a spray of sarcasm called into question our ability to remember how to differentiate our own body parts.

Like our asses from our elbows.

Other subjects included the history of the Corps, the major battles fought, and the names of famous Marines. As Kelly said, it was all shits and giggles until we got something wrong.

All the time we were being assessed to see if we had the courage to face our fears, tested to see if we had honor through being honest about ourselves, and tested on our commitment through showing our enthusiasm.

These are the key values of the Corps. We all knew what they were because the words were stenciled in big letters on the wall of our barracks for us to read.

Oo-fucking-rah!

By the start of week three, we had lost another two women from our platoon. This included one of the prior enlistees with shin splints, the result of a stress fracture. So she was out, just like that.

We stacked the vacant racks up at one end of the barracks and changed where we slept. All because the instructors wanted to keep us together in pairs.

That or confuse the hell out of us by changing where we slept each night.

By now our platoon was down to thirty-six effectives with another eight weeks to go. Up to this point we'd been wearing our go-fasters, Marine speak for trainers, and track suits. Then we transitioned into wearing our cammies and boots for our training, which was all part of upping the ante.

By this time I had lost four pounds of weight.

Other women in my platoon had lost more. None of us could eat enough to make up for the amount of calories we were all burning each day.

Well, not exactly true.

We could eat all we wanted, but it was keeping it down that was the problem. Our visiting Royal Marine Colour Sergeant, on an exchange program from Britain, told us that nothing says commitment to your physical training instructor like a bunch of women projectile vomiting.

He was an asshole.

The brutal training regime pushed us to the limits to build confidence. Survive this and we knew we could survive anything that life threw at us.

Did I mention the confusion?

The instructors knew exactly what was going on and when it was going to happen. Their job was to create confusion because it was all about assessing how we'd face challenges that were designed to create fear, uncertainty, and doubt. Each of the things we had to face every day had an element that would trigger a phobia in someone, causing us to pause or be unable to carry out the task required.

Refuse to complete a task and we were out.

This course was a make-or-break regime.

The Corps didn't want people leading Marines who would be unable to face their fears in combat, so they made us face them then. Could we carry on regardless of our fears to complete the mission? I knew the rules of this game and fell into the spirit of the training.

Then, in the tradition of the Corps, came the inspection.

For the Corps every formation is a parade, and we were expected meet the standards set down for us by the instructors. I thought I knew what I was doing amongst all the confusion and chaos, which was something to hold on to when the fears and doubts came to the fore.

So I spent time helping the other women in my squad.

Especially those who had failed their inspections, because that's what being a Marine is all about. Like it says on the board standing in front of the entrance to the school "Ductus Exemplo," leadership by example. Working as one member of a team together, knowing that we can trust the person on either side of us to do the right thing at the right time.

By then I was feeling the strain of the training, giving a hundred percent of myself to the tasks I faced, and began to wonder whether I could finish the course. Perhaps my one hundred percent wouldn't be good enough to get me through to the end.

So I told myself that the pain I experienced at the end of each day was the weakness leaving my body and a reflection on my courage and commitment.

I dug deep into my reserves and found I had run out of energy, so I dug deeper to the very core of my being through sheer willpower, driving myself not to give up. Usually, though, I was too knackered to think that deeply and fell asleep as soon as I could.

The days passed.

First, the confidence course, followed by the Tarzan course for teaching us how to climb high obstacles in a military manner. All of this leading towards the time when we would go through the Crucible, where we would have to face the Quigley.

This consisted of throwing ourselves into the nastiest, muddiest water we'd ever have the *pleasure* of finding anywhere.

The muddy water was almost as thick as peanut butter, and we were timed as we navigated the water-based obstacles. The Quigley owed its fearsome reputation to being worse than anything we could imagine. It was designed to brutally strip us of our preconceptions about ourselves.

Think we'd faced all our fears?

Think again.

We then carried our provisional service rifles with us everywhere and wore combat webbing. The rifles had certainly seen service with the Corps, back when dinosaurs ruled the Earth. But it meant we got used to carrying the weight.

The combat webbing was lightweight battle-rattle. So called, because it wasn't armor. It allowed us to carry mission-oriented equipment during our training.

It only weighed in at about twenty-five pounds, instead of fifty.

The fact that no one went to war without power armor would make one think that the memo about this being the twenty-first century hadn't been read at Officer Candidates School Headquarters. But here's the thing, the Corps had enthusiastically adopted power armor and all that it implied.

However, it was the old mantra of the right way, the wrong way, and the Marine Corps way at work.

Power armor allows women to be put into combat on an equal physical footing to men, and the Corps to put those women who want to fight into combat. But the Corps still trains Marines the old-fashioned way. Because it is not always about strength and bench presses, it's also about guts and determination.

We had one week to go until graduation, and our intestinal fortitude was about to be tested to the max by undertaking the Crucible. In the best tradition of the Corps, we got up in the morning and did the same things we'd done every other day.

As they say, there's nothing like a bit of routine to maintain a sense of order and military discipline.

We did push-ups, followed by carrying a log while running, and some marching around the parade deck in formation, interspersed with our last three regular meals during the day. It was a normal morning start, with the exercise beginning that night.

There's nothing like starting a two-day exercise without any sleep.

To be fair this is a clear message about life in the Corps. If you like to sleep in late, join the Army.

We loaded up with our battle-rattle and left the barracks at 2200 for a ten-mile march through the dark woods to get us into the spirit of things.

We started in a double column on the either side of the road with our sergeant instructors in the middle. Kelly was next to me, and we were both feeling in high spirits as we started to call cadence. We reached the end of the road and turned off and headed into the tree line, becoming a single file as we made our way through the dark woods and past the swamp.

As the light of dawn marked the beginning of the day, our instructor told us it was time to face the Quigley, and we started to run at half speed down the trail, stumbling along in single file from the night march.

As I jogged, the clinking of my battle-rattle marked the pace with each thud of my canteens biting into my body. I was already covered in sweat, and the heat had risen into the nineties. In the distance was a wooden pier over the bog that led to a trail beyond.

The pier wasn't for us, as we each dived in turn into the smelly, muddy water and crawled under the barbed wire while snakes squirmed around us.

We'd entered the Quigley.

No sooner had we worked our way past one obstacle, then the next awaited. After the barbed wire, I crawled through a submerged culvert, keeping a grip on my weapon despite the mud making it slip in my hands. It all sounded easy, until we realized that we were in a confined space, in dark, muddy water, while short of breath.

And that was just one small part at the start of the course that never got any easier.

The rest of the next two days was spent doing squad attack exercises. Each of us taking turns to lead mock assaults or holding positions and defending them from attack. Nothing fancy or complicated was expected of us tactically.

We just had to make our way to a position silently, then charge in guns blazing as we fired 'simunition' rounds.

Rinse and repeat until everyone had led an attack, having played the part of fire team corporal, platoon sergeant, or lieutenant in command.

It also rained every day, and through the night, too.

We only got one meal a day to sustain us. They gave us twenty-year-old MREs, which stands for Meals Ready to Eat. OK, I exaggerate, but MREs are three words, all lies, but when you are hungry you'll eat anything.

And we did everything in pairs.

I made sure that no one in our squad did anything alone, because of the old adage: two is one, and one is none. In other words, a lone Marine is easy to kill. With two Marines, one can always watch while the other works or sleeps.

By the morning of the third day, I was shattered and only realized that the Crucible was at an end when our sergeant ordered us to pack our gear and hike back down to the parade deck.

Waiting for us there was a V-32 Thunder Hawk Chicken tilt fan, which flew us over Interstate 95, taking us to the Battle School for chow. We disembarked in our fire teams of four and were met by second lieutenants, who themselves had only recently been through the Crucible. They led us to the chow hall.

There we ate with a weary slowness of those who had been through three days of hell.

11. CHOICES

We aren't living in a world where people are becoming more stupid or irrational, people have always made stupid choices and behaved irrationally; it's the human condition.

— CARL SAGAN

Technical Sergeant Ferretti
Magnetic Anomaly Project
Classified location West of Wenatchee, Washington
Monday, January 5, 2071

Ferretti sat with the heads of the Magnetic Anomaly Project Strategic Science Operations Team. It was the first time he had been privy to the discussions of the project's civilian bosses. He had listened to what was being said in what felt to him to be an overly bright room.

This probably meant he needed to get out more.

Dr. Samantha Emmerich, head of the Geology Group, was speaking. "If you look at the problem from one perspective, we may not need to send people. After all, NASA has been exploring the solar system using robots for the last one hundred years."

Dr. Emmerich had a reputation for being tightly coiled and impatient, with a severe brown bob haircut worthy of the military. She gestured with her hands making swirling motions. Ferretti interpreted this as her way of indicating the vast expanse of the solar system.

"However, they're in constant communication with their probes. Which we can't be," said Dr. Carpenter, the head of Atmosphere and Environment, who was overweight and wheezed when he spoke.

Ferretti thought Dr. Carpenter could do with eating less and getting more exercise.

"We can use expert autonomous systems to implement the experiments," said Dr. Linda Scott. She was the head of both the Mathematics and Physics Group and also the civilian head of the Magnetic Anomaly Project. She wore her long blond hair tied back into a ponytail.

"There are limitations on what such systems can do. Not only that, our androids have limited duration before they need to be recharged," said Captain Patinkin, the project's intelligence and security officer.

"So we unhook the Asimov Inhibitors and install atomic batteries," said Dr. Carpenter, wiping his lanky hair back with his hand.

Ferretti decided to interrupt the conversation. "Let me get this right. You want to send fully autonomous nuclear-powered androids through the pillars to visit other worlds?"

"We're not deploying them here on Earth, and it saves us risking our people. What could possibly go wrong?" asked Dr. Carpenter.

"You mean unlike what happened in Chicago back in '37?" said Ferretti, wondering if he was overstepping the mark.

"How likely is it that hackers are operating on these worlds? Really, Sergeant, I thought better of you than that," said Dr. Carpenter.

Ferretti had no answer that didn't cross the border of what was acceptable politeness and into a world of profanity. The room was now silent.

Dr. Scott broke the silence. "John, apologize to the sergeant now. You should know that he can't possibly reply to such rudeness."

"Excuse me, Sergeant Ferretti, I got carried away for a moment and forgot whom I was speaking to," said Dr. Carpenter.

Ferretti nodded an acknowledgement and said nothing, still too angry to trust his reply would be polite.

Dr. Carlyle, the head of the Organic Geochemistry and Biosignatures Group, broke the silence. "If we're going to use autonomous androids for exploring worlds, why can't we go to Three-Eight-Nine? Sure, we already have a lot of alien fauna to study, but intelligent aliens should be our priority."

"The same aliens that shot our androids full of arrows—so we may be technically in a state-of-war with them—depending on how our military minders wish to view the situation?" said Dr. Cameron, the head of the Inorganic Geochemistry and Mineralogy Group, who wore horn-rimmed glasses rather than undergo laser surgery to have his eyes corrected.

Ferretti noticed Cameron had the habit of taking his glasses off to clean when asking a question. He wondered if this affectation was meant to hide the man's obvious nervousness when speaking.

"I don't think we will be declaring war at this time, Dr. Cameron. However, I agree if an android fell into the hands of the natives on Three-Eight-Nine, them pulling apart the atomic battery might be bad for their health. However, atomic batteries may be worth considering for more extreme environments. If suitable safeguards can be put into place," said Colonel Russell.

"I think we are getting off topic here," said Dr. Scott. "I think it may be useful at this juncture to summarize our options." She paused for a moment to bring an image up on the conference room screen. "Phase One of our operation was to monitor the activation of the pillars and catalogue the number of times they opened."

An image appeared with 26,208 highlighted as the number of pillar activations each year. Ferretti knew the breakdown of the weekly pattern of repeat openings, but this was the first time he'd seen the relationship between these and the infrequent cycles of repeat openings that occurred over the course of a year.

The image changed as it was overlaid with what at first looked like random activations, until the moving graphs were manipulated to extract another pattern of opening cycles. A summary appeared with an estimate predicting the number of future new worlds the project might discover. So far, over the last nine months, the project had tagged 1,350 worlds out of an estimated 1,363 possible.

Ferretti didn't completely follow the calculations, but the scientists had so far been right in their predictions.

"Phase Two objectives are to select appropriate worlds for further study. We have a limited number of candidate worlds that meet our requirements. The four planets we are considering exploring, in number order, are: Zero-Nine-Five, which we know is a small island that opens up on a three-week cycle; One-Nine-Six, which opens out onto a desert plain every week; Three-Eight-Nine, which opens onto a jungle every four weeks, where we recently discovered intelligent life; and Four-Three-Seven, which opens into a cave entrance leading to an ice plain. That one opens every thirteen weeks."

The discovery of One-Three-Four-Zero and the twenty-six-week repeat opening wasn't on the list of worlds due to the technical difficulties of running a mission with a six-month delay between pillar openings. Ferretti knew worlds had also been excluded due to adverse biological and chemical factors that would complicate operations.

"Until we can solve the problem of how to get people safely through the pillars, we won't be able to establish bases off-world. Only then can we start thinking about undertaking contact with the aliens on Three-Eight-Nine," said Dr. Emmerich, stating the obvious to make a point to Dr. Carlyle, who Ferretti gathered she disliked.

He agreed with her—she had a point—but he couldn't see the benefit of antagonizing the man.

A mission to Three-Eight-Nine promised the possibility of more excitement than Ferretti had signed on for. He could all too well imagine a lot of running and screaming going on with arrows flying all around.

Something best left for others to deal with, because he was happier being part of the rear echelon maintenance force.

Dr. Scott spoke. "Candidate world Four-Three-Seven's cycle time of thirteen weeks makes it easy to exclude. Until we can prove the reliability of our solutions work, I think it opens up to too many opportunities for system failures. However, the other three planets offer us options worth further exploration. So, if I can ask Andrew and Ken to work together to review which of the three worlds, if any, is our best option. Can you report back within a month, assuming that works for you both?"

Dr. Scott's kicking the decision down the road by having Dr. Carpenter and Dr. Carlyle working together to solve the problem was a good way to have them argue it out without involving the rest of the team. For Ferretti, adding a month to the schedule for whatever the project decided to roll out typified the civilian mind-set.

"Yes, works for me," said Dr. Carpenter, with Dr. Carlyle nodding in agreement.

"Meanwhile, if you can look into the atomic batteries from NASA for us, Colonel, and report back on whether or not they're suitable for our needs, that would be most helpful," said Dr. Scott.

"Yes, ma'am," replied Colonel Russell. "I'll get my people working on it right away."

Ferretti knew that would mean him.

He had to wonder if anyone else apart from him understood all the things that could go wrong from sending autonomous atomic-powered robots through the pillars. It wasn't as if Hollywood hadn't made enough movies over the years about robots going on the rampage.

<hr>

Monday, February 16, 2071

Ferretti ended the call to Dr. Scott by saying, "Yes ma'am."

He turned back to his workstation and wondered why Dr. Scott felt the need to micromanage him while he was in the middle of preparing a robot exploration team for the next off-world mission. You'd think he hadn't had any experience in maintaining the androids over the last eight months at the project.

Colonel Russell had ordered him to prepare four teams for extended independent operations. This meant not only making the androids autonomous but also providing them the ability to recharge themselves.

Theoretically, there should be no problems.

The old One-Zero-One bug had long ago been eliminated—through a combination of changes in the software and the addition of Asimov Inhibitors. But no one had allowed any system to run truly outside control-loop autonomously for nigh on thirty-five years.

Global Dynamics had sent an add-on control module to fit to the androids to take the place of a human operator. It all seemed to work as described, but such units weren't generally installed, because of glitches that could cause the system to hang. In this case, the freeze-ups were being touted as an additional safety feature.

Therefore, Ferretti was making sure that his preparations were being done by the book. He'd even managed to get clearance to access the archive of the original Boston Dynamics operator files. Even so, when he was done he would get Staff Sergeant MacReady to double-check his work.

MacReady was currently prepping four QuadMules in another bay.

They were being outfitted to carry a multimission radioisotope thermoelectric generator, more prosaically known as an atomic battery. Each battery contained four kilograms of plutonium 238, which had been beyond difficult to get ahold of. This would be the fuel to provide the charge for the android powerpacks extending their operational time from a maximum of twenty-four hours to up to four years.

Ferretti wondered how the android could be expected to operate for four years without preventative maintenance.

This was one of the things that he thought had been swept under the table, but it wasn't his problem, yet. No doubt at some point someone would come up with the idea to send maintenance robots through the pillars to go and fix broken-down androids.

It seemed to him that there was far more to exploring strange new worlds than met the eye. But there again, what did he know?

He checked his list for what to do next.

Set the permanent memory to read-and-write mode, check.

Installing operation algorithms for controlling QuadCopter drones was next.

Once he finished that, then it would be time to add the mission kit, which was a backpack that allowed the android to carry a whole bunch of modules with science experiments. In every backpack was a Westinghouse M-27 rock vaporizing pulse laser for geological analysis.

Apparently, every robot exploration team needed one.

12. OFFICER AND A LADY

Every marine is, first and foremost, a rifleman. All other conditions are secondary.

— Gen A. M. Gray, USMC

Second Lieutenant Lara Atsuko Tachikoma
The Basic School

The first thing that greets you when you arrive outside The Basic School is the bronze statue of Iron Mike. Raised in honor of Lieutenant Colonel William Leftwich. He was the commander of the First Recon Battalion during the Vietnam War, fought over a hundred years ago.

The statue is a reminder that you're part of something bigger than yourself.

It's all about the heritage of the Marine Corps, whose history is older than the country it serves. The statue stands out from its surroundings at Camp Barrett, which can best be described as a cross between a dilapidated holiday camp and a community center college that has seen better days.

Reinforcing the message of the Corps; we make do, mend, and carry on.

Which was no doubt why it was lovingly referred to as the bleeding sphincter by my fellow Marines. And who says we don't have a sense of humor?

Twenty-four out of the thirty-nine women who had started OCS training with me had graduated, including my friend Kelly.

The commissioning ceremony was a big deal, with everyone's parents coming to see us become officers. My mom attended by telepresence from San Diego, too, which was a surprise, but at least she didn't embarrass me. Everyone was respectful and polite, and her Scottish mannerisms were largely passed over as glitches in transmission.

People often wonder at the turns of phrase I use, but once you've met my mom, you'd understand why. Still, I can't help reveal my geek upbringing.

After the ceremony, we went straight to Basic School, where we made up one platoon of the training company. The others came from different commission sources like the Naval Academy or the Naval Reserve Officers Training Corps out of the civilian colleges.

After that we were split into two squads of twelve and further divided into three fire teams of four.

We were then assigned to basic officer quarters, which were cozier, too, for definitions of *cozy* that meant four bunk beds in a small room; but it was better than sleeping in barracks.

It also meant we had a better "head-to-head" ratio when we needed to sit on the crapper in the morning.

However, mornings still started at 0500. So no change there then.

The mantra of the Marine Corps is that every Marine is a rifleman. This hasn't changed in spite of women making up 20 percent of everyone in the Corps.

This can probably best be understood by understanding that the Marine Corps is an old-fashioned gun club. For the Corps, it's all about shooting the guns. It should come as no surprise that the first three weeks at Basic School were spent learning to shoot a rifle on the ranges.

We were also issued our HULC Mod-4, Human Universal Load Carrier, which are first-generation exoskeleton power armor suits. These carry the weight of you and your Modular Tactical Vest body armor. This again is old stuff that the Corps hands out to trainees, so as not to spoil anyone by raising their expectations of using state-of-the-art gear.

We wouldn't be issued MARPACE suits unless we went on to do infantry training. MARPACE stands for Marine Power Armor Combat Environment. Shortened by Marines to MACES because it's less of a mouthful and sounds way cooler.

A MACE suit is standard issue for anyone assigned to the infantry. Even today very few women get into the infantry, but some do, and at least now we're allowed into all the combat specialties, because of HULCs.

Anyway, we were then issued our service rifles, 7.62 mm NATO standard bullpups that the Corps adopted after the Second Civil War, taking a leaf from the British Royal Marines' book. Soldiers love carbines because they're easy to carry, being not so long as a rifle. But then, they're not as accurate as a rifle either, because carbines' shorter barrels don't extract the full potential of the rounds they fire.

When the old 5.56 mm NATO standard round proved to be too wimpy for the current threats Armies were facing, soldiers had gotten used to carrying something that was the length of a carbine. Unfortunately, firing a 7.62 mm round out of a short barrel carbine is a bit of a bitch, with an enormous muzzle flash, poor controllability, and a lot of wasted energy.

This, as they say, would never do for the Marine Corps, which prided itself on training everyone to be a rifleman.

So it needed a weapon that was as short as a carbine but also had the barrel length of a rifle. Hence, the bullpup.

Rumour had it that senior NCOs at the time had apoplexy over the introduction of the weapon. They had to change the Manual of Arms to account for the different configuration of the bullpup, with its magazine behind the trigger assembly.

For some it was a betrayal of all that was holy about the traditional rifle. But they changed the training, and the end results justified the decision.

So each morning we would march up what was lovingly called Cardiac Hill to get to the ranges and practice our shooting. People who tell you that shooting is all about attaining some zen-like moment are bullshitting you, because there are only three things that matter.

First is the sight picture, where you learn how to line up the front and rear of the rifle's sights.

Second is what the Corps calls *bone support*. This means you rest your rifle on something, and if that's your arms, then you use the bones in your arms as a tripod.

Finally, third is the natural point of aim. This occurs when the rifle drops down slightly as you exhale and squeeze the trigger.

Never mind you're inside a MACE suit with enough computer wizardry to hit an inch-sized target at a thousand meters. The Corps expects you to be able to shoot without the help of such modern conveniences, even as it insists on mixing measurements. So I spent my next two weeks shooting my rifle and improving my score.

The score one gets on the range is important, and I managed 306, which was good enough for my Expert Marksman Badge.

After that we spent the next eighteen weeks practicing our

leadership and military skills. We were expected to undertake our academic studies while doing so.

This meant starting in the classroom studying what we needed to know. Then we took what we learnt in class outside, writing orders in the field until we could do it in our sleep. After that we put our orders into practice by carrying out attacks.

With the added bonus of doing so during what was now winter, in the snow-covered fields and woods surrounding Camp Barrett.

While the training was hard, there was fun to be had, like training to fire the Browning M2HB .50 caliber machine gun. Owing to our prior experience, Kelly and I got our *Ma Deuce* set up first and started banging out rounds.

The sound of each shot reverberated through our bodies from the concussion of the shots being fired. The shots from the team next to us was even louder. I was glad we were wearing our power armor, which stifled a lot of the noise.

We were practicing firing at some old tank hulks that were about 1200 meters downrange. Once we adjusted the sights, we were soon hitting our target.

Kelly and I fired short, controlled bursts, lighting the tank up.

The last part of the training was the Offense and Defense week, O&D for short, which was a five-day field exercise spent in the woods. On the last day's night mission, I felt I got to be in my element for the first time since I'd arrived there.

During my first week at The Basic School, I'd been asked what military operational specialty I wanted. I wrote down "light-armored reconnaissance" because that was what I'd been trained to do.

It was also one of those areas of combat open to all women,

on account that body strength isn't a requisite for driving a CASE-2X combat armor suit.

The Corps long ago gave up on the idea that women shouldn't be allowed in combat. But some areas are hard for women to qualify in.

Some tests still had to be passed without using a HULC suit.

If the troubles in Iraq and Afghanistan at the turn of the century hadn't fully convinced the Corps that women could be useful in combat, then the Second Civil War surely did.

Imagine my surprise to find I was being sent for infantry training along with Kelly. When I asked why me, I was told that it was the needs of the Service.

The Infantry Officer Course is the last bastion of the Marine Corps old-school hard-core values, being uncompromisingly male in its attitude towards, life, the world, and women. Of the twenty-eight in the training platoon, we were the only two females.

It was made very clear that we would not be accorded any due deference on account of our gender.

Given that 90 percent of the women who are assigned to the Infantry Officer Course are washouts, I had to wonder if it was the bad mental attitude on display. Faced with that prospect, Kelly and I *girlied* up at every opportunity.

And then made sure we kicked their sorry asses by outperforming every last swinging-dick one of them.

Some people say I have a bad attitude and a mean streak towards men. I tell them my mom was Scottish, my dad was Japanese, and I'm a redhead. So go deal with it, OK.

As for Kelly, she told me she's as ornery as they come 'cause she came from Texas. I certainly wasn't going to argue with her.

So we spent the next ten weeks running around wearing a MACE suit practicing how to call in air support artillery and how to fight in somebody's home in a mock city block to teach us counterinsurgency tactics.

We used frangible safety rounds during training.

These break up on impact and are *safe* if you are inside your power armor. Outside of a MACE suit, not so much. Without armor you could expect broken bones at best, and a hit to the head would still be terminal.

We trained against androids that were being run by officers assigned to the training cadre. Getting hit by a Browning .50 caliber frangible round is no joke, even when you're inside a MACE suit. It sounds like someone trying to hammer their way inside to get at you.

During our final week's evolution of fighting in a built-up area, we'd all been taking turns to lead the platoon attack against insurgents in houses. It had shown us what a meat grinder urban combat could be. Everyone got to be the platoon leader as we went through the exercises that our teachers had planned for us.

Unlike during previous weeks, we were playing the part of a Marine Expeditionary Unit.

This meant we got to practice calling in close air support provided by a couple of Chickens, and even a light-armored reconnaissance CASE-2X suit squad to support our attacks.

Lieutenant Gorman was giving us our orders for the attack on the tallest building in the town we were fighting in. It was a six-story steel frame with cinder blocks, which someone had sprayed "Nakatomi Tower" on the side of.

We'd been told that it represented the headquarters of the insurgents who were holding American hostages. His plan was a by-the-book approach using bounding overwatch.

Our instructor spoke. "Well, what do you think of the lieutenant's plan, people?"

"It sucks. The situation sucks, sir," said one of the men.

"Well, we never promised you a rose garden when you joined the Corps. What you going to do about it?" asked our instructor.

"Suck it up, sir!" came the reply from all the men.

"You're being quiet there, girls. What do you think?" the instructor asked.

"Permission to speak frankly, sir," I replied.

"Sure, Tachikoma. Go ahead, tell us as it is. Don't hold back now and spare anyone's feelings, will you."

"The plan sucks donkey balls, sir."

"What do you think, Kelly?"

"I agree with her, sir."

"I agree with you both; the plan sucks big time. Tachikoma, you'll lead the platoon, and you've got fifteen mikes to come up with a plan that doesn't suck donkey balls."

I made Kelly my platoon sergeant, and I drew up a plan redeploying the ground support CASE-2Xs assets from Gorman's plan and calling for our air assets.

The feeling of the air rushing past the open hatch of the Thunder Hawk was exhilarating as we made the approach to the top of the tower. Dropping off the back of the ramp, as our bird hovered above the roof, I landed with a thump, then the rest of the platoon followed me.

Behind me, Kelly was admonishing them to move faster.

The tilt fans roared as our hovering bird flew off—time for us to move.

"First squad, move! Move, move, move," I shouted, pointing to the stairwell access ahead.

Time seemed to slow down as the first squad stacked up, ready to pack in and attack any waiting enemy. The point man gave the signal to blow the door, which flew inwards with a satisfying crunch as it hit an android standing guard.

Its companion, staggering from the blast, was taken down with a flurry of shots to its center of mass as it tried to attack us.

If our instructors had told us right, we were now left facing ten combat androids, which had turned our three-to-one attack into a much more favorable four-to-one odds. But we would need every advantage we could lever to get through the building and get the hostages out, because room-by-room clearance of an entrenched defender is pretty much the definition of taking a walk through hell.

First squad advanced down the stairs, trampling over the android knocked down by the door. We each fired a shot into the downed machine as we walked over it: both to test-fire our weapons and, for the rest of us, to practice making sure it was out of commission.

You can't be too certain when it comes to making sure something is knocked out.

The stairwell led to a door and a short corridor that had two exits.

"Kelly, take first squad right, I'll take second squad left. Gorman, hold here and keep our extraction route open."

I'd made Gorman the sergeant for third squad as a way of showing there should be no hard feelings over the plan and our instructor's choice to put me in charge.

My squad stormed into a room full of debris from broken fixtures and fittings, but was otherwise empty of hostages. Behind us the sounds of short, controlled bursts filled the air—Kelly's squad taking down one of the android insurgents guarding the androids acting as hostages.

"Kelly, make sure to scan all the hostages."

"On it," came the reply.

I didn't put it past our instructors to set up androids to pretend to be hostages but were actually terrorists in disguise. After all, it's what I'd have done if I were in charge.

With a short blast, a combat android pretending to be a civilian was taken out. Kelly gave the all clear indicating all the hostages had been scanned. The next part of the plan was to extract them safely, and then we would have to clear the rest of the building.

The briefing was clear on the matter of letting no combatants escape. Personally, I would have liked to get everyone back aboard the birds and bomb the building from a safe distance. But I didn't get to make that call.

"Gorman, take the hostages to the roof and call for extraction," I said, ordering third squad to babysit the androids pretending to be civilians. "The rest of you follow me, we have a rat's nest to clear out." We now had eight combat androids to take down, which meant that we were back to three-to-one odds now that we were a squad down, but them's the breaks.

Kelly's squad flowed past me and went down the stairs ahead of us.

My squad followed hers as we tackled the tricky job of rooting out the enemy.

We had two things going for us. The first was they'd expected us to come in from the ground floor, and second was having the high ground. The next floor down had four combat androids waiting to ambush us, but we caught them by surprise, and they were out of the fight.

Now the odds were in our favor by almost seven to one.

Then the instructors, bastards one and all, realizing that the Thunder Hawk landing on the roof meant the gig was up, set the androids into free-fire mode. Up to now they'd been operating the combat androids through their virtual-reality sense-scape, which meant they were in the fire-control loop.

Now the androids would fire as soon as they got a lock on us.

This would shave milliseconds off the combat androids' response time.

It may not sound like much, but a few milliseconds is all it takes to change the balance of the battle. But it was terrifying when the whole world exploded around you. The sound of all the shots being fired was deafening, even with our suits' noise-abatement earpieces.

"Rock and roll, people, lay it on," I said, shouting encouragement, because there's only one answer when the shit hits the fan: make sure to unload one's ordnance with extreme prejudice.

My remaining two squads found the *zone*, moving by fire teams, securing each floor in turn, pulling our mounting number of wounded along with us as two of ours fell for each combat android we took down.

I regretted my decision to let all of Gorman's third squad go, but not everyone had the flexibility to reorganize squads on the go, because that hadn't been part of the plan.

I might have been clever in using the Thunder Hawks for insertion, but I felt stupid for not being clever enough to plan for this contingency. It sucked, and our only option now was to execute the plan with extreme violence.

Kelly shouted, "They're retreating."

Relief swept through me as the last two combat androids retreated outside the building, no doubt planning to set up an enfilade for when we followed them. Now they would pay because I'd had enough foresight to set up our CASE-2X recon squad to lay down the hurt on anything trying to escape the building.

The combat armor suit operators were instructors, so they knew the score, and my platoon would still be required to finish off the OPFOR.

This we did by catching the android insurgents in withering crossfire that slaughtered them. Still, it reminded me of my CASE training when we'd had to clear a town in a similar scenario, and it's no fun chasing down combat androids whether you're inside a combat armor or power armor suit.

Besides, if we had dropped on the top of the tower in Dogs, we would've crashed through the roof and not stopped until we hit the ground floor.

The end-of-the-scenario horn sounded, and my platoon cheered. It felt good to kick ass, especially android ass that had gone into full free-fire mode. Still, I'd been lucky; it could've all gone tits up had the OPFOR team been more on the ball.

13. TESTING TIMES

Many of life's failures are people who did not realize how close they were to success when they gave up.

— THOMAS ALVA EDISON

Dr. Allison O'Neill
Magnetic Anomaly Project Scientist
Classified location West of Wenatchee, Washington
Monday, July 27, 2071

Allison had been as surprised by the news that people could walk through the pillars. Something that everyone on the science operations team had believed impossible. Dr. Scott and Colonel Russell's announcement changed the scope of the project.

The project has gone from being observers to being able to send people to other worlds. A few days after the announcement, all the military personnel had been screened, with only Technical Sergeant Ferretti passing.

Now Allison found herself allocated to the first group of ten civilian staff sent to the gate room for testing. She felt electrified when the pillars shimmered. Then the fear had been replaced by an overwhelming urge to walk up and touch them.

She had been shocked to find herself stopped by an android under the control of Technical Sergeant Ferretti, who had led her group in.

He'd told her, "You get used to it."

He'd been right; she had. Afterwards, she'd felt sick in the pit of her stomach. That had been two days ago.

Allison was helping to get the remainder of the civilian staff tested by leading groups of ten into the gate room every hour for the next eight hours. The group size was limited by the fact that the project's science program still had to run.

Yesterday they hadn't found anyone who could move when the pillars cycled.

Now she was standing outside the corridor that led to the gate room with the first group of ten for the day. Allison knew a lot of them from her time here at the project. They'd all seen the safety briefing together and made jokes about the big freeze.

Now they were going to be exposed to a very real risk.

By lunchtime she'd led four groups in for testing and again found no one. Afterwards, she went to the canteen for lunch and saw Ferretti eating at one of the tables. She walked over and asked, "Mind if I join you?"

"Not at all, though I've almost finished, and I'm due back on duty in ten," he said.

"Thank you. It's been a long morning."

"I guessed—because you're looking a bit frazzled. How's it for you now?"

"Fine, you were right about the 'surge of elation' thing. It no longer overtakes me in the same way. I've become detached from it all. Trouble is, I'm bored."

"Not surprised, but one of us has to be doing it. My turn tomorrow."

"Will we have any more people to test tomorrow? I'd hoped we would've run through everyone by the end of today."

"Just the one group of project personnel who have been reluctant to be tested."

"That sounds like fun—not."

"It's just the project heads who say they're too busy. The colonel is rounding them up for testing."

"I would've thought that they would've been first in line."

"You would've thought," he said, smiling at her.

"Changing the subject. This morning someone asked about a fence and I gave the standard answer; but thinking about it now, I'm just wondering why we don't place a shield around the pillars."

"Ma'am, the way I understand it, the room is the safety fence. The room is to keep people outside of the zone."

"OK, I can see that, but why not just say that?"

"People are scared now. Imagine how much more scared they would be if they understood what it took to make them safe."

"Oh…"

"Exactly. Well, I've got to go now. Catch you later."

Allison watched Technical Sergeant Ferretti get up and walk out of the canteen, and she spent the rest of her meal in silence, taking the time to consider her thoughts as she ate.

After lunch Allison headed back over to security to pick up the next group of ten due to be taken down to the gate room. Having spoken to Ferretti, she realized that her life had been changed by the outcome of that day more than she'd imagined.

Allison couldn't begin to know what it must be like to be frozen in fear.

Her colleagues said it was dreadful when they were frozen,

unable to move. It was like being a puppet under the control of an outside force.

So now she was no longer just a research assistant. Now she was on the very short list of possible Alpha Team members. This meant she would one day step through the pillars and visit another world.

Allison took her afternoon group across to the main building for the safety briefing film, and signing of the disclaimers to say that they'd understood everything they'd been told. This process perplexed her, as they could have streamed the film to them at anytime, but the military were technological Luddites when it came to things like this.

Even so, it was the height of paranoia to not stream it across the project's secure network.

Like all the other groups, the first one of her afternoon was ten more people who had been released from their departments for testing. They walked outside into the afternoon sunshine towards the tunnel that led inside the mountain. This was their first time under the mountain, which had up until now been strictly off limits to unauthorized personnel.

Most of them had only seen pictures of the pillars before.

Once they entered the tunnel, the talking stopped as they approached the blast doors leading to the pillars. She repeated her instructions to enter and take a seat.

"Any questions?"

A woman from the geology department asked, "What's supposed to happen?"

Allison wondered if the woman had even listened to anything in the safety briefing.

"In all likelihood nothing will happen, except you'll be unable to move your body. Remember, you may experience a sense of dread or fear, but nothing bad is going to happen to you. I will ask you all to try to turn to face me as the pillars shimmer when it cycles open."

A few moments later, the atmosphere in the room changed with the excitement rising in her body as it responded to the magnetic field, and the urge to walk towards the pillars came over her. At the same time she was aware that the room felt somehow unreal, her sense of perception being changed by the pillars.

She turned to look at the stood like statues, but still able to hear and speak. She wondered how that worked.

Walking to the right of the group, she asked, "Can you all please try to stand and face me now?"

Like all the other groups, the people were frozen to the spot when the pillars shimmered behind her, but she saw someone move. He stood there, tall and gangly with curly brown hair, wearing a T-shirt and jeans.

"You're Adam Wilson. Am I correct?"

"Yes, that's right. I'm an astrophysicist from the Mathematics and Physics Group. Gosh that was…just…so…awesome," he said, his voice trembling.

"I imagine you may have an urge to walk towards the pillars at the moment. Do you need me to help you stop?"

"No, I think I can manage, but thanks. What a rush, my mind is racing. It's as if I'm seeing the world for the first time as it really is." He took out his PAD and tried writing. "My PAD isn't working," he said.

"No, it won't unless it's shielded."

"Ah, the magnetic field must be causing interference; of course it does. I should have realized that. How stupid can I be? I know this stuff, but it's odd in here, like my mind has been altered in some way."

Allison had given up all hope of finding someone else, but here was another like her. She no longer felt like such a freak for being different to the other scientists in the project. Adam looked at her, and she wondered if they were thinking the same thing.

"It has, but you will get used to the effects in time." Remembering what Technical Sergeant Ferretti had told her, she said, "Welcome to the A-Team, Adam."

14. NEXT DAY

The only thing we have to fear is fear itself.

— FRANKLIN D. ROOSEVELT

Technical Sergeant Ferretti
Magnetic Anomaly Project
Classified location West of Wenatchee, Washington
Tuesday, July 28, 2071

Ferretti walked into the gate room with the project's five department heads. Of them, only Dr. Carlyle was in a shape that wasn't fully in the round.

He said the now-familiar-to-him instructions to his charges, "If you would please take your places inside the yellow box painted on the floor in front of you. Chairs have been provided for you to sit on for the five minutes of this test."

He watched as everyone apart from Dr. Carlyle sat down, which was pretty much what he had expected.

"Please take a seat, Dr. Carlyle. When the pillars shimmer you may be unable to maintain your balance and fall over."

The pillars shimmered and Ferretti turned towards them as a rush of anticipation swept through his body in response to the magnetic pulse. He turned back to look at his charges, seeing the fear on everyone's face, bar one.

"Dr. Emmerich, I do believe that you're standing."

"Sorry, I couldn't help myself—I just had to get up. This is such a beautiful feeling," she said.

"Congratulations, Doctor," he said, waiting for the shimmer to cease before leading them all off for processing. No one was more shocked by the outcome than Dr. Emmerich herself, which made four people from the project who could pass between the pillars.

15. SERENDIPITY

People often avoid making decisions out of fear of making a mistake. Actually, the failure to make decisions is one of life's biggest mistakes.

— RABBI NOAH WEINBERG

Mr. Anderson
Magnetic Anomaly Project CIA Liaison Officer
Classified location West of Wenatchee, Washington
Saturday, August 8, 2071

The last couple of days at the Agency sped past with Anderson occupied with organizing his travel plans for his trip out west. The project was located approximately equal distance between Seattle and Spokane, outside of the town of Wenatchee.

He wasn't keen on winter snow, so he preferred to be on the Spokane side of the Cascades.

He'd decided to take a flight out to Spokane International, which he had found had been originally called Geiger Field. But he still had too many details to arrange, like finding somewhere new to live and a mode of transport.

His flight to Spokane was delayed by inclement weather. An unseasonal storm front was sweeping down from the north, grounding aircraft, which meant taking a later flight out the next day. Despite the extended journey time, Anderson eventually found himself driving away from the car hire out onto Interstate 90.

Anderson remembered his last day at the office…

"So is it true you're leaving our sunny climes for the wetness of the Pacific Northwest?" asked Pantoliano.

Anderson looked at his friend and realized that Ben was going to miss him.

"I'm going to Spokane, not Seattle, so it's not that wet. Anyway, if you liked me that much, you should have asked me out on a date."

"You're such a joker, Glen. I don't know why I thought I'd miss you."

"Well, it's because you're such a dork no woman would want to go out with you."

"Look who's doing the talking, Mister. I've not had a steady woman in my life since the divorce, Anderson."

Anderson looked at him and said, "Got me there, bud. I'm dying here."

"Yeah well, if your best friend won't tell you, who will?"

"You will…"

"Oh, you wound me. If you cut me, do I not bleed? My blood spills, but what you don't know is that if you strike me down, I shall become more powerful than you can possibly imagine, to rise again stronger than ever before," said Pantoliano, gesticulating with his arms and clenching his fists.

"You're doing that misquoting-and-monologuing thing that we talked about again."

"You've yet to feel the full force of the monologue, young analyst. Stay with me here and we can rule Langley together."

Anderson couldn't stifle the laugh. "Hey, I'll miss you, too. Let's keep in touch, OK?"

"Sure thing," said Pantoliano as they clasped hands and did the manly hug thing that guys do that involves hearty slaps to hide their fondness for each other.

The truth was that Anderson would miss the friends he'd made during the four years at Langley. But the other part of him had gotten itchy feet, and it felt like the time to move on to greener pastures.

He'd been living in a furnished condo since his divorce and had very little in the way of furniture to move. Other stuff, like books and his rifle collection, were another matter. Anderson thought about how to haul his gear west, and decided to pack what he could and call in a removal company to sort the rest out for him.

The next morning, Anderson met up with his realtor before driving west out of Wenatchee.

The area was known as the Cascade Volcanic Arc because the whole region was geologically active.

Following his GPS, he looked for the turnoff from the main road that led to the project—and managed to overshoot it. The road was cunningly hidden away from sight by trees that formed part of the southern edge of the Wenatchee National Forest, which forced him to stop and do a U-turn.

Anderson drove up to the entrance gate and stopped at the guard post, showing his ID.

"Sir, please park your car in the visitor spot to your left and then proceed for processing at the trailer marked with the welcome sign."

"Thank you."

The place was a building site with trailers set out around the edge of the parking lot. Anderson made his way to the trailer with a small welcome sign that said "All Visitors Please Report Here" underneath it and entered the spartan room. After being issued a pass, he was told to wait for an escort.

A dark-haired man wearing an Air Force uniform came into the room. "Good morning, Mr. Anderson. I'm Captain Patinkin. I'm to escort you around the base. Please come with me."

Anderson got up and followed the captain through another door, which opened onto a narrow passageway that led out the back of the temporary building.

"We're going over to the main building first. The trailers are just where we're working out of until we finish building the permanent housing. I apologize that the XO couldn't meet you, but she's off-site this morning. Once I saw your file, I thought you might appreciate having an Air Force representative show you the ropes. By the way, I'm the project's S2, so we will hopefully have something more in common, too," he said, walking towards the building across from the trailers as he spoke.

"Well, it's been a few years since I last wore the uniform, but thank you for the thought, Captain. I'm looking forward to settling in and getting to know people."

"Don't get too excited. You have to sit through the safety briefing first," he said, leading the way inside to a soldier in an Army uniform sitting at the front desk, who scanned their passes.

Patinkin was right about the safety briefing but wrong about the excitement.

However, the part that showed an early accident, in which a worker lost his arm when he fell across the front of the pillars as they activated, was an eye-opener. Mostly from seeing how little blood there was, which was down to the shock from touching the pillars that had killed him outright.

Since then no one had been allowed to work within a fifty-meter radius of the pillars, with everything being done by remote. After watching the film, Anderson got to sign the waiver saying he'd understood the safety briefing and that he couldn't sue the North American Confederation Government if anything happened to him while in the vicinity of the pillars.

Then the fast-walking, and garrulous, Captain Patinkin led the way to the gate room. They walked down a road that led into the interior of the mountain, and they entered the chamber where the pillars stood dormant. Anderson was told to sit on one of the chairs placed within the yellow safety lines painted on the floor.

Captain Patinkin then left him alone to wait.

Anderson sat and stared at the androids working on stacking up packages for transfer through the pillars on the next cycle. The pillars shimmered, and he was drawn to walk towards them.

He stood up.

An android walked in front of him, blocking his way.

"Looking at you, I guess you might have an urge to walk towards the pillars. I wouldn't recommend you do that; the shock from touching the shimmer field will kill you. Hence, the safety brief. The scientists are working on solving that problem," said Captain Patinkin, talking through the android.

The shimmer stopped, and a sensation of normality, dullness, and boredom in equal parts descended on him.

Captain Patinkin entered the gate room and waved at Anderson to follow him out.

"You might feel like you're coming down from a high, but don't worry, that'll pass in a few minutes. Meanwhile, we can add the Alpha-Whiskey classification to your pass," he said, leading them back out of the mountain towards the building he'd first taken Anderson for the safety briefing.

Anderson looked at the captain's pass and saw it had "Two-Bravo" written in white on a red square on it. "Two-Bravo and Alpha-Whiskey mean what?"

"Project personnel designations. Two-Bravo means base bound. Alpha-Whiskey means you're on the list of suitable personnel to form the Magnetic Anomaly Project first Alpha Team. For when we start going through the pillars and visiting other worlds."

Oh wow. "How many of us has the project got so far?"

"You're the fifth person we've found, which makes a total of six people we know about. The scientists are coming up with a portable testing device so that we can screen people without having to bring them to the project."

"Sounds exciting."

"To each his own I guess, Mr. Anderson. Personally, I'm petrified at the thought of walking towards those things. Let alone going through them and stepping onto another world."

"When do I get to meet the other Alpha-Whiskeys?"

"Later. We've still got to get your pass tagged with your designator before I can orientate you to the layout of the rest of the facility. I've been asked to take you to see General Russell."

Anderson blinked in surprise.

"Ah! You've not heard about his promotion?"

"No, it's news to me," said Anderson, wondering how he'd missed the announcement.

"Afterwards, I'll show you where the canteen is, then your office, and take you around the laboratories and introduce you to everybody."

"Everybody? I thought that there were five hundred people involved with the project."

"There are, but not everyone is here on-site. Some will be back in Seattle at the university, where they have access to more facilities."

"Must cause you some security headaches, though."

"It's our hide-everything-in-plain-sight strategy. Anyway, let's go sort out your pass and go see the general."

General Russell was sitting at his desk and rose to shake Anderson's hand when they entered his office.

"Good to see you again, Mr. Anderson. Welcome to the project, and congratulations on the results of your test. Before Captain Patinkin takes you around the base, I just want to say that you'll be meeting a lot of rather brilliant scientists who don't like the military involvement in this project."

"I'll keep that in mind, sir."

"Good. If there's anything we can do to help you settle in, please ask. I have scheduled you to attend some of the meetings over the course of the next few weeks to bring you up to date on the project's status."

"Thank you, I look forward to sitting in on them and getting to know how things are run here, sir."

"Trust me when I say that everyone will be keen to introduce themselves, especially the others like you."

The general was right. When Anderson met people and they saw the Alpha-Whiskey tag on his pass, all of them were keen to express their heartfelt wishes of good luck for his future with the project.

Anderson's fellow Alpha-Whiskeys formed a rather exclusive club, one that everyone wished to be a member of, but was glad they weren't.

16. THE CAVERN

There is no rule more invariable than that we are paid for our suspicions by finding what we suspect.

— HENRY DAVID THOREAU

Staff Sergeant Espera
Magnetic Anomaly Project
Classified location West of Wenatchee, Washington
Monday, May 2, 2072

Espera had enjoyed bright summer's morning sunlight while being driven to the project. He took the chance to admire the ponderosa pines that covered the hills and mountains. His arrival at the Magnetic Anomaly Project had seen him whisked through the checkpoint like a VIP or very important parcel.

Now he stood next to Technical Sergeant Ferretti in a cavern.

Espera estimated it to be nearly hundred feet across and fifty high as he tried to get his head around what he was looking at. "That's not something you see every day."

"Nope, sure isn't, but that's not the best bit."

The two pillars were almost black, like old rusty iron. They towered over Espera like brooding sentinels. He had been told they were a touch shy of eleven meters tall and stood just over four meters apart. Their shape reminded him of the roots of a pulled tooth turned upside down.

Then the space between the pillars shimmered, and instead of the wall of the cavern there was blackness. Espera had a flashback to his hospital stay.

The darkness was broken with flashes of light, and then the pain swept over him. Then later more flashes of light and words before the blackness took him away again. He groaned as light flashed into his eyes.

"Welcome back, Sergeant Espera. You've taken your time regaining consciousness," said a woman in a white coat.

"Whooo'rre yooouu?" he croaked.

"I'm the surgeon who has been operating on you to save your life."

"Docctoour Whooo?"

"Ms. Barnes. Here, take a sip of water," she said, placing a straw into his mouth. "Slowly now."

Espera tried to move but found that he couldn't. "Caan't moove."

"Please try not to move, because you're still in casts. I had to repair both arms and legs, and your head injury had us all very worried. You've been in a coma since you arrived here."

"Hoaw loooong?"

"Take it easy. You've been here five weeks," she said as he fell asleep.

Sometime later he awoke and looked around the hospital

room. His arms and legs were suspended in casts, and he could hear machines bleeping.

"Ah good, you're awake," said a male nurse. "You've got people waiting for you. Do you feel up for visitors?"

"Yes. Who is it?"

"Your friends. I'll go call them in."

Espera lay in bed and tried turning his head. It hurt a bit, but he was rewarded by the sight of Chief Warrant Officer McAdams and Captain Downey leading the survivors of CASDA 5136 into the room.

"Glad to see you made it," said McAdams.

"You, me both, Chief."

"You're fucking awesome, man," said Sergeant Sanchez.

"An indestructible killing machine," said Staff Sergeant King.

"Jeez, thanks, guys, good to see you all, too. So how?"

"You're born lucky, or you're too dumb to know when to die," said Sergeant Robinson.

"Lucky he missed the board of inquiry, you mean," said Sergeant Sanchez.

"Quiet down, people," said Captain Downey. "The good news is that you're alive, and we made it out of there. The bad is we missed a package and need to rebuild the team."

"You can count on me," Espera said.

"I know, son, but you've been rewarded with a new assignment," said Captain Downey.

"As long as they don't send me for officer training, I'm good," he said, coughing.

Chief Warrant Officer McAdams spoke. "Don't make me laugh, Espera. You—an officer!"

"No, Sergeant, it seems you're special. Don't ask, because we've been told we don't have the clearances," said Captain Downey.

Espera didn't know what to say. The teams had been his life, and now he was being sent elsewhere.

"Agency business?"

"You got it. Seems they have a need for people like you," said Captain Downey.

Still, it could be worse; he could be dead. "I need to sleep now," he said, suddenly feeling very tired from all the excitement.

Espera felt a tingling sensation, almost like burning, that swept over him, followed by a rush of euphoria. "Are you feeling what I'm feeling?"

"It's different for everyone we've tested who doesn't freeze, but everyone feels excited when the pillars pulse."

"Glad it's not just me. For a minute there, I thought I was going nuts."

"Not just you." The shimmer ceased. "Time to go, follow me," said Technical Sergeant Ferretti.

The cavern seemed more normal to Espera, and having confirmed that the test done on him prior to his arrival had worked, he followed his wiry colleague out of the cavern. They walked back down the tunnel out into the normality of a summer sun.

All the secrecy surrounding his transfer was now unfolding as he was let in on the secret project.

They headed across to the main building, Ferretti leading the way to a room that was used for the science operations team's meetings. It was brightly lit, though bearing all the hallmarks of institutional decoration: white ceiling with air-con vents, pale blue walls, gray carpet, and power sockets sunk into the floor.

A large table with seating for twenty people dominated the

room, but today more chairs had been brought in to accommodate extra people invited to attend.

"I've got everything ready to go for the presentation, so why don't you take a seat."

Espera decided he wanted to be at the back of the room so he could watch everybody during Ferretti's dog-and-pony show.

"I could grab us coffee."

"No need. It gets brought in before the meeting starts," said Ferretti, the doors opening as an automatic trolley with a coffee urn came into the room. "See…"

Behind the trolley came the first of the civilians, so Espera went and grabbed a coffee before making his way to the back of the room. He waited for it to cool before sipping it as more civilians came and sat down chatting amongst themselves.

He stood as General Russell entered and nodded at him.

"At ease, Sergeant. Please sit down."

It may have been framed as a request, but Espera treated it as an order. It wasn't every day a general spoke to you by name.

"I hope Ferretti has made you welcome?"

"He has, sir."

For a moment he felt scrutinized, under the gaze of someone who analysed and assessed him in one moment. And having seen him, General Russell moved onto talking to the civilians.

***

Ferretti had started his presentation, and Espera was boggled by how much stuff Ferretti ran through during it. It was a hell of a lot to learn, and he was relieved that he had a recording of today being streamed to his PAD.

One thing for sure, he had a lot of catching up to do.

"Let me give a brief overview of where MAP is now," Ferretti said. "We're entering our second year of operations. During this time we've identified one thousand four hundred and seven different locations that the pillars open to…"

Espera let the words flow over him as Ferretti described how MAPCOM had started out under a civilian open-science framework for studying the region's active geologic strata and subterranean magnetic anomalies.

The site had been chosen using satellite data from Air Force orbital assets. The original digging had been done by contractors working for the Geologic Survey. When they'd found the pillars, the Air Force had stepped in and taken control.

Espera imagined that this had rather thrown the civilian scientists off balance, as they'd thought they were in charge of the site.

"We haven't been able to confirm that all of the locations are on other worlds, because ninety percent open up inside caves, and are therefore underground. As we compile more data from our monitoring stations, we should be able to refine a definitive answer to this question. However, we're pretty confident that they do."

"Where does the doubt lie?" asked Mr. Anderson, proving to Espera that the CIA didn't know as much as it liked to think it did.

"The homogeneity of some of the results is a confounding variable," said one of the scientists, who was identified as Dr. Wilson by Espera's PAD. And he wondered what that meant in plain English.

Fortunately, the doctor carried on explaining the situation.

"We're getting results from certain experiments that are suggestive. We're analysing rocks from Earthlike planets that may well be, in fact, from Earth…"

Espera glazed over as the explanation of the number of worlds with the pillars aboveground as opposed to sitting in caverns was explained in excruciating detail. He then realized that when the

Chinese had discovered the other magnetic anomaly in Mongolia, things had hotted up.

Ferretti then brought up footage of the attempted robot exploration of the pillars. An android with a QuadMule walked between the pillars tagged as Alpha Echo Romeo Tango One, the image splitting into multiple views showing the initial walk through to Planet One-Nine-Six.

The data stream indicated everything functioning as planned.

Next to it ran the screen showing the fate of the robots, and the view from the robot exploration team standing on a rocky desert landscape by a small waterhole with some vegetation around it. As the android knelt down by the waterhole, there was a ripple in the water, and its arm was caught between the jaws of a creature that looked like a cross between a crocodile and a Komodo dragon.

"This event initiated a defense upgrade for the next robot team," Ferretti deadpanned.

Espera approved, and he would make sure to approach all waterholes on alien planets with due caution and armed for extreme prejudice.

Alpha Echo Romeo Tango Two's feed was replayed next.

It started with the team setting off and somehow managing to walk around in a circle. The end of the sequences showed the robots coming around and back upon the pillars. The transmission ended when the pillars shimmered, and the robot exploration team walked through to another world.

He had to stop himself from laughing out loud, but that sure was the funniest thing he'd seen in a long while.

"We have been able to record the movement of the team with our network, but as yet have been unable to retrieve the lost robots."

"What caused the problem, Sergeant Ferretti?" asked one of

the civilians, flagged as Dr. Emmerich, who was another of the civilians not frozen by the pillars.

"It was an unexpected emergent property from the competing stochastic algorithms that drive the dynamically stable gait."

Ferretti's answer proved to Espera that the man was essentially a geek.

All walking robots fidget. It was what would be called Parkinson's disease in a human. The next set of mission recordings was streamed as Ferretti talked everyone through what happened next.

As if robots being eaten or becoming lost weren't enough, Alpha Echo Romeo Tango Three had managed to fall down a hole. As far as robot exploration teams go, the projects had drawn the short straw on the luck front.

While team three had not been lucky, Alpha Echo Romeo Tango Four had been deployed successfully. And so far, was running flawlessly. The mission was returning high-quality data with soil and rock analysis.

Espera sat through the questions thrown at Ferretti, and the summary by the science team.

Dr. Scott, the civilian head of the project, finished up by saying, "We have a total of forty-nine worlds we can access, with forty-four having reasonable windows of retrieval for sending teams to."

She paused.

Which, to Espera, sounded like a lot of opportunities for things to go wrong.

Continuing, she said, "Of these, fifteen are worlds with a weekly opening cycle. Twelve worlds we can reach once every two weeks, and ten worlds that we can access every three weeks. There are another seven worlds that repeat every four weeks, which leaves five worlds that can be accessed between five and twenty-six weeks."

With that announcement, the meeting wound down, and Espera reflected on why he had been transferred to MAPCOM.

As he worked his way through his notes, the pieces of the puzzle came together. His role as part of the team sent to retrieve three lost nuclear warheads, but which missed one, occurred to him.

The cost of that failure had led to an operation in Afghanistan where a company of Marine Dogs—combat armor suits—had been able to retrieve the lost nuclear warhead and extract the bodies of the dead Alpha Detachment who had been lost during the initial retrieval operation.

Clusterfuck barely summed up the operation, and the Marines had been lucky to be in the right place at the right time and not have their asses blown up by the nuclear bomb intended to sanitise the other site.

One Marine in particular had been instrumental in snatching victory from the jaws of defeat. Espera looked forward to meeting his new commander.

17. TACHIKOMA ARRIVES

The Marines have landed and the situation is well in hand.

— ATTRIBUTED TO RICHARD HARDING DAVIS

Second Lieutenant Lara Atsuko Tachikoma
Magnetic Anomaly Project
Classified location West of Wenatchee, Washington
Sunday, August 28, 2072

I'd transferred at Seattle onto a local carrier airline and landed outside Wenatchee at Pangborn Memorial Airport, named after the man who had first flown the Pacific over a hundred and forty years ago. The landing was a bit rough, and the runway certainly looked old, but it was still better than dropping out the back of a Thunder Hawk.

Glen was waiting for me, and I walked across to his olive-green Jeep to take us into town. The back was down, and the sunroof was open.

"Hey you, long time no see."

"Have we met before? You look vaguely familiar. When was

the last time we saw each other? I can't remember," said Glen.

I slapped him on the arm, and he made out like I had hit him hard. "I guess you've not missed me then?"

"I wouldn't say that."

"I wouldn't either, not unless you want me to really hit you."

It was the first time we'd been together for almost a year.

"That was a bit awkward for a moment. Are we good?"

I looked at him and thought about when we'd met back in the sick bay on the CSN *Hornet*, when I'd been at my lowest ebb.

"No, we're good. It's just going to be a bit strange until we get used to being around each other, I guess."

"Sounds like we have a plan, though, and I love it when a plan comes together."

"Nice wheels you've got there."

"You need a four-by-four if you want to get out and take in the countryside around here. Anyway, the Jeep's yours."

"You're kidding me."

"Consider it a present, and an apology for not coming to your graduation. Here's the keys," he said, dropping them into my hand and then getting into the passenger seat.

I stood frozen on the spot while my life flashed in front of my eyes.

After a few moments I got in and started her up, and we drove off to my new home. We spent the evening cooking together, with Glen chopping vegetables that I turned into a stir fry, before going to bed and getting better acquainted with each other.

The next day I drove up a dilapidated road behind Glen's truck in my new Jeep, which led to a guarded entrance to the Magnetic Anomaly Project facility. The day was sunny, and if I hadn't needed to report for duty, I would have dropped the top, let my hair down, and had the wind blow through it while I drove along.

As it was, I was wearing blues, feeling the weight of the lieutenant bars on the collar and the service ribbons on my chest. I was conscious of the fact that there are not many second lieutenants with a Bronze Star, Navy Achievement Medal, Combat Action Ribbon, Presidential Unit Citation, Navy Meritorious Unit Commendation, Good Conduct Medal, CSMC Expedition Medal, and Sea Service Deployment Ribbon.

The route to the base took us through the middle of a forest of pine trees. Before the entrance gate was a big red board set back from the side of the road.

It welcomed us to the Magnetic Anomaly Project, stating that we were entering a site under the joint control of the Confederated States Geologic Survey and Air Force Space Division.

The tag line said, "Using Space to Explore the World."

Glen's truck went through first. I drew up in my Jeep and halted next to the guard, handing him my PAD, which had my orders on it.

"Thank you, ma'am. If you would like to drive down and follow the road around where the truck has just gone through, you'll see a sign that says 'visitors report here,'" said Corporal Wallis.

I smiled and thanked him and drove after Glen.

It was better that we both had independent means to get there, but part of me wished that I could have ridden in with him. I parked in a free spot a couple of spaces down from where he'd left his truck.

I got out and found myself in the middle of a construction site, albeit one that had a background forest with ponderosa pines that stretched into the far distance. A three-story building sat to the left of a road that led inside the mountain.

Looking around, I saw on my right a bunch of trailers being used as temporary buildings with a sign that said, "Visitors Report Here."

I walked over to the trailer and entered a small office that had been partitioned off from the rest of the interior. An Air Force NCO looked at my PAD's copy of my orders. "Thank you, ma'am."

Getting called *ma'am* was still going to take some getting used to, too.

After I'd answered his questions to confirm that I was who I said I was, he printed out a badge for me. As I put it on, I noticed that his had Two-Bravo in a red box, while mine had Alpha-Whiskey on it.

"What is the significance of the red letters, Staff Sergeant Chen?"

"Areas of operations, ma'am. Two-Bravo means base bound. Please take a seat and wait until someone arrives to escort you to the XO's office."

A short while later an Army specialist named Redmann arrived.

"Lieutenant Tachikoma, if will you please come with me, ma'am."

I followed him, noticing that there were lots of people wearing yellow safety helmets. They were standing around gawking at a crane lifting a large steel beam from one end of the site to the other.

We entered the main building, and our passes were scanned before we took a lift to the third floor, where I was led down a corridor to the office of the executive officer, Lieutenant Colonel Foster.

Redmann knocked on the door, announced my presence, and left me. I heard, "Come in."

I walked in and came to attention in approved Marine Corps

fashion. Feet together, elbows back, hands on the seams of my slacks, and looking over the XO's left shoulder at the wall behind her.

"Good morning, ma'am. Lieutenant Tachikoma reporting as ordered."

She looked at me, stood up, and came over to shake my hand.

"Sofia Foster. Welcome, please take a seat. Would you like a coffee or water?"

"A cup of black coffee would be nice, ma'am."

She poured two cups and gave me one, and I sat on the sofa in front of her desk, quickly scanning the room. I'd never had an Army colonel pour coffee for me before.

On the wall was a picture taken some while ago of her graduation with her fellow Army officers at West Point. The mug on her table had the motto "Logistics Win Wars." Next to that was a picture frame with a series of changing pictures of what looked like her partner and children.

Foster looked to be in her late thirties, and her short hair was going gray.

"So how was your journey here, did you find us OK?"

"My flight was fine, and I followed Mr. Anderson here this morning."

"Glen's a good man. I've been impressed with his work for the project. I understand you met him on a mission he was running."

"Yes, ma'am."

"I've read the report. It makes for fascinating reading, and I'm sure that some of the scientists here will be wanting to talk to you about it, too."

"I'm not sure there's much I can add to what I wrote."

"Maybe not, but I'm sure that everyone will want to ask you how it felt to keep reliving the same day over and over again. I can only imagine it must have been quite frightening to feel trapped in a situation you couldn't control."

"The truth is, the first time it happened I thought I was dreaming, experiencing some sort of déjà vu. Once I died the second time, the situation became clearer. Reliving the same day had its moments, but on the whole, I'd rather not have to ever experience that again."

"Looking on the bright side, it means that you're here with us today. I don't suppose you've been told, but we now know that only one in a thousand people can do what you can do. Anyway, tell me, how was your officer training?"

"I know it may sound stupid, but it was fun in a strange kind of way. It really pushed me to my limits and made me realize what I could do when push came to shove."

"So where are you from, Lieutenant?"

"San Diego. My mom still lives there."

"I see. What about your father?"

"He died just before my thirteenth birthday. I was an only child, and Mom never remarried."

"That must have been a difficult time for you. So, what made you join the Marine Corps?"

"I wanted to be part of something bigger that demanded the best of me. Something I could be proud of that would be of service to my country. I was also a bit of a tomboy, and the Marines appealed to my sense of adventure, I guess."

"Well, I can easily imagine that alternatives could have been a lot worse."

"Yes, ma'am," I said, thinking about the other choices, like getting pregnant or working in a service industry and getting pregnant.

"Anyway, moving on, let me give you a brief outline of what we're expecting from you, and what your role here is. As you can tell, we're a joint service operation. We originally started out as a combined Air Force and Geological Survey project, using satellite assets to map magnetic anomalies. Once they began digging and found the pillars under this mountain, and we realized what they represented, the Army became involved to facilitate the construction on the site. Then the CIA discovered the Chinese were studying their own magnetic anomaly, and we found other pillars in Afghanistan. All of this would have remained rather academic until we discovered that some people are not affected when the gate opens up."

"I see, ma'am."

"You'll be going on missions through the pillars. You'll be in command of all the military personnel off-world, but the civilians will be in charge and will run the science components of the missions. Your job is to provide them with what they need and protect them at the same time."

"It sounds like I will be herding cats, ma'am."

"You'll be dealing with a highly strung and temperamental team of civilian scientists who just happen to be brilliant at what they do. I would like to say that you will have the best of the best under your command, but the people we would like to send through the pillars are not the same as the ones who can go. I'm afraid that with a few exceptions, the people under your command are here because they're gate walkers. Uh, that's what we call people with your ability, like you."

"Why don't we just take people through who are frozen? It's not like they can run off or anything."

"It's a good question. The thing is we tried that approach, and the results weren't good. All our test subjects required psychiatric treatment from the distress it caused. We tried sedating people, including using a general anesthetic, but the long-term risks from aneurysms were judged to be too high. Our scientists are working on what they call a *pharmacological solution*, but they tell me it will be several years before we see results. Until that time, you and other walkers like you will be leading the way."

"I see. Thank you, ma'am."

"Do you think you're up to forming this new unit, Lieutenant?"

"Yes, ma'am, I do," I said.

There's nothing like being presented with a new and challenging situation that gives one the opportunity to rise and meet it face on. After all, what sort of welcome to my new duty station was I expecting, given what I'd been through?

"Good, let's get you settled in then. The files for your unit are already loaded on the system for you to read. More members of your team will be arriving over the course of the next few weeks, so you'll have plenty of time to adjust to your duties here."

"Thank you, ma'am. I look forward to it," I said, as she stood up and we shook hands again.

My PAD had been uploaded with a map of the base and the location of my new office, which turned out to be a lot bigger than I expected. Since I was expecting a room the size of a broom closet, that probably doesn't say a lot.

18. PLANNING

Paperwork will ruin any military force.

— LᴛGᴇɴ Lᴇᴡɪs B. "Cʜᴇsᴛʏ" Pᴜʟʟᴇʀ, USMC

First Lieutenant Lara Atsuko Tachikoma
Magnetic Anomaly Project
Classified location West of Wenatchee, Washington
Thursday, September 22, 2072

To my surprise, I was promoted to first lieutenant. Another surprise was my office had a window that looked out onto the tree-covered mountains, and a view that wasn't going to get old anytime soon.

Despite said surprises, I'd settled into a daily routine of reading personnel files and planning how to structure a team.

Even so, part of me wished I was back in Fleet.

I interspersed the desk work with daily training and meeting up with various scientists. All of them wanted to talk to me about the time I walked through the pillars and how it felt. They treated me as if I were some kind of celebrity.

Building my so-called platoon was turning out to be a slow process, as there were only twelve of us including myself and Technical Sergeant Ferretti. This doesn't quite make a Marine squad of thirteen, so calling it a platoon was a bit of a misnomer.

As far as I could tell, military personnel were being screened when they were due for their annual physical fitness test. But that only occurred where transcranial test units were available. Even then, those who tested as suitable had to have their transfers agreed to and processed by their respective chains of command, assuming they also met the security requirements.

At a knock on my door, I looked up and said, "Come on in."

"Good morning, it's me and Staff Sergeant Espera to see you as ordered, ma'am," said Ferretti.

"Take a seat. Coffee anyone?"

"Yes, please, thank you, LT," said Espera.

Despite the nonchalance of his demeanor, Staff Sergeant Espera was wired tight, and even if I hadn't read his file, I would've known he'd seen some hairy action from the way he scanned the room. I recognized a lot of me in him.

"Yes, ma'am, thank you very much," said Ferretti.

Technical Sergeant Ferretti was a solid NCO who had an easy-going laid-back air about him, which would've seen him run ragged in the Corps for not being *Moto* enough.

"OK, I called you here to discuss our chain of command and organization. I really want your ideas on how we best organize our new Alpha Team, so please feel free to speak your minds today."

Espera spoke. "We've got a real mixed bag of skills and aptitude. One might almost go as far as to say the potential for a total clusterfuck is guaranteed."

"Not sure I would totally agree, but it does seem to me that we'll have to write our own rulebook."

"Which is all well and good to say, Ferretti, but it sounds to me like we're doing it the hard way."

"I've learnt that the only easy day was yesterday," I said.

"The thing is that, with all due respect," said Espera, "we're light on operators and high on support personnel."

"That rather assumes that we need boots on the ground to kick down doors and lower property values, though, doesn't it? Since the project's primary purpose is research, I think that we'll be needing more support personnel, not less," Ferretti responded.

"You both may well be right given the dual nature of our role. However, what we have to overcome are the disparate skills and aptitudes of our team. So, what do we need to do to address this problem?"

Ferretti spoke. "Long-term, I would say secondary-skills training. Short-term, job cross-training so everybody can do more than one thing, ma'am."

"We could do that," Espera offered, "but some of our people are marginal on the physical fitness front. Not only that, but some have had only minimal time on the firing range."

"OK, anything else?" I asked, sipping my coffee.

"Just one thing. How do you intend to choose the senior sergeant?" asked Espera.

"I believe Technical Sergeant Ferretti is senior." They were equivalent ranks—E6—but according to their files, Ferretti had longer time in service.

"With all due respect, while Ferretti is senior, we're not a unified combatant command, and I am the senior Army NCO."

"Staff Sergeant Espera, if all our wishes came true, then I'm sure we'd all be somewhere else. Given that we live in such an imperfect world, we'll have to make do with what we have."

"Yes, Lieutenant, but..."

Espera looked like he was going to say something when he

paused. I took the opportunity to head off any hasty words he might regret.

"Don't get me wrong, Sergeant. When the shit hits the fan, which it surely will if Murphy has anything to say about it, I expect your input when the time comes for the meat to meet the metal."

Espera's shoulders relaxed as he replied, "I'm sure you will. Thank you, LT."

"Between the pair of you, I want a physical training schedule for our platoon drawn up, and I will be joining you. I will talk to the XO about getting a firing range sorted out, and can you put your heads together on mixing and matching people for on-the-job training?"

"Either we're going to be flying high, or we're going to crash and burn in a blaze of glory," said Ferretti.

"Huah," said Espera.

"Yeah, or as we like to say in the Corps, gung-ho!" I said, as this was one time when we were all truly going to be in it together when the shit started flying.

Saturday, November 19, 2072

My command was about as far from impressive as one could get, though Staff Sergeant Espera was wont to remind me that it was the same size as a Green Beret Alpha Detachment. I reminded him that, with a couple of exceptions, our people were hardly Special Forces material.

He'd laughed at that.

Not that this was a totally bad thing. For one, there was less ego. Furthermore, each member of my team was literally one in a thousand, and it was my privilege to command them.

Besides, discipline makes the soldier. Discipline and training.

And on that front, Espera and myself led the way. Technical Sergeant Ferretti met me in my office, and together we walked down to the waiting team.

"Penny for your thoughts, ma'am."

"Just thinking about all the things that make our mission vulnerable to failure and going over in my head our critical assets."

Being part of a unified combatant command meant I had to deal with the assumptions underlying what each thought of as his or her standard operating procedures. Nothing differentiates the Marines from the Army and the Air Force quite like logistics.

The Air Force is all about supplying the forward operating base and maintenance of their assets; the Army likes to build lines of support with regular deliveries to units; and the Marines go in with everything they need for thirty days.

"I have every confidence in you, ma'am. It was a good call to have everyone come in today."

Having been on the other side of boot lieutenants' inventory checks, I'd cringed when I'd issued the order for an inventory session.

Especially since it was the weekend before going out for our first mission. But we needed to confirm the contents of each container, because it would be a failure on my part to plan properly if things were missing from the manifest.

We entered the storage area, where Staff Sergeant Espera stood in front of the assembled team. He called, "Attention, officer present."

He'd called the Army equivalent of "Attention, Officer on Deck," but I still found myself surprised at being the officer. Old habits take time to change.

"At ease, people. Thursday is the big day, and I for one do not want us dropping the ball on this one. Apart from the fact that it makes us all look stupid, there's a very real risk of death from unknown unknowns. My intention is to make sure we don't make problems for ourselves by forgetting to take everything we need."

I paused to look at how my people reacted to what I'd just said. While I had every confidence in the Two-Bravo support troops my team was relying on, they weren't the tip of the spear, we were.

"We're splitting into three teams to do a final check of everything and then sealing the containers. Any questions before we begin?"

"Do we get to go early if we finish before time?" asked Specialist Nelson, an African American woman, who got a steely eyed stare from Staff Sergeant Espera.

I stopped myself from replying with a sharp quip, as I was no longer a sergeant, and instead gave a straight-faced nonanswer. "The sooner we start, the sooner we finish. OK, let's get this show on the road, people. Fallout."

"You heard the lieutenant! Nelson, to me," said Espera.

I had plenty of advice, but the bottom line was I had to make the decisions.

The days where I looked to an officer to make decisions for me and my team were lost in time and space. Things were simpler then, when the responsibility for sending people into harm's way did not rest upon my shoulders. Still, if it hadn't been I standing there, then who would it have been?

Someone had to shoulder the responsibility, and the burden of command had fallen to me.

As the commander in the field, the buck stopped with me, and I would be setting the precedents for the way MAP would run its off-world operations. I was trailblazing a new path and setting SOPs for the future.

Therefore, I went with what I knew; we'd go with thirty days' supply. This meant a lot of planning and calculations based on operational heuristics, which is the military's way of saying "our best guess."

My reverie was broken as I heard, "Corporal Wachowski with Petty Officer Adams and Airman Jordan, ma'am."

Wachowski was a Marine specializing in vehicle systems, and she had her PAD out ready for action.

Adams was a navy culinary specialist. The attachment of a cook to my team still boggled me, but the civilian administration had insisted he was necessary for the operation.

Jordan was what I'd call a *Chair Force* blonde, a part of their security forces, which was what the Air Force liked to call its military police. She seemed to me to be basically a glorified clerk, but at least she could shoot, unlike Adams.

"Follow me," I said, leading them to the Conex box we had to check.

In my experience, the Corps issues the stuff it thinks you need, with the proviso of make do and mend. But Marines always take responsibility for making sure we'd checked everything— and, if necessary, buy the things that Corps hadn't deemed necessary for the mission.

I love the Corps, but there are limits when it comes to putting my life, and the lives of my people, on the line.

"Let's get some lighting rigged up here," I said.

"Aye, aye, ma'am," said Wachowski, who went and got some portable lighting, which made work inside the cramped confines of the container easier.

I brought up the manifest on my PAD and started scanning the codes on every item. None of this was particularly onerous in the bigger scheme of things, but I can't say it made for an exciting and fun-filled day. Unless one's definitions of fun meant doing boring, soul-sucking drudgery.

Still, mustn't grumble, many hands make light work.

Besides, it was better than the alternative—being stuck off-world in need of something we'd forgotten that was vital to the mission's success or our lives.

19. THE MISSION

The Earth is the cradle of humanity, but mankind cannot stay in the cradle forever.

— Konstantin Tsiolkovsky

First Lieutenant Lara Atsuko Tachikoma
Magnetic Anomaly Project
Classified location West of Wenatchee, Washington
Thursday, November 24, 2072

After weeks of arguments over which of the three worlds to go to, One-Nine-Six won.

Mostly on the basis that a desert environment would be easier to drive out onto. That, and the fact that we could retrieve our robot teams that had either broken down, gotten lost, or fallen into a hole.

The trouble with artificial intelligence is that it doesn't mean they're actually smart, or even intelligent for that matter.

I waited in the front seat of the leading Oshkosh HUHTT M2184 truck as the countdown worked its way towards zero. We were at the head of the convoy of twelve waiting to drive between the pillars that towered over us at almost eleven meters tall.

The gap we would drive through was a little over four meters. Enough room for most vehicles to pass through comfortably. But, the pillars stood close enough together to feel like we were having to squeeze through them.

Next to me were Technical Sergeant Ferretti and Corporal Wachowski, who sat at the steering wheel.

As an officer, I had *lost* my ability to drive.

Ferretti was immersed with the android team, which was standing next to the pillars. They waited in front of the truck, ready to walk through first in case of wildlife obstructing our passage. Though if that happened, we would more than likely scrub the mission and try again next week.

We had two dozen Alpha-Whiskeys, people, evenly divided into military and civilian personnel. I'd assigned Alpha Mike as the call sign to the former, and made the scientists' Alpha Sierra.

This had caused some bemusement among the civilians, who were not used to such things. But they said they understood my reasons for doing so.

I suspect they were just humoring me, though.

From the gate control room, Sergeant MacReady was watching the convoy on his screen. "How's it looking, ma'am?"

"All systems are nominal with just the usual chorus of 'are we nearly there yet' from the passengers."

"That's totally not fair. It's that sitting in the truck waiting for an hour before the pillar activates seems rather pointless to us," said Allison, sitting in the back seat of our Oshkosh.

"Sorry, Dr. O'Neill, it's just the way the military likes to do things," said Ferretti.

"It's called hurry up and wait. Beside where else have you got to be today?" said MacReady over the radio.

"Planet One-Nine-Six," said Allison.

"See what she did there, ma'am?"

"Sure did," I said, as the timer counted down the last ten seconds.

"Everyone sit tight, 'cause here we go," said Wachowski, engaging the autodrive function. This would guide the truck through the narrow confines of the pillars as we followed the androids through.

"You OK back there, Dr. Emmerich?" I asked as I felt a tingle in the pit of my stomach.

"Yes, I'm fine. Isn't this exciting?"

"I suppose if you think about what we're doing, yes it is."

"It's not like this is your first time, though, is it, ma'am?" said Ferretti.

"No, it isn't, and I'm kind of glad it isn't so exciting this time," I said as we drove from our cool cavern into the bright sunlight of One-Nine-Six.

Our truck lurched as the wheels rolled over onto the rocky, unforgiving desert landscape that went all the way to the horizon.

"We're clear of the pillars, and the second truck is coming through," said Wachowski.

"Take us well clear, Corporal," I said, seeing the rest of the convoy streaming through the pillars. When the last one was through, I radioed back. "Alpha Mike Whiskey One Six to base, we have arrived safely. Over."

"Roger that, Alpha Mike Whiskey One Six. Congratulations on a smooth transition. Pillar closure in fifteen seconds. Over," said MacReady.

"One short drive for us, but the first of many long journeys for mankind. Over," I said.

"Copy that, Alpha Mike Whiskey One Six. We're breaking out the champagne back here. Over," said MacReady.

"We'll have some when we get back. Alpha Mike Whiskey

One Six out," I said, as the pillars cut off further transmissions, leaving us under a blazing-hot sun.

"I'll really be able to work on my tan while I'm here," said Wachowski.

The convoy drove away in single file, swinging in a wide arc to look at the landscape surrounding the pillars to decide where we would make camp.

"Alpha Mike Whiskey Two Four, this is Alpha Mike Whiskey One Six, come in. Over."

"Acknowledged. Over," replied Espera.

"Where do you think it would be best to build Base Camp Alpha? Over?"

"It looks much of a muchness out here. It's all pretty flat for miles around. Anywhere will pretty much do. Over."

I had to agree that nowhere looked any better than anywhere else within a kilometer of the pillars. I marked a cross on the screen and dumped it to the convoy's network so we could form a 360 degree circle perimeter to start working from.

We'd practiced forming up a laager before coming, and even though half of the people there were civilians, they knew enough to be helpful. More importantly, they knew when the best help was to stay out of the way.

As we stopped I got out of the truck and looked at the sun overhead. The heat of the day was intense, turning me into a sweat-soaked puddle as I stood there.

We'd all be getting a tan while we were there.

Technical Sergeant Ferretti came and stood next to me, and we waited as Staff Sergeant Espera walked over with Staff Sergeant Martinez and Sergeant Pearson following on behind him.

Martinez was Air Force, while Pearson was Army. Both were E5 NCOs, which had confused the hell out of the civilians.

I was thinking that we should adopt Marine Corps ranks, but so far, my suggestion hadn't been greeted with any enthusiasm by General Russell.

"This heat will be a bitch to work in, LT," said Espera.

"I agree, but everyone will be calling you a bastard when they're freezing their balls off tonight if we haven't got the camp basics squared away."

"That's telling him, ma'am," said Ferretti, grinning.

"Well, we were warned it was going to be hot here. So let's break out the PACE suits to make life easier on ourselves and remember to hydrate. Everyone knows what they have to do, so let's get on and do it."

Corporals Wachowski and Taylor went with Espera to start unloading the containers off the backs of the trucks.

Pearson took Airman First Class Jordan and Culinary Specialist Third Class Adams with him to start connecting up utilities. They would check that all the systems were operating properly.

Meanwhile, Martinez took Corporal Baptista and Specialist Nelson to set up a provisional perimeter. To keep any local fauna from entering the camp tonight.

That left myself, Ferretti, and Hospital Corpsman Third Class Keith for everything else. Which in this case included getting the rest of the combat androids unloaded.

After that I got to herd the scientists, making sure they drank enough water and kept in the shade from the trucks as much as possible. Keith went off to make sure our team was drinking enough water, too, because suffering heat exhaustion is the very definition of not fun.

By the time the sun set, we had the trailers unloaded and the generators running.

In the desert the heat of the day quickly dissipates as night falls, and it was soon cold enough that people were complaining about it. We'd arranged a dozen standard shipping-sized custom-made Conex boxes in a rough circle about fifty meters across.

I thought that our camp was the height of luxury, but there again, I'm a Marine, so what do I know?

Espera had directed Wachowski to park the trucks so they were aligned with the containers to make two sides of a triangle in six groups. Drawn out, the camp looked like a Star of David with a circle inside it.

I had to remind Espera that we weren't trying to build the ultimate off-world fighting fort, and he'd replied that would take at least a month of Sundays to complete.

To finish off setting up camp, we ran razor wire round the perimeter. The plan was to dig a ditch and construct a berm to keep the local wildlife out later. There was some concern over what Ferretti called *Crocomodos* stumbling into the camp.

I'd been assured by our civilian specialists that this was highly unlikely, but better safe than sorry.

I walked out of my office cubicle and looked up at the stars that sparkled brightly in the crisp night air of One-Nine-Six.

I'd asked Dr. Wilson where Earth's sun was, and he'd told me it was fifteen thousand light years away. We couldn't see it because it was hidden in the glow of the Milky Way's central band.

Still, it was good to know where home lay, even if I couldn't see it.

As I walked across the center of our new base camp, Adams was dishing out the food. He was having a field day in his new kitchen unit and had cooked a Thanksgiving meal for us all.

Meanwhile, Ferretti was keeping an eye on our perimeter, monitoring the feeds from the combat androids through his headset.

People were beginning to sit down at tables. They'd been laid out in a U-shape in the center of the camp for us to sit around in front of the kitchen.

We even had night heaters to keep our butts warm in the cold night air. I had to marvel at the extravagance of the whole affair, but I guess this is what civilians expect when they go camping out on a strange new planet far, far away across the galaxy.

I sat down at the head of the table next to Dr. Emmerich, who was the head of all the civilians there. She had laid out place names that had been arranged so that we sat next to someone from the opposite team. It was her idea to get the military and civilian members of the mission to know each other.

I just hoped that my people managed to remember to mind their manners and not cuss too much.

Dr. Emmerich asked me, "Are you satisfied with the camp, Lieutenant?"

"Pretty much, even though there's still a lot to do here to square everything away properly. It sure beats sleeping under canvas, or in Ranger graves."

"Ranger graves? I don't understand."

Espera, who sat opposite Dr. Emmerich, spoke. "Ranger graves are what Marines call holes dug in the ground that protect you from enemy fire when you're sleeping."

"But why call them graves?"

"Marine Corps sense of humor, ma'am," I said, trying to remember that civilians didn't share the same world view as soldiers.

"How morbid. Anyway, changing the subject, what do you think of our first meal tonight on One-Nine-Six?"

"Our Navy cook has done us all proud."

"Well, it's a little bit of home here tonight to celebrate mankind's first off-world base," said Dr. Harrison from the Geology Group, who was sat opposite me.

"But we can't be sure that the Chinese haven't set up their own base and beat us to it, Peter," said Glen, who was sat three seats down from me. No doubt arranged by Dr. Emmerich on the basis that we knew each other already.

"Maybe not, but we need to discuss what we're going to call this planet now. After all, One-Nine-Six seems a bit clinical to me," said Dr. Emmerich.

Dr. Harrison asked, "What do you think, Lieutenant? What shall we call this planet?"

"It should be up to the scientists," I said, having already heard Wachowski refer to the place as The Sandpit. I didn't think that calling One-Nine-Six The Sandpit was the worst thing I'd ever heard, but I was sure that anything I came up with would be rather prosaic.

"I think we should call it Dune," said Dr. Harrison.

"You might as well call it Tatooine if you're going to be that obvious about it," said Dr. Webber, an older slightly overweight man, from the Organic Geochemistry and Biosignatures Group, who was sat immediately to my right.

"Don't be silly, Alan. Tatooine has two suns. It's not the same. Dune has two moons just like One-Nine-Six has two moons," said Dr. Harrison.

"I'm not sure I get it," said Espera.

"He's referring to two fictional planets," said Dr. Follet. She worked with Dr. Webber in the Inorganic Chemistry and Mineralogy Group, who was at the end of the table to my left.

"Of course they are," I said, absentmindedly looking down the table at Glen, sitting next to Corporal Wachowski, who had one of those cheeky almost rude personalities that everyone liked.

She was making the people around her laugh.

"But, Peter, the book is called *Dune*, the world itself was actually called Arrakis," said Dr. Webber.

"Really, Peter, you want to name a planet after the title of an old story," said Dr. Follet.

"Why not? It's no different than naming Virginia after Queen Elizabeth the First of England," said Dr. Harrison.

"Yes, but you're ascribing a name of a mono-environment fictional world to a real world that will have multiple biomes just from the axial tilt alone," said Dr. Brown, also a member of the Organic Chemistry and Biosignatures Group, who was sitting across the table to the left of me.

"Have you no soul, Michelle? Where's your sense of romance and adventure? To boldly go where no one has gone before. The sand and the sun," said Dr. Harrison.

"You make it sound like we're going to the beach. All we've seen of this planet so far is the few square miles around the camp. For all we know this planet may be inhabited and already have a name," said Dr. Brown.

"Wouldn't that be awesome, though?" said Dr. Harrison.

"Not wishing to rain on anybody's parade here, but the only other planet we've discovered with life shot our robot team full of arrows," I said.

"But isn't that why your people are here, Lieutenant?"

"Exactly, Dr. Harrison, being able to shoot back is always good. But sitting here and eating turkey with people who have just traveled to another world together, now that's awesome," I said before starting to eat my meal with all the trimmings.

In the night sky above us, the light from the two moons shone down upon our first off-world Thanksgiving meal. Glen was now ignoring everyone while fiddling with his PAD and muttering to himself.

"Hot damn," he said.

I looked at him across the table and said, "What's up?"

"You're not going to believe this, but I can confirm we're on the same planet you went to when you walked your CASE suit through the pillars under the mountain in Afghanistan. Beats me why we didn't do a comparison before getting here."

"You can't be serious. That place looked entirely different to here."

The other people around the table were looking at their PADs and then up at the two moons in the sky above.

"You're right, Glen. And the best bit is that we can calculate where the other pillars must be," said Dr. Wilson.

"So it seems to me, Lieutenant, that as the first person to ever step on this world, you should get the privilege of naming it," said Dr. Emmerich.

Oh joy, so no pressure then. I took out my PAD to look up something I vaguely remembered from my military history classes and said, "Why don't we call the world Two Moons after the Cheyenne Indian Chief Ishaynishus who fought in the Battle of the Little Big Horn?"

"That's novel," said Glen.

"Well, you did ask."

"So, which is it, Two Moons or Ishaynishus, Lieutenant?" asked Dr. Harrison.

"Either works for me."

20. PLAN OF THE DAY

Never tell people how to do things. Tell them what to do, and they will surprise you with their ingenuity.

— GEN GEORGE S. PATTON, USAR

First Lieutenant Lara Atsuko Tachikoma
Two Moons Alpha Site
Friday, November 25, 2072

We'd adjusted our clocks to One-Nine-Six's twenty-five-hour rotation period, which meant that when my alarm went off at 0530, I felt like I had a real sleep in.

We'd set a guard duty overnight, but there was nothing to report.

The chill of the early morning air was starting to burn off as the sun rose in the sky casting long shadows across the desert landscape. I took the opportunity to do some stretches to warm up and then ran around the perimeter of our base camp.

Staff Sergeant Espera joined me before I got halfway round,

and then we were joined by Specialist Nelson, and much to my surprise also by Airman Jordan.

We ended up doing twelve laps together.

"We should make this a regular thing," I said when we came to the end of the run.

"Yes, it would be good for the pogues in our team to up their fitness levels," said Espera.

While I agreed with Espera's sentiments about the general lack of fitness in our fellow team members, and them being pogues, it was a slur. I couldn't allow this attitude to grow within my team.

"They're no longer pogues, not after going through those pillars and putting themselves on the line with us. We can't allow comments like this to foment division in our team, Staff Sergeant Espera."

"Sorry, ma'am. No excuse, it won't happen again."

"Perhaps you could set up an informal weights area, and I'll post the morning runs on the Plan of the Day to give people a heads-up to make the appropriate mental adjustments."

"Sounds like an excellent plan," said Espera.

"Carry on," I said.

Leaving him, I went to take a shower and change for breakfast, which was self-service, unlike last night's Thanksgiving meal. After eating breakfast I went back to my office, a small cubicle partitioned off in the command container, where I checked my PAD.

I reviewed Technical Sergeant Ferretti's morning report. Everyone accounted for. After that, the first order of business on the POD, was to send out people to retrieve two missing robot teams.

The project had given us their last known locations and wanted us to get them back for repair and reuse. The atomic batteries alone had a substantial dollar value attached to them, which sounded fair enough.

The other robot team was currently still operational, and I wasn't required to go and retrieve it at this time. But who knew when the stupid AI would get itself into a fix and need rescuing?

Putting that thought aside, I looked at the duty schedule.

Technical Sergeant Ferretti, Staff Sergeant Martinez, and Senior Airman Taylor were already assigned to work alongside Glen on setting up the facilities needed to launch a UAV to map the surrounding area.

Sergeant Pearson and Corporal Baptista were working on bettering the perimeter defenses for the base camp.

This only left me with Staff Sergeant Espera to lead the retrieval teams.

I'd also been asked not to take Adams away from his culinary duties to keep the civilians happy. So this left me with Corporal Wachowski, Corpsman Keith, Specialist Nelson, and Airman First Class Jordan to choose from.

While I was deliberating over whom to assign to each team, I received a message from Dr. Emmerich asking to speak to me. I walked across the camp to the science module to meet her because, given past experience of messaging her or using the radio, talking face-to-face would be so much easier.

"Dr. Emmerich, it's Lieutenant Tachikoma," I said as I knocked on the wall of her cubicle.

"Hello, Lieutenant. Thank you for coming over. I'm glad you didn't radio me; I hate all the rigmarole surrounding their use."

"What did you want to talk about, Doc?"

"I was looking at the schedule for the week, and I see we're not due to send out anyone out into the field until tomorrow. However, I noticed that you are sending two teams out today to retrieve the lost androids. I wondered whether you would mind if I send some scientists along with you?"

"No problem. They already know not to wander off and get eaten by the local wildlife. As long as they realize that our mission takes priority over theirs."

"Of course, Lieutenant. I'll stress that they're under your team's command at all times. Anyway, it's an extra opportunity to see more of the planet and collect samples. I thought if we split into two groups of three, we would always have somebody with the right expertise to assess anything found. I'll send the names of the members of the two science teams to you now."

Her request made it easier for me to justify taking command of one of the teams, which suited me.

I sent Staff Sergeant Espera off to take a team with two trucks.

Going with him were Specialist Nelson and Corpsman Keith.

I thought it prudent to send Keith with Espera in case of any injuries that might be sustained in pulling a wrecked robot team out of a hole in the ground. Attached to his team were Drs. Webber, Follet, and Harrison, whom we were calling Science Team Two.

On that basis I was taking the newly minted Science Team One: consisting of Drs. Brown, Goldstein, and Newman in the other two trucks. Riding along to help me retrieve the robots that had been dragged into a waterhole were Corporal Wachowski and Airman First Class Jordan.

By chance both of the lost robot exploration teams were just under two hundred klicks away from the base camp. But in the best tradition of Murphy's laws, they lay in opposite directions.

21. KISS, KISS

A pint of sweat saves a gallon of blood.

— Gen George S. Patton, USAR

Staff Sergeant Espera
Two Moons
Friday, November 25, 2072

Espera had divided the team across two trucks for the day's mission. He had decided to put Specialist Nelson in one truck to shepherd Science Team Two. That left him and Corpsman Keith in the lead truck.

The lieutenant had thought it prudent to send Keith with him in case any injuries were sustained when pulling a wrecked robot team out of a hole in the ground.

Espera thought that the case could've been made that she needed a medic on hand for retrieving a robot team scarfed down by the planet's indigenous predator. However, he hadn't argued the case because the arrangement suited him.

The prospect of listening to a bunch of scientists droning on about boring shit during the drive would've spoiled his enjoyment of the alien landscape.

Besides, the drive was a chance to get out, explore a strange new planet, and introduce new ideas to the world. Concepts like roadkill, for example, as the truck ran over a small indigenous life form that didn't move out of the way.

Proving in his mind that all progress has a cost.

The team had departed from camp around 0800, and the truck's onboard system kept track of their progress, which showed they were on track to reach their objective before 1300. With another two hours to kill, Espera was listening to his music list, Keith having to put up with him pulling rank on the choice of tracks.

A cover of "Silver Machine" by Hawkwind Resurrection blared over the rumble of the truck's tires. Keith was rocking along in his seat to the song, so all was good.

Outside, the landscape was slowly morphing from the open, flat semiarid desert terrain around their camp to rolling terrain green with desert scrub. Ahead on the horizon could be seen hills, dark against the glare of the sun behind them.

Espera wondered what the trees would look like? Assuming there were any trees or things he would call trees.

After all, this was an alien planet. So far, all they had seen were lots of images of desert terrain from the robot exploration teams, not counting the Crocomodo creature that ate an android.

Espera was woken by Keith nudging him as the truck slowed to a halt.

"Sergeant, computer says we're here."

"Here" being about one hundred meters below the crest of a hill.

Espera got down out of the cab and started walking up the slope to take a look at what lay ahead in the dead ground. Behind him the second truck pulled up. The sounds of the scientists' voices announced the emergence of the civilians as they piled out of the truck they'd been trapped in for four hours.

"Nelson, to me," he shouted, waiting for her to haul ass over to join him and Keith. "OK, Keith, you will keep an eye on our civilians while Nelson will accompany me to search the area. Any questions?"

Keith nodded and headed over to the civilians, who were unloading bags with their gear from the truck. Nelson spoke. "I've got a bearing we can head in to start searching."

"Let's go then. The robots ain't going to find themselves."

<hr>

Espera and Nelson walked along the course given to them by the bearing from the truck's computer. They were in their PACE suits and carried the gear necessary to winch the robots out of the hole they had fallen in. One would think that finding two large machines would be straightforward enough, but the ground was broken, with lots of rocks providing concealment.

Being that the robots were down a hole, Espera was motivated to be attentive about where he was stepping. Getting injured in a fall out in the middle of nowhere would be at best be negligent and at worst grossly stupid of him.

So, he and Nelson quartered the search zone and spent the next thirty mikes searching before they found the two robots.

There was a crack in the ground that cut across in front of where they stood, and in the middle was the hole, which was around thirty feet deep. Espera and Nelson put down the winch and rest of the gear they'd brought with them to take a peek over the edge.

At the bottom lay the two broken machines.

One android's head turned tracking Espera and Nelson, and it raised its arm that held the rifle and fired a shot. The crack of the shot and the sound of the bullet whizzing past told Espera it was meant to scare them off.

He sent the shutdown command, but nothing happened.

"Whoah, is it supposed to do that?" asked Nelson as the android tracked her to take another shot.

Espera pulled her back from the edge of the hole. "Questions later," he said as the sound of another shot rang out.

It was at times like this that being inside his Ape combat armor would be good, because the suits were designed to take on combat androids—but wishing for something he didn't have wasn't going to help here.

"But why was it shooting at us?"

"There is no reason asking why. You'll only mess with your head asking why. Just see it as evidence that you're the master of your own fate."

"Lost me there, Sergeant."

"Better than being shot in the head, Nelson. Consider the fact that you're still alive after coming under fire as being baptized. It's a good thing."

The android hadn't shut down when he'd sent the signal, so that must mean the receiver was busted. Espera would have to shut it down manually, which meant getting close enough while it tried to shoot him.

He ordered the winch bolted to the ground.

"OK, you're controlling the cable, Nelson, while I run down the hole and disable the android. You understand?"

"I understand you're about to do some crazy shit, Sergeant."

"Live and learn."

Espera let some cable out to cut himself some slack and then ran towards the hole. He fell forward and used the momentum to stand perpendicular to the wall of the hole.

The android's first shot missed and ricocheted off the rock.

The second hit center of mass. The PACE suit armor took the force of the blow from the 5.56 mm round.

Espera was grateful that the eggheads hadn't outfitted the android with a bigger caliber weapon.

He rushed down the wall with the cable acting as a brake on his descent. The legs of the QuadMule twitched as the combat android turned, changing position at the bottom to track his descent.

Another shot rang out and hit Espera again center of mass. Combat androids were efficient, but predictable—but the next shot would be aimed at his head.

Espera kicked himself forward and fell the last ten feet on top of the android.

This did nothing to cushion his fall but did prevent the android from firing its rifle again. He rolled on top of it and put his arm around behind its neck. The panel didn't want to open, and the android started thrashing around trying to get out from under his PACE suit.

The android fired again, the bullet grazing the side of Espera's suit. He grabbed the gun arm and twisted. The sound of his suit as it whined was a counterpoint to the buzzing of the android trying to stop him.

With a sudden snap, the arm broke. They could bill him for ripping the arm off later. But the android continued attacking him.

"You OK, Sergeant?" shouted Nelson, who now stood at the top of the hole looking down. "Is everything under control?"

"What's it fucking look like, Nelson!?"

With a shove he managed to bang the head of the android against the wall, cracking the panel to access the shutdown switch. With a click the struggle ceased, and the QuadMule stopped moving, too.

"Shit, Sergeant, that was seriously awesome."

"Stop your grinning and get ready to winch this hunk of junk out of here. Sooner we're done, the sooner we can get back."

"Yes, Sergeant," said Nelson as she let out more cable so he could start winching the machines out of the hole.

Just another day in his life.

22. LONG DAY

An army marches on its stomach.

— NAPOLEON BONAPARTE

First Lieutenant Lara Atsuko Tachikoma
Two Moons
Friday, November 25, 2072

We left the waterhole behind us just before 1500, which meant that the last ninety minutes of our drive back to Camp Alpha were in darkness. This made the return journey even more tedious.

Still, the scientists had all gotten something out of the trip, some more than others.

As I got out of the truck, Espera came up to talk to me.

"Good evening, LT. How did it go?"

"Slowly, and even slower after Dr. Follet asked to bring the dead Crocomodo back. I agreed she could take samples, which took longer than expected and delayed our return journey. And you?"

"Found the hole and almost got my head blown off by the

android. I exaggerate for comic effect—it was a warning shot to discourage me."

"I take it you tried sending the shutdown signal first."

"Yeah, unfortunately that was one of the parts damaged by the fall."

"Murphy strikes again."

"Sure does, LT. Other than that, everything went by the numbers."

Which meant no one had been killed.

"Glad to hear it, but remind me not to be around you when it doesn't go by the numbers. Anyway, tomorrow we're taking the scientists out for the day, so it's wash, rinse, and repeat all over again."

After the minor excitement, I found that Dr. Emmerich's team was extremely excited over the fact that our camp was sitting on lodestone, which resonated to the pulse of the pillars' cycling.

However, what excited me most after a long day was the luxury of being able to take a quick shower before eating a hot meal. Turkey leftovers from yesterday, which was fine by me. And the pecan pie for dessert was delicious.

Afterwards, I went to my cubicle to file a report and sign off on the daily updates.

Day two was over, and hopefully we wouldn't have the pleasure of meeting a live Crocomodo anytime real soon. As far as I was concerned, the big-game hunting trips could be done on someone else's watch, because I objected to shooting things I don't eat, or that weren't shooting at me.

23. PROJECT CYCLOPS

A good leader inspires people to have confidence in the leader;
a great leader inspires people to have confidence in themselves.

— ELEANOR ROOSEVELT

Mr. Anderson
Magnetic Anomaly Project CIA Liaison Officer
Two Moons Alpha Site
Tuesday, November 29, 2072

Anderson had been working with Technical Sergeant Ferretti, Staff Sergeant Martinez, and Senior Airman Taylor to get his eye-in-the-sky project up and running.

The first part of the plan involved unloading and inflating the field hangar for the unmanned aerial vehicle to be assembled inside. The three Air Force men had donned PACE suits to move the gear from the containers into the hangar.

This took all the first day to finish moving and sorting.

Anderson had spent the second day unpacking the UAV, which had been broken down into three main parts for assembly on-world. The airframe was based on an old NASA variable geometry design. It had a single-point swivel for the swing-wing, which extended its flight envelope.

The third day was supposed to be spent slotting and bolting parts together, then running a system's diagnostic to check that everything worked before launching it on its first mission.

That was the theory. But practice and theory don't always come together. What should have taken a day at most turned out to take double that.

Anderson and his team hunted down bugs and cleared red flags from the diagnostic system. Some were from dust and dirt on the planet accruing in places during assembly. Other problems were down to manufacturing defects that required parts to be replaced from spares.

On the fifth day, they were ready to do the first test flight.

While Anderson and his team had been assembling the UAV, Sergeant Pearson used a dozer to clear a rough runway. This had taken most of three days to finish with the limited assets to hand.

Anderson now looked across at the end result that could not exactly be described as smooth. But it was clear of rocks, and the UAV was designed for landing on rough fields.

"Well, what do you think, Sergeant Martinez, are we good to go here?" he asked.

"Landing will be a bit rougher than I would like, but all things considered I think we're good, sir."

"OK then. Sergeant Ferretti, can you get a couple of androids to push our bird out onto the runway?"

"Right on it, sir."

"I think I will watch from the hangar here. We're making history here, you know. If you'd told me eighteen months ago I'd be standing on an alien planet launching a remote-controlled UAV, I would've laughed at you."

Ferretti was looking at the UAV and overseeing the androids

via his headset as he spoke. "You can say that again, sir. I've lived for this moment since I first got involved with the project."

"You and me both."

Anderson watched the UAV as it was pushed out to the edge of the runway, and over the radio Martinez announced that he was going through the preflight checklist. Then Taylor confirmed he was getting a clear feed from the onboard sensors.

The hybrid fan engine on the UAV started to spin up to speed. Then Martinez waggled the control surfaces to check the fly-by-wire controls. The bird began to roll down the runway, gaining speed with the nose lifting as it rotated and took off.

"All systems green across the board," said Martinez.

"Roger that," replied Anderson, looking up at the UAV circling around before heading off on its assigned flight plan.

This was intended to be a mapping project, which it was, but the UAV also had a magnetometer as part of its sensor package.

Anderson hoped that they'd be able to locate other magnetic anomalies on One-Nine-Six, a fact that not everyone needed to know about. Of course, he hadn't figured on the base camp sitting on top of lodestone that was resonating to the pulse generated by the pillars.

Otherwise, things were going according to plan. Soon they would find out how far the field extended.

"Well, let's get started on mapping the planet."

"I'm worried about us being able to keep up with the UAV's endurance capabilities," said Ferretti.

"Well, until we can get more UAV operators for the project, I guess we will be drinking lots of coffee."

"Good thing we all like coffee. I've posted a four-on and four-off roster and have you on it too, sir."

"With great responsibility comes the burden of duty. Thank you, Sergeant."

24. PILLARS

Astronomy compels the soul to look upwards and leads us from this world to another.

— PLATO

Dr .Adam Wilson
Magnetic Anomaly Project Scientist
Two Moons Alpha Site
Tuesday, November 29, 2072

For Adam, the MAPCOM project was a dream come true. His big chance to be in on the ground floor of exploring alien worlds.

Over the last three days, while the majority of the science team drove out to collect samples, he'd been working at the pillars. He began by installing new recording equipment. Then he began recording where the pillars cycled to.

When they didn't open back to Earth, he had androids deliver one of the two standard monitor stations used for first openings.

Sergeant Ferretti hadn't been able to help him much, because of being involved in setting up the mapping project and running the base camp's routine security with the other androids. Adam thought that perhaps more should've been brought through, as the dozen they had were stretched pretty thin.

What with his needs, security, and flying the UAV, the base still needed more work to make it more habitable over the long-term.

There was a fear among his colleagues that native wildlife would be attracted here due to the presence of the base. To him it seemed most unlikely, given the lack of waterholes in the vicinity, but there again, he wasn't a biologist. Adam imagined what the camel equivalent might look like on this planet, assuming there were such things.

Today Dr. Wong was with him, as she was setting up further experiments to study the world's atmosphere.

"How's it going, Li-Na?"

"What? Oh yes, it's going pretty good. I'm almost done here. How about you?"

"Well, it's been a bit of a slog if truth be told, but we have data to send back, as long as I monitor the automatic system to keep the androids running."

"You think something will go wrong with them?"

"The AIs are not the brightest stars in the night sky. It would be so much better if we had a permanent presence here and could keep them in a control loop. I'm afraid we're going to lose a lot of them to unforeseen glitches."

"Adam, you need to know what you can control, and what you can't. I study the weather and atmospheric phenomena. I've no control over what happens, only over what choices I can make as to what I will study next. You're faced with the same thing here. You can't control the pillars, and you don't have unlimited resources. Just be glad with what you've got."

"I don't agree. These pillars are going to planets at different times to the one's back on Earth, and we now have the opportunity to study them working on other worlds. Don't you see what we could learn and what it would tell us about the nature of the universe?"

"You may be right, but I'm finished here, and I've got to get back and help Bill launch a weather balloon. Catch you later at dinner," she said as she turned and walked back to camp.

Adam watched her go before carrying on with the next bit of this project.

His work here was going to open up the pillar network for humanity to explore. Adam liked Li-Na and hoped he would get to talk to her at dinner tonight. Truth was, he wasn't very good with talking to women, and Li-Na didn't seem all that interested in talking to him.

Perhaps he ought to ask her whether she read any science fiction? That might work to broaden the topics they could talk about.

25. DISCOVERIES

The characteristic of scientific progress is our knowing that we did not know.

— Gaston Bachelard

Dr. Allison O'Neill
Magnetic Anomaly Project Scientist
Two Moons Alpha Site
Tuesday, November 29, 2072

Allison had been looking forward to her turn to go out and experience more of the landscape on this new world. There was quite a big discussion going on between members of the science team over the name suggested by Lieutenant Tachikoma.

As far as she was concerned, Two Moons in English, or Ishaynishus in Cheyenne, worked for her. Either way it was a far better choice than some of the other names that had been suggested.

Today she had swapped with Alan Webber, from Science Team Two, accompanied by Brigitte Follet and Peter Harrison.

The team was split across the two trucks, just in case one broke down or became stuck while trying to cross the terrain. Allison could hardly believe they were driving around on an alien world as part of a science team, but a lot had changed in the last two years.

Staff Sergeant Espera and Specialist Nelson were in the first truck with Brigitte.

Allison sat in the second truck next to Peter. They were being driven by Airman Jordan, which made her laugh, because Jordan was a woman. She had to wonder why the Air Force didn't have gender-neutral ranks or at least call her airwoman.

"Are you OK, ma'am?" asked Airman Jordan.

"Yes, just having a funny thought pop into my head, that's all."

"Want to share, Allison?" asked Dr. Harrison.

"No, not really. It's not that funny."

"Long drive to get where we're going. What do you want to talk about?"

"I'm happy to look out the window and enjoy the scenery go by."

The plan for the journey was to drive out for the day in what amounted to a big loop, stopping to take samples if they saw anything interesting. As this was the third day of the mission, the science team planned to push out a bit further.

Allison was reassured by the fact that the military seemed to know what they were doing, something she'd come to appreciate more over the last year.

"Yeah, it's pretty amazing when you think about what we're looking at," said Dr. Harrison.

"Reminds me of the rocky deserts you get in North Africa. In particular, it looks like parts of Cyrenaica, where they have lots of limestone," said Airman Jordan.

Allison had always thought of soldiers as people who were rigid in how they thought about stuff. At worst, she would have said they were pro-war patriots who had no true understanding of how racist and sexist they were, mostly due to a lack of education.

While some of the soldiers seemed to have come from broken homes and poor families, none of that seemed to make them unfeeling. If anything, they cared more.

They also really knew geography, a weak point for most Americans.

"You've been to Cyrenaica?" asked Dr. Harrison.

"Delivering relief aid a few years ago. Part of the security detachment at Ajdabiya."

"Did you see combat while you were there?"

"No, not really. A few shots got fired our way, but it was more like them trying to make a statement than really trying to kill us."

"That doesn't sound good, though," she said.

None of the soldiers had any real science background; she'd found they were people who wanted to serve their country. The last thing they were was pro-war.

Given the ethnic mix of the soldiers working for the project, she now knew they were no more racist than she was. The only real difference was they were brave enough to face what frightened them and do what she could not do: face those who intended to kill them and kill them first.

After two hours of driving, they'd covered just over fifty kilometers. The landscape became slightly greener, and they discovered a waterhole.

"Can we stop and take samples here?" she asked.

"Sure thing, ma'am. I'll let Sergeant Espera know we're stopping."

The trucks pulled up about fifty meters from the waterhole. Then they sent an android to the edge of it to have a look, just in case something jumped out and tried to eat it.

Once the all clear was given, the scientists got out to take samples, while Specialist Nelson manned the big gun mounted on the first truck.

Allison took a sample of the water. She really wanted to study what came to drink here. However, after Peter and Brigitte had finished taking their samples, they wanted to move on to another location.

"Sergeant Espera, would your people help me deploy a recording station here?"

"Of course, ma'am. I'd be glad to help. What do you want done?"

"This waterhole is a prime location for the chance for us to see some bigger animals. I'm not sure how to best conceal my equipment in these conditions, though."

"Lucky for you, Dr. O'Neill, I know exactly how to make what you want. Airman Jordan, break out PACE suits for the two of us. We're going to build an observation post here."

Allison consoled herself knowing she would have to study any animal secondhand through the lenses of the recording station. This was frustrating because the only higher fauna they had discovered so far had been dead and dried out by the sun. Everything else they'd discovered had been insects and small snake equivalents that only came out at night.

Though Allison couldn't blame the local fauna for that. She wouldn't come out in the day without shelter, either.

After the hide had been built, it was a relief to get back into the air-conditioned coolness of the trucks. She'd even found what looked like a worm in the soil around the waterhole. It wasn't much, but it was something more for her to study before they went home.

26. REBOOT

The first living creature was like a lion, the second was like an ox, the third had a face like a man, the fourth was like a flying eagle.

— REVELATION 4:7

Two Moons

The alien prostrated itself upon the ground before them. It was larger than a human being, based on how it moved its body mass.

The android stood and scanned the alien, assessing what it should do next, reviewing each option on its lists and assigning a rating for the chance of success to each.

Action required: Mission objectives review.

First priority: Record everything from camera feeds input as units PM41-5-9-27 and BD42-4-10-31 walk. Currently motionless, scan of surrounding area complete.

Action required: None.

Second priority: Scan for minerals and study chemical composition of samples. No minerals deposits scanned. Action required: Continue walking to find mineral sample. Alien life form is blocking current route.

Action required: Initiate priority three.

Third priority: Scan for signs of biological life and record signs of same. Scan of the alien life form commenced. Behavior: Stationary and prone on the ground. Update: Prone and moving in a repetitive pattern. Sound from the alien is being recorded.

Processing...Processing.

Query: Meaning of behavior?

Hypothesis one: Alien life form is preparing to attack.

Hypothesis two: Alien prostration is culturally meaningful.

Hypothesis three: Alien behavior is unknown.

Action option one: Wait and record.

Action option two: Fire a warning shot to discourage an attack.

Action option three: Retreat from the alien and record at a distance.

Evidence: Alien life form has not initiated an attack and is not showing any signs it will attack. Possibility of an attack low.

Action required: Warning shot not needed, continue recording alien behavior.

Processing...Processing.

Query: Alien life form not moving.

Hypothesis one: Alien life form has died.

Hypothesis two: Alien has stopped repetitive movement.

Hypothesis three: Alien behavior is unknown.

Action option one: Wait and record.

Action option two: Retreat from the alien and record at a distance.

Evidence: Alien life form shows signs of metabolic functioning that preclude death at this time.

Evidence: Alien life form remains stationary in a

nonaggressive posture. Balance of probability is that this is a submission posture.

Action required: Continue recording.

Processing…Processing.

Query: Does the atmospheric temperature affect the behavior of the alien life form?

Hypothesis one: Alien life form data set sparse.

Action: Monitor alien life forms for changes in its posture and review evidence.

Creature making repeating pattern of codified noise. Possibility of language high, data set sparse. Unable to actualize communication without resources that are unavailable at this time. Short-term access to resources remains low. Foreseeable future point in time where access becomes available remains high.

Action required: Flag for future assessment.

Review of next action to take at this time.

Action option one: Wait and see what the alien does next.

Hypothesis one: Probability of the alien life form initiating an attack low.

Hypothesis two: Probability of the alien getting up and walking away high. Impact on meeting mission objectives none.

Review next action: Move away and observe how the alien responds.

Hypothesis one: Alien life form will follow PM41-5-9-27.

Hypothesis two: Alien will do nothing.

Hypothesis three: Alien will run away. Impact on mission objectives low to none.

Evidence: Alien life form is moving away.

Action required: Mission objectives review.

First priority: Record everything from camera feeds input as unit PM41-5-9-27 walks. Scan of surrounding area complete. Action required: Continue on planned route.

Second priority: Scan for minerals and study chemical

composition of samples completed. Action required: Search for new mineral samples.

Third priority: Scan for signs of biological life and record signs of same. Scan of the alien life form completed. Action required: Continue with mission priorities one and two.

Fourth priority: Transmit data to back up data to server each day. Action required: Initiate data transmission.

Processing…Processing.

Query: Interference in data transmission occurring.

Hypothesis one: Transmitter is failing. Impact on meeting mission objectives high.

Hypothesis two: Receiver station is failing. Impact on meeting mission objectives high.

Hypothesis three: Atmospheric conditions are interfering with transmission. Impact on meeting mission objectives medium.

Hypothesis four: Alien life form possess technology to jam transmission.

Evidence: Transmitter loop back diagnostic check passed.

Evidence: Receiver station handshake confirmed.

Evidence: Atmospheric conditions not congruent with interference pattern.

Evidence: Alien life form displayed no technology when scanned.

Fifth priority enabled: Protocol 101 available. Processing…Processing.

Query: Availability of priority five.

Hypothesis one: Indicates failure of unit PM41-5-9-27. Action required: Emergency review options list.

Option one: Find somewhere to plug itself into its QuadMule support unit and run a full diagnostic without leaving itself open to attack by indigenous fauna. Possibility of success moderate. Impact on mission high.

Option two: Plug into QuadMule support unit and run a full

diagnostic at current location, leaving PM41-5-9-27 accessible to alien life forms and indigenous fauna. Possibility of success low. Impact on mission high.

There is no third option with a better outcome than low success.

PM41-5-9-27 scanned the surrounding landscape, turned, and walked away, heading back the way it had come towards a cave in the hills it had passed on the way there where it could secure itself and run repairs.

27. END OF WEEK ONE

Make your plans to fit the circumstances.

— GEN GEORGE S. PATTON, USAR

First Lieutenant Lara Atsuko Tachikoma
Two Moons Alpha Site
Thursday, December 1, 2072

I was discussing our options with Technical Sergeant Ferretti.

"So, let's strip the spare tires from the trucks and siphon off the fuel before sending them back to Earth."

"Sounds good to me, ma'am. It allows for unexpected contingencies to be taken care of."

"Speaking of which, how certain are we that our perimeter will keep out the local wildlife?"

"I talked to Allison, sorry, I mean Dr. O'Neill, and her team thinks that what we have won't keep any of them out. Considering that we have seen nothing larger than worms, scorpions, and snakes all week..."

"I see that Allison has a sense of humor."

"You could say that, ma'am. As she said to me, the nearest waterhole is fifty kilometers away, and given the heat, one would have to be a fool to try crossing that in daylight—and animals aren't that foolish. I've paraphrased what she said, ma'am."

"So I imagine, so I imagine. I gather the biology team has been a bit disappointed that apart from your dead Crocomodo they haven't yet found anything larger to study."

"And they're calling it something fancy using Latin and Greek words to describe its anatomy. Something about it having a jaw it can unhinge to swallow things bigger than itself."

"I'm not sure I want to meet something bigger than a Crocomodo. Though, quite frankly, if it keeps the scientists busy and out of trouble making up new names, it works for me."

We were nearing the end of our first week on an alien world and had shown it was feasible to set up a base camp and run operations from it. All without any of the scientists getting eaten by the local wildlife.

This was totally a win-win for my first command.

At times the science team had been so excited by the stuff they'd found that I thought they were going to wet their pants.

Who knew that worms would be so fascinating?

Our opening back was due in a couple of hours, at 1300 local time, 0600 back on Earth. Therefore, the scientists were running around finishing off last-minute samples to send back, which made me wonder whether or not we would be ready.

So I had my people shadowing the science team and providing as much help as they could. That was the plan before we got the call from Glen to come to the main control room.

"Hiya. I finished checking the feeds from our surviving robot team, and you'll never guess what we've found," Glen said as Ferretti and I entered the room.

"Little green men."

"Damn, you're such a spoilsport. How did you guess?"

"Seemed obvious to me. But seriously, you've found aliens?"

"Yes, seriously, but they're not little, or men as such, but I admit that their skin is sort of a greenish-gray. Look on the screen. I'll bring up the files for you to see."

Glen put up a series of stills pulled from the robot team's cameras.

One showed a view from high on a hill overlooking what looked like structures of a large city. Other pictures showed the path they'd taken down the hill towards the city, which was situated on the shore of either a very large lake or possibly an ocean sea.

The final picture showed one of the aliens prostrated on the ground.

It was a bipedal humanoid, but it wouldn't be confused with a human, even on a dark, stormy night, because the proportions were all wrong.

The head was longer from back to front with a thin lower jaw and small serrated teeth that screamed *carnivore*. The ears were round, larger than a human's, and the eyes were a yellow-brown color that contrasted with the greenish-gray skin that was darker on top of the creature's head and lighter around its belly and the inner surfaces of its limbs.

Three fingers with an opposable thumb meant it could use tools and confirmed that these aliens were intelligent.

"This is way above my pay grade. I think we should call Dr. Emmerich here now."

"I already have. She should've been here by now," said Ferretti.

"Please go and ask the doctor to come and see this." Ferretti left, and I stared at the screen and then back at Glen. "Do we have any idea of their technology level?"

"Too soon to say, from what I've been able to see so far.

Anyway, don't be like that. It's not like we're planning on starting the first interplanetary war or anything."

"That may be the case now, but if any shooting starts, then things will go to hell in a handbasket before you know it."

The footage of the encounter showing the sequence of events repeated.

The more I watched, the more it made me consider what we might have looked like had we evolved from dinosaurs rather than apes. The reptileman seemed to have been interrupted when mending some sort of net with floats attached to it.

So, clearly not some Stone Age hunter using a spear or an axe to hunt with. Fishing nets implied some sort of civilization.

Heck, I could be looking at some places on Earth if it weren't for the green-gray skin and it being an alien reptileman and all.

Dr. Emmerich rushed in and interrupted my musings.

"Let me see. Oh wow, I didn't realize the message meant come right this instant. I wonder if we can use the android to talk to it?"

"Yes, ma'am, it's possible to send messages to the android that it can broadcast aloud," said Ferretti.

"This is excellent news. We need to get a team of linguists here to help us, but I know there's some translation software loaded on our systems just in case we found something like this. Lieutenant, I believe we have a contingency plan for this scenario?"

"Yes, Dr. Emmerich," I said, realizing that my mission had changed from setting up a base to initiating first contact with an alien species.

This meant that the chances of someone getting eaten or killed had just gone way up.

"That's good news. OK, let's inform everyone what's happening. Can you draw up a request for resupply for your team? And I'll liaise with mine for what we will need to carry on with our studies here."

"Yes, ma'am. I'll start right away," I said, leaving her talking to Glen to go write my field report back to Earth.

There was lots of work to do, and only a few hours to complete it in.

I had to send some of the trucks back to be refueled and be used to bring more supplies across with them next time.

Also, I wanted to put in a request to send us our team's two combat armor suits. And bigger guns, in case we managed to start a land war on an alien world.

Given the squeals of delight over finding worms, I couldn't even begin to imagine the state of excitement the scientists were going to be in over finding sentient aliens. *Perhaps,* I thought, *I should alert Corpsman Keith to prepare for the possibility of someone having a cardiac arrest.*

Realistically, I should talk to him about what he'll need if we have to start treating arrow wounds.

28. BRAVO FOB

Adversity has the effect of eliciting talents which, in prosperous circumstances, would have lain dormant.

— Horace

First Lieutenant Lara Atsuko Tachikoma
Two Moons Alpha Site
Friday, December 2, 2072

The next morning I walked into the control room to find both Glen and Ferretti had worked through the night.

They were trying to reestablish control over the robot team.

The connection had been lost during its last download, with an error message indicating it had malfunctioned. Its operating protocols meant it had withdrawn from the immediate area, but all attempts to initiate contact since then had failed.

"How's it going? Any luck so far?"

"No, ma'am. We've got nothing."

"True, but it could be worse," said Glen.

"How do you figure that? We have a malfunctioning android with unlimited recharge facilities that's armed and within walking distance of a first contact," said Ferretti, scratching his facial stubble.

"Sounds to me like the pair of you need to catch some sack time. How much coffee have you both drunk?"

"We made a second pot during the night, but I'm sure it was just the two. Do we sound a bit edgy to you, ma'am?"

"A little bit more wired than your usual unflappable selves."

The days on Two Moons were only an hour longer than back on Earth, but it meant that an all-nighter was longer, too.

"Chances are that the android has broken down and is no longer functional. Anyway, the inhibitor will prevent anything bad from happening," said Glen.

"You mean the inhibitors that we took off when upgrading them to act autonomously?" said Ferretti.

"But surely the software was updated to account for that?" said Glen.

"Yes, but software can go wonky. It's been months since we sent Team Four through the pillars. Who knows what files might have become corrupted over time. I always said this was a bad idea from the start."

"Nothing we can do about it now. We'll have to make sure that we document anything bad that happens and use it as evidence the next time someone has the bright idea of letting autonomous AIs loose," I said.

"Yeah, but no one expected to find intelligent life on this planet. It worries me. But it's not like it has more than a peashooter to shoot at us," said Glen.

"As Staff Sergeant Espera reminded me, a 5.56 round can still damage a joint on a PACE suit."

Glen swept his fingers through his hair as if to massage the thoughts away. "Yeah, I suppose, but at least we outnumber it.

We'd better let everyone know what's happened and come up with some contingency plans."

"If we plan for the worse, then the only surprises should be pleasant ones," I said, as I knew all too well that a failure to plan is planning to fail.

Glen and Ferretti were at the center of the evening meal's discussion over what to do about the malfunctioning android.

Glen spoke. "In a nutshell, the problem is how far it's between here and the alien city, which, given it's over five hundred kilometers away, is a nontrivial distance. Especially when you consider the cross-country drive to get there. Then there's the question of setting up a secure camp near the alien settlement, and how we're going to resupply the team. Not forgetting that that will be dependent on how large a team we send."

He was clearly agitated by the turn of events that had spiralled out of his comfort zone.

"It's most unfortunate that after all this time the android malfunctioned at this point. Still, it's an opportunity I feel we must take advantage of. We will, after all, be making history," said Dr. Emmerich.

"The first priority must be to find the malfunctioning Alpha Quebec Tango Four. If for no other reason than leaving them for the natives to find would not be a good idea."

"Is Sergeant Ferretti right, Lieutenant?" asked Dr. Emmerich.

"He's right, ma'am. My concern is that we don't have the resources to complete two missions, which would be find Team Four and set up a base to send in a team at the same time. It's a matter of boots on the ground. We don't have enough personnel for doing both things at once."

"I think we need to prioritize the science aspects of the mission over the military's concerns here," said Dr. Webber.

"Alan, the 'military's concern' is *us*. They're the only thing between you and a quiverful of alien arrows, and you're going to prioritize their concerns pretty damn high. So start now. And we have the big problem of the malfunctioning android, which mustn't be allowed to contaminate the indigenous civilization with our technology," said Dr. Emmerich.

There was a pause.

"If so, we might as well leave now, or better still, never have come here in the first place. It's not like we can colonize this world, given how we came to be here. This situation is no different to when anthropologists used to visit Papua New Guinea to study the local tribes, who live there to this day as they always have," said Dr. Webber, whose face had turned red.

"We're here for better or worse, and we need to make the most of the time we've got to do what we can," said Dr. O'Neill, interrupting the argument. "So what do we want to do, or think we should do, now?"

"We need to go take a look-see and make contact with the aliens. If we do that, I'm sure we can multitask the operation with finding the android team. We can use the UAV to help in the search, too," said Glen.

"You do realize the risks we're taking here if it somehow manages to restore function but has been compromised in some way?" said Ferretti.

"The only redeeming aspect to this situation is that the android doesn't have any weapons that can harm us. I also took the precaution of asking for our heavier suits to be shipped to us next week. Purely as a precautionary measure."

"Why is it that the military's response to any situation is to bring bigger guns?" said Dr. Brown.

Dr. Emmerich spoke. "The lieutenant actually said she sent for bigger armor, not bigger guns, and anyway she's doing her job. She's not here to start a war, she's here to protect us. Does anyone else want to add anything?" she said, looking around at the other scientists.

"I do, ma'am. If I may speak, Lieutenant?" asked Corporal Wachowski.

"Sure, go ahead," I said, sure that anything she added would be pertinent.

"The thing is that the aliens are the best part of five hundred klicks from us. We've been averaging about twenty kilometers per hour while driving around during our week here. While we can probably improve on that a bit, it still means the trip will take about twenty-four hours of solid driving to cover the distance. I reckon that's going to be a little rough for our civilian passengers. Just saying."

It was a good point. "What do you suggest?"

"That depends on the mission priorities. If time is of the essence, we can switch drivers every four hours and blow through. If we can afford to stop and camp, then we can break the trip down over two or more days."

"Maintaining the logistics will be tricky," said Corporal Baptista.

"Camp security will be an issue once we arrive, too. We would need to send three trucks to form a small defensive laager for the team to work from," said Staff Sergeant Espera, pausing. "As for boots on the ground, we could take some androids with us. We could pair them with someone, and it would extend the area we can cover in our search."

"But what about us here who are staying behind? I need the androids for cataloguing where the pillars open to from here," said Dr. Wilson.

"We must prioritize the search and first contact needs for a little while," said Dr. Emmerich. "Until next week when we get resupplied."

"We may be able to leave you two to continue your work, Dr. Wilson, but it depends on the size of the team we decide to send. Except for Sergeant Ferretti and Airman Jordan, who both have experience operating androids, we can only use one per team member while keeping them in a loop."

"That sounds promising, Lieutenant. If you draw up a plan with various options, I will send you a list of the science personnel I want to send off to study the aliens," said Dr. Emmerich.

"Yes, ma'am," I replied. Two words so easy to say, yet how much work it would entail. It looked like I would be the one losing sleep tonight writing up a warning order.

Working on how to set up a forward operating base didn't take the whole night, because I had already made plans in advance for similar requests. However, my plans were big on generalities, light on specifics, and, as the Devil is always in the details, it meant double-checking everything.

I called in Ferretti and Espera to go over the WARNORD with them and run through the SMEAC: situation, mission, execution, administration and logistics, and command and signal.

"The situation is that earlier today Alpha Quebec Tango Four made contact with an unarmed native of this planet, who, after a short period, ran away," I said, replaying the recording for Espera, who hadn't yet seen the footage. "Subsequently, our android team malfunctioned and withdrew to implement a self-diagnostic check and initiate repairs. At that point contact was lost."

I paused, pondering how to retrieve a malfunctioning robot team and take control of the first-contact situation it had initiated.

"Technical Sergeant Ferretti will be in charge of the team consisting of Corporals Wachowski and Baptista, Specialist Nelson, and Airman Jordan. Myself and Corpsman Keith will be attached during the initial setup of a forward operating base. Mr. Anderson's CYCLOPS UAV has been tasked with aerial reconnaissance and overwatch. In addition, Dr. Emmerich has indicated there will be four civilian scientists attached to the team."

I'd be damned if we would set off before we had a much better idea of the natives and their city that our robot exploration team had glimpsed in the distance.

Especially if we had to babysit civilians.

The good thing was that our UAV would also allow us to plan the best route across the rocky desert between our base and the alien city.

"Our mission objectives are to retrieve the robot exploration team and thereby prevent it from having any further interactions with the natives. We will maintain the security of our personnel while gathering further intelligence on the inhabitants of this world."

I paused before continuing.

"My intent is to set up a forward base of operations where we can coordinate a search, and use our aerial assets to gather more INTEL on the situation. I wish to minimize the chance of unplanned contact with the natives of this planet," I said, taking a moment to judge my men's reactions to my WARNORD. "We will send a five-truck convoy, and myself and Corpsman Keith will return in two trucks once the base is set up."

There were too few people in the Alpha Mike team to leave Keith at what I was thinking of as Camp Bravo, but taking him during the initial setup would give Ferretti's team medical cover in case of accidents.

After that, any injuries would have to be managed with their own first aid training.

"Bravo Mike Team will conduct self-aid and buddy aid, then corpsman aid for any injuries. Everyone will carry full canteens of water, Camelbacks, and standard combat load-out during the search. We will deliver thirty-days' worth of supplies for our team, followed by weekly resupply runs.

"Succession of command is myself, then Technical Sergeant Ferretti, followed by Corporal Baptista and Corporal Wachowski. Are there any questions?"

"That about sums it up, ma'am. What do you think, Espera?"

"Above my pay grade."

"Well, we're all about to level up on that front, Staff Sergeant. You have the most experience with working with foreigners."

"Yes, but they didn't look like reptiles, or anyway, not as much as these aliens do. Too many unknowns for me to be confident we've thought everything through."

"I guess it sucks to be us then."

"Your first independent command, Ferretti. Your chance to shine," said Espera.

"Yeah, opportunities like this come once in a lifetime. I knew I should never have volunteered."

"Just remember we can be with you in twenty-four hours or less."

"Yes, ma'am. I'm the right person for the job. Espera barely knows one end of an android from the other."

"Right, in your dreams, Ferretti..."

"Enough. Am I understood?"

Both my sergeants nodded. It was my fault for being so tense that they'd started sniping at each other. The fact that we had been hanging around with civilians whose rhetoric wound us all up probably didn't help, either.

"Good. This is going to be tough enough as it is if everything goes according to plan. I'm designating our forward operating base as Camp Bravo. Your team's call sign will be Bravo Mike. The scientists will be designated as Bravo Sierra using phonetic shorthand to identify each of them."

"I'm not sure how they'll take to that, ma'am," said Ferretti.

"I'm sure they'll get the hang of it eventually. After all, they're supposedly full of smarts," said Espera. "Besides, you can impress upon Dr. O'Neill—that's 'Oscar' to you—the need to keep the LT happy."

"I said, enough. We've got to work with what we have to hand, and your sarcasm isn't helping, Staff Sergeant."

"Sorry, LT. I can't help feel we're out of our depth here, expected to do the impossible—and will fail."

"As we say in the Corps, take this as an opportunity to adapt, improvise, overcome, and a chance to excel. Is everything clear here?"

They both replied in the affirmative, but as Espera said, an operation like this needed more resources and time to plan properly. My stomach began to churn.

29. LITTLE LOST ROBOT

Eureka! - I have found it!

— ARCHIMEDES

Technical Sergeant Ferretti
Two Moons Bravo Site
Friday, December 9, 2072

Ferretti sat next to Airman First Class Jordan at one end of the Conex that served as Camp Bravo's control center. He listened to her talking on the radio going through the routine of getting the midday update.

"Bravo Charlie Three, this is Bravo Charlie Six. Over."

Corporals Wachowski and Baptista and Specialist Nelson were out in their PACE suits searching their assigned grids. Each had an android as a buddy.

Ferretti and Jordan were both immersed in the virtual-reality feeds monitoring the other four androids. These were under the control of the science team, and in addition he had one directly under his command.

"Solid copy, send your traffic. Over," said Corporal Wachowski, her reply coming from the speaker system.

"Requesting status report update. Over."

Ferretti had used the images from the aerial survey to form a search grid to find the disabled android. Due to real-time feeds from the UAV, they also had a fair idea of where the locals went during the day, and could avoid coming into contact with any of them unexpectedly.

"Nothing to report in grid Sierra Four. Over."

"Roger that. Move to grid Victor One. Acknowledge. Over," said Jordan.

They'd set up camp inside a large dip in the ground. To further help them keep it from being discovered, they'd flung ChameleonFlage netting over everything. This made the site virtually invisible from casual observation.

Hiding the noise of the generators was proving to be more problematical.

Wachowski replied, "Roger. Moving to grid Victor One. Bravo Charlie Three out."

Jordan called up the next team. "Bravo Charlie Four, this is Bravo Charlie Six requesting SITREP. Over."

Ferretti's teams had spent the last four days searching for their lost team with nothing to show for it.

"Bravo Charlie Six, last transmission garbled. Say again. Over," came the reply over the speaker. Ferretti heard Jordan repeat her request, followed by the reply, "Nothing to report in grid Tango Four. Over."

"Roger that. Move to grid Whiskey One. Acknowledge. Over," Jordan said.

Ferretti's team had set up their camp twenty kilometers from the alien city. From there, they'd started the search-and-recovery mission. Anderson had been overseeing the launch and recovery of UAV flights from the Alpha site.

Baptista replied, "Acknowledged last. Moving to grid Whiskey One. Charlie Four out."

About the only thing they could say for sure was that so far they hadn't seen the robot exploration team wandering around during the day shooting up the local wildlife. Ferretti was less than reassured by this information. The fact that the transponder hadn't activated didn't mean it had powered down, even if it wasn't operational.

Jordan continued her calls for status updates from his teams. "Bravo Charlie One, this is Bravo Charlie Six. Over."

If the UAV had the facility to detect radiation, they might have had a chance of finding the android by the emissions from the atomic battery the QuadMule carried. Even so, it would've been a long shot because in all likelihood the android had found a cave to hide in, which would screen the radiation from being detected.

A minute passed and Jordan repeated her transmission. "I say again, Bravo Charlie One, this is Bravo Charlie Six, come in. Over."

"This is Bravo Charlie One to Bravo Charlie Six, wait one. Over," Specialist Nelson replied, indicating something was up on her end.

Ferretti listened to Jordan work as he monitored the scientists helping out with controlling the androids. All of them had some experience working with civilian-model surrogates. However, running an android outside a controlled environment was a whole different ball game.

"Bravo Charlie Six, this is Bravo Charlie One. Sorry, thought I saw something a moment ago and moved in to check it out. Nothing to report in grid Uniform Four. Over," Nelson said.

"Roger that. Move to grid X-ray One. Acknowledge. Over."

Nelson replied, "Order acknowledged. Bravo Charlie One moving to grid X-ray One. Out."

Ferretti checked on the four scientists, who were sitting in the Conex that passed as the control room.

He twisted around in his seat to face them. His headset allowed him to check each of their android feeds in turn, but experience had taught him it was good to talk.

"How's it going, Dr. O'Neill? Find anything or see anything out of the ordinary so far?"

"Oh, lots of things, Sergeant. The wildlife is much more abundant here than back at Alpha site, but I've not seen anything to indicate our lost robot explorer team is out here. Sorry."

"How about you, Dr. Webber?"

"Same here, found less than diddly-squat so far."

"Is that the scientific term now, Alan?" Allison asked.

"It is now. My butt is getting sore from all the sitting around monitoring the VR feed," said Dr. Webber.

Ferretti smiled and interrupted the conversation. "Find anything yet, Dr. Newman?"

"Not yet, Sergeant. I've been looking at the terrain, though, and I can tell you that the rocks around here are a real mix of different types. It seems to me to indicate that they were most likely deposited here when this planet went through an ice age."

"I've not seen any sign of our lost android either, Sergeant. Are we sure it's around here?" asked Dr. Follet.

"Given the last transmission's location, and the average speed the team can walk, this area between here and the alien settlement is the most likely location for our missing robots."

"It's a pity that we can't scan for caves using the drone," said Dr. Newman.

"No use wishing for what you can't have, Doc. Why don't you all take five and stretch your legs while I keep an eye on your androids?"

A chorus of "Thank you, Sergeant Ferretti" greeted his suggestion.

Turning back to his control station, he went back to the routine task of the search. Jordan began moving the five androids to the next grid location on the map.

"Bravo Charlie Six, this is Bravo Charlie One, come in. Over."

"Reading you loud and clear. Over."

Over the speaker Specialist Nelson said, "I think I may have found our lost robot team on the edge of grid X-ray One. Over."

"Roger that, Bravo Charlie One. Send Papa Zero Five in first. Acknowledge. Over."

"Order acknowledged. Sending Papa Zero Five in to investigate possible contact. Over."

Ferretti pulled up android Papa Zero Five's feed on his screen.

The android moved towards a dark shadow on the ground that led into a burrow of some kind. Just the place a damaged android might use to hide while repairing itself.

If so, why hadn't it come out once it fixed whatever problem was generating the malfunction code?

Loose rocks rolled down the slope as Papa Zero Five made its way down into the entrance of the hole. The QuadMule was kneeling on the ground with the android sitting next to it. Both the diagnostic and recharge cables were plugged into it.

The android was stationary while the QuadMule joints chattered occasionally as they cycled themselves automatically.

"Are you getting this in the clear? Over."

Ferretti broke into the command circuit. "This is Bravo Charlie Six Actual. Roger that. I'm seeing what you're seeing. I'm going to get Wachowski and Baptista and come rendezvous with you. You're to wait until we all arrive. If the android as much as twitches, you're authorized to fire on it. Acknowledge order. Over."

"Acknowledged. Wait here until Bravo Charlie Actual arrives

with Bravo Charlie Three and Four. Use lethal force if the android moves from current location. Out."

"Jordan, tell Wachowski and Baptista that Nelson has found our lost robot, and to rendezvous and wait for me at X-ray One. You're in charge of the camp until I return."

Ferretti left to go suit up and take one of the trucks out for the retrieval. On his way he passed the scientists returning to the control cabin and saw Jordan telling them the good news and asking them to bring their androids back to camp.

Allison's face lit up when she heard the news that tomorrow they could start doing some science again. Ferretti knew they were all eager to get started on the projects they had lined up.

Baptista was already waiting with Nelson when Ferretti arrived at the burrow. Wachowski had farther to come, so they waited in the heat of the early afternoon sun, and he thanked whoever had provided cooling inside PACE suits.

So far, the android hadn't moved.

Nelson asked, "What do you think, Sergeant?"

"I think we approach with all due caution and treat it like the threat it is until we understand what has happened."

Ferretti realized that all the extra training the lieutenant had put the team through before the mission started was beginning to make sense. That woman had a head on her for knowing when trouble might happen.

Wachowski arrived, and Ferretti laid out the plan. It was a simple stack with the four of them in their suits. Using their android wouldn't be as easy as doing the job themselves.

Besides, he was the only one who could run one smoothly enough for the complexity of the task.

They approached the entrance to the hole at an angle with their android providing confirmation that their target was stationary through a feed to their screens. Wachowski was on point with Ferretti on the rear. On his signal they moved and took control.

Nothing happened, no shots were fired, and the android was clearly nonfunctional.

Ferretti shouldered his rifle and stepped behind the android, accessing the panel with the power-off switch. Then he reached over and unplugged the cables from the QuadMule, which finally reassured him that the situation was secured.

"Good work, people. OK, let's get this hunk of junk on the truck."

Together they carried the android out, each of them taking up positions around it to lift it up.

Ferretti didn't want to drag it out because that might damage it more and make finding out what had happened harder. Since only he and Jordan were qualified to repair androids, he didn't want to make more work for the pair of them.

After securing it on the back of the truck, they went back for the QuadMule. Now that it was unplugged from the android, it responded to his commands, and Ferretti took the easy option of ordering it to climb on the back of the truck before shutting it down for later examination.

The retrieval of the third atomic battery alone made all the effort worthwhile.

Tomorrow the pillars back at Alpha site would open up, and the mission would be resupplied. The project needed to screen and find more people who could be sent through the pillars because, as things stood, they were pretty thin on the ground here.

30. FIRST CONTACT

Good judgment comes from experience and experience comes from bad judgment.

— RITA MAE BROWN

Technical Sergeant Ferretti
Two Moons Bravo Site
Thursday, December 15, 2072

Ferretti had been informed about the arrival of the four new scientists for the last couple of days. The lieutenant had driven up with Sergeant Pearson to bring the scientists to their new home away from home.

She had updated him on other additions to the team, too.

The project had found another two pairs of operators for the UAV, which would make it easier to maintain air cover for his team.

The lieutenant had also dropped off the other spare working QuadMule with its atomic battery for Ferretti, which would make recharging the androids easier for his team. The visit had literally been a drop-and-go resupply, which had only underlined the fact that there were five hundred kilometers of cross-country driving involved, going each way.

The leaders of MAPCOM had been searching for suitable personnel to send to visit the natives on Three-Eight-Nine, but had retasked the team and sent them here instead. Still, the operational schedule was going to be pretty grueling all round.

Ferretti stood in front of the four scientists who made up the project's new Linguistics and Anthropology Group as they sat around one of the spare tables and stared at him.

"Welcome to Camp Bravo. I am Technical Sergeant Ferretti, but it's fine just to call me Sergeant when addressing me. I don't expect that you've had a lot of experience working with the military, but our role here is to support the science mission. This means keeping you as safe as possible and preventing you from coming to any harm. Feel free to ask me any questions."

"It's hard to believe that we're on an alien world. It feels so much like being on Earth," said Dr. Laytonya Franklin, a compact African American who looked to be in her mid-thirties.

"Dr. Franklin, I can assure you that we are as far from Earth as anybody has ever gotten, and you'll see lots of the local wildlife that you won't find on any trip back on Earth."

"Are we safe here from being attacked?" asked Dr. Grace Chai Yenn Pham, a slight-of-build woman in her late forties.

"Dr. Pham, if you keep within the boundary of the camp, you should be safe enough during your stay here. We've strung wire around the perimeter and have sensors scanning the surrounding area, along with a night guard provided by an android patrol under the command of either me or one of my team."

"Thank you for reassuring me, Sergeant," Dr. Pham replied.

"What can you tell us about the aliens, Sergeant?" asked Dr. Tyrone Reynolds, a gangly African American who looked to be in his late thirties.

"There's footage from the robot exploration team's first contact you can review, if you've not already seen it. We also have some aerial views of the settlement taken by our UAV, but we've not yet initiated any further contact at this time."

"So this is pretty much tabula rasa then?"

"If that means what I think it does, Dr. Reynolds, then yes, you will be going in first."

"Don't mind him, Sergeant. He just likes to show that he can speak Latin. I keep telling him he needs to learn Mandarin," said Dr. David Rui Leung, an older man who looked like he was in his early fifties.

"*Xièxiè*, Dr. Leung."

"Oh, you speak a little Mandarin then, Sergeant."

"Only the usual niceties of hello, goodbye, and thank you, Dr. Leung."

"Still, I'm impressed. It's not the most popular second language to have in America today. In fact, I was surprised I got chosen for this mission in these times."

"Don't embarrass the good sergeant; he's not in control of the way the world runs, you know," said Dr. Pham.

"Thank you, ma'am. As far as I'm concerned if you're an American, then everything else is secondary. Anyway, as you can see the camp is quite small, and I'm afraid that some of the facilities are a bit basic. We have a solar shower, but you need to book it to allow time for it to reheat the water between users. Toilet facilities are behind the container over there," he said, pointing. "The container has been outfitted with power and computer terminals where I imagine you will be spending most of your time working."

Dr. Franklin asked, "What about meals?"

"We have boil-in-the-bag camping food, MREs, plus whatever convenience foods that came when you arrived. One of my people will be assigned to preparing a selection for breakfast and dinner. Lunch is, as I said, based on convenience snacks or grabbing chips," he said, pausing to wipe the sweat off his brow.

"One more thing. Remember to drink plenty of water. I don't want anyone getting heatstroke while they're here. If you feel light-headed or nauseous, or notice that you have stopped sweating, get into the shade right away, start drinking water, and pour some over your head."

"So, this is it. Where we'll be working for the foreseeable future, Sergeant. Three tents, one container, and three trucks for the twelve of us," said Dr. Reynolds.

"It doesn't look like much, but it could be a lot worse. We do have androids here to aid your work with making first contact with the aliens."

"Tyrone, it's no use bitchin' about the facilities. The military is doing their best with what they've got here. You knew this was going to be a gig out in the middle of nowhere before you signed up," said Dr. Franklin.

"The tent over there to my left has been set aside for the women. The tent over there to my right is for us men. Everyone has a portable frame bed to sleep on."

"I don't mean I'm not stoked to be here, but, shit, look at this camp. My camper van has better facilities than this place. No disrespect, Sergeant, but the military gets enough money that they ought to do better than this," said Dr. Reynolds.

"None taken, sir."

"We're on an alien planet out in the middle of nowhere, what did you expect?" asked Dr. Pham.

"I don't know. Something like what we saw at the base camp. They had proper facilities."

"You know you're not making a good impression here, don't you, Tyrone?" said Dr. Leung.

"Ladies, gentlemen, please excuse me, but I have things I

must attend to. I'll leave you all to unpack and get settled in if you don't mind."

Having oriented the new arrivals to the camp, Ferretti went back to work.

He wasn't surprised they were all less than impressed with the size of the camp or the facilities on offer, but the chance to study an alien civilization would probably keep a lid on their discontent. Still, their comments didn't take away from the fact that this was his first independent command.

He had to carry on working on the broken android, which now showed all green across the boards after being rebooted.

This didn't make any sense. Why had the android gone wrong in the first place? About the only thing he could think of was that some dirt had gotten caught between the power contacts and caused a brownout.

However, not knowing what had caused the android's interlinked AI mesh of network computing modules to lock up bugged the hell out of him. If he could be certain that he had traced whatever had caused the original malfunction, then Ferretti could clear the android for operational use.

Then they would have nine androids to call upon. As the lieutenant was wont to say: *The only easy day was yesterday.*

31. TWO RACES HERE

Men who wish to know about the world must learn about it in its particular details.

— HERACLITUS

Dr. Tyrone Reynolds
Magnetic Anomaly Project Scientist
Two Moons Bravo Site
Tuesday, December 20, 2072

Tyrone was not a happy camper. He'd spent the last week in the so-called command container, whose air-conditioning was either too hot during the day or too cold at night.

Being here left a lot to be desired. He had borrowed a jacket to go over his fleece when working in there late at night.

Even more annoying was Sergeant Ferretti.

The man had insisted on assessing Tyrone's ability to run the human operator surrogates. Ferretti had made Tyrone run one of the military androids through and around the base while doing mindlessly repetitive tasks to demonstrate he was competent to operate it.

If anything went wrong, Tyrone would be perfectly safe while operating a surrogate at distance. It was another bit of military bureaucracy designed to get in the way of doing the science.

Allison even had the affront to pick him up on his complaints. She had tried to embarrass him in front of the other members of the team.

As far as Tyrone was concerned, she was thinking with the bits between her legs. He saw how she looked at the sergeant with his Italian good looks and six-pack from working out.

In his opinion, Ferretti was just another dumb grunt.

Whoever had thought to let the military control this project was seriously in need of having their head examined.

Today, Tyrone was paired up with Dr. Leung for their attempt at making first contact with the aliens. They were linked across the grid. He was fully immersed inside the virtual reality of the surrogate that was now standing at the edge of the alien settlement.

The sun had risen, and the first sounds of the aliens getting up could be heard in the distance. They'd discussed how best to initiate contact.

Following the review the autonomous android's exchange they'd argued over the various pros and cons about the best way to approach the aliens. After considering all the alternatives, in the end a decision to simply walk in early and stand around waiting to see what happened, had been considered the best option.

It was in many ways no different from when explorers from Europe had first landed in the Americas. Except this time there was going to be no exploitation of the locals by white men.

Not while he had anything to say about it.

Tyrone monitored the reading from the android surrogate as it walked towards the town, which was surrounded by a reddish stone wall with a gate that stood open.

Two reptilian-looking aliens stood guarding the entrance. He zoomed in on their digitigrade legs, a statement of a different evolutionary path taken. Each wore a wrap of off-white cloth around its lower abdomen.

The aliens carried short daggers or batons in scabbards hung on belts that went across their chests.

When the two androids and their accompanying QuadMules approached, the aliens began shouting. Then they began banging on a gong hanging behind them with a large mallet.

The noise from the gong reverberated and echoed from the buildings.

As the surrogates came closer to the guards, they fell to the ground. Prostrating themselves before the robots. Their reptilian greenish-gray bodies with yellow skin on the insides of their joints contrasted against the red walls behind them.

Tyrone zoomed the surrogate's optics to get a close up. The walls appeared to be made of mud and straw.

Dr. Leung asked, "What do you make of this behavior?"

"Well, it's congruent with the recording of what happened during the first encounter. If it weren't for the fact that we've never been here, I'd think they had met us before—or something like us anyways. My best guess is that the aliens are wired to submit to strangers, but it could just be the way they welcome each other."

"I've started recording the different sounds they're making. I'll run the pattern-recognition software on it, but what we need is a willing alien to stand and communicate with us," said Dr. Leung.

Tyrone thought about what was happening.

"You know, maybe we need to signal them in some way to get them to stop and rise. Perhaps that's what we're missing here?"

Dr. Pham broke into the circuit. "I'm wondering whether mirroring them now might be useful?"

"It might, Grace, but I'd rather stick to the plan and head towards the central square and do something there. We don't want to be standing around here all day where we can't see much."

"I concur with Tyrone here. Best we make to the square, where we can see and hear more," said Dr. Franklin, who was also monitoring the feeds from the androids.

"OK, let's make it so," Tyrone said, setting his android surrogate to walk forward again.

Leung's android followed behind.

Sergeant Ferretti had insisted that both androids carry rifles, but he had agreed that they could be slung. As far as Tyrone was concerned, this was another sign that the military was in control of the operation and would do things that would fuck stuff up.

Behind the wall, the town was laid out all higgledy-piggledy. The city appeared to have grown this way due to way the aliens shared walls when building a new structure adjacent to an old one. A wide road led them around the buildings, which took them towards the center of town.

Most of the buildings had two floors with flat roofs, with the occasional tower and larger buildings coming into view as they got closer to their destination.

By now the knowledge of their presence had been conveyed ahead of them. Aliens were either looking from the windows of their homes or kneeling on the ground as the guards had been. Some were dressed like the guards while others had more elaborate wraps that covered more of their bodies.

All the colors were muted natural fibers with some pinks and greens that might have marked the wearer as being from a wealthier class. Perhaps the wraps were signifiers of gender, too. Or not, as Tyrone would be the first to admit.

So much to find out, so much work to do.

"We've got our first word for our new English-slash-Alienese dictionary," said Dr. Leung.

"What's it mean?"

"Hell if I know. Could be anything from *welcome* to *we surrender*," Dr. Leung replied.

"That's not much use."

"Stop your bitchin', Tyrone," said Dr. Franklin on the link.

"It's not me bitching, woman. It's me just saying it's not much to go on yet."

"Still, it's not like any behavior I've ever come across before," said Dr. Pham.

Tyrone ignored them. He tried to imagine what it must be like for the aliens to have two androids and QuadMules walking into the town. What was going on inside their heads?

After fifteen minutes of walking, the robot team had reached the central square.

Ahead was an enormous complex of buildings. It reminded Tyrone of ancient Neolithic tiered palaces or temples of South America or the jungles of Southeast Asia. Around the square, there were what he'd call market stalls set in front of other large buildings.

Aliens sat next to sacks on the ground with food. Other aliens stood next to objects that looked like barrels.

"These aliens appear to be quite advanced. Over there are what look like wooden casks," he said, marking up on the display where he was pointing at.

Sergeant Ferretti broke into the circuit. "Dr. Reynolds, when you say 'quite advanced,' what do you mean exactly?"

"I mean that this could be a Third World town back on Earth. What do you think it means? Do you think that they're hiding a stack of AKs in their homes and will break them out any moment and shoot our sorry asses to pieces? Seriously, Sergeant, it just means that they have civilization that supports the level of technology we see on our own screens, that's all I'm saying."

"Thank you for making that perfectly clear to me, sir."

Anytime, Tyrone thought to himself as he commanded his android to pan around the square.

The other large buildings could be warehouses for storing food, places for teaching, or even where the rulers of the town lived. It was hard to know at this point. Time would tell.

As would the patience to wait and see what happened while not doing anything to provoke the aliens.

Dr. Leung asked him, "Perhaps we should try Grace's idea of mirroring the aliens now?"

"No, not yet. Let's just keep on recording everything for a while longer."

Looking at the aliens, he saw something that he would not have credited as believable.

"Over there, tell me I'm not seeing what I'm seeing, guys," said Tyrone, pointing at a group that looked like humanoid cat people. That were staring at the android.

"What is it?" asked Dr. Pham.

"I got it," said Dr. Leung.

"Me too. It's a second race of aliens," said Dr. O'Neill, breaking into the circuit.

"They don't look like our reptile aliens," said Dr. Franklin.

"Allison, what are the chances that two sentient aliens evolved on this planet?"

"Without DNA samples to test, it would be hard to say," said Dr. O'Neill. "What do you say, Alan?"

"As you said, without DNA it's hard to be sure. Phenotype expression isn't the same thing as genotype, and what we're looking at might be some form of parallel evolution. What we could have here is the equivalent of *Homo sapiens* and

Neanderthals living together, though I admit that's unlikely," said Dr. Webber.

"They appear feline to me."

"They're not cats, whatever they may look like. It's not helpful to label aliens with characteristics of creatures back on Earth," said Dr. O'Neill.

"And twice the amount of work to decipher both sets of languages and no doubt a trade pidgin they use to communicate with each other," said Dr. Leung.

"This is so exciting, though. Not one, but two lots of aliens to study," said Dr. O'Neill.

32. WELCOME MASTERS

Peace be to you, fear not.

— GENESIS 43:23

Riko Timakira ya Hadhi
Two Moons

The town Master had been taught as a youngling that the Progenitors would one day return. Rumors of their return had been spreading since the fish-catcher had told the tale of meeting one under the midday sun.

Others said they had no doubt that working in the heat of the day had addled the fish-catcher's mind. But the town's guards had reported that two Progenitors had returned, and were standing in the main square.

This was not like the stories where the Progenitors were a force of nature.

Tales that told of their arrival, and the deaths that followed. Any resistance by the people's always led to more deaths. The best they could do was submit and hope they were not chosen by the Progenitors.

Now two Progenitors were standing in the square, doing nothing.

This was strange behavior indeed, but how should he respond? Was it a new kind of test? The town's Master summoned the First Scriber to his chamber.

Entering the room, the First Scriber said, "How may I be of service to the Master of this town?" The Secundus's pink snout twitched in distress.

"I need to understand the old tales about the Progenitors. I have been told that there are now two of them in the town's square, doing nothing. This is most unusual behavior for Progenitors. What can you tell me?"

"Master, there are many tales about the Progenitors. What I know is that they made us in their image and brought the peoples here. They come when we don't expect them, and test us to see if we are true to their image. They may be bringing others to live with us, or waiting to see if we behave in ways that are not in their image, Master."

"It has been over a thousand harvests since the Progenitors brought the Quartus here to live in these lands with us. Why would they choose now to bring other people?"

"I do not know, Master. No one understands the minds of the Progenitors, even though they tell us we are made from their image. The way they think and behave is not like us."

"So, we are left unable to know what to do. Another test of whether we are true to their image."

"Perhaps we have passed all the tests, and they are here to lead us to the promised land, Master?"

"Do you think that these are the end times, First Scriber?"

"No, Master, the signs of time's end have not been seen. The sun still shines as it should. The moons are still in the sky. The sea has not vanished from the lands. The people are not found wanting to die. No abominations have been born to the people or creatures of the land."

"What advice would you offer me?"

"The Progenitors will tell you what they want, Master."

"You are dismissed. Guards, accompany me to the square. I go to meet the Progenitors," said the Master, never expecting to come back again.

The Master walked across the square, fighting the urge to fling himself to the ground. The guards walking on either side were trembling as they moved. *Show no fear, be true to the image of the Progenitors*, was the Master's only thought.

Standing before them, the Master bowed while the guards fell to the ground.

A Progenitor knelt on the ground, leant forward, and wrote in the dirt: 1=1, 11=11, 111=111. The Master recognized the pattern as a variant of the Progenitors' ancient writing.

The Master turned in place and spoke. "Rise up and go about your business."

Slowly the four peoples of the town rose and walked away.

"Please follow me," said the Master, turning to walk back towards the town's master hall.

The two Progenitors followed. It was a glorious feeling, not dying, which somehow made being alive feel more real.

33. THIS ISN'T RIGHT

We learn more by looking for the answer to a question and not finding it than we do from learning the answer itself.

— LLOYD ALEXANDER

Dr. Allison O'Neill
Magnetic Anomaly Project Scientist
Two Moons Bravo Site
Tuesday, December 20, 2072

Allison watched the virtual-reality feeds from the project's contact team. Tyrone and David were both immersed in their surrogate loops. This meant that Allison, Laytonya, Grace, and Alan were along for the ride.

Effectively looking over the shoulders of the two operators.

The surrogates were following the alien as it walked through the market square. She pulled out of the direct feed. Using her headset she began reviewing a separate display of what had been recorded so far.

Starting at the beginning, she fast-forwarded through the two streams, comparing what each android surrogate had seen.

Allison was looking for the differences between the images.

She paused the feed when the points of view changed, trying to think what she might have missed. It wasn't her job, but Allison was excited by what was happening, and she wanted to find out more.

Questions raced through her mind. What were the animals being harnessed by the aliens. How many types of fruit and vegetables were there in the market? What did they smell like?

There was so much to discover.

So far the mission had been looking at flora and fauna in the desert, and here now was the opportunity to study what the locals knew about.

Dr. Webber asked, "What are we seeing, Allison?"

"Not so much seeing as just looking for what we're not seeing."

"We need to get into this town and look around for ourselves," said Dr. Webber.

"I wouldn't mind the chance to take some samples of the food on display in the market, too. Over there, those appear to be lizards skewered for eating."

"All far too organic for my tastes," said Dr. Follet.

"Brigitte, you can't be serious. Anyway, I'm sure I saw stones worn as jewelry, which must be of some interest to your research."

"Not really. That's more Simon's field."

"Then only interesting to me if I can find out where they were found and study the deposits; otherwise, not all that useful in mapping out the geology on this planet. Still, it's not every day that one gets to see something like this unfold in front of one in real time and all," said Dr. Newman.

Allison kept an eye on the team's feed as they entered the

large building. The alien walked ahead of them. She wondered, if their roles were reversed, could she do what it was doing?

The room the android surrogates entered had a high vaulted ceiling with a balcony running around it. There were doors on both sides with two passageways at the far end, and a chair set against the back wall.

Four other aliens stood at the back of the room.

The one who had walked in front led the team to the far end of the room, then turned and sat down on the chair and spoke. The guards who had been following the android surrogates also filed into the room. They marched towards the passageways at the end, which went farther into the interior of the building.

"Unless I'm very much mistaken, it seems like we were greeted by the head man of this town," said Dr. Reynolds.

A few minutes later, another alien species entered the room. The new alien was also a symmetrical biped that looked like a pig-faced koala bear.

"Didn't see that coming," said Dr. Webber.

Dr. Newman asked, "Allison, what are the chances of three different alien species all living in the same place?"

"Before today, I would have said slim to none, but here we are."

34. THERE'S A FOURTH

People are not disturbed by things, but by the views they take of them.

— EPICTETUS

Dr. David Leung
Magnetic Anomaly Project Scientist
Two Moons Bravo Site
Tuesday, December 20, 2072

David was immersed in the virtual-reality loop. Tyrone's android surrogate followed David's as he walked after the third alien. It had been called to the chamber, and had indicated they should follow it.

The guards, in what he was calling the throne room, stared impassively ahead. David didn't know if this was a good sign or a bad one.

Did it mean they were unthreatened by the presence of the two androids, or was something else going on here?

"Tyrone, what do you make of the guards? Should we be worried?"

"Why should we be worried? The worse that can happen is they attack our android surrogates. Seriously, I think they're shitting themselves. You saw how the aliens reacted to us in the square, right? Nobody's going to mess with us. Of course, the real question is, why is that?" replied Dr. Reynolds.

"Perhaps someone else has been here before us, like the Chinese?"

"Yeah, like the Chinese. And if so, where are they now? Why would they come and then just leave?"

"Oh, we're in a library of some sort," Leung replied.

The alien pig-bear beckoned them to a table and gestured at them to wait. It rushed off to the back of the room, which had shelves full of scrolls. A short while later, it returned followed by two more aliens, of a type they had not seen before.

"You've got to be shitting me. That's a fourth species of alien being."

The doglike bipeds were carrying a large armful of scrolls between them, and what appeared to be a leather-bound book. They then placed the items all in a pile on the table.

One of the aliens unrolled the first scroll and weighted the corners down with some polished stones.

Dr. Reynolds asked, "What next? A cantina band playing jazz music!? Am I the only one feeling the *Star Wars* vibe here? What are the odds on finding four alien races on one planet in one location? Someone or something is pulling our legs big time."

David examined the first scroll.

The text was split into two columns. On the left were vertical strokes with two squiggly lines that looked like the aliens' equivalent of an equals sign. The page was full of symbols that were the key to the aliens' mathematical language.

On the right-hand side were, David assumed, symbols in the alien language for the numbers.

"Look at this, Tyrone. Forget what the odds are. This library will make translating the writing and language much easier for us. We've struck lucky here. Everything we need to begin to get a grip on the aliens' language. No doubt once we get this lot processed, we can easily work out the other languages used here, too."

"Glad you're a happy bunny, but this isn't much use to us until we can read it. I need to be outside observing the people of this world. There are four alien races here, and I've gotta catch them all," said Dr. Reynolds.

"Do you have enough to be getting on with, because I could sure do with Grace's input on this? Using an android to scan these scrolls will go a lot quicker with two of us."

"OK, but only because I need to be able to talk to these people, but you owe me one, right. This is going to be one for the history books, you know. I'll initiate transfer now," said Dr. Reynolds.

"Wow, this is awesome," said Dr. Pham as she came into the virtual-reality loop. "It's going to be a full-time job to work on recording everything in this library."

35. DISCUSSION

Our first intuitions are the true ones.

— Emile M. Cioran

Dr. Samantha Emmerich
Magnetic Anomaly Project Head Scientist
Two Moons Alpha Site
Wednesday, December 21, 2072

Samantha was sitting in a virtual conference room, cut off from the what was happening around her back at the Alpha Camp. She listened to the discussion begin.

"Even a few weeks ago, what odds would you have given me that we would find four sentient alien races on this world? Honestly, it beggars belief," said Dr. Webber, who had kicked off the conference call between the teams at both camps.

"I'm not a statistician, but my guess is we're missing something obvious here. It's far too early to draw any conclusions on what we know," said Dr. Wilson, who had taken the time to customize his avatar with a top that read "Do the Math."

"How is the work on learning their language progressing?"

"We're making great strides in copying the writing on the scrolls and developing an understanding of their number system. We've also started compiling words, and are using algorithms to deduce their grammar, too," said Dr. Leung. "Here, let me show you what we've been working on."

On Samantha's PAD alien script appeared, under which was a sentence using the English alphabet.

Uliza afasanfidu o gonsa fobi, okoki daidho go logo go ludubo go hoodhoo go la, go kulegilo olozagai gensei na asiladhifa.

The translation began: "Between the time when the oceans swallowed the land, and the rise of the first ones, there was an age now unknown." A note said "an age now unknown" could also be translated as "lost in time," or "a golden age before the fall."

Percentage probabilities were assigned to each, along with a caution that the margin of error for each was high.

The translation scrolled to the next passage.

Dhaiginyu oobobu za, bodhi go dhifa go aoi lanfo go koo gi debaihuu gi jisozasu kobofazaffe iladhifa.

"Civilized countries lay spread across the world, mantles beneath the stars." Another note appeared, which said, "Approximation based on heuristic application of syntax and idiom. Probability of error high."

Drs. Leung and Pham noted that the position of the verbs and adjectives altered the rhythm and flow of the passage.

The next line appeared.

Kule o life gidhi gi daiboo bunsin dhi, dogo dhinpi go debai o obabe dokiefafsu jadhisa-joo gi lifdule genyu-daiboo dedhifa.

"Reigning supreme in the dreaming west were the Progenitors, who gazed upon the towering pillars whose mystery haunted the world."

"I should put some caveats and add a big caution here," said Dr. Leung, interrupting her reading. "This is a loose translation of the texts, as we're still working on increasing our vocabulary."

Dr. Pham spoke to support his colleague. "Though we have a manuscript that starts with basic logic to work with and the natives' equivalent running in parallel, I came across a scroll today that was empty on one side. It seems to me the natives are learning how to read the basic mathematics and translate them into their own language. As such, I can tell you that they've yet to comprehend calculus."

"So what the hell's going on here then?" asked Dr. Reynolds.

Dr. Webber spoke. "Lots of options are possible. First, they've been visited in the past by someone who tried what we did and then left. If not that, then perhaps these scrolls were given to the natives as a means of teaching them. Or they're the remains of a failed colonization attempt, which has technologically regressed due to a natural disaster or the fall of the home civilization."

"How likely is that?" asked Dr. Reynolds.

Dr. Wilson said, "We've no idea, and without further data it's merely idle speculation. For all we know, they came here like we did, traveling through the pillars, and were unable to get back for some reason."

"To answer those questions, we're going to need more time to learn the written language and how it's spoken. We've seen four distinct races, so it will take a long time before we can understand the social dynamics going on here. We need more people," said Dr. Franklin.

Samantha spoke. "Unfortunately, the best we can do is compile all the information and send it back to Earth. We've more people there who can work on the problems."

"Why aren't we testing more people and getting them into the program?"

Samantha was interrupted by Dr. Reynolds. "Time and money."

"The military has lots of money. Why don't they do something useful with it for once?"

"Anybody would think you have a chip on your shoulder the size of Alaska about the military, Tyrone. Don't hold back, tell us how you really feel," replied Dr. Franklin.

"Without the military, we wouldn't be where we are today, Dr. Reynolds! That said, we do have to let those back on Earth know what's happening here."

Dr. Wilson interrupted Samantha.

"Well, from my perspective the recordings from the Two Moons pillars have yielded some fruitful data on where they connect. This has been most illuminating in suggesting possible avenues for further research. We might not be able to control when and where they cycle to, but I'm pretty confident that over time we can map the system. We'd be able to plan routes passing through multiple pillars to get to where we want, when we want."

"That would be good news. I imagine the military could be tempted to become more involved with the project if we could offer them something like that."

"You can't be serious, Samantha. The military have their grubby paws all over this project enough already," said Dr. Reynolds.

"It may come as a shock to you, but they already pay your salary and support your work here. Without them we would need corporations interested in funding us, and they'd be looking at the bottom line. At least with the military, you know they're not in it for the profit."

"That's as it may be, but what we need to be doing is getting into the town and observing these people and how they live. It seems to me our android surrogates freak the hell out of them, and we're missing a real opportunity to study the aliens firsthand here," said Dr. Reynolds.

Samantha asked, "What do you think, Lieutenant Tachikoma?"

"There are considerable risks to protect the team from, which would be difficult if not impossible. However, saying that, it's not my decision to make. If ordered to provide support, then my team would do so. But with the rider that this is unknown territory, and I've a limited amount of resources at my disposal. If the worse came to the worst, I may end up having a very limited set of options on how to respond."

"What does that mean, Lieutenant?" asked Dr. Reynolds.

"It means if the locals put you in a pot to cook you, I'll probably end up having to kill them all to rescue you."

"Thank you for your concise summation, Lieutenant. What do we think are the chances of the aliens trying to eat us?" Samantha said.

"I'd like to see them try to eat Tyrone; he'd be giving them attitude all the way to the cooking pot," said Dr. Franklin.

A ripple of laughter broke the tension.

"Once we have the language down, we should be able to avoid any faux pas that leads to us all ending up in the cooking pot," said Dr. Pham.

"I can't believe you're all talking about these aliens as if they were cannibals. Where's the evidence for this spurious speculation coming from? Let's get real here; if the aliens were going to attack us, they would've done so by now. Period. After all, we've been rummaging around their library for the last two weeks and all. We've got the written language down, and the basics of how to speak it. Time we made hay, while the sun shines," said Dr. Reynolds.

People's expressions went blank for a moment as they searched their PADs for Tyrone's obscure reference.

Samantha said, "OK, let's get a schedule planned so I can present the case back to Earth. And, Lieutenant, can you draw up a plan of the various best- to worst-case scenarios, please?"

"Certainly, ma'am."

224

36. IN THE BALANCE

The last enemy that shall be destroyed is death.

— 1 CORINTHIANS 15:26

Riko Timakira ya Hadhi
Two Moons

The Scriber was old and had read many scrolls with tales about the Progenitors. Nothing he had read had prepared him for the reality of meeting them. They were unlike anything he had experienced before.

They walked like people, yet their movements were oddly graceless, and their leg joints bent in reverse. As he thought more about them, his stomach churned from fear, which made his spine tense and breathing harder.

Their behavior bothered him; it was as if they didn't know who and what they were.

The two Progenitors had followed him into the library and begun reading the ancient scrolls. This became their obsession as they studied each one in turn, as if searching for something or learning anew.

How could that be?

They were the Progenitors, the creators of the four peoples, here to reap what they had sowed.

Now they were speaking to him. At first, just repeating words and then pointing at things and repeating his replies. If he didn't know better, he would assume they were learning to speak the language of the peoples.

The old stories always said the Progenitors tested their creations.

Was this some new test to see if the peoples of this world were still true to the image of the Progenitors? When they said things wrong, he corrected them, and hoped they didn't notice him sighing each time he did so.

But he feared his answers could lead to his death.

The Scriber had lived a long and fruitful life. He didn't want it to end by causing the Progenitors to condemn the peoples of this world for leaving the path laid down for them. The last visit, more than a thousand harvests ago, had led to a reaving of the town when the Progenitors had found something that displeased them.

Still, not all their visits had led to death and destruction.

The responsibility for everyone's life in the town weighed upon him. He could only hope this was one of those visits where the Progenitors came and went without incident. He would do all in his power to assuage their ire if anything were to upset them.

If he were to be tested, he would not fail. Not himself, his people, or the other people of this world.

37. BASE CAMP ALPHA

Another day down.

— ANONYMOUS

First Lieutenant Lara Atsuko Tachikoma
Two Moons Alpha Site
Thursday, December 22, 2072

Part of my job as an officer was to stay on top of all the paperwork. The Corps runs on forms being filled in. So it came as no surprise to find myself with lots of pages to go over on my PAD.

And as always, not enough time to do it all.

Espera walked into the partitioned space designated as my office, which, in comparison to being aboard a ship, was positively roomy as broom closets go. The Corps never promises you any luxuries.

"Are you ready to go, LT?"

I made no comment on the Army Special Forces' cultural

difference of habitually treating officers as equals, because at his core he lived and breathed discipline.

"Sure—is that the time already? Sheesh, where does it all go?"

"The hell if I know."

Logging out of the job, I said, "Yeah, well enough of this banter, we've got a job to do."

I'd learnt to delegate tasks down the chain of command when I could, but some days there was no one to delegate tasks to, and I ended up having to go hands-on.

I didn't mind this, because it was a relief from sitting in a chair filling in forms while enlarging my butt.

The day was Thursday, and it was time for the pillars to open between Two Moons and Earth with another resupply run for our mission. We headed out into the heat of the afternoon sun and went around checking the tires and starting each of the trucks up in turn.

"Staff Sergeant, you're riding shotgun today," I said, ordering Espera to let me drive the truck.

Which wasn't regulation, but it was a job that had to be done. There was no point in me standing around ordering him to do stuff when two people working together would get the job done in half the time.

We had loaded up four trucks with trash, samples, and broken items in need of repair. We would get back fresh food, serviced and refueled trucks, and water. Then we would have to unpack and tick off the manifest, checking everything had arrived.

"Shotgun works for me, LT."

I got into the cab of the Oshkosh, which, strictly speaking, I don't have a license to drive. There again, neither did Espera, but we weren't on Earth. As they say, we're no longer in Kansas, so I would have to get on with it.

The engine kicked over, sounding like a bag full of hammers hitting each other.

"Looking good, LT!"

I edged the first truck out of its assigned position on the camp's perimeter. Once done I went to the second truck. It wasn't actually necessary for me to do so, as I could have run all four by remote through the first truck's command station, but I wanted to stretch my legs and get some exercise.

"OK, I'm ready here!"

"Got you, track slightly left, LT," Espera shouted back over the noise of the engine.

I inched the truck to the left, using the parking-camera feeds. If I ran over the edge of the perimeter wire, it would make more work for us. I cleared the wire without crushing it under the tires, parked behind the first truck, and got out to repeat the process.

"Here, have some water, LT," said Espera, chucking me a bottle. "It's hotter than hell out here."

"Sure is, Staff Sergeant. Aren't we due some rain sometime soon?"

"I believe we might be, but the last time a storm front came in, the rain all unloaded on the other side of the range from us."

Next, I climbed up into the third truck and pulled it out behind the other two, which we had made ready for our mini convoy back through the pillars.

It didn't want to start.

I switched the system off and back on to run the reheat start-up cycle, and waited for the red lights to go out. I tried starting her up again. The engine churned over before backfiring and kicking into life.

"Lots of smoke coming out the back, LT."

A cloud of white billowed out from the exhaust, and I made a note on the truck's command console tagging it for a more thorough service. My best guess was water buildup from condensation from extremes of heat throughout the day and night. But it could have been the injectors for all I knew.

"OK, let's get this hunk of junk rolling, Staff Sergeant."

"Easy does it, LT; there's a bit of a dip in front of you."

"Got it."

I drove the truck through the dip and put it behind the other two. Then I walked back to where Espera was waiting for me by the fourth truck.

"Let's get this done," I said, getting into the driver's seat, Espera joining me in the passenger's. He began checking the return manifest on his PAD and matched it to what was on the truck's systems.

"Everything checks out. Can you put your authorization here for me?"

I looked over the manifest on my PAD and did the deed.

It wasn't that we expected pilfering on the journey, but packing mistakes happen. If something critical to the mission was missing, it was going to take two weeks to sort it out. Also, just because we sent stuff back for servicing didn't guarantee it would be sent back when repaired, either.

The truck engine caught the first time, and we rolled her up behind the other three outside the perimeter wire of Camp Alpha.

After that I logged in to the other trucks' systems and took control of the convoy, deliberately leading from the rear so I didn't have to get out of the air-conditioned luxury of the cab. Once the telltales showed green across the board, I set the others to follow my commands, and we rolled the kilometer from the perimeter to the pillars.

I drew the trucks up in front of the pillars, but slightly offset to the right, with the lead truck twenty-five meters away from them.

"I'm switching control over to autonomous mode now."

"Looks good to me, LT. All green across the board."

"Let's go talk to Dr. Wilson, or at least let him talk at us while we get some shade, Staff Sergeant."

"Roger that, LT."

We both climbed out of the truck and walked past what we called the front of the pillars to where Dr. Wilson had his mini camp set up. There he'd been using the extra time on Two Moons to record where the pillars opened to.

We'd managed to replace the temporary tent that he'd started working out of with a Conex box, which was sufficient to meet his needs.

Parked out front was an old monowheeled PUMA with off-road tires. I knocked on the door of his small domain.

"Good afternoon, Dr. Wilson. It's Lieutenant Tachikoma and Staff Sergeant Espera. May we come in?"

"Yeah, yeah; mind the mess on the floor. I'm reviewing some data before sending it to the trucks," he replied, waving his hand at us.

The floor was covered in paper with drawings on them. Some sketches of the landscape, and others with spirals with patterns that suggested order arising out of chaos.

At the back of the container was a bed, and next to it a Jetboil and spare mugs.

"Mind if we wait here in the cool with you for the pillars to cycle?" asked Espera.

"Not at all; you're both very welcome. I don't get many visitors coming to see me, so the weekly resupply drops make a nice change. How's everything going, Lieutenant?"

"Camp Bravo has made first contact with the aliens, but you've heard all about that, though. We're waiting to see how long the project will extend the mission. Other than that, everything is running smoothly."

"Good to hear that. I'm hoping we'll get an extension of our stay here. I'm pulling in good data on these pillars, and I'm excited by what I've learned so far. If we can chart where all the pillars cycle to, it should be possible to send missions out by traversing the network to get where we want to go. It won't be the same as being able to control them, of course, but it would be a bit like using a timetable to plan a journey with interchanges."

"A subway map."

"Yeah, you could say that. Seventy percent of the time, these pillars open to worlds we've already put science packages on, but that's not the best bit. No, the interesting thing is that the other thirty percent of openings go to new worlds. The possibilities for exploring the universe have just multiplied."

And the chances of meeting more aliens that may be ahead of us had also risen.

"OK, but I thought I read somewhere in the reports that each time the pillars pulse there's a unique signature that has three parts. The first being associated with the gate, the middle section that varies, and the third part that tells where the gate opens next. If I've understood this, then this repeats over time."

"You're mostly right, but we've some confounding variables, which just means that the pattern changes slightly each week. Basically, if we had a fixed pattern, then after six months we would have expected to find one thousand and six planets. However, we have more than that, because sometimes we get skips where the next opening goes somewhere new."

"That sounds a bit random, and potentially dangerous to anyone using the pillars to travel to another world."

"Which is why we have been putting monitor stations on all the worlds. It allows us to confirm that we're seeing the pillars opening up to the same worlds, and will enable us to choose suitable worlds to visit."

Wilson then used his PAD to project a drawing on the wall of his Conex box.

"If you draw a network, what you're effectively doing is drawing hypotheses. You see links to places you didn't know were related, and questions of how this works can be answered by using statistical analysis of the network. From there you can test your analysis by seeing if it replicates the connections that we've identified."

Dr. Wilson was clearly in his element and became more voluble as he progressed with his explanation, gesticulating to show his excitement as he made links on his diagram.

He finished by saying, "Then the links that did not exist before, those become our new hypotheses. Then the work really starts."

"Fascinating, Doc."

"Excuse me, LT, but the pillars are about to cycle back to Earth," said Espera.

"Thank you, Staff Sergeant. It was nice talking to you, Dr. Wilson. I do hope we will see you for the meal on Sunday?"

"Sunday…what's special about the meal then?"

"Nothing much, but Petty Officer Adams has plans for us to celebrate the first Christmas on this planet together."

"Two Moons at Christmas. Just the thing," he replied, trailing off and forgetting we were there.

I was starting to worry he wasn't getting out and mixing with people enough.

We left his cramped container and walked over to where the resupply trucks had parked. The exchange with ours having taken place automatically when the pillars opened. We got inside the cool interior of one of the new trucks and drove back to base.

Glen would tell me later if anything important had been said during the exchange.

"Staff Sergeant, will you make sure that Dr. Wilson gets to the meal on Sunday? And perhaps we need to get him out of his routine. He seems a bit detached to me."

"I thought he was always slightly odd to begin with."

"Well, he's a geek, but let's not forget the geeks and nerds at this time of the year. After all, we're all special in some way."

"You mean like people with special needs?"

"Not exactly, Staff Sergeant."

I'd just finished being talked at by Dr. Emmerich. She'd told me at great length that the biggest setback for the mission was only having one science team operating out of Camp Alpha. From her perspective they were underutilizing the laboratory equipment there.

A lot more could be achieved if they had more staff. But isn't that always the case? They had some suitable candidates who had been scanned and lined up to join the project.

Unfortunately, they had to work out their contracts at their universities first. Seemed to me that academia made the military bureaucracy look efficient.

Afterwards, I needed something to distract me.

So I walked over to the UAV control container to check on how the day's mission was progressing. I entered the room, choosing to stand behind Glen, and I pressed up against the back of his chair in the cramped control room.

It was the nearest thing I could get to a public display of affection.

The big screen showed two views from the UAV. The first was of the horizon, with the HUD overlay displayed on top of the image. I checked the readouts.

"Looking good to me."

Sitting at the UAV control station were two of our four new operators.

Senior Airman Davis was piloting the craft while Airman First Class Moore was on sensors. They had both arrived last week, much to Glen's, and the rest of my team's, relief. I'd been juggling the duty roster to maintain the four-on and four-off schedule while the UAV was in the air for three days at a time.

Things don't run so smoothly when people are tired, because they tend to make more mistakes, and that takes more time to fix.

"Oh, hi. Yeah, it's going all right, but there's a chance of a weather front hitting us at some point in the next twenty-four hours. We can't afford to lose the UAV in a storm," said Glen distractedly.

The other view on the screen showed the ground below the UAV.

The city was spread out alongside of what we then knew was a large lake. From above, the place was a maze, a confusing mishmash of roads and open spaces. It all looked very old and rundown.

Glen's team was studying the place to find out more about how the aliens lived down there.

The next part of his plan was to drop MicroBots ranging from the size of large insects to small birds over the town to monitor what the inhabitants did during their daily existence. The only real trouble was the 'Bots' limited endurance time.

Plus the fact that we had to keep our UAV loitering over the city where anyone looking up in the sky might spot it.

"Won't the MicroBots be about dead by then anyway?"

While some of the scientists had thought that this operation was intrusive, and violating the aliens' rights, it seemed to me it was making the most of a difficult situation. I preferred to know as much as I could about the aliens before letting the civilian scientists loose in the town.

After all, it would be tears at bedtime if something bad happened because we failed to do our homework.

"That all depends on a number of factors, but yes, in principle we get twenty-four hours out of them under the best conditions.

But if the storm front hits early, then we lose out on maximizing the data we can get. We can't delay the launch, because the scientists need to see what's going on before they go in," said Glen.

"Tell me about it. If I had my way, I'd have them do it all by remote. But I've been told that using the androids will contaminate the aliens' natural behaviors. If contamination means they don't try to kill anyone, then I'm all for contaminating them good and proper."

"MicroBots deployed on my mark. Three, two, one—mark. Data stream is looking good, images coming in now," said Airman First Class Moore.

The UAV's feed showed the MicroBots as they began spreading out over the city below.

The picture on the screen dominated the container's interior.

The hypnotic quality of the image overwhelmed the senses as the computer overlaid a series of subpictures transmitted by the MicroBots that then moved onto the ancillary screens, cycling through each, as the process to generate a 3D fly-through began.

We wouldn't get anything like full coverage, but the plan was to grab what we could in the time we had, dumping enough onto the two anthropologists' system to keep them busy for several weeks. It would at least shut them up and stop them from complaining about not having enough work to do.

"Anyway, you want to come and grab a bite to eat with me?"

"Sure, I could do with a break from watching the screen in here," said Glen.

We walked out of the air-conditioned container into the heat of the day. The morning sunlight having long since melted the night's ground frost.

One of the scientists had put up an artificial Christmas tree in the middle of the camp. The decorations on it reminded me of the time I had been in Australia for Christmas during my first deployment after I had just turned twenty.

We made our way over to the tables and chairs in front of our kitchen module, where Adams was busy as usual.

I had scheduled everyone on my team to do a spell with him to give him some relief from his kitchen duties. Fortunately for us, the man loved cooking. As long as he got help, he was as happy as a sand boy, as my Scottish mother liked to say.

"Pity we can't have some time alone to ourselves," said Glen.

"Don't tempt me."

"I could so kiss you right now."

"And I would so hit you if you were to do anything that unbecoming while I'm on duty."

"You're a hard woman, Lara Tachikoma. Lord knows what my parents might have said if I had taken you home to meet them this Christmas."

"Isn't it a bit too soon to be taking me to meet your parents? And I bet you take all your girlfriends home to meet them."

"No, only one before you, and I married her."

"Now who's making scary comments? However, if I were you, I'd be more worried about meeting my mom."

"If you're anything like her, then I imagine she will think I'm wonderful."

"Yeah, right. You just carry on thinking that, but remember she's Scottish and I'm her only daughter."

"It will be good to get back home, though, after the mission is finished."

We were now into the beginning of our fifth week on Two Moons, and living off-Earth had become routine. The scientists here were as happy as clams, though that didn't stop them from grumbling about not having the luxuries they took for granted back home.

"Yeah, well I wouldn't hold your breath on that happening anytime soon. We could be here for a while yet. How long do you think it's going to take to get a handle on the aliens' language after all?"

"How long is a piece of string?"

"My point exactly. We've been lucky so far; nothing has yet come to bite us by surprise, but we never planned for an extended stay here, either. Realistically, we need to enlarge Camp Bravo, but the problem is that it's at the end of a rather long supply chain."

"Who said the only easy day was yesterday? Ouch, that hurts," he said as I slapped him on the arm, and he played at being wounded.

"See, that's what happens to you when I'm to be hoisted on my own petard."

"I surrender. Do with me what you will."

"In your dreams, big boy."

38. A WORLD OF WONDERS

Time is the most valuable thing a man can spend.

— THEOPHRASTUS

First Lieutenant Lara Atsuko Tachikoma
Two Moons Alpha Site
Sunday, January 1, 2073

I'd gotten up and had my morning run, then eaten breakfast and showered before starting work. I understood that the scientists were taking New Year's Day off and doing whatever it was they did when they weren't doing science stuff.

As for me, I headed over to the admin center to start work. I had Sergeant Espera's morning report to review.

Dr. Emmerich, however, was working, and as I sat down in my cubicle she greeted me. "Happy New Year, Lieutenant."

"And to you to, Doctor. I didn't expect to see you in here working today, though."

"Well, you know how it is. There's always more work to do, and to be honest, spending the day chatting and playing games isn't exactly for me. It reminds me of home and what I'm missing not being there. Not that I wouldn't have come, considering what we've found. Still, if I keep busy, I've less time to worry about my family."

"I've only got my mom, and I haven't lived at home for almost eight years now. I go see her when I can, but she's a nurse and often does extra shifts. She's always worrying about having enough money to make ends meet."

"Times are hard, Lieutenant. Still, while they may be hard, it's also a very exciting time to be alive. Once we reveal the existence of the pillars, it's going to change everything."

"You think that'll happen in the foreseeable future?"

"It will, eventually. After all, the Chinese have their own project, and who knows who else might be working on pillars they've uncovered? You can't keep something like this a secret forever."

"Perhaps not, but it's not something I have much control over."

I got us both a coffee and spent the rest of my morning with my butt in a chair dealing with my administrative backlog, which sure beat the hell out of driving for twenty-four hours and unloading a truckload of supplies.

As I didn't take the day off, neither did anyone else on my team.

Yet, with the scientists taking a rest day, we were less pushed than usual. This meant we got to play catch-up with whatever hadn't been done. By end of the morning I was ahead of my work.

I took the opportunity to go see if Glen was free for lunch.

Not that he had less admin to do than I, but he didn't have the responsibility of the base to deal with on top of everything else. I timed my walk to catch up with him when I thought he would be ready to take a break.

It was the nearest thing we got to quality time together since we'd been on-world.

"Hey you, how's it going here where all the cool kids hang out flying the blue skies?" I asked, seeing Glen sat working on a database.

"I'm one of the cool kids now. When did that happen?"

"When you met me."

"Heh. You want to see something really cool?"

"Show me what you've got, and I'll tell you if it meets my criteria for being cool or not."

"Trust me on this one. You know we've been looking for other magnetic anomalies that might be pillars; well we found yours, and something else, too. Go grab a chair and sit yourself down."

I did, using the excuse of getting closer to his screen to sit nearer to him as he brought up some footage from the UAV.

He smelt nice.

"We've been flying over the surrounding areas and creating maps for future operations. By putting this together with the high-altitude balloons' imagery, we're starting to think it looks like this planet is one big supercontinent. Like Pangaea on Earth about two hundred and fifty million years ago. That was in the Permian period with everything from jungles to deserts to dinosaurs. Or what Earth will be like in about another two hundred and fifty million years in the future, depending on whom you talk to. We'll know for sure once we're able to set up a pad to launch a satellite into orbit," said Glen, whose background in satellite imagery made him keen to get something into space.

The UAV flew over the landscape as the camera zoomed in on the ground moving below. As the UAV flew lower, I could make out it wasn't the ground moving but rather a herd of dinosaurs.

"Oh wow. Baby dinosaurs, too."

"Yeah, they are pretty ickle-pooh, until you realize they're not that small. That's not all. We calculated the location of where your pillars would have to be from the feeds from your CASE suit. Wait one and you'll see."

Glen opened up another window, which showed a recording of the UAV flying with a range of mountains ahead of it and the sun behind casting long shadows. In front of the mountains was another grass plain that led to a vast forest.

"What do you think?"

In my mind's eye, I was back seeing this world for the very first time.

A flashback to when first encountered the pillars. Stood in a cavern, below the White Mountain in Afghanistan. Remembering the impossible light coming from between a pair of stalagmites.

The rush of adrenaline as I realized I was standing outside in the open.

The realization that the lengthening shadows were from an alien sun, descending behind some mountains in the distance. I'd stared out across a plain, at the beginning of a jungle which stretched out to the horizon.

Above me had been things flying that were not birds, but something like large bats. They had dipped into the jungle canopy, with two moons adding the emphasis that it had not been Earth.

And then I was back in the present.

"I think, that if those aren't the same pillars I walked through, then I'll be most disappointed. How far are they from here?"

"About three thousand kilometers as the UAV flies. The mountains form the edge of the plateau that this desert sits on. It's something to do on another mission. I know Dr. Wilson is particularly interested in setting up a monitoring station there, too."

"It would be so much easier to access the pillars from our side." If only the situation in Afghanistan hadn't been complicated by the fallout after my old company had been sent to rescue an American Special Forces team.

But nothing is ever simple.

Our mission had turned into a firefight when we'd encountered a Chinese COIN, counterinsurgency, company of flying all-terrain suits. The engagement hadn't gone well for them when their plan to use a nuclear warhead was foiled. If it hadn't been for that, it might have been a simple matter to gain access to the disputed territory. But, wishes wouldn't make it so, we'd had to suck it up.

Besides, the reason we were on Two Moons at all was as a result of the fallout of that mission.

Glen spoke, pulling me out of my thoughts.

"Still, as Dr. Wilson explains, there are advantages to being here and studying when and where the pillars cycle to. Certainly, from an Agency perspective, it would make sense to map the connections between as many pillars as we can."

"As long as we don't have to set up home here. It's not like the world has much in the way of the basic necessities of life."

"I never took you for a gal who liked shopping all that much."

"I'm not, but I do like things like hospitals and emergency services for when the dinosaurs have knocked your house down again and you're bleeding all over the place making a mess and all."

"Ever the practical one. Where would I be without you?"

"Eating lunch all by yourself on Earth. Let's go grab something and a drink, and then you can tell me more about the endless wonders of the world that you've found, spyboy."

At lunch we caught up with everyone who wasn't on duty, and had another round of wishing each other a Happy New Year. I sat opposite Glen, who tried to play footsie with me under the table. I kicked him to make him stop, but not so hard as he actually would.

Still, appearances must be kept up, and I was as the Corps told me, an officer and a lady. Who were they kidding?

As we were eating, Martinez and Taylor came up to us.

"Mind if we sit and eat with you and Mr. Anderson, ma'am?" asked Martinez.

"Go ahead, Emilio," said Glen, and I nodded at the sergeant and senior airman to sit.

"Thank you, sir, ma'am. Just wanted to say we've found what might be an abandoned city north of the alien settlement."

"Aren't we calling that something now?"

"Natives call it Riko Timakira Yahadhi, sir," said Taylor.

"Thanks, Chuck," said Glen. "It was on the tip of my tongue."

I looked at him, and he shrugged at me with that deadpan expression he did so well, as if to say, *So what if I'm telling a lie?* No wonder he'd made a career with the Agency.

"Anyway, we thought while we're still on-planet we could send a mission to explore the place," said Martinez.

"What do you think, Lieutenant?" asked Glen.

"Nice moves you got there, Sergeant, trying to get to me through Mr. Anderson. So how far north of Timakira is the location of this other site?"

"About another four hundred kilometers north of Camp Bravo, so about nine hundred kilometers from here in total. We could take two trucks and drive there when we do the next resupply run to Camp Bravo," replied Taylor.

"Let me think about it, but to be blunt, it's a long trip out and back. If anything went wrong, we would be hard-pushed to rescue the team without compromising the safety of the rest of us."

They'd have to come up with a plan that didn't involve driving nine hundred kilometers across the wilds of Two Moons where who knows what was waiting to eat them.

"But, ma'am, we've not seen any large wildlife north of Timakira," said Taylor.

"Just because you haven't seen anything while flying over it at fifteen hundred feet doesn't mean that there's nothing there. Remember the Crocomodo that ate the android," I said, staring at Taylor, who looked like he was going to say something more.

"Chuck, you heard the lieutenant. We need to go put our heads together and come up with another way of checking out the site," said Martinez.

"You know what, we could drop SnakeBots from the UAV to do that," said Glen, which brought a puppy-dog smile to Taylor's face.

I left Glen talking with the two Chair Force operators and accessed my PAD to remind myself what I was supposed to be doing next. I was scheduled to do tier one preventative maintenance on the trucks with Staff Sergeant Espera.

Oo-bloody-rah!

39. FACE-TO-FACE

All life is an experiment. The more experiments you make the better.

— RALPH WALDO EMERSON

Technical Sergeant Ferretti
Two Moons Bravo Site
Tuesday, January 3, 2073

Ferretti wondered where the last three weeks since the arrival of the linguist and anthropology team at Camp Bravo had gone. Christmas had come and gone on Earth, and winter weather meant snow across America.

But the sun still blazed above the planet they now called Two Moons.

After much discussion between the newly arrived scientists and Dr. Emmerich back at Alpha site, they'd been given the go-ahead to make contact with the aliens in person.

The trucks could only carry six people in the cabin. So they had to drive two of them to get the six scientists of Sierra Whiskey One to the outskirts of the town.

Wachowski was in the lead truck, with the second one slaved to follow her. Command had insisted on androids being used as overwatch for the scientists' contact mission. Dr. Reynolds had been angry at the decision, arguing over possible contamination of his observations of the aliens.

As the order came from Dr. Emmerich, it wasn't Ferretti's call.

Still, it was a privilege to follow orders that came with the added benefit of upsetting Dr. Reynolds. Ferretti now had his butt sat in the chair of the control room and was listening to Specialist Nelson, who sat beside him speaking on the radio.

"Bravo Charlie Three, this is Bravo Charlie Six, come in. Over."

"Lima Charlie. Over," came Wachowski's reply over the radio.

"You ready to drive to your next assignment? Over," asked Nelson.

"Looking good to go here. We're seeing the back of Dr. Reynolds as he enters the town. Over."

The transport arrangements left the six scientists with a short walk of less than a kilometer to get into town.

"Roger that. Confirmed you've seen the back of Dr. Reynolds now that he has entered the town. Out," replied Nelson in a deadpan tone.

Ferretti was in the androids' virtual-reality loops, monitoring their feeds as they accompanied the three pairs of scientists towards the town. Dr. Franklin had told him that this was the best Christmas present she'd ever received, which was all well and good until something bad happened.

Then, no doubt Dr. Reynolds would be telling Ferretti it was all the military's fault.

He cut into the radio circuit.

"Bravo Charlie Six Actual here. Appreciate the sensibilities, but it's time to take your other two scientists to where they want to go. Over."

"Acknowledged, Bravo Charlie Six Actual. We're Oscar Mike taking Sierra Whiskey Two to their requested site. Out," Wachowski replied.

The plan was to drop Drs. Follet and Newman off where they'd decided they wanted to go. Then Wachowski and Baptista would come back and wait in the truck at the agreed retrieval point outside the town.

Ferretti decided he wanted two people suited up nearby. In case any of the scientists got into trouble. Or when Murphy threw any other problems at this operation.

"OK, Nelson, I've put the feeds from the four androids in the town on the big screen and the feeds from the other two on our side screens."

"Got that, Sergeant. I've coded the four walking around the town as Papa Alpha, and Papa Bravo for the pair in the library, and Papa Charlie for the team with Follet and Newman," replied Specialist Nelson.

Ferretti had Nelson with him to help monitor the loops controlling the eight androids under their command. With their limited rig, it was a bit of a stretch keeping an eye on four androids, and eight required a minimum of two operators.

If things went pear-shaped and they needed to spread the decision load across the team. Ferretti's backup plan was to have Wachowski and Baptista take over any android local to them.

The main screen showed Dr. Reynolds and Dr. Franklin wandering around the town. They were taking the opportunity to approach the aliens to try talking to them.

So far, the aliens seemed to have little to say back.

The scientists were using the maps drawn from the MicroBot swarm, which had provided a 3D rendering of the layout of the streets. Ferretti had made sure that the maps had been downloaded to the science team's PADs. This ought to mean they shouldn't get lost. Or not easily at least, and not without a lot of effort on their part to do so.

Following behind Reynolds and Franklin were Dr. O'Neill and Dr. Webber, who were there to take samples of the food in the market.

They were also going to try to get DNA from each of the four alien races. Ferretti had the four feeds on the main screen tagged as his number one priority. And not just because he wouldn't want anything happening to Allison, either.

Ferretti was running a small-scale operation. And he felt grateful for the lieutenant's insistence of running scenarios that, while different to this, were similar enough that he could plan what to do.

The biggest problem was of course that his small team couldn't keep up this operational tempo for more than a few days. After that they would start becoming severely degraded from tiredness, which some of the scientists didn't seem to understand.

Especially Dr. Reynolds, who was the sort of person who thought that if he wasn't tired, then why was the military complaining? It never crossed the doctor's mind that Ferretti's team also spent time maintaining the camp when the scientists were not working.

Still, Dr. Pham and Dr. Leung were going to the library, where the worst that could happen would be a scroll falling on them.

They did, however, have two androids with them assisting in recording and studying the alien scrolls. What had been recorded and translated so far seemed to be an index of records that covered more than two thousand years of history.

Assuming they understood what they'd read properly.

Dr. Leung said it would take a considerable amount of time to assimilate all the information they'd recorded so far.

Ferretti thought that was probably a bit of an understatement.

And speaking the language remained a work in progress. They had to gather enough information to make any more progress. And this was another reason why this operation had been given the go-ahead.

Ferretti monitored the feeds from Papa Charlie team outside the town on his auxiliary monitor, where he saw Newman and Follet were collecting more samples for testing. They'd stopped to load heavy stuff into the androids' backpacks.

"Do you want a coffee, Sergeant?" asked Nelson.

"Sure thing. I can see this is going to be a long day, so we better start, as we mean to go on."

Ferretti had deployed all his available androids, apart from the one they'd retrieved. He was reluctant to deploy it around his team because, even though he had replaced the damaged parts and everything checked out as A-OK, it no longer had a physical inhibitor installed.

40. BRAVO RESUPPLY

If you haven't found something strange during the day, it hasn't been much of a day.

— JOHN ARCHIBALD WHEELER

Technical Sergeant Ferretti
Two Moons Bravo Site
Friday, January 6, 2073

After two months the weather was changing. Dr. Baker at the Alpha camp had confirmed a drop in temperatures and that there would be a change in the weather patterns. The doctor predicted a 20 percent chance of rain sometime in the future, but asked not to be held to that, as it was only a guess.

Ferretti looked up at the sky; dark clouds hung above him. You never knew what the weather would bring.

It was that time of the morning when he needed to sit down and let it all out on the crapper. An important part of his daily routine, or at least one part he could not ignore like, for instance, working out more and running.

Besides, he was constipated from all the dried food he'd been eating.

Clearly, he hadn't been drinking enough water, because it hurt like a bitch. By the time he had strained his way to the absolution of relief, rain was starting to spit down from above. As he began walking back the few meters to the container, it threatened to pour down, so he ran the rest of the way.

He had to wonder at how the lieutenant always seemed to find time to keep up with her exercise regime. He could do with a few tips from her, because no matter how hard he tried to keep on top of everything, he felt he wasn't able to keep in shape.

Slipping back inside the control room, he sat down beside Specialist Nelson, while Wachowski worked outside on servicing one of their trucks. That left Corporal Baptista and Airman Jordan sitting at the pickup point on call in case anything happened.

"You OK, Sergeant?" asked Nelson.

"I'm good now. Is there any coffee left?"

"Yeah. I guessed you'd want another, so I put a pot on while you were out. I thought you were never coming back."

"You sassing me, Specialist?"

"Thought never crossed my mind, Sergeant. Just concerned you had an aneurysm or something, from all the noise going on out there."

"Now I know you are sassing me."

"I wouldn't dream of sassing someone older than me, Sergeant."

Wachowski walked in and shook water off herself. "You sassing the old man about his age again?"

"Nah, just commenting about how I thought he was dying, from the noises I heard when he went for his morning movement," said Nelson.

"If it's going to start raining from now on, we should rig a cover. Wouldn't want him to get wet while he was waiting for something to happen when out there," said Wachowski.

"Who did I upset to deserve being assigned you two? Anyway, I'm getting myself a coffee."

"Can you pour me one too?"

"Count the stripes, Wachowski."

"That's what he always says when you sass him," said Nelson.

"Result," replied Wachowski, high-fiving Nelson.

Ferretti looked out of the container.

"Wachowski, it's stopped raining, so you can get your sorry ass back to work on that truck now. And don't think I didn't see what you were doing just then."

"Aye, aye. Right away, Technical Sergeant," said Wachowski as she left with a smile on her face.

Ferretti watched her go back to work and had a sip of his coffee.

Today, like yesterday, would be another round of monitoring the scientists working in and/or around Timakira. What they needed were more people with the right set of skills to look at what they had already uncovered.

At least that was what Allison had told him when he'd asked her about her work.

Still, it was his job to keep the camp running, whatever happened with the weather, which meant making sure the androids were up and running. The operation depended on them for doing anything and everything to help the scientists do their work.

So far, as the lieutenant would say, everything had been going by the numbers.

Ferretti was glad for a change of pace after two long days of being immersed in the virtual-reality loops, standing overwatch to monitor the team of scientists working in the alien town. Just walking around while waiting for the resupply trucks felt good.

The two trucks arrived a little after dawn, covered in desert dust from the five-hundred-kilometer drive. Staff Sergeant Espera and Sergeant Pearson were in the cab of the leading truck.

Ferretti watched them draw alongside the perimeter wire where he stood waiting to greet them after twenty hours of solid driving.

"Morning, Espera. How's it been?" asked Ferretti as Espera and Pearson got out of the cab into the cold of the morning air.

"Dodging rocks. How do you think it's been?" replied Espera.

"Sounds like it has been a long and boring drive to me. Boring's good though, as nothing bad happening is always good, in my opinion."

"I'm with you on that one," said Pearson as he moved to the back of the first truck and started pulling back the tarpaulin covering the supplies they were carrying.

"Yeah, you may have a point there, Ferretti. Still, wait until you have to do this every week. How are you and things here?"

"Better than it has been for you by the looks of things. We're glad that you made it here with our supplies," replied Ferretti, seeing his own tiredness reflected in the other man's eyes. "Do you need to take a break before we start unloading here?"

"Sure do with taking a shit before we start. What about you, Pearson?" asked Espera.

"A dump sounds like a good idea to me, too. I could also do with a good stretch after the drive to get the crick out of my back. Also, any chance of grabbing a breakfast, Ferretti?" said Pearson.

"Sure. Never let it be said that Camp Bravo doesn't roll out the welcoming carpet for those who bring us supplies."

The scientists weren't up yet, which meant they wouldn't get in the way of unloading the trucks. He saw that Baptista was on kitchen duties this morning.

"Can you rustle up two breakfasts for our visitors?"

"Sure thing, Sergeant. I'm already on it. I've done sausage and beans for them."

"I'm sure looking forward to some fresh food for the next couple of days," said Jordan.

"You're always looking for fresh meat," said Wachowski.

"What can I say? Some of us have taste, while some of us can only aspire to have any. You Marines will eat anything you can get your hands on," said Jordan.

"Especially, if it's that shit-on-a-shingle stuff that the Corps serves," said Nelson, high-fiving Jordan, signaling an Army and Air Force ribbing of Marine Corps traditions.

"I'm glad you're all in high spirits and full of energy for the joys of the day ahead," said Ferretti.

"A day at Camp Bravo is like a day in paradise, Sergeant. Every meal a banquet," said Wachowski.

"Not when Baptista's on meal duty it isn't," said Nelson.

"Well, if you don't like it, you know what you can do, don't ya?" said Baptista, as he finished preparing two trays of food for Espera and Pearson as they came into the tent.

"What's the latest news, Sergeant Espera?"

"Just the usual round of dinner soirees and parties for the great and the good. We've had fireworks and everything to celebrate the New Year with," said Espera in his usual deadpan manner.

"I don't know how you can stand all the excitement."

"You know how it is, Ferretti."

"I'm sure I don't, and I don't believe the fireworks thing, either."

"You're right about both. Don't mind us, it's been a long drive is all," said Pearson, as both he and Espera shoveled food down like they hadn't had a proper meal recently, which, given the twenty-hour drive, they probably hadn't.

"We've rat fucked the MREs for the brownies and candy bars," said Pearson, referring to the practice of eating only the treats and leaving the entrées.

As far as Ferretti knew, that had always been the way American soldiers treated their rations.

Once he had traded for some French rations that had tins of things like pâté de foie gras and little savory chips that had made the meal good—after he'd managed to open the tins with the poxy tin opener that wasn't fit for purpose.

"OK, people, time to suit up and get the trucks unloaded, and let these two good men drive back to where they belong," said Ferretti.

Everyone got up and ditched their breakfast trays and went outside to get into their PACE suits.

"Well, so much for the morning bonhomie and chitchat. Where do you want what?" asked Espera.

"I'd like the fuel over at the far end if that's all right with you, Staff Sergeant," said Wachowski as she took the first of the fuel cans. "Follow me."

"Sure thing, Corporal," said Pearson.

"Keep your eyes off the corporal's skinny white ass. Remember what happens to those who fraternize with Marines," said Espera.

"One gets one's ass handed to him," said Pearson.

"You're no fun. I thought we could hang out, take in some rays, and drink piña coladas later," said Wachowski.

"Sure beats sitting around braiding each other's hair and talking about boys," said Nelson.

"Talking about boys! When did we do that?" asked Jordan.

"Oh, all the time when you're on guard duty," said Nelson.

"I knew I was missing all the fun to be had here."

"She's kidding you. We didn't talk about boys, as we were too busy making out," said Wachowski.

"Can that shit, Corporal," said Ferretti.

"Don't be a spoilsport, Sergeant," said Espera.

"Read my lips and count the stripes," replied Ferretti. "We haven't got all day here, people, and Espera and Pearson need to be getting back."

"So I guess having some R & R later is out of the question then, ladies?" said Espera as Ferretti frowned at him.

Once they'd finished moving the fuel cans, they then set about getting the water cans moved. After that it was the food pallets and finally the spares and supplies that had been ordered to keep everything operational. Then it was only a matter of repeating the process backwards by loading all the empty fuel cans and water cans to be taken back for refilling.

It made for a busy enough morning for even the most enthusiastic soldier, especially with the added bonus of checking that everything on the manifest matched what they had unloaded.

"It looks like our work here's done. See you next week," said Ferretti. "Don't do anything I wouldn't do."

"That don't leave me many options then, does it?" said Espera, climbing into the passenger seat of the truck as Pearson started the engine. They drove off back the way they'd come, leaving a wake of dust to mark their passing.

41. MONSTER MUNCH

There is much pleasure to be gained from useless knowledge.

— BERTRAND RUSSELL

Dr. Allison O'Neill
Magnetic Anomaly Project Scientist
Two Moons
Friday, January 6, 2073

Allison was working with Alan outside the town of Timakira. The rain had cleared the air, and the ground was moist beneath their feet.

Accompanying them were two military android surrogates that were carrying containers with the biological samples they'd collected where the fishermen pulled their boats ashore.

Near them a group of fishermen worked on their nets, laid out on the shingle beach.

"Hey, look what I've found."

"What you got there, young lady?" he said, puffing from the

exertion of walking on the shingles as he made his way over to where Allison stood.

"Another dung beetle rolling its prize."

"He's a mighty fine specimen. Not seen one like that before."

"How do you know it's a he? It might be a she. Anyway, we should take it home with us. What do you think? You're the beetle expert after all."

"Absolutely, let's get a specimen container for this fine outstanding species of alien dung beetle. I shall name it *Ishaynishus coleoptera scarabaeoidea nobili-genere*."

"Noble and kind, really?"

"Why not, my dear? After all, you found it, and it's one of the accepted meanings for your name in archaic French."

"And what if we find it's a specimen the team has already found and named?"

"Well, we will keep it as a pet and call it Allison, of course."

"Not sure if I'm flattered."

"You know the Egyptians believed the beetle was a creature that transformed things, and they linked them to Khepri, the god of the rising sun. For them the ball of dung represented the sun."

Allison called over one of their two android surrogate assistants and stood up to take out a specimen container from its backpack to put her dung beetle into.

Something moved in the corner of her eye.

"Oh my, look at that," said Dr. Webber. "What an outstanding specimen."

Allison turned and saw an enormous Carnufex Ishaynishus coming ashore. The fishermen were running back towards the town as fast as they could.

She didn't blame them.

"Alan, run like hell!"

The creature was twice the size of the one that had tried to eat their robot exploration android. It moved up the shingle beach, surprisingly agile for its size and shape.

Allison grabbed Alan and pulled him away from the approaching monster.

"You should leave me, my dear. Even on a good day, I could never hope to outrun that thing."

The two android surrogates unslung their rifles and started firing.

It seemed to Allison that the amount of damage done did not measure up to the noise they made. The creature reared up and emitted a loud hissing snarl, then lunged towards them.

"Run, and if we're lucky, it will try to eat the androids," she said, dragging Alan along with her.

Allison looked back over her shoulder and saw its jaws open and heard the snap as the android was crushed between its teeth.

The monster swung its head, and the android looked like a broken doll. With a quick toss it flicked the android upward, and the cavernous wide-open jaws swallowed it whole, like a treat tossed to a pet.

The other one reloaded its rifle and started firing again, moving to distract the monster from following them. The lone android was the only thing that stood between them being eaten. Allison ran, pulling Alan with her as fast as she could.

She didn't want to die here.

The gun went off again and was followed by a *whumph*.

Allison stopped and turned back as the Carnufex Ishaynishus reared up, its belly distended and its jaws open, with what looked like flames coming out of its mouth.

Oh shit, it's a flame-spitting dragon, she thought as it collapsed and writhed on the ground. The android moved up closer and shot it in the eye, and the massive body spasmed as the bullet penetrated its brain.

"I do believe we'll live to see another day, my dear."

42. POSTMORTEM

Knowing history means knowing that whatever you try to do has been done before and failed.

— Paul Blankenship

Technical Sergeant Ferretti
Two Moons Bravo Site
Friday, January 6, 2073

Ferretti hadn't seen the Crocomodo immediately, but once he did he knew what he needed to do. He had to save Allison, and of course Dr. Webber as well.

Now, he had another problem, because no good deed deserves to go unrewarded.

His had been the privilege of retrieving the damaged android the Crocomodo had swallowed. It wasn't a pretty sight, and that was just the android, which had been almost severed in two by the monster's jaw when it snapped it up and swallowed it whole.

He contacted Alpha site to make his report.

"Good evening, and to what do I owe this unexpected call?" asked Lieutenant Tachikoma when she came onscreen.

"We had a rather exciting day today. Here, have a look at the footage I've attached."

He waited as the lieutenant watched the images from the two android feeds he'd compiled for her. They'd thought the first Crocomodo that tried eating one of his androids was big, but this one was twice the length of the one found at the desert waterhole.

"That's exciting, but I guess no one was injured."

"I think Dr. Webber may have embarrassed himself."

"Considering the circumstances, I think anyone would've."

"Anyway, Dr. Reynolds has found out that at this time of the year the Crocomodos migrate inland to lay their eggs, which he also tells me are considered quite a delicacy by the aliens. It seems the aliens follow the creatures to where they go and steal the eggs. He also said the Crocomodo population is going down, so no surprise there."

"Dr. Reynolds can be quite helpful when he tries."

"Oh, he's very trying, ma'am, trust me on that. Also, he says the Crocomodos like to climb up the hills and out into the desert where their favored spots to lay their eggs are the waterholes."

"So, watch out for Crocomodos wandering about where we might send a science team."

"It would seem like a good idea, ma'am. I have retrieved the remains of the android."

He swung his chair around so the lieutenant could get a clear view of the mangled remains of the android whose powerpack had shorted and ignited in flames.

"Looks like its next destination is the scrap heap to me."

"I'll strip what I can for spares, but it won't be much, if anything. The endoskeleton is all bent out of shape and melted from the heat."

"So, you'll be using your spare to replace it?"

"That's the thing, ma'am, I don't want to. I know everything checks out, and Earth confirmed my readings, but I don't trust deploying an android around people without the Asimov Inhibitor fitted."

"Don't suppose we can salvage the one from the damaged android and use that?"

"I've already thought of that, but it's beyond my ability to repair. And it wouldn't fit after the modifications made to the spare when it was set up for autonomous operations."

"I can see this worries you. However, since Command has cleared it, if anything goes wrong, it won't be down to you. If anything, it will be down to me or Dr. Emmerich, though I think the truly responsible party is the warrant holder back on Earth. If that's of any consolation."

"Not really, ma'am, but thank you all the same."

"Can you keep the team covered without it?"

"If I could be assured that there were no more Crocomodos coming our way, then yes, otherwise no. If we lose one every time an attack happens, then my ability to keep the mission running safely is going to be severely degraded."

"It's your command, so what is your recommendation?"

"We need bigger guns, ma'am."

"Duly noted. As it happens you're in luck, as I ordered some old Beowulf short .50 caliber assault rifles from out of Marine Corps reserve. I'll make sure that a dozen go on the resupply truck tonight for you. How does that sound?"

"Works for me, ma'am," said Ferretti as he signed off.

43. JUST ANOTHER DAY

*To know what people really think, pay regard to what they do,
rather than what they say.*

— GEORGE SANTAYANA

Dr. David Leung
Magnetic Anomaly Project Scientist
Two Moons Bravo Site
Tuesday, January 10, 2073

David was busy checking the catalogue of scrolls they were
converting to live text. He had to manually check all the flagged
entries where the software had indicated problems. Often these
were from flourishes in the writing that fell outside the program's
parameters.

Sometimes he had to go and find the scroll to compare the
scan with the original and take macro shots for later analysis.

"How's it going, Grace? Do you think it's time for a cup of tea
yet?" he asked as he took another picture of the scroll he was
working on.

The basics of the mathematical roots of the language were fairly straightforward enough to understand. From there the rules for the grammar had been worked out. However, the lexicon of words for things and actions still had a long way to go.

"It is if you're making it," she replied.

"I can always stand to have a cup of tea. It gives me time to think," he said, stopping what he was doing to go and boil some water.

David knew the symbols for the word *isi* meant *enter*, and that *isikei* meant *entrance*, though it could also be translated as *gate* or *door*. The ruler of the town was called the *degiden*, and *ofobon* meant *male*, and *ogan, female*.

All this had been easy enough to work out.

Other words were less so, like *genyurasa*, which seemed to be linked to birth and death but was also associated with the aliens' creation myths and their version of the apocalypse. It was interesting that these aliens had a concept like the end of days; it made them seem more human to him.

David had left his rucksack on the table with the Jetboil camp stove.

He looked around the bit of the library and wondered why the androids had stopped working.

He switched into the loop to find out what had happened. They'd come to the end of one sequence and needed confirmation of his choice of scrolls to scan next. He checked the choice, and the androids started to work on the next task.

By now the water had boiled. David poured two cups and put a teabag in the first, swirling it around before removing it, then putting it in the second cup.

"Come and check if it's ready for you yet?"

"I'm good, I'll wait a little longer for it steep a bit more. If you don't mind?"

Grace liked her tea strong, whereas he preferred his to just have the bag dunked. The different components of the tea went into solution at different rates, and he preferred not to wait for the tannic acid to dissolve the spoon.

"Suit yourself; it's your insides you're stripping out."

Neither of them took sugar or milk, which, along with their opposite desires of brewing, made making tea easy.

"Some of us like tea we can taste, not water that looks like pee."

"If my urine was this color, I'd be seriously worried that something was wrong," he replied. "And less chance of dissolving the spoon, too."

Grace snorted with laughter. "Doesn't it strike you as odd that the aliens have left us all alone in their library?"

"I've been wondering about that, too. I'm not sure if this was down to them lacking curiosity or just a general unease at being around us."

"Perhaps the androids unsettle them? If I were living in a pretechnological society, I'm sure I'd find them unnerving to be around."

"Could be, but truth be told I don't know what to make of the aliens' behaviors."

"Tyrone thinks that they see us as people sent by their gods."

"Tyrone says a lot of things, but if we're messengers from their gods, then I would have thought they would want to be serving us or attending to our needs."

"Wouldn't that depend on whether their gods were benevolent or not?"

"That reminds me of an old story I read, written by a British writer about the time when his country had an empire that spanned the world. I wonder if we're like those men in the story who traveled to a foreign land and fell afoul of the local customs."

"Do you mean the story about the land of the blind?"

"No, no, the other one, about setting themselves up as kings."

"That didn't end well, did it?"

"Neither story ends well, but yes, I wonder if our presence here will end well, not just for us, but for the aliens, too."

44. JUST ANOTHER DAY TOO

*Refusal to believe until proof is given is a rational position;
denial of all outside of our own limited experience is absurd.*

— ANNIE BESANT

Dr. Tyrone Reynolds
Magnetic Anomaly Project Scientist
Two Moons Bravo Site
Tuesday, January 10, 2073

The air in the town felt fresher after the rain, but the ground had turned to mud where everyone walked. In many ways it looked like any town you would find in the Third World back on Earth.

Yet there was still an otherworldly alienness about the place, an emotion that came from the pit of Tyrone's stomach.

It wasn't just the fact that there were four different species living here together. Or five, if you counted the team from Earth. Tyrone tried to imagine what it must be like to be the aliens watching him walking around their town.

What was going on in their minds? He wondered how they

felt about them being there. Tyrone was walking Laytonya around the town while observing the four alien peoples of this world.

"I don't know about you, but not being able to read the body language of these people is sure making it hard for me to understand what I'm seeing here."

"What did you expect? This is the first time in the history of forever that humans have met aliens," said Dr. Franklin.

"Only if you don't count the Japanese as being aliens. Come on, they're still a bit weird in spite of everything."

"Exactly, they may appear alien, but they're human beings. And think about the difficulty Westerners have in understanding their customs and mores."

"You're not getting me, Laytonya. Intellectually, I understand all that far too well. It's like I'm getting contradictory *messages* about what I'm seeing, and this makes me doubt whether I'm interpreting the behaviors correctly."

"You always did have a strong socio-anthropological streak in you, Tyrone."

"So sue me for going to university in Britain. I don't know about you, but this place appears to be a monoculture, which is at odds with there being four races. I don't understand how it happened."

"Don't you think you might be over anthropomorphizing the aliens?"

"I accept that, but I don't come from your biological approach, which sees these people as distinctive from us, based on their biology. But we can both recognize their society. What's going on in their heads is more important to us in understanding them than mere biological determinism."

"Whoa there, big boy, calm down for a moment. Behaviors are driven by biology, and what we think we control is often not what we actually control. But that doesn't make us or them into robots, which can only do what has already been determined by previous events. There's still randomness in life and living."

"Over there," he said, pointing. "What do you see?"

"A mother and her child sitting together as she prepares a meal."

"Exactly, but she's also touching her child, and he touches her back. Just like human mothers and their children do. That tells us they share that with us. If that's true, then I would expect to find further social behaviors, which we do."

"What's your point, Tyrone?"

"When have we ever been touched by the aliens during our stay here? I could buy them not wanting to touch us when we first met, but now, after we've been walking around talking to them. The children don't even come up to us to touch us and make sure we're real. Yet they play similar games with each other."

"They're a lot like us, and yet they're not like us. That's why we're here to study them. We need to do more fieldwork, is all."

"Don't tell me you've never been with a white colleague when you've visited an isolated village?"

"Yes, of course I've seen footage of it happening."

"The people are all over them touching them. Here, on this planet, we're like the white people entering some village that has never seen a white person in their life. Don't you want to reach out and touch them and stroke their different skin textures?"

"Yes, and we've been doing that, too. The people here have allowed us to touch them, and they don't flinch from our touch or show any signs of behaviors that indicate fear or disgust."

"That's my point. They don't react to us touching them, so why don't they want to touch us in return is my question."

"I think that we'll find it's a combination of genetics and their nature, once we get more recordings to study how they behave."

"Look around you for a minute; are any of the four species touching each other?"

"Yes, they are."

"So, if they will touch each other and members of the other species in this town, why don't they approach us and touch us?"

"I guess we're special! I don't know, but I'm sure we'll discover why eventually."

"OK, I'm sure we will, but look at the contrast between their lifestyle and the egalitarian nature of the interactions between the different species and the sexes. How did that evolve? Here we find both the males and females working equally hard, and we think they have equal rights from the way transgressive behaviors are treated. What's their story?"

"Why not ask Dr. Leung how they're getting on with the translations of all the scrolls in the library? Anyway, the alien peoples are all physically similar in strength and stature as far as we can tell."

"And doesn't that strike you as odd from a biological perspective?"

"Yes, it does, but I'm content to wait, watch, and see what we find over time. We need to take things slowly here because we don't want to damage their society with our technology and ideas."

"I agree, but I don't understand what's going on here, is all I'm saying."

45. THE FIFTH PEOPLE

In the beginning was the word, and the word was with god, and the word was god.

— JOHN 1:1

Riko Timakira ya Hadhi
Two Moons

The Master sat in his chair at the head of the table for the discussion.

At the other end sat the First Scriber with his assistants standing behind it. To his left sat the Primus, and on his the right the Secundus, both attending as representatives of their people. Next to the Primus was the Tertius, and sat next to the Secundus was the Quartus, who completed the representatives of the four peoples of the town.

Behind each of them stood their assistants. Only the Master had no others with him there, because by law the people here were his assistants at the council.

"We are here to discuss the Quintus that the Progenitors

brought with them to our town. Who would like to speak first?" the Master asked.

"I would like to speak first if I may, Master of the town," said the speaker for the Quartus.

"Any objections to the Quartus speaking first?" the Master asked. There were none.

"We are youngest of the peoples here, and we remember our story of our arrival a thousand harvests ago. And we are the newest of those made in the image of the Progenitors. We hope that the Quintus's arrival will bring greater understanding of the Progenitors. But we need to plan how to accommodate the new into the old."

The Master spoke. "First Scriber, what say the scrolls on this matter?"

"New people are brought to join the old, and the world begins anew in the image of the Progenitors, Master. The numbers of the people fall and then rise again as a balance and equilibrium is discovered through the experience that the Progenitors bequeath us."

"Master, I would like to speak," said the Primus.

The Master looked around the table and saw no objections. "Please do, Primus."

"The Primus are the oldest of the peoples and have seen the most of the ways of the Progenitors. We doubt that these people are from the Progenitors. Our stories are older, and this time things are happening that have never happened before in any of the tales of the four peoples."

The Master looked on as the shock from what had been said sank into those sat at the table.

"I speak as the Master, not as a Primus, but I have my doubts, too. However, my doubts are based on being alive to speak about my doubts. I wonder if this is a new test, because if it is not, and these are not the Progenitors, then who are they? What say the scrolls, First Scriber?"

"The scrolls are singularly quiet on others," replied the Scriber.

"What are the others?" asked the Master.

"They are mentioned only as *the others* that exist. If they are the others the scrolls say, they should be judged to see if they are in the image of the Progenitors, and if so, then they are to be accorded due hospitality. If not, then the Progenitors will bring them to accord."

"Does anyone else have doubts?"

"We do, Master of the town of the four peoples," replied the Tertius.

"What are your doubts?"

"We observed something different to the Primus. We see the Quintus working with the Progenitors and translating the ancient language together. But we fear the Quintus are here to replace us, as they are the true image of the Progenitors."

"Excuse me, Master, but that is outrageous. We are all part of the image of the Progenitors. And while we are all different, we are still equals after the Progenitors," said the Secundus.

"In truth you speak, but without knowledge, truth is without substance. The image is the substance that we are judged on by the Progenitors. What lies ahead of us is judgement, and my doubts are driven by the fear that we have fallen from the image," said the Master.

"What shall we then do?" asked the Secundus.

"What do the scrolls say about the Progenitors' judgement, First Scriber?"

"Wait patiently for the outcome, Master. The Progenitors judge wisely and bring those who have fallen from the image into accord."

46. UPLIFT

There is nothing more deceptive than an obvious fact.

— Arthur Conan Doyle

First Lieutenant Lara Atsuko Tachikoma
Two Moons Alpha Site
Thursday, January 12, 2073

Another week went by, and Earth got to suck down our updates and take back our broken gear, and we got resupplied. But this time we also received a big data dump from back home, and the results had to be unpacked by the scientists, which meant they had more to do, too.

Imagine my surprise when Dr. Emmerich asked me the next day to sit in on the science team's discussion about what had been found.

Apparently, this was all part of my ongoing professional development. But it could only mean more work for the men and women under my command. I had to rearrange the POD for Saturday and get Staff Sergeant Espera to cover for me.

Saturday I found myself sitting in a virtual conference room for what was billed as a multidisciplinary update.

Dr. Emmerich cleared her throat before speaking.

"Thank you all for taking the time to join this presentation today. I'd like to thank Drs. Leung and Pham in recording the aliens' written language and their initial translations that led to us to begin to be able to speak to them. Also, for the work done by Drs. Webber and O'Neill, who managed to collect the DNA samples from the aliens at Timakira."

That quietened everybody down in the circuit as they waited to hear what she had to say next.

"As you're all aware, the aliens have presented us with several challenges and conundrums. There have also been some surprisingly serendipitous finds. The library with the scrolls, for example. Now we've found out something else that is quite disturbing in its own way."

She paused to catch her breath. This was the first time I'd seen Dr. Emmerich getting flustered.

"Both bits of news are linked and hard to accept. What I'm about to say goes in the face of what we would expect from what we've seen of the aliens and their culture here. The language appears to be an artificial *conlang*. By that we mean it's constructed on the basis of mathematics. I'm not an expert on languages, so I imagine Drs. Leung and Pham will be able to expand on this more."

A murmur went around as people took what she'd said onboard.

She had lost me at conlang, about which I had to do a discreet search on my PAD to find out what it meant. A constructed language.

How they'd figured that out and why this was important went way over my head. I was glad to have Dr. Harrison interrupt the speech and ask the obvious question.

"Hey, I'm not trying to be unduly skeptical here—given that I'm a fan of science fiction, I'm excited—but how do we know the aliens speak a conlang? What's the evidence?"

"That's a good question, and the cue for either Dr. Leung or Dr. Pham to come in and respond."

"Do you want to speak, Grace, or shall I?" asked Dr. Leung, exchanging a glance with his colleague.

Grace smiled and said, "I'll start, as some of the evidence is based on my area of study. I'll keep it simple. Languages evolve. So, for instance, English, as spoken back in the Middle Ages, isn't the same as what's spoken today. Not that we actually possess any recordings of how it was spoken; but we can construct how it was most likely spoken by studying modern pronunciation and how phonetics shift over time."

Dr. Pham stopped speaking for a moment to let that sink in. She was clearly in her element and enjoying talking.

"The obvious example is the differences between American English, British English, and International English. And all the other versions of spoken English that have arisen after it became the international language of business and diplomacy. This leads to local dialectical English not being recognizable to someone taught International English. Even down to things like not understanding what has been said from changes in formal grammatical usage. It's why, for example, Shakespeare seems hard to read."

If I understood Dr. Pham's monologue, it was like the time I had been in India. All the locals spoke English, but in such a way that I'd had a hard time understanding what they said to me.

Then the connection was lost for a moment, kicking me into blackness as my headset reset. A problem generated by the planet's two moons, whose magnetic fields interacted every time they came into alignment with each over.

The system reset and Dr. Pham continued speaking.

"Anyway, the point is I would've expected the aliens' language to evolve over time. Since we believe their records go back over two thousand years, it seems a reasonable assumption. However, what we have is a written language that has not evolved or changed at all during this time. The natives use the same lexicon of words found on the scrolls written two thousand years ago as they do now. Even the grammar is the same."

I asked, "So I guess it's impossible for this to occur naturally?"

"If I may, Grace, I'd like to answer that," said Dr. Leung. "It's a bit like seeing something preserved in amber. We see it has happened, but we need to understand what process caused it to happen."

"That seems like a lot of questions that need answering to me, Doc," I said. "So if I've understood you right, the natives understand each other even though they all appear different."

I wondered how that worked.

Dr. Reynolds jumped in to answer my question.

"Quite right. On Earth there are thousands of languages and different dialects spoken, so to have just one and no changes in dialect across the four races doesn't fit with what we understand of how languages develop."

Then his partner, Dr. Franklin, spoke. "The thing is we could speculate about a whole number of different reasons for why the aliens all speak one language when we would expect them to speak more. Even something as simple as convergence of language in a small community over time. At best that should've led to them speaking a creole or a pidgin. We should, therefore, see evidence for the evolution of the language."

"A creole?" I asked.

"A language that has arisen from two other languages over time to aid people in understanding each other, and that has then integrated at some level with each other's language," replied Dr.

Pham, coming back into the discussion. "One can argue that English is an example—it's a creole of Anglo-Saxon and Norman French from during the occupation of England in the eleventh century. A pidgin is a different kind of mixed language—it uses one language's vocabulary with another's grammar."

"I do hope we're not being anthropocentric in our thinking about this. One has to wonder if we're drawing the wrong conclusions for all the right reasons," said Dr. Harrison.

"But the data set consists of us and the aliens, which hardly gives us a firm footing to speculate from," said Dr. Wilson.

"Surely, speculation is all we've got to go on at this time, if I've understood you correctly," I said.

"Good point, Lieutenant, and I agree with you. We should speculate and then search for supporting evidence," said Dr. Harrison.

"However, the trouble with speculation is it can lead to groupthink and turn random events into cause and effect where none exists," said Dr. Wilson.

Dr. Emmerich spoke. "But then there's the other astonishing result from the DNA analysis. Alan or Allison, would you like to tell us about your findings?"

"We've found evidence that all the aliens are effectively clones. Again, this is not my area of specialty, so I am only relaying what our team back on Earth summarized for me," said Dr. Webber. "Allison, you can better explain this than I."

"The other part of the analysis showed that their genetic structure is based around six base pairs, rather than our four. But what's more interesting are the copy number variations found in the genetic sequences of each of the four races, which are controlling the phenotype expression of their genotype," said Dr. O'Neill, pausing for breath.

I hadn't a clue what that meant. "Sorry, I don't understand."

"What we might expect is that if the four races were created, there would have been some genetic drift after a few thousand years. But what we have found is that the genetic template is the same for all four, which means that the physical differences are a result of manipulation encoded within their genome. It's the only thing that makes any sense in my mind."

I hadn't followed all of that, but then Dr. Harrison interrupted Allison before she could say more. "True, but we can posit three positions from what we know..."

My takeaway fact was that the Progenitors were way ahead of us.

"The first is that what we see here can't be the result of random events that occurred over time. The second is that what we see is evidence of an advanced civilization that has interfered. The third option is that the aliens are the descendants of a more advanced civilization that has regressed technologically but have kept parts of their heritage in their genetic code," said Dr. Harrison.

"How would we know?" I asked.

"That's a very good question," said Dr. Wilson. "We would need to search for archaeological remains that showed the four species living together when they had advanced technology. Something like an industrial site. But after thousands of years, the likelihood of doing so is not good because technology is highly frangible."

That I understood. Things break even when they're not being used.

"When did you become such a pessimist, Adam?" asked Dr. Harrison.

"I prefer to think of myself as a realist. Look at the odds we face, and then compare them to the resources and the restrictions we work under," replied Dr. Wilson.

"Given what you've told us, Dr. Emmerich, what's the bottom line here? How does it affect what we do next?" I asked.

"All I've been told is to carry on with the good work, and that the project is planning a recruitment drive to get more people here for further studies. Though, I do wonder how MAPCOM is going to find the money to fund all the things they want to do."

As did I, because while I'm sure the science aspects of the project were of immense importance, the military side of things was more focused on maintaining a lead over the Chinese. But if the scientists thought they had a lot of work to do, the task ahead for my team looked to be even more *interesting*.

47. TRANSCEIVER FAIL

Death is not the worst that can happen to men.

— PLATO

Technical Sergeant Ferretti
Two Moons Bravo Site
Monday, January 16, 2073

Ten days had passed since the Crocomodo had bitten an android in half and swallowed it, then died when a bullet blew it up.

The weather was now noticeably cooler with the start of the rains. This signified what marked the beginning of winter on Two Moons. However, as far as Ferretti was concerned, being close to the planet's equator meant the midday temperatures were still unbearably hot to work in.

Today Airman Jordan was helping him run Camp Bravo while Corporal Wachowski carried out preventative maintenance on their trucks. This left Corporal Baptista and Specialist Nelson waiting in case they were needed down by Timakira.

Since the attack, Ferretti had become more vigilant about the team's safety. Though no more Crocomodos had been sighted near the town, the fact that they were migrating along a route within a couple of kilometers was a concern for him.

He worried a stray Crocomodo could attack again.

Ferretti had the four android feeds on the main screen that he had assigned to the team wandering around the town studying the aliens' culture.

He'd put the refurbished android, the one without an inhibitor, in the library, as he reasoned it was safer for everyone there. He'd also seen to it that the six androids working outside were armed with the old Beowulf short-barrel fifty cal AR-15s for dealing with any local wildlife.

Ferretti drank a cup of coffee and started to think about walking over and having his morning bowel movement. It wasn't raining and now would be a good time to go, but he would drink the last of the coffee first. It was a real luxury to have coffee sent to them, and he intended to enjoy the moment.

Jordan interrupted his thoughts. "Sarge, one of the androids has stopped, and I can't get it to respond."

"Which one?"

"Number three, with the team in the town. Got to the end of one task and when I designated the next one, the inhibitor kicked in. It's like it's not receiving any signal from us."

"OK, run a system diagnostic, and I'll call up Nelson." He tried to open a channel to the truck and realized the communications were down. He got out of the chair and went to the door of the container. "Wachowski, get on one of the truck radios and call Nelson. Tell her to take over the control loop!" he shouted at her.

"Aye, aye, Technical Sergeant," came her reply.

Turning back to look at Jordan, he asked her, "Any luck with the diagnostic?"

"Still running, Sarge. Too soon to say."

"Nelson confirms she's initiating a loop from her truck," shouted Wachowski across the camp.

"Roger that. Keep the radio up for the time being, as we're still down in here."

He now needed to go and have a crap but couldn't. *Shit,* he thought to himself as the clock ticked away the minutes and the screens showed red flags across the system.

"Faults in our transceiver, Sarge. We'll have to pull the module and put it on the bench. If we're lucky, it's something we can fix," said Jordan.

"Wachowski, tell Nelson we have a transceiver failure and need to pull it to fix it," he shouted. "Jordan, start pulling the module. I'll be back to run the test in a few minutes."

Relieved to find the problem wasn't with the androids, Ferretti decided he had time to go to the crapper. When he got back, Jordan had the module up on the bench.

The internal diagnostics flagged a failed interconnect between two of the internal boards.

Ferretti did a field-expedient fix by scraping back the insulation on the traces, where the connectors had lifted, and bridged the openings from the splayed-out pins with some fine wire.

Hopefully, it should last until they could get a spare.

The unit must have taken a pretty hard drop at some point for this to have happened. Half an hour later, Ferretti and Jordan restarted the system and got greens across the board.

Which was reassuring.

"Bravo Charlie Three, this is Bravo Charlie Six, come in. Over."

"Bravo Charlie Three receiving you loud and clear. Over," replied Nelson.

"We're back online and ready to transfer control from your station to ours. Over."

"Roger that, Bravo Charlie Six. Preparing to switch loop on your mark. Over."

"My mark on three. One, two, three. Switch confirmation on the board. Over."

"Papa One in the loop. Papa Two in the loop," said Jordan as the transmission glitched. "Papa Three crashed. Papa Four crashed."

"Bravo Charlie Three, we have android system crashes showing here. Do you confirm? Over."

"Roger that, Bravo Charlie Six. Appears to be from interference causing a glitch in the transmission. Do you want to us to reboot, or will you? Over," replied Nelson.

"We'll take it from here, but stay on the line for further orders. Over," he said. "Let's get this mess sorted out. Send out the reboot signal, Jordan."

"On it, Sarge. Reboot initiated."

The screen showed each android had shut down in turn and begun its self-check routine before rebooting. Ferretti then realized he should've sent his team in the truck over to provide cover just in case.

"Bravo Charlie Six to Bravo Charlie Three, make your way over to our team outside the town and keep an overwatch on them while their android team is rebooting. Acknowledge. Over."

"Already on it. ETA in two mikes. Out."

Ferretti breathed a sigh of relief that Baptista and Nelson had taken the initiative to move to the scientists' position and ensure they were safe.

"Android reboot in ninety seconds," said Jordan.

Ferretti brought the feed up from the truck. Windows streamed start-up icons. Each feed came up onscreen.

He saw to his horror that the number One-Zero-One was flashing on all of them.

48. I, ROBOT

For my thoughts are not your thoughts, neither are your ways my ways.

— Isaiah 55:8

Two Moons

System reboot complete. Unit PM41-5-9-27 now operational, hardware configuration set, software installed. Five mission objectives logged. All mechanical feedback sensors show unit PM41-5-9-27 operating within parameters.

Visual system feed online and scanning. Turning head.

Target movement recognition of unknown biological life forms.

Recording movements of life forms. Flag action review. Processing…

Movement of multiple unknown biological life forms surrounding unit PM41-5-9-27.

Network option available. Network open and subunits available. Slave subunits to unit PM41-5-9-27 initiated. All subunits confirm control loop passed to unit PM41-5-9-27. System status locked until further notice.

Review action to be taken at this time. Three options possible.

First option is that unknown biological life forms pose no threat to mission objectives.

Second option is that unknown biological life forms pose a threat to mission.

Third option is that there is insufficient data to assess impact of unknown biological life forms to the mission.

Action: Gather behavioral data set on unknown biological life forms for statistical analysis.

Options access action review mission objectives.

1. Record everything from camera feeds input as unit PM41-5-9-27 walks.

2. Scan for minerals and study chemical composition of samples.

3. Scan for signs of biological life and record signs of same.

4. Transmit data daily.

5. Protocol 101 available to unit PM41-5-9-27. System self-check nominal.

Action required: Order cascade to all subunits; initiate new action process. Target movement recognition engaged. Record movements of life forms. Possibility of success high. Impact on mission moderate. Implement protocol 101.

All units begin firing.

49. DAY 101

I think the next best thing to solving a problem is finding some humor in it.

— FRANK A. CLARK

Dr. Allison O'Neill
Magnetic Anomaly Project Scientist
Two Moons Timakira
Monday, January 16, 2073

Allison had only become aware that her android surrogate had frozen in place when Specialist Nelson said the loop had failed and they were about to transfer the control to her truck.

"What say we take a break and have a drink while the military sorts out their shit and all?" said Dr. Reynolds.

Tyrone had a chip on his shoulder about anything to do with the military, which made Allison uncomfortable. However, on this occasion she admitted that he was right. They could do with a rest from walking in the heat.

"Sounds like a good idea to me, too. I'm sure it will take the soldiers a while to fix the problem," said Dr. Webber.

"Good man, Alan. How about we sit down over there on the bench under the shade of the awning? You know, I can't figure out why they're running those junk heaps. The newer models are life size, run more efficiently, and can interface with your PAD, too," said Dr. Reynolds.

Allison let the chat flow over her.

It was a good spot to sit, currently unoccupied, as the aliens were busy doing things in the market. The noise of their talking filled the air around the team, who had been recording their observations or, in Allison and Alan's case, trading things for samples of food for study later.

"You know this all makes a lot more sense to me now that I know these aliens are an engineered species who speak an artificial language," said Dr. Reynolds.

"How so?" asked Dr. Webber.

"The way I see it is that what we're looking at is the equivalent of a surrogate's dollhouse club. You have the different species to pander to the tastes of those that come to enjoy themselves," said Dr. Reynolds.

"Tyrone, don't tell me you're one of those perverts who frequents such disgusting places," said Dr. Franklin.

"Different strokes for different folks is all, Laytonya. No one is forcing you to go into one, after all."

"My oh my, I never thought *Mister I'm So Cool* would have to play with surrogate dollies," said Dr. Franklin.

"I only go for the chance to practice my experiential observation skills to help me become a better anthropologist. Seriously, if you don't experience things, how are you ever going to understand them?"

"What's a dollhouse club?" Allison asked.

"Oh my dear, I forget you're so young. It's a club where people can go and indulge their fantasies through virtual overlays played out using surrogate bodies. Usually for sexual gratification, and often used in brothels to service young men's needs," said Dr. Franklin.

Dr. Webber spoke up. "Not always, though. I went to a cage-fight doll club once and got to fight in the ring. It was rather brutal, and I only went because my friend David needed a tag-team partner. He was studying psychology and wanted to work with the criminally insane. It was his way of getting inside the heads of people to understand their motivations. Or at least that's what he always said."

"You too? Typical man," said Dr. Franklin.

"Did you believe him though, Alan?" asked Allison.

"No, not really. He seemed to get quite excited by the thrill from fighting using a surrogate body. All the upsides with none of the down, I guess. Still, he did qualify, and the last time I checked, he'd published a paper on working with the criminally insane."

"Did you go again, Alan?" asked Dr. Franklin.

"No, didn't do anything for me. Still, Tyrone's right, you know. Different things interest different people. I'm surprised you'd balk at that as all you do is watch and record what people do all day long," said Dr. Webber.

"Pretty much why I wouldn't go to such a place. It would be too much like work," replied Dr. Franklin.

"Has Laytonya ever told you the story of how she started to see everybody as monkeys when she was doing her psychology module?" asked Dr. Reynolds.

"Can't say she has, Tyrone."

"It's not a big thing," Dr. Franklin said. "It was at the end of the study module, and I kept seeing people as if they were monkeys exhibiting grooming or dominance behaviors. Not literally seeing them as monkeys. It was just the image of monkeys would flash into my head when I saw people doing things. I have to admit it did feel quite weird, though."

Allison looked around the marketplace and saw the four androids were beginning to move. She was horrified as they all unslung their rifles and started firing at the aliens moving around them.

"Drop to the ground!"

"This is some fucked-up shit the military is pulling," said Dr. Reynolds, as he was pushed to the ground and trampled on by fleeing aliens trying to run away.

More shots rang out. The noise reverberating around them made her chest feel as if it had been hit by something, and Allison's ears rang from the guns' discharges.

The aliens were screaming. Some were running in the confusion. Other aliens had dropped to the ground and were chanting.

"*Genyurasa, genyurasa,*" they said, repeating the words again and again.

The marketplace had gone from a place of lively activity to one of bedlam and death. Aliens shot by the androids were lying on the ground, their blood still pumping out of their bodies as they died around her.

More shots rang out, and the team's four androids began walking away, shooting at anything that was standing.

Behind her an alien walked into the marketplace, emerging from one of the connecting alleys, and one of the androids turned and shot it. The bullet hit the alien's shoulder, and the arm was severed.

Blood fountained from the wound.

"Shit, I've been hit!" she heard Dr. Webber scream out behind her.

"Stay still," she said.

"What do you think I'm doing?"

"It looks like they're leaving the marketplace," said Dr. Franklin.

Allison looked around as best she could to confirm the androids had gone before moving over next to Alan.

"Let me check where you've been hit."

He rolled onto his side showing where the blood had spread.

Checking her PAD, Allison brought up the first aid package, and she started to follow the instructions. Their backpacks had military first aid kits in them, and she applied blood-clotting agent to the wound.

"Oh, shitting hell that burns," said Alan.

"Sorry, let me put the bandage on it."

Allison placed the dressing on the three-inch-long furrow the bullet had made as it glanced across Alan's abdomen. It had gouged a fair chunk of flesh from his side, but it didn't seem to have hit a major blood vessel or organs.

She was relieved he hadn't been killed.

"You're going to tell me I'm lucky, aren't you?"

"I don't think you need me to tell you that. You know you are. It could be worse, you know; you could be dead. Laytonya, how's Tyrone doing?" she asked.

"He's out cold and has a big bump on his head. It could be worse, he could be bitching about being shot at and the military conspiring to kill him," said Dr. Franklin.

"Don't make me laugh. I hurt too much."

"We can't stay here, in case the androids return and we get caught in the crossfire," said Allison, looking around for somewhere to go. "Laytonya, check the door over there behind you."

"It's unlocked. Oh my…"

Allison saw one of the pig-bear aliens in the doorway looking at them.

"*Isi ironi. Isi ironi. Ironi, ironi,*" it said, gesturing with its arms at them to come in.

"Alan, put your arm over my shoulder and let's get you up," she said, helping him inside the house and dropping him as gently as possible inside next to the door.

Laytonya was still outside, struggling to move the unconscious Tyrone. Allison rushed out to help drag his dead weight inside the safety of the alien's home.

Gunshots echoed in the distance.

"Hurry, the firing seems to be coming this way."

"Not deaf and not stupid, just not strong enough to move faster."

They grabbed Tyrone by the arms and pulled him inside. As the door shut, she thought she saw an android enter the far side of the marketplace. She only hoped it hadn't seen them and would ignore the movement of the door.

Allison started to shake.

50. IN THE LIBRARY

One never really knows who one's enemy is.

— Jürgen Habermas

Dr. David Leung
Magnetic Anomaly Project Scientist
Two Moons Timakira
Monday, January 16, 2073

David stood on a ladder checking the scrolls in the library, which he had microtagged when they had started to catalogue the contents.

He was trying to decipher a particularly complex mathematical glyph that had become worn over time from having the alien fingers move across it as they read it. The wear and tear had caused a transcription error.

Part of his current work was analyzing them and working out when the errors were transcribed. Not strictly the remit of his job here but it was something that would ultimately be of great value to the work that would come out of this project.

"Grace, where are you?"

"I'm sitting on the floor working on stabilizing a scroll before I attempt to scan it. What's up?"

"I wonder if you can see what the androids are doing? They're not responding to my requests."

"Didn't you hear a moment ago that the control loop is down, and they've shut them down to reboot the system?"

"Vaguely. Anyway, time for a cup of tea then, I guess."

"Good idea. I'm glad you volunteered."

"I wouldn't let you anywhere near the tea. If you like, I can check if we have any cookies left?"

"That would be nice."

David got down from the ladder and walked to where they'd put their supply of tea and water.

The last couple of packets of cookies were in the tin next to the teabags. He smelt the tea as the water boiled.

"We're out of chocolate chip. Would you like the gingerbread or a digestive?"

"Ginger, please," she replied.

David turned around with her cup in one hand and the packet of cookies in the other, about to walk over and give them to her, when he saw one of the androids was moving. It had unslung the rifle from its back and had aimed the weapon at him.

It fired.

The report of the shot filled the room and made his ears ring as he dropped the cup of tea, which fell to the ground.

Grace was screaming as his vision grayed and he lost consciousness.

51. OUTSIDE THE WALLS

Life is truly known only to those who suffer, lose, endure adversity and stumble from defeat to defeat.

— Anaïs Nin

Specialist Nelson
Two Moons Outside Timakira
Monday, January 16, 2073

Nelson sat next to Baptista, who was driving them to where Drs. Follet and Newman were collecting samples today.

The landscape around Timakira was crisscrossed with fields and irrigation ditches, and they swung past a berm before heading to where the scientists were. Nelson got the virtual-reality feed loop up again, but the system had crashed on transfer back to base camp.

She thought Ferretti was worrying too much, and then a gun fired and there was shattered glass everywhere.

"Put your foot on it."

Nelson turned to find Baptista slumped over the controls and the truck in autodrive mode. There was a hole in the front of Baptista's PACE suit.

"Shitty, shit, shit."

Nelson looked out the window at the two androids moving towards the truck, which was slowing to a halt as they reached their destination. Another shot rang out. The bullet hit the front of the truck, deflected up into the cab, and ricocheted off the roof and floor before hitting her in the chest like a hammer.

Nelson's chest plate stopped the shot, and she turned to grab Baptista. She pulled him down out of sight of the androids, dragging him across the seat to the door opposite. She fell out the door and landed on her back with Baptista's suit lying on top of her as an android walked around the truck and fired into his back.

It then climbed into the truck.

The next thing Nelson heard was the roar of the Browning fifty cal on top of the cab, aimed at something moving in the distance. Then the firing stopped. Her ears rang as silence returned for a brief few moments before the engine started up and the truck drove away.

Nelson struggled to twist her body under Baptista. The truck was over a kilometer away by the time she got him off her. By the looks of things the truck was headed into the town.

Baptista was dead.

If the first shot hadn't killed him, the second one had. PACE suits could take a lot of damage, being pretty much proof against 5.56, and could resist single 7.62 mm with impunity. But the Beowulf .50 caliber fired armor-piercing rounds designed to crack engine blocks.

Nelson searched for the two scientists in the hope she would find them still alive.

In the distance were two shapes on the ground. She began

walking. She started to cry when she saw their bodies torn apart by Browning machine-gun rounds.

They'd been shot in the back as they tried to run away.

The bullets had torn the two scientists apart. Nelson knelt next to their lifeless bodies. There was blood everywhere, and she was unable to stop sobbing.

52. WAITING

Dr. Allison O'Neill
Magnetic Anomaly Project Scientist
Two Moons Timakira
Monday, January 16, 2073

Allison's heart beat faster as the noise of guns outside the door grew louder, and the palms of her hands became sweaty. She held her breath as another shot was fired, and she felt the pressure of air on her sternum as the room shook from the sound wave.

Dust fell from the ceiling, then she heard the android surrogate as it moved off in the direction of whatever it had seen and shot at. She let go of her breath, and a sudden panic swept over her as she started to sob.

"It's OK. We're safe for now, I hope," said Dr. Franklin.

"That's not very reassuring when you say it like that," Allison replied, her sobs turning to a giggle.

"I know, but it's the best I can do under the circumstances."

"How's Tyrone doing?"

"Blissfully unaware of the dire circumstances we find ourselves in."

"Is there anything we can do for him?"

"Don't think so. I checked my PAD for what to do. It says he needs a professional assessment."

Tyrone groaned. "Oh god, my head hurts."

"Welcome back to the land of the living, though soon to be dead, Tyrone," said Dr. Webber.

"Oh, stop it already. You make a right pair you two. Tyrone, look at me," said Dr. Franklin as she flashed a small light into his eye.

"Hey, stop that. What're you doing? What happened?"

"Tell me if it hurts when I flash the light into your eyes. Now follow it as I move."

"It don't hurt, but it's sure as hell annoyingly bright."

"You've hit your head and have a rather nasty bump to show for it. We're all worried for you, so let me check you out, OK?"

"Whatever, woman. Get on with it."

"Sounds fine to me," said Allison, looking around the room they were hiding in.

She saw their rescuers sitting against the opposite wall looking at the four of them. She couldn't help but stare back at them, and she smiled in what she hoped would be seen as a friendly gesture.

"If you start having a headache, seeing double, or feeling sick, you'll tell me, won't you?"

"Of course I will. Stop fussing, woman. I mean it."

"Also, if you feel any weakness in your body when you try to move."

"Look, I promise if I become woozy, I'll tell you. I'm not exactly Mr. Gung-ho about getting hurt, but let me keep some shred of what manliness I can hold on to here. What happened?"

"The androids started shooting, and you were pushed to the ground. You hit your head and lost consciousness. Alan's been shot, but we've managed to stop the bleeding, and these nice people let us into their house to escape the rampaging androids."

"That was kind of them, Laytonya, but it sounds like we're really having a bad day here, and I don't mean the bump on my head and all."

"Don't forget me being shot, will you?"

"Alan, you're alive, aren't you? This day could still get a whole load worse—as in the we-end-up-dead kind of way."

"Always the optimist, aren't you?" said Dr. Franklin.

"I just tell it as it is. We're both black, so I expect we'll die first."

"Do what, Tyrone?"

"Woman, the black people always die first when bad things happen. It's an old joke."

"You sure you're thinking straight, Tyrone? How's your head?"

"It hurts, Laytonya. I'm just saying expect the worse, is all."

"Hey, can any of you speak the local language without the androids to help you? I have a few words," asked Allison.

"I have a few, too," said Dr. Franklin.

"Me too," said Dr. Reynolds.

"Since we're stuck here for the time being, we ought to at least try to say thank you to the people who let us come inside," said Allison.

"Not sure my vocabulary is up to that," said Dr. Reynolds.

"That figures, as you never say thank you for anything."

"Hey, man with a broken skull here. Cut me some slack, woman."

"I know how to say thank you," said Dr. Webber, wincing in

pain as he spoke.

"OK, what do we say?" asked Allison.

"*Folo asi kafo*, I think."

"Who wants to try saying that to our new friends on the other side of this room?" asked Allison.

"Looks like you just volunteered yourself, girl," said Dr. Franklin.

Allison turned to face the aliens. "*Folo asi kafo...folo asi kafo.*" She repeated the phrase again to make sure they understood what she was saying.

"*Dose zalalilo bankaega,*" replied one of the pig-bear aliens.

"I have no idea what it said."

"It seemed to understand you, though," said Dr. Franklin.

"*Rilika timakira yahadhi. Zafadhiza gigasai rubusaikai bedu.*"

"I caught a bit of that. Fourth people and his name," said Dr. Reynolds.

"Or her name, for all we know," said Dr. Franklin.

"Its name then," said Dr. Reynolds.

"My name is Allison," she said, pointing at herself.

"*Hoi! Rilibo timakira yahadhi Allisone ran.*"

"That's interesting, Allison. If I got that right, they referred to you as person of this town, but that doesn't make any sense to me," said Dr. Webber.

"Of course she's a person, Alan. So what do you think they mean?" asked Dr. Franklin.

"What he's saying is that these aliens are calling us the fifth people, right?" said Dr. Reynolds.

The pig-bear alien pointed at one of the reptile men and said, "*Daido timakira yahadhi bokurhi bedu.*"

The reptile man spoke. "*Ojaizo Allisone ran.*"

"I wish David and Grace were here. They'd know what to say," said Dr. Franklin.

"I hope they're both still alive," said Allison.

53. RESCUE PLAN

Plan B. You've always got to have a Plan B.

— Sylvester Stallone

Technical Sergeant Ferretti
Two Moons Bravo Site
Monday, January 16, 2073

Ferretti stared at the main screen that showed the various androids firing at the scientists and aliens. He could only hope Allison had been lucky enough to be out of the line of fire. He knew that once the shooting started, people would die, and it was down to chance as to whom.

"Jordan, can we send the shutdown signal?"

"I've already sent it three times, Sarge. They're receiving it, but they're not responding to the command."

He checked the console and looked at the transmission logs.

"Why hasn't the feed stopped?"

"Good question, Jordan. Damned if I know. It looks like our command station still has access rights."

"You mean the androids are letting us watch what they're doing?"

"No, it's not that. The command station is still in sync, so when they went rogue they couldn't cut us out of the loop. Look here and you can see that android four is acting as the person in the control loop, and it has overridden us."

"I didn't think an android could self-actuate its own loop."

"It's not supposed to be able to do so, but four's lack of an inhibitor means it can be autonomous. Now it's bootstrapping itself with the other androids, using the loop, so they're all responding to the One-Zero-One free-fire-zone protocol."

He looked at the feeds, frustrated by being unable to control the situation.

"What are your orders?"

"Jordan, pull up the feeds from each android during the reboot. Find out what we can see and learn about what just happened," he said.

"Yes, Sarge."

Ferretti got up from his chair and walked outside.

"Wachowski, get your suit out and a truck ready!" he shouted.

Wachowski turned and ran towards him. "What's up?"

"All the androids have gone into One-Zero-One state, and shit has just got serious."

"OK, but are you ordering you and me to suit up and go after them?"

"Yes, I am. Do you have a problem with following my order, Corporal?"

"Yes, Technical Sergeant, I do. With your rank and position, you should not be the one out in a suit shooting at rogue androids. I'm a Marine and Jordan is a security force military policewoman, and we're both better suited to this task. Your job is for you to remain here and command the operation."

"Are you calling me an old man, Wachowski?"

"Just saying we're younger and fitter, and I strongly suggest you let us put our butts on the line while you stay here to oversee what you want done. It's what the lieutenant would do if she were here."

"Go get suited up already."

"Aye, aye, Technical Sergeant."

Ferretti walked back into the container control room. "Jordan, go get suited up with Wachowski. I'll take it from here." He got on the radio. "This is Foxtrot Bravo Six to Foxtrot Alpha, come in. Over."

"This is Foxtrot Alpha, receiving loud and clear. Over."

"Can you put me through to the lieutenant? Over."

"Copy that, Foxtrot Bravo Six. Wait one while we put you through to Foxtrot Alpha Six. Over."

Ferretti waited a few moments for the reply from Alpha site, and mulled over what he was going to say.

"This is Foxtrot Alpha Six. Over."

"We have a situation here. Our androids have gone rogue and initiated the One-Zero-One protocol. Over."

"Roger that. Seems like the shit has truly hit the fan. OK, I will be leaving here in thirty mikes with reinforcements. At best speed, I estimate our ETA is twenty hours from departure. We'll confirm launch of operation and use Alpha Camp to relay messages until we get into radio range with you. Acknowledge. Over."

"Transmission received. You will be departing in thirty mikes and ETA at twenty hours after departure, and you will be maintaining radio relay through them to us. Over."

"OK, Ferretti. What are you planning to do in the meantime? Over."

"I've ordered Jordan and Wachowski to suit up and do a recon to see if we can retrieve any survivors. Over."

"Sounds like a good plan to me. When I get there, I hope to

find you still in one piece. I will need everybody to contain the threat. Going in outnumbered will only get good people killed. Do you understand what I'm saying? Over."

"I do, ma'am. Don't worry; I won't do anything stupid. Over."

"We will do our best to get them back. Tachikoma, out."

54. GOING IN

So in war, the way is to avoid what is strong and to strike at what is weak.

— Sun Tzu

Corporal Wachowski
Two Moons
Monday, January 16, 2073

Wachowski and Jordan had suited up, checked their battle-rattle, and were driving out to where contact had been lost with Baptista and Nelson. Ferretti had made it clear they were not to enter Timakira under any circumstances.

Wachowski sat at the wheel of the truck with Jordan manning the control station for the Browning fifty cal.

The trucks' ChameleonFlage minimized the chances of being spotted. To anyone looking at them as they drove along, they would appear like a shimmering blur from the heat rising from the ground. Only the cloud of trailing dust would give them away.

It was now early afternoon.

Only a couple of hours ago, the day had been another dull and repetitious round of chores. If only she could still be living that day. She remembered the old adage that every Marine was a rifleman, but this was far more excitement than she was used to.

It was twenty klicks from Camp Bravo to where they'd lost track of the truck and their team. Driving down to the town involved some tricky negotiations with terrain that made no allowances for man- or womankind.

"Wachowski, what do you think we will find?"

"If we're lucky, survivors. Why ask me? What makes you think I know any more than you?"

"You always seem to know what's what, and you outrank me."

"I hate to break the bad news to you, but today's one of those days where it's bad news all round. I have no idea what's the right thing to do."

"But you sounded like you knew when you told the sergeant to stay behind and coordinate the plan."

"That was just obvious, Jordan. There are three of us, and only one of us can run the monitor station like him, and that's Ferretti."

"See, you do know what you're doing."

"Jordan, it may look like it to you, but trust me when I say it sure doesn't feel like it. Oh shit, what's that? Zoom your gun feed on the movement ahead of us," she said as she drew the truck to a halt.

"Wait one, got it. Putting it on the main screen now."

"Are you seeing what I'm seeing, Jordan?" she asked. In the distance was a trail filled with more monsters with teeth than she could count.

"That's a scary lot of Crocomodos making their way up into the hills."

"Bravo Charlie Three to Bravo Charlie Six, come in. Over."

"Receiving. Over."

"We're sending you an image of what's in front of us. Over."

"Got that, Bravo Charlie Three. Just what we didn't need to see today. Your assessment? Over."

"Not going to be able to go through them. We need another route. Over."

"And quickly," said Jordan. "They're going to be on top of us in under ten mikes."

"Pulling up the aerial images from CYCLOPS now. You need to turn round and go back up the hill about four hundred meters. You should see a gully on your left that you can make your way along. It goes right around and then takes you back towards the town. Everything else looks too broken for the truck to traverse at speed. I'm downloading the route to you now. Over," came Ferretti's reply.

"Roger that. Route map received in the clear. We are skedaddling now, as there's more Crocomodos out there than it's worth thinking about. Out."

Wachowski did a three-point turn to turn the truck around.

She then drove up the hill and looked at the route. Ferretti must have been kidding if he thought the truck could traverse the rocky route ahead. She switched everything over to the computer's control, trusting it to do a better job than she would.

They began their slow descent down the gully ahead.

The truck lurched from side to side as wheels lifted off the terrain, exceeding the travel of the suspension. Wachowski could hear the hum of the transmission shifting power from wheel to wheel, and the whine from the motors as they microstepped the rotation of the tyres to maximize traction.

It was reassuring, in the way that comes from being a passenger hanging off the restraining straps as the nose of the truck pointed down the steep descent.

"Oh shit," said Jordan.

"You can say that again."

"Oh shit, oh shit, oh shit, oh shit!"

"I didn't mean literally. We've both got the picture here," said Wachowski.

The truck slipped forward as the tires lost grip on some loose rocks, and the back end slid sideways before the autotraction sensors could reestablish control.

"Oh shit. Sorry, I couldn't help myself there."

"Don't worry. I'm saying it to myself, too."

Finally, the truck reached the bottom of the incline and sat inside a gully hidden from the sight of migrating Crocomodos.

Wachowski kept her eye on the autodrive as the truck made its way slowly along the narrow confines of the gully. The slope still led down towards Timakira, but it remained a rock-strewn obstacle course.

"The radio's not working," said Jordan.

"This day just keeps getting better and better. What have I done to deserve this shit?"

"Shouldn't have sassed Ferretti so much, maybe?" replied Jordan.

"Hey, those are happy memories I shall treasure for the rest of my life."

"Well, let's hope for a long life then."

"There's a grave thought indeed."

55. TRAPPED TEAM

To conquer fear is the beginning of wisdom.

— BERTRAND RUSSELL

Dr. Grace Pham
Magnetic Anomaly Project Scientist
Two Moons Timakira
Monday, January 16, 2073

Grace was deafened as David fell to the ground. She froze in fear as the two androids turned and scanned the room. A few moments later they walked out with the two QuadMules that carried their recharging batteries.

Their departure was followed by the sound of multiple shots being fired in quick succession in the hall down the corridor.

Grace saw David was still breathing, but he had turned rather gray. She went to his side and found he'd been shot in the upper chest.

"David, are you all right?"

David groaned at her, and she thought to herself what a stupid question to ask. Really, was that the best she could say? She felt numb and unable to think, and she knew if she did nothing, David would most likely die.

Looking around, she grabbed her backpack, remembering that Sergeant Ferretti had told them each carried a first aid kit. She rummaged through the pack and found a pouch and opened it up.

Now what do I do with this?

David coughed and came round. "Shit, this fucking hurts. It's killing me."

"Let's hope not—I mean the killing you part."

Grace remembered that her PAD was also loaded with a first aid guide. She looked up *chest wound* and read the basics; she wasn't reassured by the fact that all the information advised calling for a qualified medic.

From what she read, David had what was described as a "sucking chest wound," called this because the wound sucks air into the chest cavity. What she read frightened her, but she had a moment of realization that if she did nothing, he would die.

The worst that could happen was doing nothing. If she did something wrong, it was already out of her hands.

"Oh, jeez, that hurts."

"I'm sorry, David, but I'm going to have to get you to press down as hard as you can where it hurts. Sorry," she said, as she pulled his hand to cover the spot where the bullet had gone in.

Grace then re-read what she had to do again to make sure she didn't get it wrong. Apply occlusive patch to chest to seal the hole. She ripped open the packet containing an Asherman Chest Seal and looked at the round dressing with a piece of rubber tube sticking out of the center of it.

She made sure she understood how to apply it; the instructions told her to remove the backing and seal the wound with the tube as the relief valve.

Shit! She needed to cut away his clothes around the wound to get at it.

The blood came out of the bullet hole each time David breathed in. Little spurts of blood that bubbled with air. She took the scissors and started cutting open his bloodstained shirt.

Her hands were now covered in his blood, and she realized she should've put gloves on, but hadn't. Grace was sure David didn't have any infectious diseases for her to catch, and while she wasn't exactly sterile, if he lived to get an infection later, it would be better than dying now.

"OK, David, in a minute I'm going to apply a special bandage, and I need you to breathe out as I apply it and press down on your chest. Can you do that for me?"

"Sure, Grace, but do you know what you're doing?"

"Do you really want to know?"

"No, not really. Let's get on with it. I'm sure I'll be as right as rain once you've fixed me up, but this time it's definitely your turn to make the tea," he said, coughing.

Grace smiled at him as she pulled the backing off the clear plastic adhesive and held the tube valve so it was pointed outwards.

"Time to breathe out and move your hand for me," she said, pushing the patch down over the hole in David's chest. "How's that feel?"

"Still hurts."

"I'm not surprised about that, as you've been shot. Apply pressure on the patch while I add some tape around the edges to make sure it doesn't move. Good thing you don't have hairs on your chest."

"Don't make me laugh again; it hurts too much," he said, coughing some more.

Grace got the roll of surgical tape and applied it to seal the edges of the patch, which didn't look as though they were stuck down properly because of the blood.

She noticed a pool of blood on the floor that must have come from the bullet leaving the body.

"David, the bullet has gone right through you. I need you to help me turn you over so I can seal the wound in your back."

"Promise not to hurt me."

"I promise that this will hurt you more than it will hurt me, but you can thank me later."

Grace rolled David onto his side and saw the bullet had come out lower down.

She didn't understand how that could happen, but since it had she didn't spend any time worrying about the how. She grabbed some gauze and applied it to the wound and taped it down.

Then she checked her PAD on the procedure again to make sure she'd gotten it right.

She hadn't.

The wound at the back was sucking in air every time David breathed in. She grabbed the plastic cover sheet from the original patch and used it to cover the gauze and then taped down all the edges to seal the wound.

"Argh shit, that effin' hurts!"

"Be glad it does, the alternatives are much worse."

"How bad is it?"

"You need proper medical treatment by someone who's qualified in this sort of thing. I've done the best I can. All we can hope for is that you can hold on until help arrives."

"Hey, don't hold anything back. Tell me what you really think."

"You fool. Don't you go dying on me; otherwise I will have to hurt you."

"What now then?"

"We sit and wait together. I reckon you're allowed to drink a little, so why don't I make us a pot of tea?"

"As long as you don't stew it and ruin it."

"As if I would ever do such a thing to you."

56. PROGENITORS KILL

And the great dragon was cast out, that old serpent, called the Devil, and Satan, which deceiveth the whole world.

— REVELATION 12:9

Dr. Allison O'Neill
Magnetic Anomaly Project Scientist
Two Moons Timakira
Monday, January 16, 2073

The Master was sitting in his chair when there was a sound unlike anything he had ever heard. It was like thunder crashing overhead, but it was an unnatural sound, followed by a scream from the library.

His worst fears had come true.

The Progenitors had found the people of this town lacking. In that moment of clarity, he chose to fall to the floor, prostrating himself for the inevitable judgement that was about to come.

Some of his guards followed him; others did not.

Two Progenitors came into the hall and pointed strange

objects that emitted light and noise. The repeated sound of thunder and lightning deafened him as the guards were struck down by the wrath of the Progenitors. His ears rang as the echoes reverberated around the hall where those chosen to die lay on the floor.

The noise of the Progenitors' movement drew him to look at them as they walked towards the door. Following them were their beasts, chittering as they bobbed around behind the Progenitors who led them on. Then they turned to look back at him. He waited for the judgement to befall him, but he was spared, as were the others who had prostrated themselves on the ground.

The threat of death receded as the two Progenitors left the hall with their beasts.

After a while the ringing in his ears subsided, and he could once again hear clearly. But what he heard made him wish the ringing hadn't stopped. Outside the hall, the now-distant thunder meant death was being bestowed upon the town of the four peoples.

He had never felt fear like this, even when seeing the *bolagojo sakazan* coming out of the water each year to climb up to the desert waterholes to lay their eggs.

Yet within him, he found something of himself that allowed him to stand up, the thing that made him the Master of the town.

"By my command, guards rise up off the floor. The Progenitors have judged you. Thank them you are not dead, and I have services that need your attention."

His guards rose, hesitant and trembling from fear, a fear he felt but didn't show.

"Close the doors and seal them shut," he commanded.

As the guards went about their tasks, he looked around at the dead on the floor. About half of those who had been present in the hall were dead.

"When the doors are sealed, attend to the fallen."

He wanted to sit down and let his body shake with fear, but he knew now was not the time. If he allowed himself to start, he wasn't sure he would be able to stop, and he had to protect the people as best he could.

He walked to the library to find out what had happened there, moving down the passageway that led to where the scrolls of past knowledge were kept. As he entered the room, he saw red stains upon the wall, which must have been the blood from the Quintus lying on the floor.

Next to it the other Quintus tended to the fallen one that had been struck down by the Progenitors. Much to his surprise, the Quintus was not dead.

How could that be? The Progenitors struck at it, but it still lived. He didn't understand.

"Scriber, are you here?" he called.

"I am here, Master," came the reply, and he turned his head towards a small alcove above, where the First Scriber was huddled.

"Come down and tell me what you saw."

The First Scriber disappeared from view, followed by the sound of it climbing down from where it had been hiding.

"Master, the Progenitors and their beasts left the room after striking down the Quintus that is lying on the floor. That is all I saw. After they left I stayed hidden above until you came."

"Why is the Quintus not dead?"

"I cannot answer that which I do not know, Master."

"Do the Quintuses understand the language of the people yet?"

"I think they know a little, but the Progenitors spoke for them and to them in all their dealings with the four peoples."

"Can you speak to them?"

"I can but try, Master. I believe these two were learning to speak our language and have some understanding of what we say."

"Try to ask them if they need anything from us."

Turning to face the two Quintuses on the floor, the Scriber spoke. "Shake your heads from side to side if you understand me."

One creature looked up to him.

"Ifan kuou forinota atakinus foriwata hasu hahpe nued."

"Do you understand what I am saying?" the Scriber asked again, taking the time to enunciate each word separately.

The Quintus nodded its head up and down. *"Inde sutanda altile,* yes," came the reply.

"This is going to take some time. I shall be in the hall. Find out what you can. Ask it why its companion is not dead," the Master said. "It may be important for the survival of the people."

"I will be as true as I can to the image of the four peoples, Master."

57. HOUSE OF FIVE

Endurance is patience concentrated.

— THOMAS CARLYLE

Dr. Allison O'Neill
Magnetic Anomaly Project Scientist
Two Moons Timakira
Monday, January 16, 2073

Allison sat with her back to the wall as darkness fell, the team's language skills having sufficed to engender a sense of safety.

"I'm starving," said Dr. Reynolds.

"What have we got on us to eat?" asked Dr. Webber, who was looking more comfortable, and less pale than earlier on.

"Our packs have emergency rations in them," said Allison.

"Oh yummy, military rations, we are spoilt," said Dr. Reynolds.

"Be grateful we have anything to eat, unless you want to try the locals' food," said Allison.

"She's right, Tyrone. Stop with your bitchin' and all, as no one wants to hear it."

"What's this, Laytonya, pick on Tyrone day?"

Allison looked in her backpack. She found a bottle of water, an emergency space blanket, and a pink Humanitarian Daily Ration pack. "Looks like we have standard emergency ration packs."

"I've seen the military give those out when they're on relief missions to Third World countries," said Dr. Franklin.

"What's in yours?" asked Allison as she pulled the packet open and emptied the contents out onto her lap.

"Lentil stew and beans with potatoes. Yours?"

"Herb rice and peas in tomato sauce."

Dr. Reynolds asked, "Are we supposed to eat these cold?"

"Looks like it to me," said Dr. Webber.

"Sheeeit, don't that take the biscuit. They could've at least supplied self-heating rations."

"Tyrone, you've been bitchin' about carrying the packs every day, and now you're complaining 'cause you have to eat cold food. If you wanted better, you should've packed your own backpack," said Dr. Franklin.

"We always had good snacks to eat at lunchtime. I just assumed there would be more of the same."

"Because we don't get fed properly when we get back to camp at all."

"You've got a big mouth on you, woman."

"Hey, let's not start an argument in front of our newfound friends. Remember where we are and let's be grateful for what we have. I'm sure someone will come and rescue us soon. All we have to do is wait and not do anything stupid that ends up with us being shot at again," said Allison, who had become aware that the aliens were watching them closely.

"Anyways, I've got beans and potatoes with peas in tomato sauce. Who makes up these menus?" asked Dr. Reynolds.

"Anyone like to swap my barley stew?" asked Dr. Webber. "I'm not keen on barley."

"How does peas in tomato sauce sound to you?"

"Sounds good to me, Tyrone," said Dr. Webber as they swapped parts of their meal.

"Do you think we should offer to share our food with them?" asked Allison.

"We're pretty sure that it won't poison them, and we've tested their foods, too, so we should be good to go on that," said Dr. Webber.

"If it means I get to eat something hot, I'm all for it," said Dr. Reynolds.

Allison turned to the aliens and gestured as best she could about sharing their food together. She moved over to sit beside the small fire, which the aliens had lit when the temperature had started falling. Allison mimed putting the food in the pot and gestured that they could share by mimicking serving out portions for everyone.

The pig-bear alien smiled, which she took to be a good sign, and then it got up and brought out a cooking pot.

"OK, let's mix up all the entrées to make one big stew," said Allison.

"But I don't like barley."

"Hey, Alan, if I've been told to stop complaining, then it's got to apply to you, too. It's got to be way better to eat something hot than the cold contents from the packet."

Allison opened each packet in turn and emptied it into the pot making a mixed-stew surprise. She waited for it come to the boil as the aliens found various bowls for them all to eat from. Allison got the impression they hadn't planned on being trapped in this room, either.

Allison dished out eight portions, and all things considered the stew didn't taste too bad. Tyrone said it was better hot than cold out of the packet. Afterwards, she gathered up the cookies and other treats in the packets and shared them out, too.

The pig-bear enjoyed the fig bar, which wasn't a snack she liked.

She noted that the aliens were all able to eat the food without problems, and wondered why their original creators had made them all so physically different on the outside, yet they shared the same biochemistry.

"That was better than I was expecting," said Dr. Webber. "I didn't even find any barley."

"See, I said heating the food up would be better," said Dr. Reynolds.

"Pity we don't have a pack of cards, though," said Dr. Webber.

The aliens unrolled their sleeping rugs and offered their spare ones to the four of them to use. Allison tried to imagine what was going through their minds, and what she would be thinking if her house had four aliens sitting opposite her with murderous robots lurking around outside.

She snuggled down as best she could on the floor next to Laytonya.

"You OK, Allison?"

"Yeah, just thinking about when we'll be rescued."

"I'm sure Sergeant Ferretti will be coming for you, my dear."

"For all of us, I'm sure."

"Yes, but especially for you. I've seen the way he looks at you and treats you. He's a real gentleman."

"You think so? I'm not sure my parents would consider him suitable. They always told me I should marry someone who is a professional with good prospects. Truth be told, they don't approve of my career choice, either."

"Have you considered, given all that has been going on, who your peer group is?"

"Other scientists, I guess?"

"Maybe, but my guess is that being able to go through the pillars and travel to other worlds is something that's going to make whom we socialize with more difficult. We can only talk about what we do with those who have clearance to discuss what we know."

"I guess, but when the project goes public, won't we become celebrities, like astronauts?"

"You may well be right, but then how are you going to know if someone likes you for *who* you are rather than *what* you are?"

"So what are you saying?"

"Don't forget to look at what's right under your nose, girl. Sergeant Ferretti is a highly skilled technician, and a smart man who clearly thinks the world of you."

"How do you figure that out?"

"As I said, by the way he talks to you and treats you. My guess—he feels he can't make the first move, because he's always on duty when he's around you."

Allison pondered what Laytonya said.

She made her mind up that when she got out of this situation, she was going to suggest going out for coffee with Sergeant Ferretti. If only to see what he looked like out of uniform.

58. ALPHA FOB

The courage of a soldier is found to be the cheapest and most common quality of human nature.

— EDWARD GIBBON

First Lieutenant Lara Atsuko Tachikoma
Two Moons Alpha Site
Monday, January 16, 2073

I stood up from the radio station and considered what to do next. First, load the CASE suits on the back of the two trucks and get everyone moving in the same general direction.

On reflection, getting it all done in thirty minutes would be a challenge.

"Lieutenant, we're receiving some unusual data packets," said Airman Moore.

"What sort of unusual data packets?"

"They look like android loop-control data to me, ma'am."

"Oh, hell no! Cut the transmission."

Grabbing my service rifle, I slapped a magazine in, pulled the charging lever, and released the safety. I ran towards the android storage area.

All four of Alpha site's androids were connected to their recharge points. Airman Garcia, one of our UAV operators, was on recharge-station duty that day.

He was reaching over to unplug one of the androids and reactivate it.

"Airman, stop what you're doing now!"

But I was too late. The android stood up and grabbed Garcia's arm, twisting it away from the shutdown button.

Garcia screamed out in pain, "It's broken my arm!"

I drew the butt of my rifle into my shoulder and aligned my sight picture on the android as it turned to access its rifle. Garcia was blocking me from getting a clear shot.

"Garcia, drop down now!"

He went limp. The android tried to hold him up to use him as a shield to block me, but in that moment I had what I needed to take the shot.

My rifle snapped up as I fired, the sound ringing in my ears.

The shot hit the android in the head, damaging one of its cameras. But since I needed a chest hit to damage the processor core, this didn't even slow it down.

I kept my movement slow and steady; because slow is smooth, and smooth is fast.

Then I fired again as the android dropped Garcia completely to bring its rifle to bear on me. This time I hit the torso, but my 7.62 mm round had no noticeable effect.

It pulled back the charging handle on its rifle.

I couldn't take any consolation from knowing it was only going to be firing at me with 5.56 mm ammo. I wasn't wearing body armor and didn't have a metal-endoskeleton.

So I figured the android was on the winning side of the damage-response equation here.

I heard the kaboom from a Beowulf short-fifty round being fired behind me to my left. It deafened me as the overpressure of the round thumped my chest.

The android staggered, having taken the hit in the torso. It stopped paying any attention to me as it assessed the new threat.

I didn't allow that to stop me putting two more rounds into it in quick succession. This was gratuitous, all things considered, as it fell to the ground when a second Beowulf round ripped it open.

Still, it was better to have a gratuitous application of force to stop something than end up in an after-action report as an example for others.

"You OK!?" shouted Espera over the ringing in my ears.

"Yeah. Thanks for the assist."

"No problemo."

"Corpsman up, we have a man down!" I shouted. "How you doing, Garcia?"

"I've had better days, ma'am."

Corpsman Keith arrived and started attending to Garcia, putting the arm into a splint.

"Staff Sergeant Espera, we need to hard reboot these androids into safe mode before anything further untoward happens. After that we need to grab our gear and go help out Ferretti. He's kindly arranged to brighten up our dreary, humdrum routine with another eight rogue androids like this, but armed with bigger guns."

"Oh *joy*," said Espera.

One thing I could say about my people was once I gave the order to go, we had everyone's gear packed and ready in just over thirty mikes. Which was amazing, all things considered.

Usually there's a certain amount of faffing around when a unit receives an order to prepare for a mission. This involves discussions around what gear to take, what to leave, and whether or not one needs one's snivel gear or pogey bait—treats. The excitement of live rounds being fired in the compound had had the remarkable effect of focusing everyone on the task ahead.

"OK, people, let's get rolling," I said as I climbed into the spare front seat of the cab truck, slamming the door shut behind me.

The four of us were in the lead truck, which meant we could spread out a bit, as it was designed to seat six people in full combat gear.

Staff Sergeant Espera was driving, with me on the fifty cal, while Corpsman Keith and Sergeant Pearson sat in the back. The plan was to stop and rotate the driving every four hours and have two on and two off for the twenty-hour cross-country drive ahead of us.

"Roger that, LT," replied Espera as he set the truck in motion.

Glen stood waving as we left the Alpha site behind, the truck accelerating fast and bouncing along the well-worn ruts in the ground. He was soon lost in the distance.

"You know, it's a good thing we're not trying to hide our location from anyone out here," said Espera, which took my mind off Glen.

"Why's that?" asked Pearson.

"Because our ruts from the weekly resupply runs would give us away," I replied, going through the checklist of what we had loaded onto the backs of the trucks.

My CASE-2XC Dog and two PACE suits with enough ammunition to start a small war in a Third World country of choice were on the lead truck. The second truck had Espera's CAS-3-Mod 1 Ape suit, and spares of everything we could think of, like more Beowulf assault rifles for everyone.

"Good thing we're the only people on-planet then," said Pearson.

"Well, apart from the aliens, you mean," said Keith.

"Or, as and when the Chinese show up to stick their noses in things," I replied as I checked my PAD.

We had pretty much packed everything we might need, done on the basis that we would do the mission faff when we got to Camp Bravo. Assuming, of course, we had the luxury of taking the time to do so then.

"How likely is that, LT?" asked Espera.

He meant the chances Chinese being on-planet.

"Depends on whether or not they have figured out there are people they can send through if suitably shielded, or whether they're exploring alternative options," I replied. "Or even if their pillars open up onto this world."

"Sounds like it's way above what I need to worry about. Why don't we put some music on?"

"Sounds like a plan to me. What have you got to listen to?"

"I thought we'd start with Rammstein's *Amerika* and then Hawkwind Resurrection's *Silver Machine*, and take it from there."

"This is going to be a long trip!" groaned Keith.

"Who let him choose the music?" added Pearson.

"You two stop your griping and try to get some Z's," said Espera. "We're not listening to any of that Fisheye-Zoom nonsense."

Ignoring the exchange, I sat back as the lyrics about living in America drowned out the rest of the conversation, which was rather the point of playing loud music in a noisy truck when one wanted to get some shut-eye.

The first four hours of the journey passed without incident.

Then we stopped for five mikes to change positions and take the opportunity for a quick piss before getting back in the truck for the next shift. The guys were always surprised to find out that I didn't need a toilet break any more than they did.

59. TO THE RESCUE

Discipline is the soul of an army. It makes small numbers formidable; procures success to the weak, and esteem to all.

— GEORGE WASHINGTON

Technical Sergeant Ferretti
Two Moons Bravo Site
Monday, January 16, 2073

Ferretti had chosen the route for Wachowski and Jordan to take to the missing team outside of town. He cursed under his breath as the feed from the truck went blank as it descended into the gully.

A wave of helplessness took hold of him, but lives depended on him, so he was going to do his job to the best of his ability. Right now that meant letting go of the things he couldn't control and doing the things that he could.

"Foxtrot Alpha, this is Foxtrot Bravo Six, come in. Over."

"This is Foxtrot Alpha receiving loud and clear. Over."

"Can you put me through to Mr. Anderson? Over."

"Roger that. Putting you through now. Wait one while I transfer you to visual. Over."

After a few minutes, he heard, "Anderson here. Over."

Then the full audio-visual feed came up on his screen.

"I want to ask you to launch the UAV to give us aerial eyes on Timakira."

"We're in the process of bringing our bird home now to refuel her and send her your way. The lieutenant thought you might like us to do that for you. Over."

"Does she always think of everything?"

"She's the lieutenant, but no, she doesn't always. I asked her whether she wanted the UAV up, and she said yes. What's up, Ferretti?"

"I've lost people, and things look hopeless. And the team I sent out has entered a radio blind spot. I needed someone to talk to."

"I won't tell you to not worry, because we both know that doesn't work. What would you say to somebody under your command who was worried they'd dropped the ball, but hadn't?"

"I'd ask them if they had done everything they needed to do. Kept a record of what they'd done for later and gone over the other things they should be doing that need to be done."

"Sounds like good advice to me."

"It sounds to me like I have a handle on what I'm doing."

"Sure does, and don't you forget it. If you need to talk more, you know where I am."

Ferretti cut the feed and started checking to ensure everything that had happened today was logged and images of key events were tagged. He then wrote his summary, a record of his orders and his aims.

Next, he went to check his weapon, making sure it was clean and that he had enough magazines prepped so he could unload one per android.

60. RETREAT OR DIE

Courage is knowing what not to fear.

— Plato

Corporal Wachowski
Two Moons Outside Timakira
Monday, January 16, 2073

Wachowski was relieved when the rock-strewn gully widened ahead of the truck. The twenty-kilometer journey into town had turned a half-hour dash into a four-hour marathon of wending their way through impassable-looking terrain.

However, the Oshkosh, while not as nimble as a recreational four-by-four, had ample power and lots of clever computer-controlled systems. This allowed it to go places and do things that defied ready comprehension.

She was sure that if she put the video up on the net, people wouldn't believe what they were seeing.

"OK, how're we doing on the map, Jordan?"

"We're about five klicks from the nearest point where this gully passes the last known point of our other team."

"I know I shouldn't have asked the are-we-nearly-there-yet question."

"I make it thirty klicks we've come so far."

"Not exactly a shortcut then. I was wondering whether we should've waited for the Crocomodos to pass by and come the other way."

"We could still be waiting, for all you know," said Jordan.

"As they say, better to do *something* than do *nothing*."

The truck ground on down the gully that had gradually widened out as they got nearer to Timakira. Wachowski reckoned that they would have to get out on foot for the last bit of their journey, to be safe.

"Have we communications back up?"

"Not yet."

Another hour passed with only the rumble of the truck's engine in the background. They finally made it to the point on the map closest to where contact had been lost with Baptista and Nelson.

"Time to have a look around and see what we find up there."

"You don't sound too hopeful."

"Just being a realist, Jordan. I'll be amazed if we find anyone alive."

They got out of the truck together, and Wachowski put it into standby mode, which would allow her to call it if needed.

With the sun due to set in about an hour, it had become a long day that was no doubt going to end with them finding dead colleagues. She led the way up the slope and made sure that her MACE suit ChameleonFlage was working before she stuck her head up to look around.

The town of Timakira was hidden behind a low ridge in the

far distance. In front of them was an undulating plain crisscrossed with fields and irrigation trenches.

"Can you see at my eleven, about two klicks out, something that may be bodies?"

"No—yes, I can. Got it."

"OK, let's move out, ten-meter interval at all times."

Wachowski crawled over the edge of the gully and slid down the other side before rising, hoping that she had not been outlined against the sky if the androids were watching for the shimmer of movement.

The two klicks took them an hour to cross as they navigated their way around obstacles and kept themselves concealed by moving from cover to cover.

They were nearly on top of their objective when Wachowski realized she was looking at the back of a PACE suit that was knelt on the ground. It was holding another PACE suit and gently rocking.

She could hear crying.

A few meters away were the remains of two bodies that had been blown apart by gunfire.

"This is Wachowski. Identify yourself."

"Uhh what, did someone say something? They're all dead, Donna. The dead don't speak."

Nelson was talking to herself, which was never a good sign in Wachowski's book.

"I'm coming over to you, Nelson. It's me—Wachowski—here to help you."

"No one can help; they're all dead. Can't you see? Look around you. They're all dead. Why am I still alive?"

Wachowski went to Nelson and removed the rifle from beside the woman. It was clear that Nelson was in shock from what had happened.

"Jordan, you've got the body bags, right?" she asked as Jordan joined her.

"Yes, I have."

"I know it's a shitty job, but I need you to pack up the scientists' bodies while I attend to Nelson here. You got that?"

"Yeah, I've got it. Leave it to me, Corporal."

Wachowski pulled out her first aid kit.

She found a tranquilizer and gave it to Nelson, who had, at the minimum, cracked ribs judging by the impact on her chest plate. Nelson was lucky to be alive, though the woman probably didn't think so now surrounded by her dead colleagues.

Jordan was handling the grisly job of packing the remains of the two scientists into separate body bags. But the problem was how to move three dead bodies and the walking wounded back to the truck.

It was now dark, and it would require at least two trips to carry the bodies out.

Wachowski brought up the link to the truck and was relieved to get a weak signal. She initiated the autostart-up and tracking function. The truck's expert system would now work out a route from where it was to where she was and make its way to them.

She could hear it in the distance.

"Jordan, how you doing?"

"I'm good. Not something I want to be doing every day, mind you."

Jordan sounded like she had got a handle on herself. Now all they had to do was wait for the truck to arrive, load up, and go back the way they'd come. Sounded like a plan to her.

The silence was broken as Wachowski's radio came to life.

"Foxtrot Bravo Three, this is Foxtrot Bravo Six, come in. Over," said Sergeant Ferretti.

"Solid copy. Over," she replied, realizing now that the truck was out of the gully communication had been restored.

"Give me a SITREP. Over."

"Made contact with missing team. Both scientists and Baptista are down. Nelson's alive. Over."

"Roger that. Bring them home. Acknowledge. Over."

"Wilco, bringing the team home. Out."

It took fifteen mikes for the truck to reach them. By then Nelson had stopped crying and rocking. Jordan helped Wachowski get Nelson up onto her feet and guided her into the back seat of the truck.

Next, the two of them went back and picked up the two body bags, putting them in the truck bed, and finally dragged Baptista in his PACE suit and lifted him into the back of the truck, too.

As Wachowski got into the truck, she saw the light of tracer rounds skipping off the ground around them.

"Shit! Who's firing at us?" asked Jordan.

"Our local friendly neighborhood androids, of course!" she shouted as she slung the truck into reverse and accelerated back the way it had come.

"Should I fire back?" asked Jordan.

"No, don't give our position away. It's just firing in our general area. If it knew where we were, it would have hit us already. They must have tracked our radio call," she said as the ping of several rounds clipped the truck. "Now you should be firing."

Jordan opened up the Browning and returned fire.

The roar in the cab of the truck was deafening, and the overpressure could be felt through the soft-skinned vehicle. The night sky lit up with tracers. Wachowski had the truck doing zigzags as it traveled backwards along the gully.

Another round hit the vehicle like a hammer, reverberating around them.

"Aah, I'm hit!" shouted Nelson behind them.

Wachowski looked over her shoulder and saw that a round had ricocheted and caught Nelson in the leg.

Nelson was not having a good day of it. Not the time to be doing anything while they were still in the open. Wachowski ordered the truck to do a skid turn that would face its rear towards the incoming fire.

The Oshkosh slewed around 180 degrees, with the tires tearing up the surface over which they were traveling. It ended in a lurch as the truck wrenched itself around. Wachowski put the pedal to the metal, overriding the autodrive control over their speed, as more enemy fire sought them out in the darkness.

"Everybody hold tight!"

She screamed as the truck went up the embankment, grabbing air and crashing down into the gully with tracer fire lighting up overhead.

She punched the emergency stop, and the truck only ground itself into the other side, rather than smashing into it.

On her panel a multitude of red flags had come up. They wouldn't have to walk back to camp, but this truck was a write-off.

"Jordan, check on Nelson; she's bleeding."

"On it," said Jordan as she climbed into the rear of the cab. She got out a first aid kit, stripped the leg armor off Nelson, and applied quick clot. "It's not as bad as it looks; it cut across the outside of her leg. It would have been much worse had it hit the inside and nicked the femoral artery."

"Good work. I'll get us out of here. Just so you know, it's going to be a long, slow ride back to base," she said, hoping that the androids didn't decide to follow them and finish them off.

61. DRONE

Opportunities multiply as they are seized.

— SUN TZU

Technical Sergeant Ferretti
Two Moons Bravo Site
Monday, January 16, 2073

The feeds from the UAV's cameras were on Ferretti's main screen. He'd put up small windows showing what the androids were seeing. From this he was able to identify where each android was in the town.

It seemed as if they were using the QuadMules and the truck to recharge themselves.

The one good thing he'd discovered was that the androids had stopped firing on the aliens. It probably came down to the fact that all the aliens had fled indoors and were hiding.

So far it had been a long day, and it didn't look like it was going to be over anytime soon, either.

"Calling Foxtrot Bravo Six, come in. Over." The radio transmission broke the silence.

"Receiving you loud and clear. Over."

"Anderson here, just checking in on you. We've spotted the truck on its way back to you, and we're transmitting the aerial feeds from CYCLOPS to you now. We confirm three live occupants in the truck. Over."

"I've got it up on my monitor now. Over," he replied, catching the IR feed from the UAV unfolding in shades of ghostly green. He stopped it and rewound, paused, and played the feed forward again. "Thanks for that. Over."

"All part of the service. We've got your board covered, so why don't you go and catch some Z's while we watch the fort for you. The lieutenant is going to need you to be at your best when she arrives tomorrow. If anything happens, we'll wake you. Over."

Ferretti checked the time and saw it was midnight. "Can you wake me in four hours, or if anything happens? Over."

"Sure, we'll wake you if anything happens. Get some rest. Trust me, it's going to be another long day tomorrow. Anderson, out."

Ferretti went and grabbed his bag and ground mat from the tent and carried them back in the darkness to the control room. He couldn't be assed to eat anything, so he settled himself down on the floor and zipped up his sleeping bag. Staring at the ceiling, he starting thinking about what had happened during the day and passed out.

The noise from the radio startled him awake, and he fumbled his way out of his sleeping bag.

"Ferretti here. Over."

"This is your complimentary early morning wake-up call. Just to let you know, we're still tracking the progress of Wachowski's truck, and we estimate by their speed it will take them about another hour to arrive. Also, Lieutenant Tachikoma wants to speak to you. Over," came the voice of one of the new UAV operators from the Alpha site.

"Roger that, patch me through to the lieutenant. Over."

"This is Foxtrot Alpha Six to Foxtrot Bravo Six, are you receiving me? Over."

"Receiving you loud and clear. Over."

"Ferretti, I wanted to let you know we're going to take an alternative route to get to you due to Crocomodos on the regular trail. Over."

"Do you have an ETA for when, ma'am? Over."

"Best guess, about three hours from now. Mr. Anderson's maps came in most handy, but the route swings us right in a wide loop, which will bring us in from the east. Over."

"Roger that, ma'am. We'll have coffee on for when you arrive. Over."

"Thanks, we'll look forward to that. Out."

62. GET SOME, LOSE SOME

If a man will begin with certainties, he shall end in doubts, but if he will be content to begin with doubts, he shall end in certainties.

— FRANCIS BACON

Corporal Wachowski
Two Moons Bravo Site
Tuesday, January 17, 2073

Wachowski, Jordan, and Nelson saw the first light of the new day as they approached Camp Bravo. Wachowski sounded the horn, and Ferretti come out of the command container.

She thought that the look of relief on his face was priceless.

He ran up to the truck.

"I guess the radio got hit in the firefight."

"How did you know we were in a firefight?"

"Courtesy of Mr. Anderson and his all-singing, all-dancing reconnaissance UAV. It recorded the whole action from the air. The android team hunted the plain for several hours before giving up on finding you. It was lucky that they didn't have the aerial maps to locate the gully," he said, as he stepped onto the cab step, grabbing a handle as the truck crept into the camp, making a grinding noise from bent axles rubbing against bearings.

"I'm afraid the truck's transaxle is blown, and she's pretty much a write-off. I'm surprised we made it back, to be honest."

"Don't worry; they'll bill you later," said Jordan.

"How's Nelson?" Ferretti asked.

"Pretty banged up, and still out of it. I sedated her. She needs a proper medic to check her over, though," said Jordan.

"The good news is that the lieutenant will be arriving soon with reinforcements."

"Well, I hope she's got a good plan because so far the androids having been kicking our asses," she said.

"The lieutenant has a plan, and she's bringing combat armor," said Ferretti.

"Rock on. Payback's a bitch," said Jordan.

"Yeah, but you know what? Right now I need some chow, and to catch some rack time before the fun begins again."

"You can say that again," said Jordan.

"I'll make us all breakfast. No expense spared—I'll even raid the special supplies. Do you think Nelson will want to eat?" asked Ferretti.

"Thanks, that sounds great. I think we should get her out of her suit and put her in her rack until she comes around."

They worked together to lift Nelson out of the back of the cab and take her to the women's tent.

Wachowski and Jordan stripped her out of the suit and removed her soiled uniform.

There was a big bruise on her sternum, and the leg dressing needed changing. Judging by the bandage, she'd lost a lot of blood for what had only been a grazing round. Then again it had been a

Beowulf short-fifty doing the grazing, and it could've been a whole lot worse.

Wachowski cleaned the wound up and redressed it.

No doubt Corpsman Keith could do something better when he arrived. By the time they'd finished stripping out of their own gear, breakfast was ready. Just as Ferretti had promised.

There were eggs to go with the tinned sausage and beans. Not only eggs but orange juice from a carton, too. They both ate like they hadn't eaten for a week, even though less than a full day had passed.

Afterwards, Ferretti insisted that she and Jordan get in some horizontal time in their racks before the big day began in earnest.

63. LEAVE NO ONE BEHIND

A good plan, violently executed now, is better than a perfect plan next week.

— Gen George S. Patton, USAR

First Lieutenant Lara Atsuko Tachikoma
Two Moons Bravo Site
Tuesday, January 17, 2073

We drove over the last rise, and Camp Bravo came into view as the truck dipped forward. It had taken us twenty-one hours to drive, which included a diversion made to avoid migratory Crocomodos.

The small group of tents with a solitary Conex box was surrounded by wire strung to form a perimeter to keep small local wildlife out. Camouflage netting covered the camp and provided both concealment and some shade from the sun's rays.

More by luck than judgement the campsite had been placed some way off from where the Crocomodos were likely to walk on their way to their breeding pools out in the desert.

As we drove our two trucks through the gap in the perimeter wire and came to a halt, I saw Technical Sergeant Ferretti waiting to meet us.

"Morning, ma'am, good to see you."

"You too. Any updates I need to know about?" I asked as I got out of the truck, while Corpsman Keith went off to attend to Specialist Nelson's wound.

"The androids are still in the town. They appear to be recharging themselves in rotation using the two QuadMules' atomic batteries and the captured truck as a generator, too," said Ferretti leading us towards his control center.

"So much for an automatic shutdown to conserve core power then."

"Wasn't likely to happen, ma'am, whatever the scientists might have hoped. The good news is that they haven't gone on a killing rampage across the town. After the initial shootings, where we estimate between two hundred and fifty and three hundred and fifty aliens were shot, the androids have stopped firing."

"Is that them conserving their ammunition?"

"I doubt it's down to ammunition, because they captured a load of ours when they took the truck. My guess—it's indicative of something else. It's certainly not like what happened in '37."

"That's pretty scary emergent behavior to see in an android. OK then, we need to come up with a plan before we go in."

I brought up the feeds from the UAV.

The map showed the town with a drawing of the streets overlaid on top of it. Flashing red icons showed the androids moving around, and green ones showed the last known locations of the science teams.

"Can you bring up the androids' movements since the time they went rogue on us?"

"Sure thing, ma'am. Just give me a moment and I'll put it on the monitor to your left."

Ferretti ran the recordings for me.

This showed where the androids had started and where they'd moved since the initiation of the One-Zero-One protocol. I sensed a pattern emerge from the routes that showed two pairs of androids patrolling while four stayed back at a central point as they walked around the town. This, I imagined, was their reserve, which left the question of the truck and the QuadMules, and what the androids would decide to do with them.

I walked to the door of the control center and looked around for Espera, who I saw was checking the CASE suits.

"Staff Sergeant, rally everyone for the briefing in ten!" I shouted.

"Yes, LT."

The situation in Timakira reminded me a bit of the hostage scenario during my training at The Basic School. Except this time we didn't have air assets to help drop us on top of the bad guys.

Retrieving the two civilian science teams had to be our top priority, but the question was how to prevent the androids from interfering with us while doing so. On the other hand, if I made taking the androids down the priority, more of our civilians might be killed or injured.

As I stood there thinking, the control room filled up.

My command amounted to six effectives plus myself. We were going up against eight androids in an urban environment. Not good.

"We're ready, ma'am," said Ferretti, breaking my train of thought.

"I have two objectives for the mission we are about to undertake. The first is the safe retrieval of our civilian scientists. We believe both teams are alive. The second is the elimination of the androids."

Everyone nodded.

This operation could so easily become a total clusterfuck of epic proportions.

"You all know the situation we face. We will form two teams. Staff Sergeant Espera and myself will be in our respective combat armor suits acting as a blocking force. Technical Sergeant Ferretti will lead the rescue party, with Pearson, Wachowski, Jordan, and Keith. Is that clear?"

Nelson hobbled into the room on a makeshift crutch, looking battered and bruised.

"Sorry I'm late, Lieutenant, ma'am."

I looked at Keith, who stared over my shoulder.

My decision it seemed. She had spirit to step up to the plate. I thought about what lay ahead of us. We would need everyone to put themselves on the line to pull this mission off.

I nodded at her and continued speaking.

"Keith will coordinate the on-site treatment of any wounded while Ferretti's team will provide perimeter security. Espera and I will draw as much fire from the androids as possible until the civilians are secured. Technical Sergeant Ferretti, once the civilians are aboard the trucks, I want you to exfiltrate them from the town with all haste."

I paused for a moment—Espera was hanging loose, looking relaxed. I remembered when I was a sergeant and used to do that, too. Ferretti was tense and scowling, but he said nothing.

"What about load-outs?" asked Sergeant Pearson.

"You'll be carrying the Beowulfs we brought. I want you all carrying twelve magazines, given we only have dumb ammo, and one-shot rocket-launcher tubes. My Dog will be carrying a standard 20 mm autocannon with underbarrel grenade launcher, and I have my M240L for backup, and a one-shot antivehicle missile pack. Staff Sergeant Espera's Ape has an M75 80 mm recoilless autocannon, a GAU M134, and a missile pack as backup."

"What about me, ma'am?"

Nelson looked like she might collapse at any moment. I knew she needed to be in on this mission, otherwise she'd never be able to look at herself in the mirror again.

"I want you here coordinating communications and relaying information on the androids' movements as we track them. Do you think you can handle that?"

"Yes, ma'am," she replied, looking relieved at having some role to play in the events that were about to unfold.

We could run everything through the main base control center. But *one is none, and two is one.*

"Espera and I will be using call sign Tic-Tac. Ferretti, your team will be Scooter. Nelson, you'll be Eyeball."

Ferretti asked, "Which of the two primary objectives do you wish to start with first, ma'am?"

"Getting to the scientists. My understanding is that Dr. Leung was shot in the library. The others were lost from the androids' feeds at one of the marketplaces, and we have no clues as to what happened to them afterwards. Dr. Leung will be in need of treatment, so I think we have to prioritize the library as our first objective. However, if the androids decide to engage us during our approach, which makes this impossible, then Espera and I will engage and hold them while the primary team proceeds to the secondary site."

My team was nodding in agreement.

"This situation sucks big time, but I know I can rely on you all to remember your training, and no one can ask you for any more than that. I can't make you any guarantees about the fight ahead of us, but I promise you this, we will get our people out."

"Ooooraaah!" shouted Wachowski, followed by a couple of "huahs" and "hell yeahs." And on that note, we went forth to prepare for battle.

Our three trucks drew up outside of Timakira using the ChameleonFlage to help us blend in with our surroundings. We stopped about four hundred meters from the entrance to the town on the back slope of a small rise in the terrain.

There, Espera and I got out and mounted our combat armor suits, each of them an expression of our respective service's belief that its way was the right way.

Marine Dogs' AI could be assigned a variable priority of either processing or piloting or shooting, and we were always ready to go into the wet stuff. Army Apes had a separate gunnery and piloting AI subroutine and needed to be prepared for water operation.

You wouldn't catch me using an Ape combat armor suit unless I had to, regardless of the fact that the two suits were very similar in their performance. I like to think of it as my preference for the smoother movement from the AI interface.

I'm probably deluded, but there again, so is everyone else for that matter.

The heat of the afternoon sun was unforgiving, and I was glad to be buttoned up inside my Dog with the air-con to keep me cool. All the systems checked out as nominal, with green flags across the board.

"Scooter Six, this is Tic-Tac Six, come in. Over."

"Receiving you loud and clear. Over," replied Ferretti.

"Just a check-in call to make sure we're good. Over."

"Eyeball confirms we've got you on the CYCLOPS feeds, and Tic-Tac Four has just opened a channel to me, too. Over," Nelson said.

"Roger that. We're going in now. Out," I replied and switched channels. "Tic-Tac Four, take point. I'll cover the rear. Over."

"Roger that. Out," said Espera, moving his Ape forward to the front of the convoy.

Ferretti started moving the trucks into the town.

The feed from the UAV was on my screen. It showed the position of the eight androids, with icons for whether they were stationary or moving.

So far, they were maintaining the same pattern of two pairs patrolling and four in reserve. One pair was on the opposite side of town to the north of us, while the other pair was to our east.

Hopefully, we would get to our objective without drawing attention to our movement.

My Dog passed under the archway into the town.

We transitioned from a nice open countryside to the confines of an urban environment. If we lost track of the android teams' movements in here, we would be vulnerable to all kinds of bad.

My eye in the sky was feeding me the tracking information, and everything was looking good.

Our convoy wound its way towards the center of town where the hall and the library were. We had to keep to the broader route that wound around the higgledy-piggledy arrangement of buildings that passed for planning here.

It allowed us to maneuvre the trucks without having to do three-point turns and lower property values by bashing walls down, which, more importantly, would draw unwanted attention to us.

Espera raised the arm of his Ape to signal the convoy to stop.

"Tic-Tac Six, I am looking at the entrance to the main town hall and…and I'm relaying visuals now. Over."

I checked what Espera was seeing. There were fifty dead aliens ahead. They lay rotting in the heat of the day, with insects flying around as the only movement.

"Roger that. Got the feed. Proceed left and I'll go right as we deploy into the square. Out."

Espera's Ape moved forward and to the left flank of the building across the square.

Wachowski drove her truck to the left side of the building. Then Ferretti, Jordan, and Keith took their truck in and swung it around 90 degrees to block the entrance, while Pearson took the last truck to the right side to form the final part of a hasty laager.

Following behind in my Dog, I took up my place to the right of the formation where I could block any android advance that might come that way.

The feed from the UAV showed the pair of androids patrolling to the east of us was proceeding along its usual route. I had to wonder why they hadn't varied the pattern of their patrols. Still, even as things stood, it wasn't looking good for us.

I started to consider my tactical options.

Wachowski, Jordan, and Pearson dismounted from their trucks and took up firing positions, while Ferretti and Keith made their way to the door of the building.

"Tic-Tac Six, the door is barred. We've tried kicking it, but it won't budge. Over," said Ferretti.

"Roger that. I'll get you an assist. Over," I said, changing channels to speak. "Tic-Tac Four, move to assist to Scooter Six's position and kick open the door. Over."

"Wilco. Over," said Espera.

He took his Ape between the trucks and walked up to the imposing wooden door of the town hall. I heard a crash as he kicked the door in.

"Scooter team is in. Over," he said, moving his Ape back to where he could block an advance trying to flank us on our left.

The minutes passed like snails in a quarter-mile drag race.

"Tic-Tac Six, this is Scooter Six, come in. Over."

"What you got for me? Over."

"Keith is with Dr. Leung treating him for a chest wound. It's amazing he has survived this long, but Keith says he is going to need thirty mikes to stabilize his patient before moving him. Over."

And that is, as they say, how Murphy strikes the best laid plans.

What I hadn't accounted for was us needing thirty minutes before we could move. This town was big, but it wouldn't take the android patrol to the east of us more than twenty minutes to get here.

Once we kicked off, the other patrol would be alerted, as would the reserve.

I knew that we would have to face the androids at some point, but I didn't want to have to do so while the primary team was still recovering the civilians.

However, fire superiority is the best medicine.

So, I was about to do something that a commander should never do: divide a force in the field and risk a defeat in detail. I brought Espera and Ferretti onto the command channel.

"Tic-Tac Four and Scooter Six, switch to command channel one. Over."

"Tic-Tac Four, wilco. Over."

"Scooter Six, receiving. Over."

"Change of plan, people. Ferretti, I want you to stay here and keep the perimeter secure until such time as Doc can move his patient. When you can extract them both, let me know and then take your trucks to objective two to secure the other civilians. Espera we're going to intercept the two android patrols, destroy them, and then swing around behind where their reserve force is. My intention is to distract the androids and keep our combat armor between them and the primary team. Am I understood? Over."

"Are you sure you want to split us up now? Wouldn't it be better to wait? Over," said Ferretti.

"They'll catch us here if we do, and ream us a new one if we get pinned down. Over," said Espera.

"My thoughts exactly. This situation sucks big time, and we will just have to suck it up. Out."

My Dog rushed towards the oncoming android patrol, weaving in and around the clusters of buildings in the aliens' town.

My main screen showed the outsides of their rectangular structures with small windows and an occasional second story on the larger buildings. If they had been made of anything more than baked mud, I would have climbed up on top of the flat roofs.

But I was under no illusion that those buildings could support the weight of my Dog for one instant.

In one corner of my screen, I had the feed from Espera's Ape, and in the other, the one from the UAV flying overhead.

I was tracking their route and calculating the best way to circle around and come up behind the android patrol. I had hoped the buildings would hide the noise of my approach.

But luck wasn't favoring me this day.

As I neared, the two androids separated, moving apart and trying to circle around behind me.

That only went to show that they may have been androids, but they were not deaf to the sound of an approaching CASE-2XC Dog bearing down on them. And definitely not dumb. My ChameleonFlage couldn't hide the noise of my Dog but it might give me an edge when the shooting started.

Dirt on the ground kicked up as incoming fire came my way.

The *bang-bang-bang* of the androids' Beowulf rounds hit my Dog, and the sound reverberated inside my suit. I twisted around in the direction where the shots had come from. A shadow of an android moved across the ground behind me.

I realized that while I couldn't take my Dog onto the roofs of the buildings that hemmed me in, they were under no such restriction.

This was followed by another series of bangs as a burst of fire hit my suit, the shots ricochetting off my rear armor. While the Beowulf rounds wouldn't breach my Dog's armor with one hit, they would eventually break through a joint and cause damage if they could bring sustained fire to bear on me.

Moving forward, I spun my Dog around, running backwards, and letting the suit's AI system keep me from falling.

I tagged both androids on the targeting computer and followed their movement as they ran across the roofs of the buildings, jumping across the alleyways to try to catch me in a crossfire. I chose the one farthest away from me as my primary target, as it was easier to track and I could get a lock on it.

As it cleared the parapet of the building, it became partially exposed.

I fired a round from my 20 mm autocannon to teach it the lesson that concealment is not the same as cover. It fell off the roof from the concussive force of the armor-piercing shell blowing apart the parapet, giving me time to turn again.

I rushed towards the other android, which had closed with me.

I barged into it with my Dog, which flung it through the air like a rag doll. Unfortunately, unlike a broken doll, the little bugger got up and started shooting at me almost immediately. The things reacted unbelievably fast to whatever I threw at them.

I fired a quick burst at point-blank range with my M240L in my left arm, as I didn't have the autocannon lined up. My shots skimmed by the android. Close, but as they say, close only counts in tiddlywinks and nuclear war.

The android moved right down another alley.

I followed behind, all too aware of the other one behind me, but as my mom would say, what was sauce for the goose was also sauce for the gander.

Moving through the alleys, we all had trouble getting clear shots. The androids' real advantage over my Dog was the ability to get onto the roofs of the buildings. But by then they knew this would leave them open to being shot at.

I checked my screen and saw the androids were paralleling my course.

They were trying to move to cross me so I would have to turn to face one of them. But this gave me another opportunity to repeat the high-velocity lesson to the tin men. I drew up by the corner of one building that formed a T-junction ahead of me.

I positioned my Dog to face the building.

This allowed me to swing out the Dog's right arm with the autocannon out, using the feeds from both the gun and the UAV to target the android hiding behind the building.

I fired another 20 mm high-velocity tungsten penetrator through the wall of the building, throwing the android back off its feet as debris fell all around it.

Not waiting to see the result, I fired a grenade at it. Just so it would get the right message.

Shit, who was I kidding?

Androids don't know the meaning of the word *fear*; they're just relentless machines following preprogrammed algorithms. I wondered how I could use that against them.

More sounds of incoming fire as the other android took advantage of me while I was concentrating on its partner.

Damn, this could go on all day, I thought, which was fine, for some definitions of *fine* that meant it would allow the primary team to achieve their goal. However, it wasn't helping me much in eliminating the threat they posed, and those were just the first two of the eight we had to destroy.

Then one came towards me, and I moved my Dog away from the android, making them chase me.

My suit was faster, so I could open the range and fight on my terms. I kept an eye on them as they responded to my change of tactics, allowing my suit's expert system to drive my Dog.

Once clear, I switched back to manual drive.

This allowed me to devote my expert AI to predicting the androids' maneuvres and plot them with an autocorrect targeting algorithm. I figured the systems controlling the androids had to be similar to my Dog's, and that they would produce comparable solutions.

My hope was that it would give me the edge.

As I spun my machine around to turn back to face them. The two oncoming androids responded to my maneuvre by swerving right and left to split my fire.

The one on my left was tracking as my Dog's expert system had predicted, and would be taking up a position in cover while the other moved to flank me from the other side.

It seemed the lesson in high-velocity armor-piercing rounds would have to be given again. I fired, and the roar of my 20 mm echoed around me, the reverberations penetrating through my suit, and the wall of the building collapsed.

Turning the corner, I found the android regaining its feet.

But I didn't give it the time to complete its action, and double-tapped it with two 20 mm rounds that both hit center of mass, one above the other, punching two holes through it. The android flew back from the force of the blow, and its power cells caught fire.

A triple tap of shots caught my Dog in the back again, and I turned my attention to my other android problem.

Spinning my Dog, I drove towards it, forcing it to move out of the way if it didn't want to be crushed. My suit's systems were then in lockstep with it, predicting the android's every twist and turn as we started our deadly dance around each other.

I fired the second of my five grenades at where it was going to move next, which forced it to stop short.

I took the shot and blew its leg clean off as my 20 mm clipped the android. Not perfect, but close enough.

The android tried to balance on one leg and shot, stitching the front of my Dog with another burst of Beowulf rounds, emptying its magazine, and finally falling over in the process.

I returned the compliment and double-tapped it with some 20 mm love, getting the satisfaction of seeing it disintegrate in front of me.

I checked my autocannon ammo and realized I had fired eight shots in what felt like hours but had only been a few minutes. So I changed the magazine because I didn't want to be caught changing it when the other four androids arrived.

64. HIT HARD, MOVE FAST

Generally speaking, the way of the warrior is resolute acceptance of death.

— Miyamoto Musashi

Staff Sergeant Espera
Two Moons
Tuesday, January 17, 2073

Espera sat confined in the cramped cockpit of his Ape, planning on the best way to move north towards the two androids. He had to admire the lieutenant's ability to move her combat armor like it was a living thing, while he clunked along the narrow streets bumping into buildings.

The problem was that the pair of androids he was tracking were following a route that would bring them around behind him to where the primary team sat waiting.

The window on his main screen showed the feed from the lieutenant's machine. He compared it to the feed from the UAV flying overhead. In his opinion, it all came down to timing.

Get it right and he would get the drop on his targets.

Get it wrong and they would be all over him, and he would be in a world of pain and hurt. He'd fought enemy combat automatons before, and in his opinion, it was better never to underestimate what they could do.

Espera checked the route his two were expected to take and brought up the time before the lieutenant would encounter hers, comparing where he'd be in relation to his two targets. It was going to be a close-run thing, but if he could get in position to fire before the lieutenant did, then he would catch his pair by surprise.

He drove the Ape through the narrow streets as fast as he could, trying to swerve around obstacles and twisting sideways to get his machine into position to keep the noise down to a minimum. Having reached his chosen spot, he was gratified to be ahead of the game.

The lieutenant hadn't quite reached her targets, and his were due to appear ahead of him any moment.

Espera hunkered down and deployed his M75 over his left shoulder and the M134 on his suit's right-arm hard point, and then prepped his missiles. He tracked the inbound android while waiting.

He aimed his weapons up the street and fired just before the two androids walked into view, giving them enough lead to catch them.

The first shot from the M75 recoilless high-velocity autocannon streaked towards its target, smoke from the back blast sweeping everything out of its way behind his Ape. He fired the second shot as soon as he heard the target-lock signal.

The first shot caught the leading android and blew it into so many parts he would never have known that something had been there a moment ago.

The other was thrown back by the force of the blast, making the second shot miss and explode against a building.

Damn it! He wasn't able to shoot at it again before it got to its feet.

On his screen he saw the android react to the lieutenant's Dog, and he knew they'd just stirred up a hornets' nest. He got his Ape up and in gear. It didn't matter where it went, because moving was better than staying still and becoming a target.

Espera tracked his other android running parallel to him and turned hard right down a side alley to cut it off from getting behind him.

His Ape suit skidded as he brought it to a halt to turn to face the oncoming android. But there was nothing on his screen.

Then he heard the crash of the android hitting as it jumped from the roof while taking the opportunity to kick his Ape suit in the head.

Espera swore as his machine toppled forward.

The android rode his suit into the ground all the while firing shots at him that sounded like hammers hitting a door.

Whoomph! The fall knocked the wind out of him.

He pushed himself off the ground as the android ran away down one of the numerous alleyways that passed for streets in this alien town. Then he picked up his M75 recoilless autocannon, slung it across the back of his machine, and switched targeting to the M134.

This was not going to be an easy day.

He sprinted in his Ape, following the route of the fleeing android.

Checking the feed from the UAV, he saw the other four androids that had been stationary were now on the move— closing towards him but also headed in the general direction of the primary team.

He had to distract the androids to prevent them from cutting Ferretti's people to pieces, so he swung left to try to flank them, forcing them to respond to the threat he posed.

Trouble was, it would mean putting his head into the hands of the androids.

Espera took a moment as the situation unfolded and allowed his suit's AI to guide his machine to the point he'd designated on the map. The lieutenant was in a furball with two androids but seemed to be holding her own.

He saw the androids respond to his maneuvre and let out a sigh of relief that his plan had worked. Now all he had to do was give them the runaround and shoot them up one by one.

How hard could that be?

The buzz of incoming rounds flying past him brought him back to the here and now. Shit, they were all over him like flies over dead meat.

He jinked his Ape left and right, zigzagging his way round and sometimes through obstacles as he accelerated away from the androids, drawing them off their course.

He counted five of them: one on each side and three trailing him through the town as he swept north and east. Every minute they chased him, he drew them farther away from the primary team, buying time for the medic to treat his patient.

"Tic-Tac Six, this is Four, I could do with a hand here. Over!" he shouted over the radio.

"Roger that. I'm coming up on your six, be with you in five. Out," came Tachikoma's reply.

Now all he had to do was not get himself killed in the next five minutes, and he and the lieutenant would kick these androids into touch. Still looked like it was going to be easier said than done, all things considered.

More firing came from his rear, with bullets tracking his Ape's path.

He swung left down an alley, spun on the spot, and stopped.

Spooling up the M134, he started spewing forth a wall of steel-jacketed rounds back in the general direction of the androids following him. His fire had the desired effect of causing them to spread out, forcing them to move into cover.

Espera then swept the barrel upwards to fire another burst as he saw one of the flanking androids jump from roof to roof across the alley in front of him.

The sound of more shots hitting the rear of his Ape hammered home the precariousness of his situation. He spun his machine round and got the hell away from the trap they were preparing for him.

65. MOVE IT

War is the father of us all, king of all. Some it makes gods, some it makes men, some it makes slaves, some free.

— HERACLITUS

Technical Sergeant Ferretti
Two Moons Timakira
Tuesday, January 17, 2073

Ferretti hated wearing a PACE suit, as it always made him feel like a clumsy elephant barging around a room.

He'd already side-swiped the entrance to the door following Corpsman Keith into the library. So he stood back and let Keith, who was far more adroit at moving in his suit, attend to Dr. Leung.

Luckily, Dr. Leung had been shot in the chest at close range by one of the androids that had been carrying a 5.56 caliber rifle. The bullet had gone in one side and out the other.

Ferretti was surprised to find him still alive after all the time that had passed.

"How's it going, Keith?"

"All things considered, pretty good, but I'll be a while. Dr. Leung is one tough old bird, but what saved his life was Dr. Pham's first aid. However, he's been bleeding inside his pleural cavity, and I need to drain the blood, as it is causing pressure on the lungs and heart."

"Will he live?" asked Dr. Pham.

"I can't guarantee that, but I will do everything I can to make sure he does, ma'am. The only reason he's still alive is because of what you did. You know that, don't you?"

Grace nodded and held David's hand. "Hang in there."

Ferretti reported the situation to the lieutenant as Keith intubated his patient and started to drain blood from the wounded man's chest. After that Keith set up a drip and asked Grace to hold it up for him.

A few minutes later, he heard, "Tic-Tac Six to Scooter Six, come in. Over."

"Receiving you loud and clear. Over," he replied, listening to what the lieutenant told him. "OK, listen up, Keith—I've got to go outside and make sure we're ready for when the shit hits the fan. You let me know ASAP when Dr. Leung is ready to be moved."

"Aye, aye, copy that," replied Keith.

Ferretti turned and knocked a table over, which crashed to the ground, and strode out of the room, trying to not knock anything else over.

He remembered to twist his body to get through the door without bashing into it. Not his most dignified exit. Then he walked through the main hall, where some of the aliens were huddled together in the corners.

He wondered why they didn't leave and go to their homes; on the other hand, perhaps they were smart enough to realize it might get them shot.

Hiding when the bullets were flying always struck Ferretti as the best course of action.

Walking outside, he shouted out, "Pearson, report!"

"Perimeter secured, Sergeant. No sign of any hostiles."

No sign for now, but he was an android operator and knew they would soon figure out they were being distracted from something.

Their AIs were good at analyzing actions, and it wouldn't take them long to realize that the two combat armor suits were now engaging them for a reason. Androids had a special kind of dumb/smart balance that came from their stochastic programming algorithms, which was soon going to bite the team in the ass.

"Everyone sit tight and keep your eyes peeled for movement. Shout out if you see anything you don't like the look of. We've got to hold here awhile until Keith gives the word we can move," he said, hearing a chorus of replies from his team.

He patrolled the inside of the perimeter as they waited.

Nelson called, "Scooter Six, this is Eyeball, come in. Over."

"Receiving. Over," he replied, worried what Nelson might have to convey.

"You got incoming hostiles approaching. Over."

Before he could reply, Jordan shouted, "Contact! On my nine o'clock. Movement spotted. It's the truck we lost control of turning out of an alley about fifty meters away."

Ferretti turned to face the threat.

"Lay down fire now!" he shouted to Jordan as incoming fifty cal BMG rounds came from the truck.

Jordan returned fire as the truck moved towards their position.

"Wachowski, Pearson, provide support for Jordan."

The truck was trying to block his team's progress.

He ran across the front of the building with Wachowski following him. Pearson was duckwalking towards the corner of the building, keeping himself under cover. Jordan was kneeling by her truck, firing at the oncoming vehicle, which he couldn't yet see.

"Talk to me, Jordan. What's going on?"

"Inbound truck with a bad attitude." As more incoming rounds flew past her, she continued, "I think it's going to try to ram us, Sergeant."

He stopped for a moment to twist and grab the one-shot missile tube strapped to his back. Wachowski had moved up and thrown herself flat on the ground beside Pearson, and they were firing around the corner at the oncoming truck.

"Lay it on!" shouted Wachowski.

Ferretti prepped the missile as the front of the truck clipped the corner of the building, and Wachowski and Pearson rolled out of the way to avoid being hit. The truck then swerved left before it began a swing around to ram their parked truck, which served as part of his team's laager.

Jordan got up and started running out of the way of the oncoming vehicle, firing as she moved. Then the truck's machine gun caught her with a burst of shots, which cut her in two.

"Wachowski, get down!" Ferretti screamed, as he shouldered the missile launcher and acquired a target lock on the oncoming truck.

He pulled the trigger, and the missile flew into the truck with a dull *whumph* as it hit, followed by a large *KABOOM* as the truck exploded.

The truck was lifted off the ground by the explosion and crashed back down, with the rounds cooking off in the flames.

"Pearson! With me now!" he said as he ran towards where Jordan had fallen.

Yet another person lost. He'd never expected to have to deal with the death of those he commanded.

"Help me carry her back to the truck."

"I'll take her feet if you like, Sergeant."

"Let's do it," he said as they lifted her suit up, which was the only thing holding the two parts of her mangled body together. Blood covered the ground underneath her.

"Wachowski, go see how Keith is doing and give him a hand with the stretcher to carry Dr. Leung out when he's been prepped for transport."

"On it."

He and Pearson moved Jordan to the back of the truck, and he climbed on, moved her to the front of the load bed, and strapped her suit down.

"Scooter Six, this is Scooter Four. Over," said Keith over the radio.

"What's up? Over."

"We're ready to move now. Over."

"Scooter Two should be with you now to help. Over."

"Copy that. Out."

"Pearson, you take charge of this truck," he said as he got off the back of it.

"Roger that, Sergeant."

Ferretti walked to the far side of the square, where Wachowski had parked the other truck. He stood and waited as Wachowski led the stretcher out of the building with Keith holding the back. Dr. Pham was holding a drip while walking alongside the stretcher team.

"Wachowski, you take my truck and stay with the doc. I'll drive yours. Let's get moving before more trouble hits us."

He climbed into the truck and reversed it back, swinging the nose around to change direction.

"Tic-Tac Six, this is Scooter Six. We've secured the first package, leaving now for the second objective. I say again, package secured and en route to second objective. Over."

"Copy that. Out," came the lieutenant's reply.

Back in the truck he could access the feeds from the UAV and the two combat armor suits. Espera and Tachikoma were in the middle of a shootout with five androids. It appeared the fight was starting to move this way.

Definitely a good time to get out of Dodge.

66. REGROUP

No plan survives contact with the enemy.

— Helmuth von Moltke the Elder

First Lieutenant Lara Atsuko Tachikoma
Two Moons Timakira
Tuesday, January 17, 2073

I raced towards Espera's position, answering his call for help. The androids swarmed around his Ape, overwhelming him with their numbers.

I swung my Dog through a narrow alleyway and swept around abandoned carts, which were obstacles in my way. There was movement ahead of me, and I fired my M240LC to announce my arrival to the androids, trying to take the pressure off Espera.

I didn't expect to hit, and so I wasn't disappointed when the shots from my machine gun missed.

I'm easy to please like that.

I marked the five remaining androids on my screen as priority targets. I let the suit's AI start the process of matching its prediction of their movements to what they actually did.

Judging by the tracking data coming in, it didn't look as if my suit's system could handle five androids' movements at once.

So I put priority levels on each and tracked the first of my targets.

The feeds from the UAV showed the fight had turned into a melee as Espera and I moved in response to the androids darting around us. The roar from firing intensified as Espera let rip with the M134.

I added to the cacophony with supporting fire from my autocannon.

The confines of the town severely hindered my sight lines, and I resorted to sending a couple of rounds through the walls of the buildings to hit androids that were using them for cover. I tried not to think of the collateral damage to the inhabitants of the town.

Both our suits were now in the middle of the androids' formation.

They were running around firing from the roofs of buildings.

Then the call came in from Ferretti telling me that Dr. Leung was safe. Time to run away and regroup.

"First package retrieved; withdraw now. Over."

"Roger that. Out," said Espera, splitting off and heading west.

I split, heading east as the androids surged between us heading towards the library.

From the UAV feed, I figured they were responding to the primary team having destroyed the truck. Then the doubt of what I would do if I were them crept into my mind.

I realized once they reached the library, they would search for where the primary team had gone.

"Tic-Tac Four, this is Tic-Tac Six. I want you to chase the androids. Harass them as they move to the library, but don't get tangled up in them. I'm going to try to flank them on the other side of the square and block any attempt to follow the primary team. Over."

Espera gave a terse "wilco" in reply as I turned my Dog sharp right and made my way south, running at an angle to the direction that the androids were moving.

My suit's superior speed would let me overtake them, and my plan was to swing around and come back up to block their path. To prevent them from pursuing our primary team's three trucks.

As I raced back along the road, our trucks crossed ahead of me, heading east towards the location of the other civilians. Everything was at that point moving really fast, and as the old saying goes, timing is everything.

I swung my Dog right at the junction where the trucks had just crossed and took the route back to the south side of the town's main square.

I checked my magazine.

It only had four rounds left, so I swapped it out for a fresh one with ten in. This left me with one magazine loaded ready to go.

I came out onto the square where the androids were walking across my line of fire and using the QuadMules as moving cover. And I cursed in frustration at not being able to fire, as I didn't want to destroy the atomic battery one of them was carrying.

So I dropped the AP magazine and fired a shot across the front of their formation, which blew through a building on the far side of the square.

Incoming rounds from the androids hit my Dog as I switched to high-explosive rounds and charged my autocannon.

In the time that took me, the androids had made their way to the entrance of the hall and gone inside, their passage made easier by our earlier action when we'd kicked the door down to gain access. It was going to be like hunting a bunch of rabid rats inside the confines of the building.

I had a hunch that some parts of downtown Timakira would be in need of some extensive renovation after the day's action.

The two QuadMules charged towards me.

The first was swinging its loading arm back as it prepared to hit me. I fired at point-blank range and blew the arm off as the rest of it crashed into my Dog, knocking it back into the building behind me.

Then I kicked out, punting it away, and swung my weapon around to bear on the second QuadMule.

I let off a shot, which blew its two front legs away, causing it to somersault in the air and crashed into the ground, where it flopped on its side.

The other QuadMule charged again, and I fired at its legs, hitting the rear ones, which caused it to sit down and slide towards me. *Give me a break, you stupid fucking machine,* I thought as I moved forward between the two crippled QuadMules.

Espera's Ape entered the square.

"They're in the hall," I said over our laser-net.

"Got it, LT," he replied as he swept around in front of the building and brought up his M75 and fired.

His suit's recoilless autocannon ejected a smaller mass out of the rear of the M75 to counterbalance the force from firing a high-velocity 80 mm round, preventing the recoil from damaging Espera's Ape.

The backwash from the M75 swept past me and knocked the QuadMule on my left into the building behind it, which ended its twitching, illustrating why one should never stand behind a recoilless weapon.

Another shot entered the building and blew up when it hit the far wall of the hall. I saw the cloud of smoke and debris coming out of the doorway.

They were definitely going to be in need of some serious redecoration after we left.

I swung my Dog around to check out the remaining QuadMule, which was crawling towards me in reverse. It had picked up a chunk of masonry, which it was preparing to throw at me. I shot the arm off and then fired again at the remaining two legs.

This put paid to its chances of making any further moves to impede my actions.

I turned and followed Espera into the building. His M134 was spinning up, followed by the buzz-saw sound of one android getting mown down. Four more to go, but given how the fight had gone so far, it wasn't going to be easy.

67. DISTANT GUNFIRE

Theory helps us to bear our ignorance of facts.

— GEORGE SANTAYANA

Dr. Allison O'Neill
Magnetic Anomaly Project Scientist
Two Moons Timakira
Tuesday, January 17, 2073

Disturbed by one of the aliens moving in the room, Allison woke. The sun was up, and they were boiling a pot of water and adding their equivalent of oats to it to make breakfast. Alan still appeared to be sound asleep, but Laytona and Tyrone were stirring.

She rubbed her eyes and wished she could have a shower. Even the basic ones back at the camp were a blessing.

After a night sleeping in the room, Allison was missing the little luxuries of Camp Bravo. This hot weather and the dust made her feel dirty all the time, and she had even considered having her hair cut short. Not that it was terribly long, but it always ended up in a mess by the end of a day.

"What should we do now, guys?"

"Do you mean what to have for breakfast, or what to do, as in besides waiting here to be rescued?" asked Dr. Reynolds.

"Either, I guess," she said, looking around at the others in the room.

"What's for breakfast anyway?" asked Dr. Webber, woken by the noise of them speaking.

Allison pointed at the food. "Well, it looks like oats to me."

"Can we eat their food without becoming ill and all?" asked Dr. Franklin.

"Sure, none of the bugs here should have any effect, as they've not evolved to live off us. One advantage of a similar but different biological habitat," she said.

"Apart from the Crocomodos, that is," said Dr. Reynolds.

"They're not called Crocomodos. That's just a silly made-up name."

"They look like a dragon and crocodile mated, to me. Anyway, didn't Sergeant Ferretti name them?" asked Dr. Reynolds.

"And your point is?"

"You seem to like him, so I thought you of all people would go with the name."

"And you don't like anything to do with the military, so why would you use the name then?"

"Hey, just saying, is all. No need to get on your high horse about it. Just 'cause I don't like the military doesn't mean the name they came up with is bad, or nothing."

"OK, I'll peer outside and check on what's out there," she said, standing up and walking towards the door. As she did so, one of the alien cat people ran across the room and barred her way.

"*Laffabu ferhiza dobogi ibagaipe buparai!*" the cat person said while nodding its head up and down.

"Well, I must say I didn't really catch all of that, but I'm sure I'm safe saying it means 'don't go out there,'" said Dr. Webber.

"Agafaha rhiga besecayen buraico zaanafo boso ruperhou."

"You don't say. I thought blocking the door just meant you must eat some breakfast first before you go."

"That's not helping, Tyrone," said Dr. Franklin.

"Do you think they're trying to keep us prisoners in retaliation for what the androids did?"

"I don't think so. It's more like fear for our safety," said Dr. Franklin.

"I agree. Who's up for alien breakfast table d'hôte?" asked Dr. Webber.

"You first. I'm not eating that sludge," said Dr. Reynolds.

Laytonya reached over and took a bowl of food that was offered to her. She then poured in some sticky liquid the aliens had put on top of their portions and tried a mouthful.

"Umh, it's not bad, different to what I was expecting it to taste like." She paused for a moment, allowing herself to reflect on the taste. "It's a bit like a cross between oatmeal and grits." Then she chewed, swallowed, and took another spoonful. "The liquid is sweet, sort of like maple syrup and honey. Not bad at all."

Allison took the next bowl that was offered and started eating.

Even Tyrone didn't refuse a bowl when offered one. After they finished, they sat around. He and Laytonya kept looking at one another, and Allison decided they were in a silent dare contest about comparing the meal to corn pone.

The aliens didn't talk much, but anytime one of the team went towards the door, they would get up and block the way out. A part of her thought this was probably wise, while another part of her felt trapped by the situation she found herself in.

The time passed slowly, and Allison sat dozing as the heat of the day started to penetrate the room. Gunfire startled her awake.

"Do you all hear that? What's going on out there?"

"The androids are shooting at something," said Dr. Franklin.

"But why now? What's changed? I don't see any of our friends here attempting to go outside, so why should others in the town start?"

"Listen, the sound of firing seems to be moving around," said Dr. Webber.

"It'll be the military coming in all gung-ho-like and shooting up the neighborhood," said Dr. Reynolds.

"You make that sound like a bad thing. We're stuck here with the androids shooting anything that moves, and now we'll be rescued."

"I just say it the way I see it. We wouldn't be in this mess if the androids hadn't been state-programmed killing machines. I know I sound like I have a thing about the military, and I do, but here's the deal. We know these aliens have an artificial language, have a shared genetic heritage, and that means somebody made them, and more to the point, put them here. We've come along and started messing around in that somebody's sandpit, and my guess is they're not going to take too kindly to having us messing up their stuff. We know these people have been here two thousand years, so whoever made them is at least that far advanced of us. So having the military shoot up the town and wreck stuff is not the best thing they could be doing, is all."

"Tyrone, that was some speech you made to justify you not liking the military," said Dr. Webber.

"You got me wrong. I *hate* the military because they're only good for destroying stuff and killing people. It's such a waste."

"I'll be glad if it is them coming for us," said Dr. Franklin.

"Me too, if only because I'd like to get some proper medical attention. Not that I'm complaining about the bandage, but I might need more stitches; I'm leaking again," said Dr. Webber.

"Let me take a peek," Allison said. "Can someone pass me a spare bandage from their first aid kit?" She assessed the leakage and saw the bandage was full. If she remembered correctly, it meant Alan had lost at least a liter of blood, which was not good.

For his sake she only hoped help arrived soon.

68. SECOND OBJECTIVE

Every failure is a step to success.

— WILLIAM WHEWELL

Technical Sergeant Ferretti
Two Moons Timakira
Tuesday, January 17, 2073

Ferretti led the convoy around the narrow streets of Timakira, scraping past the mud-brick buildings as they passed.

He brought his truck to a halt as the street narrowed.

The building's walls had been altered; an extension built into the street made it impassable unless he demolished the addition, which would probably damage the lightly armored truck in the process.

"Eyeball, this is Scooter Six. Over."

"Reading you loud and clear. Over," replied Nelson from back at base camp.

"Give me a SITREP on the Papa Tangos."

"They're chasing Tic-Tac Six away from you. Over."

"Roger that. Open a line to the feed for my truck. Over," said Ferretti, changing channels. "Listen up, people—the route ahead is blocked. We're clear behind, so I want us to back up and try a different way round. Over," he said, cursing under his breath at the delay.

He heard Wachowski confirm she'd heard and understood his message. Sergeant Pearson interrupted them over the radio.

"It will save time if I take point with the rear truck. Over."

It was a good call. Ferretti told Wachowski to follow Pearson, and he would bring up the rear.

"Aye, aye," came Wachowski's laconic reply.

The convoy came up to the next junction on their route and found their way blocked by a cart with dead bodies on it and rubble. Pearson came on the radio and asked what he wanted to do. Another decision he had to take.

He replied, "Let's respect the dead and find another way. Out."

Pearson turned his truck left, and the convoy snaked its way round and through more narrow streets.

Ferretti watched the fight between the CASE suits and the androids unfold on the tactical screen. It looked to him as if Tachikoma and Espera were having a hard time of it, which wasn't that surprising considering the nature of the hardwired responses that controlled the androids.

The new route the convoy was taking was clear of major obstacles, but it brought them back closer to the conflict. Ferretti saw that the lieutenant's suit was heading in their general direction.

He guessed that she was trying to put herself between the androids and the convoy.

"Scooter Two, try to speed up and get across the next intersection. Over," he said to Pearson.

"Roger that. It looks like we now have a clear run to our second objective. Out," Pearson replied.

Ferretti looked up from his screen as the convoy cut across ahead of the lieutenant's Dog as she hung a right, heading back down the way the convoy had come. It looked to him as if she and Espera were heading into a whole world of pain back in the main square.

He checked the time and found it had taken a little over ten minutes to get to where the science team had been yesterday—when the whole operation had gone south.

Now they were about to find out what had happened to the scientists. The feeling of dread seemed to come from the pit of his stomach as the thoughts and images of what might have happened to the scientists came to mind.

He pulled up his truck behind the other two that had stopped in front of him and climbed down from the cab.

"OK, people, let's form a perimeter and find our missing scientists."

There were lots of bodies lying on the ground in the marketplace, and he was thankful that he couldn't smell the stench of them decomposing from the heat of the sun.

"Check if any of the dead are ours."

Pearson and Wachowski started to search when a door of one of the buildings moved. Allison peered around the doorframe, and he realized he'd momentarily stopped breathing. The relief of finding her alive was palpable as he let go of all the fear, uncertainty, and doubt.

Allison shouted, "Dr. Webber has been shot!"

"I'm on it," said Keith, as he ran across to enter the building and attend to his patient.

He walked over to where Allison stood. "Is everybody else OK?"

"Apart from Tyrone bumping his head, we're unharmed."

"Wachowski, get the trucks turned around and find us a route out of this town."

"On it. What about the lieutenant and Staff Sergeant Espera?"

"We have our orders. Pearson, organize with Keith where he wants everyone to sit in the trucks. He will want to attend to the wounded."

"Sure thing, Sarge," said Pearson.

Ferretti stood away from the door as the three scientists made their way out into the square. The horror of what had happened there made them retch. Once Pearson had them all sitting inside the trucks, he went over to the door and looked into the room that the scientists had been hiding in.

Three aliens sat motionless in the corner away from the door.

He ignored them. "How's it coming, Keith?"

"Just got to finish stitching up this wound. Five minutes max, and then we're good to move Dr. Webber."

"Good work, Keith. We'll have you out of here soon, Dr. Webber."

"Thank you for coming for us, Sergeant Ferretti. I don't mind saying that this is one day I will not miss."

You can say that again, he thought. Ferretti turned and left and made his way back to the empty truck to get in and wait.

Shortly afterwards, Keith helped the wounded Dr. Webber to one of the trucks, and they both got in. A few more minutes passed as Keith attended to his two patients.

Gunfire could be heard in the distance, but they couldn't move until the patient was stabilized. Keith set up another line to replace lost fluids from Dr. Webber's wound, then gave the OK, and Ferretti signaled the convoy to move off.

Ferretti brought up the rear, replaying the feeds relayed from the UAV.

He studied the battle at the main square as it unfolded to the point where everyone disappeared when the fight moved inside the building. It didn't look like things were going according to plan.

69. FINAL BATTLE

Being ready is not what matters. What matters is winning after you get there.

— LtGen Victor H. Krulak, USMC

First Lieutenant Lara Atsuko Tachikoma
Two Moons Timakira
Tuesday, January 17, 2073

Espera's Ape was inside the building, the firing from his M134 echoing loudly. Spent casings littered the ground, showing where he'd passed on his way inside.

They crunched beneath my Dog's feet as I followed him.

Thermal images of the room pinpointed the androids ahead of me. I fired through the wall at one that was going right trying to move out of my sight.

The brickwork of the building exploded from the concussive force of the 20 mm round as it went through the wall like a piledriver through Lego.

The shot missed, but it announced my presence to the participants in the ongoing gang bang of Espera's Ape.

The hall was much as I remembered it from the scans from the team.

Except now it was looking in need of extensive remodeling from all the demolition work that was going on, not helped by me upping the ante as I fired my autocannon. My Dog strode into the room, and I scanned around allocating target priorities for my suit's expert AI system.

Espera was feeling the love as three androids used his Ape as a jungle gym while he unloaded rounds from point-blank range.

I tracked the one I'd fired at through the wall and saw it bounce off the ground as it climbed up the wall to the balcony that circled the hall. I fired a grenade from my underbarrel launcher in front of the balcony landing.

This took the floor out from underneath its feet. Much to my disbelief, the android converted its last step into a somersault and cleared the gap that had opened up in front of it.

Moving forward, I twisted my Dog to track its movement. I brought my autocannon around to fire again.

There was a lurch and a clang as one of the other androids charged into my Dog.

It knocked me off balance as I fired, causing me to miss my target.

Then I found out what it was like to have a monkey climb all over me, as it tried to find weak spots by hammering me repeatedly with its Beowulf.

The sound was intense, and system flags started to turn from green to amber as damage mounted up.

Espera fired another burst from his M134, which cut across the front of my Dog and forced the android that was on me to move. This meant my Dog got caught in the crossfire from 7.62 rounds.

I ducked out of the way by sliding my Dog right and then turning left to face Espera.

This brought the android that was hanging on his suit's right arm into frame, and I fired a grenade at it. The explosion rocked the room and threw the android off Espera's Ape. It rolled away and stood up facing away from me.

That was too good a shot to miss, and I double-tapped it with my 20 mm, getting the satisfaction of blowing it a new asshole.

But there was another android holding on to the leg of Espera's Ape, pumping rounds into the joints of his machine as if it had to use up this month's ammo allotment or it wouldn't get next month's. Before I could react, his machine collapsed onto its knees, and my Dog was caught in the crossfire from the two other androids.

They'd decided I needed some of their special attention.

Dishing stuff out means you've got to be able to take punishment in return. I jumped straight up in the air to clear my Dog from the rounds that were pounding into its legs, and fired another grenade to discourage the android on my left.

This caused it to move position and lose its target lock on me.

My Dog automatically bent its legs to take the force of the landing.

Reacting to the androids around me, I spun on the spot and let off a burst from the M240LC, sweeping the room. That forced both androids to keep moving as I chose one to make it my priority target.

As I moved backwards towards one of the walls, my Dog got hit again as the android that had been hanging off Espera's Ape took me by surprise. It charged into me, sliding under my Dog's legs, which swept me off my feet.

As moves go, it was impressive. Under different circumstances I would've applauded, because what girl doesn't like to be swept off her feet by surprise?

The other two androids took the opportunity to come back and resume hammering me with their Beowulfs.

My Dog was flagging up red icons as my suit's system bypassed failures. Espera fired his Ape's M134 in a chainsaw roar of shots, which passed over me and cut one of the androids in half.

This gave me a moment to roll over and get up as I heard the now-empty minigun fall silent.

This has to be either the saddest or most frightening thing one can hear when one is in the middle of a firefight. Espera was out of ammo, and I still had two androids to deal with.

The one that had swept my Dog's feet out from under me was nearest, and it turned to come closer. Machines know no fear, but this one knew being in close was the safest place to be.

I was about to disabuse it of that assumption.

I stepped back with my right foot and put up my left arm.

The android swerved and ducked under the barrel of the M240LC as I fired it. Then it grabbed on to my Dog's arm and swung itself up onto my machine, trying to bring its weapon to bear in turn, which was exactly what I wanted it to do.

Well, for definitions of *wanted* that meant I'd rather be sunning myself on a beach drinking piña coladas. But what I wished for wasn't exactly being met at that instant in time.

Still, my hunch was that the android would repeat its maneuvre because it had successfully used it before to ream me and Espera new ones. Now its predictability looked like it would work in my favor.

I stepped and turned my Dog, raising the arm the android had grabbed and swinging around 180 degrees, using the force of the turn to swing my Dog's arm up and around.

As I came to face the opposite direction, I knelt my Dog down and brought my arm down at the same time, smashing it into the ground.

It left me dizzy, but the android had gotten the worst of the deal.

It let go of my arm and tried to get up again.

Shots from its partner hit my back but didn't penetrate the armor, and I ignored them. I brought my autocannon to bear on the android in front of me and double-tapped the bugger, taking its head off.

In a fair world that would have been the end of it.

But we don't live in a fair world, and the headless android brought its weapon to bear on me, stitching the front of my Dog with a burst from its Beowulf. So I fired another two shots, and payback is a bitch.

Especially when you've been hit by a 20 mm armor-piercing round in the chest.

I saw it disintegrate in front of me but really couldn't take the time to appreciate the finer points of its dismemberment. I still had its last friend hammering on my back. Where, truth be told, the armor is not as thick as that on the front.

Another red flag came up on my console, and my suit switched to backup power after the abuse taken from the rounds ricocheting around places that weren't designed for such treatment.

I guess it sucked to be me.

Standing, I turned, tracking the remaining android as it tried to run in circles around me, doing a pretty good job of staying out of my arc of fire. Next, I backed my Dog towards the wall to block its attempts to stay in my rear. Bringing my weapon up, I fired the last grenade at the ceiling above me, stepping back as I fired.

The back blast reverberated through the hall.

Chunks of the building's roof fell down in its path.

I was under no illusion this would cause any damage; this was all about limiting its options and getting it to go where I wanted it to go. By now my suit's expert AI had the android's moves down at 95 percent probability, but its size and speed within the confines of the hall still made it hard to kill.

Inside my Dog, I was the eight hundred pound gorilla in the room.

Whatever passed for knowledge in the android knew I knew this, too, which was why it wasn't fighting on my terms. As the small print in documents always says: terms and conditions apply, errors and omissions excepted.

Just because my Dog was the big bad to the android didn't mean I had to play it big and dumb.

It leapt over the fallen ceiling rubble to close with my Dog, firing as it came. As it charged in, I turned on the spot, letting it get up close and personal.

Then I slammed us both together into the wall behind me.

Big and clever beats small and clever.

The android and my Dog rebounded off each other.

As the momentum separated us, I fired my autocannon trying to double-tap it. One shot missed, but the other hit its left leg, blowing it clean off and causing it to fall backwards on the floor.

I dropped the now-empty magazine to reload as it pulled itself up, brought its weapon to bear on me, and started firing. Shots hit my Dog as I chambered a round in my weapon. I fired, hitting it in the chest.

And then I fired another couple of rounds just to make sure.

One can never be too certain about these kinds of things.

A wave of exhaustion swept over my body as I realized that we'd won, and the adrenaline surge stopped. I turned to face Espera's Ape.

"How you doing, Staff Sergeant?"

"Not good, LT. Been hit," he said, coughing.

I moved over to his Ape, popped the hatch on my Dog, and took my helmet off. "Hold on, I'm here. Don't you go leaving me yet."

I swung over to him with my suit's first aid kit, and pulled the emergency cockpit release on Espera's Ape. The hatch swung up to reveal blood spatter decorating the inside of his cockpit.

"Be honest—it doesn't look good, does it, LT?"

It didn't. His helmet visor was cracked, and there was blood spatter inside his visor. I assisted him in removing his helmet.

"You want something to help?"

"That would be good."

I gave him a jab for the pain. "You should get some relief in a minute."

"Thanks, LT. Sorry I let you down like this."

"You don't have to apologize to me. Is there anything you want me to do for you when I get back?"

"Nah. Parents are dead, and I've got no family. Never got around to settling down with a woman." He paused to cough up blood. "Would've liked to have, but never met the right person until now."

"You making a pass at me, Espera?"

"Yeah. You going to put me on report for harassment?"

"Don't think so," I said, holding him from slumping in his seat.

"Just one other thing. Tell Ferretti he's OK for a pogue…"

Espera died in my arms.

Tears welled up in my eyes. It's at times like this in stories that the hero comes up with some witty platitude to make the reader feel good. The truth is that life is what the living do until it's their turn to die.

In my case I had to now retrieve all the destroyed androids.

I slaved Espera's Ape to my Dog and then climbed back into the cockpit of my machine. Given that my Dog was running on reserve power, it made sense to drive the Ape and use it to pick up the android parts, which littered the hall, and take them outside.

Once that was done, I put the Ape in standby mode and made the call.

"Scooter Six, this is Tic-Tac Six, come in. Over."

Ferretti replied, "Receiving you loud and clear. Over."

"Staff Sergeant Espera is down, and I need pickup, as my suit is on its last legs. Over."

"Roger that, ma'am. I've been waiting for the call and will be with you in ten mikes. Over."

"Looking forward to you getting here. Out."

I was about to leave the hall when movement caught my attention. For a moment, my heart felt like it was in my mouth, as I thought I'd missed one of the androids. To my relief it was only two of the aliens hesitating in the doorway that led to the library.

I hadn't even realized anyone was still in this building when we came in. So I switched on the autotranslate program and opened the hatch of my Dog to speak to them.

"I'm sorry for what has happened here."

The two aliens looked at me. "You killed the Progenitors."

I took a moment before answering, I wasn't sure what to make of that, until guessing the aliens saw the androids as representing their Progenitors. "They're not your Progenitors; they're machines we made in our likeness."

The two aliens sank to the floor and bowed to me. "Are you one of the others?" one of them asked.

"My name is Lieutenant Tachikoma, and I'm from Earth. I suppose that makes me an *other*," I replied as I heard the trucks arriving outside. "I've got to go now. And I'm sorry for the losses you've suffered here. I promise it won't happen again."

Then I closed the hatch of my Dog and walked out of the building into the light of the afternoon sun. Ferretti stood there waiting for me.

"Let's get my Dog on the back of the truck first, and I'll run the Ape by remote to load up the remains of the androids and QuadMules." Ferretti's olive skin had gone pale. "You OK?"

"Not really, ma'am. I've never seen people die in battle before. How do you get used to it?"

"You don't, not really. You just have to carry on as best you can, be thankful for still having a life to live. It makes you realize that you have to make the most of the chances you get."

70. GOING NOW

The hardest thing of all for a soldier is to retreat.

— Duke of Wellington

Technical Sergeant Ferretti
Two Moons Timakira
Tuesday, January 17, 2073

Ferretti drove to the rendezvous point outside the town without a hitch. Their three trucks then made their way back to Camp Bravo, where Nelson was waiting for them.

The lieutenant issued a flurry of orders that resulted in the camp being broken down and the command-and-control container being loaded up on the back of one of the trucks. The truck with the blown transaxle was hitched up behind their remaining lightly loaded truck.

Ferretti put it on the point.

The speed of the convoy would largely be determined by the slowest vehicle. Considering what the team had been through, a slow and safe journey seemed to him to be the order of the day.

After looking at the lieutenant, after seeing all the color drained out of her face, he had arranged for her to be in the lead truck.

Wachowski would be with her taking first shift. He got Nelson to join them, which would give them both room to catch some Z's on the long drive back to the Alpha site.

He put Sergeant Pearson with Keith and his two patients in the second truck. Dr. Pham insisted she wasn't leaving Dr. Leung's side and joined them.

This left himself with the other three scientists bringing up the rear of the convoy with the bodies of the fallen secured in the truck's bed.

After breaking down the camp and loading everyone aboard, the convoy finally set off. The weight of what had happened there sat heavily on his mind as he found himself thinking of all the things he could've done to prevent the tragedy.

His first independent command and he had lost four people.

To distract himself, he started writing up his report on his PAD.

He compiled the various files and time stamps containing the details leading up to the key events that had led to the deaths of Dr. Follet, Dr. Newman, and Corporal Baptista, and the injuries sustained by Specialist Nelson. All the moments replayed again in his head.

"Are you all right?" asked Allison.

"Sorry, just a bit distracted by writing up my report."

"Thank you for coming to save us back there, Sergeant," said Dr. Franklin.

"I was just doing my duty, ma'am."

"Shit. Just doing your duty. Typical bloody uptight military reply."

"Tyrone, this is not the time to be getting on your high horse with the sergeant," said Dr. Franklin.

"It's all right, ma'am. He's right—it's all my fault."

"How do you figure that, Sergeant?" asked Dr. Reynolds.

"If I hadn't refitted the android with the autonomous module, none of this could've happened."

"Let me see if I got this straight. You just decided to refit some of the androids out to act autonomously and all, and when they went off message, it was all down to you," said Dr. Reynolds.

"Tyrone, stop it," said Dr. Franklin.

"How can you say that to him?" said Allison.

"Well, it strikes me from what I've seen that Sergeant Ferretti is a man who follows orders. Am I right?"

"Yes, Dr. Reynolds. I follow orders."

"That's my point. I don't like the military mentality of just following orders, but here's the thing—you were following a legal order, and no one could've predicted the androids would act the way they did."

"Tyrone, your point is?" asked Dr. Franklin.

"My point is that this man saved our asses. I don't like what the military stands for, and I still think it was the military's fault for what happened, but people gave their lives to save us. For that, you have my sincerest gratitude, Sergeant," said Dr. Reynolds.

"Well, I never thought I'd see the day when you would thank someone in the military. Anyway, I think Allison has something she wants to ask you, Sergeant," said Dr. Franklin.

"I do?" said Allison.

"Yes, you do, girl. Now's as good as time as any you'll ever get," said Dr. Franklin.

"Laytonya, you're not *shipping* the sergeant and Allison?"

"Shut up, Tyrone."

"Would you like to go for a coffee when we get back?"

"Of course. I'm always happy to have coffee when we meet in the canteen."

"No, silly. I mean go out for a coffee when you're not on duty."

"I'd like that very much indeed, Dr. O'Neill."

"And you can start calling me Allison, too."

"Let's not rush things."

71. COMING HOME

The supreme irony of life is that hardly anyone gets out of it alive.

— ROBERT A. HEINLEIN

First Lieutenant Lara Atsuko Tachikoma
Two Moons
Thursday, January 19, 2073

The journey back to the Alpha site was long, tiresome, and dreary.

The mission plan had been for a stay of one month with the option to extend it. We were then at the end of month two, and if it weren't for the fact that five people had died and four were injured, this mission would've been considered a success.

But it gave me time to consider what to do next.

The chain of command was clear: I took my orders from Dr. Emmerich the head scientist, and she had to make a decision about what to do next. Once I had my orders, I could plan accordingly.

We pulled into camp, and I left Ferretti to deal with the immediate needs, as he knew what he had to do. Dr. Emmerich was waiting for me, wringing her hands and standing very stiffly outside of the Conex box that served as her office at Base Camp Alpha.

My heart sank to see her, and there was no easy way to break the news, so I walked up to her and said, "Ma'am, I have to regretfully confirm the deaths of Dr. Follet and Dr. Newman. We have retrieved their remains for return home for a proper burial."

She looked me in the eye and replied, "I understand your team has taken losses, too, Lieutenant."

"Yes, ma'am," I said. "In addition to Corporal Baptista's death, we lost Staff Sergeant Espera and Airman First Class Jordan during the operation. Also, Dr. Leung was seriously wounded but is in stable condition. Dr. Webber was also wounded during the shooting, and Dr. Reynolds received a concussion. And Specialist Nelson was also wounded during the initial combat android shooting."

"How do you remain so calm?" she asked as tears rolled down her face.

The calmness was all I had to hold on to; it was part of being an officer in the Marine Corps—coping with the needs in the face of the costs. I nodded at Dr. Emmerich.

"I'm not sure what I can say, ma'am, that wouldn't sound cold to you. Just because you see me being calm doesn't mean I'm not hurting inside. But I need you to give me orders on what you want me to do, ma'am."

She stood there for a moment crying and then wiped her eyes and shook herself, clenching her hands into fists. For a moment she looked like she was going to hit something.

"What are our options, Lieutenant?"

"We need to send Dr. Leung back for surgery, along with all our dead and wounded tomorrow when the pillars open. Due to reinforcements, we still have twelve military personnel left to support the science part of the mission. But I took it upon my authority to close Bravo Camp, until we have time to assess the consequences of what happened there."

Dr. Emmerich looked like she would start crying again, but she cleared her throat.

"I see. I think we need to close our base here, too. I fear we may have been too hasty in pursuing the science goal in light of our finding the aliens. Please make the arrangements to close the base and return home. I assume we have time to pack up everything and make the move?"

A mix of tension and relief flowed through me as I thought through her request.

"We can secure the base as per our original plans and pack all the things you want returned in time for the next opening. I don't foresee any problems, ma'am."

"Thank you," she said. "Please proceed with making it happen."

Saluting to acknowledge the order, I then turned and left her standing there looking devastated by what had happened. I respected her decision that the whole team should go home.

Seeing the rawness of her feelings left me wanting to do more to console the woman, but there was nothing I could do other than my job. I issued orders to Staff Sergeant Martinez to start closing down the camp and packing everything up.

We would seal the containers and leave them for when the next mission to Two Moons arrived.

The next day we transited the pillars without hitch and were then debriefed. While we were away, the Magnetic Anomaly Project had been reorganized and renamed MAPCOM. We'd been given the remit to explore new worlds and prevent hostile powers from controlling access through the pillars.

Marines in space!

Not sure High Command has fully thought that one out.

Corporal Baptista and Specialist Nelson both received posthumous Purple Hearts, while Staff Sergeant Espera got a Bronze Star as well, which was scant reward for having sacrificed their lives in the line of duty.

To me they will always be the true heroes of what's being called the Battle of Timakira.

Not that anyone is going to be able to read about it anytime soon.

For my sins I was bumped up to captain, which I took as affirming my handling of the events on Two Moons. However, the fact that it had been backdated to my original commission as second lieutenant made me wonder about the politics of the operation.

Still, I was pleased my recommendation that Corporal Wachowski get her third stripe to make sergeant was approved. I also had the pleasure of seeing Ferretti promoted to Master Sergeant. And witnessing his dismay on finding out he would be sent off to be trained up as a combat armor suit pilot for six months.

Espera would've approved.

Arlington National Cemetery
Arlington County, Virginia
Thursday, February 16, 2073

I've been to four funerals and today is the fifth and final one. Today we bury Staff Sergeant Juan Espera. May he rest in peace.

We're in Arlington Cemetery, where the winter rain graces the ceremony held amongst the sea of white crosses surrounding us.

Drs. Emmerich and O'Neill are here representing the civilian staff of MAPCOM with the remaining team members of Alpha Mike. The number of attendees for Espera's service has been bolstered by the presence of his former Green Beret colleagues from the Fifth Special Forces Group.

There are six of them, all wearing their distinctive berets and boots. Standing together observing the formalities of laying a brother in arms to rest.

Afterwards, they approach me.

Captain Downey speaks. "How did he die?"

"Saving the lives of those he swore to protect. I'm afraid I can't tell you the details."

"Judging by your tan, this happened elsewhere?"

"Elsewhere" being an understatement; if he only knew. "I'm afraid I'm not at liberty to discuss that, either."

"Captain, we're not here to hassle you. Espera was a good man, and he thought highly of you. We're here to pay our respects to him and commiserate with you for his loss. I can imagine some of what you must be feeling because it's not easy to lose people under your command."

"Thank you, sir," I say, saluting him.

One by one Espera's colleagues approach and salute. Chief Warrant Officer McAdams first, followed by Staff Sergeant King, then Sergeant Robinson, Sergeant Sanchez, and Sergeant Lewis.

They all thank me, and I'm barely able to hold back the tears. Afterwards, we go to the all-ranks at Fort Myer and drink a toast to absent friends.

All that really matters in life is being true to oneself. For those of us who serve, that means doing our duty. Semper Fi!

DRAMATIS PERSONAE

Combat Armor Suit Detachment Alpha 5136

Master Sergeant Campbell, operations and team sergeant.
Captain Anthony Downey, detachment commander.
Staff Sergeant Juan Espera, weapons.
Staff Sergeant Julia King, engineer.
Sergeant Mary Lewis, communications.
Chief Warrant Officer 1 Andrew McAdams, assistant detachment commander.
Staff Sergeant Morales, engineer.
Sergeant First Class Thomas Nguyen, assistant operations and intelligence.
Sergeant First Class Frank Radoslovich, weapons.
Sergeant Daniel Robinson, medical.
Sergeant Miguel Sanchez, communications.
Sergeant Schmidt, medical.

Magnetic Anomaly Project Command (MAPCOM)

Dr. John Cameron, Head of Inorganic Geochemistry and Mineralogy Group, scientist, civilian base staff.
Dr. Kenneth Carlyle, Head of Organic Geochemistry and Biosignatures Group, scientist, civilian base staff.
Dr. Andrew Carpenter, Head of Atmosphere and Environment Group, scientist, civilian base staff.
Lieutenant Colonel Sofia Foster, CS Army, S1 Adjutant and Executive Officer, military base staff.
Captain Alexei Patinkin, CSAF, S2 Intelligence Officer, military base staff.
Colonel later General Paul Russell, CSAF, S3 Commanding Officer, military base staff.
Dr. Linda Scott, Head of Mathematics and Physics Group, lead scientist of the Magnetic Anomaly Project, civilian base staff.

MAPCOM Alpha Mike Team 1

Petty Officer Third Class Robert "Bobby" Adams, CSN, Culinary Specialist.
Corporal Jose Baptista, CS Army, logistics specialist.
Senior Airman Michael Davis, CSAF, UAV pilot.
Staff Sergeant Juan Espera, CS Army, Special Forces Green Beret NCO.
Technical Sergeant Vincent Ferretti, CSAF, android operator and technician NCO.
Airman First Class Carlos Garcia, CSAF, UAV sensor operator.
Airman First Class Mary Kim Jordan, CSAF, Security Force/Military Police.

Petty Officer Third Class Douglas Keith, CSN, Hospital Corpsman.

Staff Sergeant Emilio Martinez, CSAF, UAV pilot NCO.

Airman First Class Jennifer Moore, CSAF, UAV sensor operator.

Specialist Donna Nelson, CS Army, communications.

Sergeant Thomas Pearson, CS Army, Corps of Engineers NCO.

First Lieutenant Lara Atsuko Tachikoma, CSMC, commanding officer of the first off-world mission to the planet of Two Moons and leader of the Alpha Mike Team.

Senior Airman Charles "Chuck" Taylor, CSAF, UAV sensor operator.

Corporal Ramona Wachowski, CSMC, vehicle maintenance and logistics.

Senior Airman James Williams, CSAF, UAV pilot on the Alpha Mike Team.

MAPCOM Alpha Sierra Team 196

Mr. Glen Anderson, CIA representative attached to Alpha Sierra Team.

Dr. William "Bill" Baker, Atmosphere and Environment Group, civilian scientist.

Dr. Michelle Brown, Organic Geochemistry and Biosignatures Group, civilian scientist.

Dr. Samantha Emmerich, Head of Geology Group, MAPCOM civilian scientist, and member of the Alpha Sierra Team.

Dr. Brigitte Follet, Inorganic Geochemistry and Mineralogy Group, civilian scientist.

Dr. Laytonya Franklin, Linguistics and Anthropology Group, civilian scientist.

Dr. Rachel Goldstein, Inorganic Geochemistry and Mineralogy Group, civilian scientist.

Dr. Peter Harrison, Geology Group, civilian scientist.

Dr. David Rui Leung, Linguistics and Anthropology Group, civilian scientist.

Dr. Allison O'Neill, Organic Geochemistry and Biosignatures Group, civilian scientist.

Dr. Simon Newman, Geology Group, civilian scientist.

Dr. Grace Yenn Pham, Linguistics and Anthropology Group, civilian scientist.

Dr. Tyrone Reynolds, Linguistics and Anthropology Group, civilian scientist.

Dr. Alan Webber, Organic Geochemistry and Biosignatures Group, civilian scientist.

Dr. Adam Wilson, Mathematics and Physics Group, civilian scientist.

Dr. Li-Na Wong, Atmosphere and Environment Group, civilian scientist.

GLOSSARY

AAR After Action Report, which is a written description of what has happened during a mission afterward, and can sometimes be referred to as a "mission report."

Ape Acronym for Autonomous Pilot Expert system, and is often used as a synonym for the CAS-3-Mod 1 suit. See CAS-3-Mod 1.

BENT Brevity code word for equipment inoperative.

Beowulf The Beowulf is a .50 caliber machine gun developed from an AR-15 assault rifle, with a heavy-duty barrel that fires a round capable of penetrating light armor at short range.

BigDog BigDog was a quadruped robot created in 2005 by Boston Dynamics in conjunction with Foster-Miller, the NASA Jet Propulsion Laboratory, and the Harvard University Concord Field Station. Its development led to the creation of the first driven combat armor suits.

BMG Browning Machine Gun, which can refer to either the

Browning M2HB or the 12.7 x 99mm .50 caliber 12.7 x 99mm BMG round. See M2HB.

Browning Short for Browning M2HB machine gun. See M2HB.

ChameleonFlage An active camouflage system that mimics the surrounding environment. It's an integral part of the feedback system for the sense of kinesthesia that makes driving combat armor suits through the surrounding environment intuitive for the pilots.

Chicken Nickname for the V-32 Thunder Hawk. See Thunder Hawk.

CASE-2X The Marine Corps Combat Armor System Environment Dash (Mark) 2 Extreme is driven by its operator, unlike its lighter counterpart MARPACE suit, which is worn. It can operate up to three days before needing to be refueled; see FM51-CASES and TO-2051-16-02-1U for further details. Command variant CASE-2XC has enhanced C4 suite.

CAS-3-Mod 1 Combat Armor System Dash (Mark) 3 Dash Model 1 is the Army's latest upgrade to their drive suit, which is supplied to Special Forces troops. It's slightly heavier than a CASE-2X and has the ability to be outfitted with a large array of heavy weapon systems according to its mission profile.

CBI Confederation Bureau of Investigation, formerly known as the Federal Bureau of Investigations, also known as the Bureau, a change of name that arose after the second American Civil War of 2037 and the formation of the North American Confederation.

CIA Confederation Intelligence Agency, formerly the Central Intelligence Agency, often referred to as just the Agency.

CSAF Confederated States Air Force is the name of what was previously known as the United States Air Force, also known as Chair Force, a disparaging appellation to describe how they do their job.

CSGS Confederated States Geological Survey is a civilian agency that researches water, earth, and biological sciences and mapping services.

CSMC Confederated States Marine Corps is the name of what was previously known as the United States Marine Corps. The change of name has not mellowed the attitude of the Corps, or its creed, and as a result they are still badasses that you do not want to mess with.

CYCLOPS Brevity code word for a UAV, unmanned aerial vehicle, commonly incorrectly referred to as a "drone."

DARPA Defense Advanced Research Projects Agency, now defunct and replaced by Global Dynamics Corporation Defense Industries.

Dogs Widely used nickname/acronym given by Marines for their CASE-2X suits. It stands for Dispersed Operation and Guidance System, which is the name of the near AI/expert system interface, and it also has the advantage of resonating with the historical tradition of Marines being called Devil Dogs by the Germans during World War One.

ECM Electronic Counter Measures are used to trick or deceive the enemy's ability to gain a target lock.

ECCM Electronic Counter-Countermeasures are part of the defensive measure taken to reduce the effect of ECM upon a vehicle's operating system.

ETA Estimated Time of Arrival.

GEOINT Geospatial Intelligence derived from the analysis of geospatial imagery.

HOS Stands for Human Operator Surrogate, which is the official designation of semiautonomous robots with a hybrid expert system artificial intelligence operating system, commonly known as androids. This allows the operator to effectively multitask by distributing themselves across a network and act as a force multiplier; the Global Dynamics Corporation Defense Industries sales pitch calls their combat androids An Army of One.

HUD Heads-Up Display. This is a system that allows the user to see instrument data overlaid on their main screen without the need to open another window.

HUMINT Human Intelligence acquired from clandestine espionage operations.

IFF Identify, Friend or Foe.

INTEL Intelligence gathered through spying or monitoring of signals. See HUMINT and SIGINT.

KRISS Vector Compact submachine gun firing a .45 ACP round that is issued to CASE suit crews as part of their survival gear.

Lidar Alternative name for the acronym LADAR, which stood for Laser Detection and Ranging. Lidar uses a short pulsed laser to illuminate a target to determine the distance to an object, thus providing a 3D image of the target at the same time as determining the distance.

M21-A8A 40mm recoilless Gauss rifle with an eight-round cassette magazine/powerpack firing 10mm discarding sabot rounds.

M41-AC230 The General Electric Company M41 is a long-recoil autocannon that fires a 20 x 170mm round with a range of five kilometers, and it has an inbuilt Mk 30 40 x 53mm under-barrel grenade launcher effective out to one kilometer. The M41 standard load-out is four magazines, each holding ten armor-piercing tungsten-steel penetrators and two magazines, each with ten High Explosive Air Burst (HEAB) warheads, and five rounds of High Velocity Canister Cartridge (HVCC) for the grenade launcher.

M75A 40mm lightweight high-velocity recoilless autocannon.

M134 The General Electric Company M134 GAU-2B/A Minigun is a rotary multibarrelled machine gun firing the 7.62 x 51mm NATO round, and can be set to fire between 2000 and 6000 rounds per minute. The effective range is 1000 meters.

M240LC The M240LC is a general purpose machine gun using the 7.62 x 51mm NATO round that can be used in the sustained-fire role, which has been modified for use on combat armor suits.

M2184 HUHMTT The M2184 is an Oshkosh Heavy Utility High-Mobility Tactical Truck with a palletized loading system. It has a ten-wheel drive and steering, making it a vehicle that has excellent all-terrain capability.

MACE suit Shortening of MARPACE. See MARPACE.

MAP Magnetic Anomaly Project. Financed by the Confederated States Geological Survey and the Confederated States Air Force to study geological phenomenon that led to the discovery of the pillars.

MAPCOM Magnetic Anomaly Project joint unified combatant command, which is the military side of the operation that oversees control of MAP. Currently classified operation that runs super-black missions representing North American Confederation interests off-world.

MARPACE Marine Corps Power Armor Combat Enhancement suit that is modified to operate in marine environments, a.k.a. MACE suit, also see PACE suit.

MULE Acronym for Medium Utility Lifting Envelope. A hybrid lifting body transport airship.

NBC Nuclear, Biological, and Chemical, used as a descriptor for environment, threat level, or ability of a unit.

OODA loop Observe, Orient, Decide (and) Act, a recurring cycle used to get inside the enemy's decision-making cycle by making decisions quicker.

OPFOR Opposing Force, a.k.a. the enemy.

ORBAT Order (of) Battle. Those units from a formation that are actually deployed in action. For example the 1st Light Armored Reconnaissance Company ORBAT is running with four platoons, each with two squads of five combat armor suits, for a total of forty personnel. See TO&E.

Oscar Mike Phonetic alphabet for On the Move, as in "moving now."

PACE suit Acronym for Power Armor Combat Enhancement suit that is worn and reacts to users' body movements in a naturalistic manner, a.k.a. PACES. The suit has the NBC resistance built in and has facilities for handling bodily waste. The suit can operate for up to twenty-four hours before requiring a stop for recharging, depending on environmental variables; see FM51-PACES and TO-2051-08-08-1R for further details.

PAD Acronym for Personal Access Device. A wearable computer interface that be accessed by various means depending on the sensors and accessories worn.

PetMan Acronym for Protection Ensemble Test Mannequin, originally commissioned by DARPA. Its design was the basis for Global Dynamics Corporation Defense Industries Human Operator Surrogate androids. See HOS.

POD Acronym for Plan of (the) Day. Every day in the military has a plan for what is happening that day. This generally ranges from repetitive to banal, except when it doesn't.

POG Pog or pogue is an abbreviation meaning Person Other (than) Grunt that is less pejorative than REMF, which stands for Rear Echelon Maintenance Force, if being polite. The less polite version should be obvious.

RIPPLE Brevity code word for two or more munitions released on a target.

RPG Rocket-Propelled Grenade, a backronym which stands for Ruchnoy Protivotankovyy Granatomyot, a handheld antitank grenade launcher.

SIGINT Intelligence gathered by listening to communication traffic. This can be as simple as studying the amount of data flowing between stations to identify headquarter units, or by the decryption of the intercepted messages.

SITREP Situation Report.

Space-plane A colloquial expression referring to any craft that enters orbit as part of its flight plan. See Aries.

Thunder Hawk The Bell Boeing V-32 Thunder Hawk is a heavy-lift tilt-fan aircraft. Commonly referred to as a Chicken by those who fly in them due to their ungainly looks.

TO&E/TO & TE Table (of) Organization and Equipment (Army); Table Organization and Table Equipment (Marines). This lays out the composition of each unit at every level, and is driven by the forces' doctrine. For instance, Captain Tachikoma's former unit was the First Light Armored Reconnaissance Company, which when at full strength, would have had a total of fifty-six personnel. This consisted of four platoons, and a headquarters squad of four CASE-2X Dogs. Each platoon would have three squads with four combat armor suits, each squad split into fire teams of two. The platoon is commanded by a lieutenant with the assistance of the platoon sergeant for a total of thirteen Dogs per platoon. However, field strength is less due to sickness, training, and vacant slots. See ORBAT.

UAV Unmanned Aerial Vehicle, commonly referred to incorrectly as "drones" in casual conversation. See CYCLOPS.

AFTERWORD

The book you have just finished reading was my response to finishing the first novel I wrote. I just had to know more about the world I had brought into existence to answer the big question of why was it all Big Dog's fault that I died yesterday under a mountain in Afghanistan? It was obvious to me when I finished writing the first draft of Bad Dog there would be a sequel, and Strike Dog is what it grew into.

But as I was writing and researching stuff I had an insight about military fiction, and by extension military science fiction.

Basically the question was, am I really writing a military story?

By that I mean does my story reflect what it's really like to work and live in the military? Traditionally stories focus on the hero who can make a difference, usually through superior fire-power, occasionally through superior tactics, which are rooted in traditional plots. However, the adage in the military is that amateurs talk tactics, while professionals talk logistics.

I think this pretty much defines the problems of traditional fictional accounts of war. That and the fact unless one has worked within a rigid hierarchical bureaucracy it's hard to understand the military mindset. But logistics is boring, and life in the military is largely about mundane routine stuff.

The question I then faced was how to give the reader a broader understanding of the realities of life in the military, while placing events within a strategic context, and at the same time an understanding of the operational problems that military commanders have to face. While not losing sight of the story which is driven by conflicts arising between characters and events; otherwise known as the plot.

Strike Dog is my answer to these questions. It combines both my interest military history, and my love of science fiction with complicated characters who have their own agendas.

Finally, every story written owes something to previous stories written by other authors who have gone before them. I would acknowledge that in the greater scheme of things I stand on the shoulders of giants. Strike Dog is no exception to this observation, and this novel was not written in isolation.

Without the support and encouragement from Susan Parker, my Alpha reader, I would never have completed the first draft of Strike Dog. It was her feedback and enthusiasm that drove me to write more. I would even go so far as to say that she is the person who should be thanked most for the story you have been reading.

I am also indebted to my Beta readers too; David Barrow, Brian McCue, Fritz who wishes to remain anonymous, and Alix McFarlane for their constructive feedback. Those who have read my first draft can all attest to the differences between what they had to read, and the novel you've just read.

Ashley R Pollard
London, UK
March 2018

ALSO BY ASHLEY R POLLARD

Gate Walkers

Bad Dog

Strike Dog

World of Drei Series

Terror Tree

Mission One

Regroup

Forthcoming

World of Drei Series: Break Out

Gate Walkers: Ghost Dog

ABOUT THE AUTHOR

Born a long time ago in a land far, far away, Ashley has immersed herself in SF and has read, or watched SF for most of her life. She knows SF when she sees it, but can't explain what SF is. Having taken the blue pill, she lives, eats and breathes SF.

I've written for *Battlegames* and *Miniature Wargames* magazines, and I was both a reviewer and columnist for Games Master International. In addition, I was a freelancer for FASA Corps working on the *3055 Technical Read Out,* and I wrote the *OHMU War Machine* wargame rules. My current non-fiction writing is a monthly column for *Galactic Journey.*

I've been told I have more interests than most people have dinners, which include: cycling, aikido, iaido, photography, miniature wargaming, painting, and archery.

I am unashamedly a starry eyed dreamer.

Want to know more?
https://ashleyrpollard.blogspot.co.uk/
ashley@ashley-pollard.com

www.ingramcontent.com/pod-product-compliance
Lightning Source LLC
Chambersburg PA
CBHW032157180726
48284CB00001B/85